The Priest's Wife

"You've been down to see Kevin?"

He pulled a chair close to the bed and sat down but said nothing. There was something about his demeanour that caused me to look straight into his face, but he didn't meet my gaze. His look was distant and obscure as though a veil had descended. Why couldn't he bring himself to meet my eyes?

"Finbarr! What is it? What's wrong? Tell me."

Did I need to ask? The answer cried aloud from his expression of doom. I leaned toward him, trying to reach his face and make him look at me.

"What, Finbarr? What?"

"I've just been down there. It's not looking good, Susan. Not good."

To Shane and Mary

With best wishes

Paddy

Wings

THE PRIEST'S WIFE

by

PJ Connolly

A Wings ePress, Inc.

Mainstream Novel

Wings ePress, Inc.

Edited by: Camille Netherton
Copy Edited by: Jeanne Smith
Senior Editor: Joan Afman
Executive Editor: Marilyn Kapp
Cover Artist: Trisha FitzGearld

Wings ePress Books
http://www.wings-press.com

ISBN 978-1-61309-845-5

Published in the United States Of America

September 2013

Wings ePress Inc.
403 Wallace Court
Richmond, KY 40475

Dedication

To my wife Joan, who walked the long road with me.

Acknowledgements

Thanks must go to my editor, Camille Netherton for inspired advice as also to David Toft, Jackie Morrissey, Oliver Duhl and Imelda McDonagh for unwavering support. Also to Claire-Emmanuelle Balay for advice on French usage.

One

The frame froze right there. The reader stopped reading, the other sisters forgot their food and all eyes focused on my blazing embarrassment.

Inexplicably the tray had tilted and I could only watch in horror as a snow-flurry of salt and pepper scattered across the old knotted pine floorboards. All eyes turned towards Mother Mercy, sitting on her raised dais, presiding, taking everything in as we, her minions, waited in submissive silence for her reaction.

"I'll go get a brush, Mother," said Sister Carmel helpfully. I sensed my fellow novice was simply trying to shift attention away from me. She was a good friend, Carmel.

"No need for a brush. Sister Susan will clean it with her tongue."

I stared in silent disbelief at my superior, convinced I glimpsed a semblance of spite in that austere face. I stood there, isolated, like an actor on an empty stage. My audience sat like the disciples in Da Vinci's painting, all facing inwards on either side of the refectory. Alone and aloof as befitted her station, Mother Mercy sat below the large crucifix which dominated the scene.

"Get down on your knees, Sister, and lick the salt from the floor."

Never since I entered the convent had my humiliation been so public or so degrading. Even now, looking back over all the years, I see it as the most demeaning thing one human being could seek to impose on another. But I was in no position to refuse. You obeyed an order from your superior, no questions asked. I was painfully aware of the total silence in that room as the whole community watched and waited to see what I'd do. There was no way out. I had to do as I was ordered.

"Yes, Mother," I said, and dropped to my knees on the floor.

I brought my face close to the cracked boards and started to lick the salt pepper mixture. I was nauseated with the taste of salt and pepper and the feel of the dust and grit in my mouth. But it was the sheer degradation more than anything else that found me fighting back the tears.

Mother Mercy gave Sister Veronica a curt command to resume reading from The Imitation of Christ and everyone went back to their food. From my crouched position, I saw Sister Consolata leave her place to whisper something in the Superior's ear. I caught the serious expression on both women's faces, but of course I'd no notion what was going on. When Consolata went back to her place, Mother Mercy looked straight down at me and said Benedicamus Domino. That brief Latin invocation told me I'd been reprieved.

"*Deo Gratias*," I answered and struggled to my feet.

Two

I turned the door handle and stepped inside to be met by the clean lavender smell that always hung about the parlour. The long room with its bay window at one end was dominated by a large mahogany table and set of matching chairs. This is where visitors to the convent were usually brought, but tonight the room was being used for confessions. The minute he saw me, he got up and came over. I felt the firm warm grip of his hand.

"And who have we got here?" I could feel his eyes on me and his interest seemed special. I wasn't used to this kind of attention.

"Sister Susan, Father."

"Forget the 'Father' bit. Finbarr will do just fine. Finbarr Gray." The wavy black hair and boyish grin told me he couldn't have been more than six or seven years older than me.

I was surprised, slightly taken aback, I have to say. I'd heard that some of the younger priests were affecting a new trendy persona but this was my first experience of something like that. All I'd ever known was a 'yes Father, no Father' attitude to the clergy. Best china taken out of its dusty isolation and tea served to the local priest in a room barred to everyone but special visitors.

"No need to kneel, Susan. You'll be more comfortable in that chair. Let's forget the formalities, what do you think? You don't mind me calling you Susan, I hope?"

"No…no, not at all." I didn't think I could ever bring myself to call him Finbarr though.

So there I was, making my confession sitting in an easy chair, a long way from the lines of penitents waiting outside the confession box for their turn to whisper anonymous sins in the ear of a shadowy priest on the other side of the wire grille.

It suddenly struck me that here was a man I might be able to talk to.

"Is it true," he said, "you're taking your final vows in a couple of months? I suppose you've given it a lot of thought."

"Sister Consolata gave me a book to read, 'Poverty, Chastity, Obedience'. The book explains everything."

"Poverty, Chastity and Obedience. Let's talk about chastity. I presume you know what you're getting yourself into on that score?"

I was taken aback, a bit embarrassed, to tell the truth. But I could still hear Sister Consolata's words in my head. *The vows set you apart, mark you out, make you one of the small band of the elect.*

"I'm committing myself to Jesus. That's how I see it."

"Don't you think you might ever need the love and companionship of a man?"

I felt the blood rushing to my cheeks. I was raised in a family where this kind of thing was never talked about.

The Swinging Sixties had passed us by without as much as a nod in our direction. As for sex education, I had to depend on what I'd picked up from my school pal, Molly Featherstone, who had a habit of sneaking out to the local hop when the nuns thought we were all safely asleep in our beds. Molly kept me up to speed on her exploits with a succession of lads from the town, though I have to confess I barely understood what she was talking about. As for my past two years in the novitiate, I think they assumed I already knew everything there was to be known about boys and girls and what they might get up to. There were big gaps in my education.

The priest was studying me, waiting for an answer.

"Sister Consolata says I'm going to be the bride of Jesus and as long as I keep that before my eyes, I'll have no problem".

He smiled.

"Sister Consolata must never have any bad thoughts, then. I'll tell you something for nothing, Susan. Celibacy's the thing that causes the biggest problems for priests and nuns. Priests leave the church over it. And I've no doubt it's just as hard for the nuns. There's a case to be made for doing away with celibacy altogether."

"It frees you up to devote yourself to God's work."

"Is that what they told you? Just don't think it's going to be easy, Susan. That's what I mean."

"You're not saying I should pull out before it's too late?"

"I'm saying you don't seem to be getting the full picture, that's all."

He must have noticed my eyes moistening. He waited.

"There's something I wanted to talk to you about. It's got nothing at all to do with...with, you know..."

"Take your time."

It all came pouring out. How Mother Superior made me go on my knees and lick the salt from the floor. A look of concern spread across his face as he listened.

"You're telling me she made you do this in front of whole community?"

"And she knew it was my twenty-first birthday. She always opens my post."

"But that's incredible."

"I felt like dirt. And I'm supposed to accept it's God's will."

"Take it easy, Susan."

"How can I vow obedience to this woman? We don't hit it off at all. I don't want to find myself taking orders from someone so totally...so totally inhuman."

"Can't say I blame you."

"I ask myself how much more of this I can take. God alone knows how long she'll be in charge here."

"I'm going to let you in on a little secret." A faint smile. "This is just between you and me, mind. I've had to deal with the same kind of thing myself."

"I can't imagine..."

"I belong to a religious order just like you, so I know what you're talking about. Give some people a little power and it goes to their heads. Take my own situation. I say, 'yes Mike, sure Mike, you're dead right, Mike.' That keeps him happy. Sort of feeds his sense of importance. Then I just go off and do my own thing anyway. You're shocked?"

I couldn't believe my ears. That a priest would talk like this about his superior and then take a novice like me into his confidence. I took a deep breath.

"I'm having second thoughts about my vocation." There. I'd said it.

Suddenly I was ready to open up in a way I'd have found impossible a few minutes before. It all came tumbling out. How we got the news of Mam's cancer the same week I got my Leaving Certificate results. How I turned down the chance to study English Literature to nurse Mam through the final months of her illness. How my whole attitude changed as I watched my mother bear her suffering with silent fortitude. 'Now I can die happy,' she'd said when I confided my intention to join the nuns.

"You decided to sacrifice your life as a sort of tribute to your mother?"

"I'm afraid if I give up on it now, it'll be...I don't know...a kind of betrayal."

"Your mother only wants what's best for you. You'll know what to do."

The time came to kneel and receive absolution.

Ego te absolvo ab omni peccatis tuis...his hand rested lightly on my head *...in nomine Patris et Filii et Spiritus Sancti. Amen.*

As he raised his hand in blessing, something intangible passed between us and I realised a new peace inside me.

~ * ~

"What did you make of him, Susan? Isn't he gorgeous?"

We'd sneaked off to our secret spot in the grounds, Carmel and I, to compare notes on the new chaplain.

"Well, he's certainly not your regular run-of-the-mill, I'll grant you that."

"I felt I knew him all my life."

"That's just you, Carmel. You'd feel perfectly relaxed with the archbishop."

"Oh come on, tell me what you thought of him. I'm dying to hear."

"He wanted me to call him *Finbarr.*"

"Finbarr, imagine!" She giggled.

The groan of a bus labouring up the hill on the other side of the high convent wall. A wall built to keep people in or to keep people out. On the outside, people in the real world made their way home from town, worn out by their day's work, maybe to face worse problems at home. Just inside that wall our excitement fluttered around silly school-girl gossip on the merits of the young chaplain.

"Tell me something, Susan, do you fancy him?" I caught the mischievous glint in her eye.

"Will you stop it?" Once Carmel got on this tack, there was no holding her. "Would you like to marry him?"

"He's a priest, for heaven's sake! I wish you wouldn't go on like that."

"All the same, you can't help wondering what it'd be like, you know, married to a priest."

"Look, Carmel, priests can't marry and neither can nuns. You know I don't like that kind of talk."

"I was just wondering, that's all. No harm in wondering."

"You'd be better off trying to keep your thoughts pure and holy."

"Imagine a good-looking young fellow like that joining the priesthood. I wonder why he did it."

"And why wouldn't he?"

"But what about all the disappointed women he must have left behind? Did you never think of that?"

"Oh, for God's sake, Carmel!"

She laughed. I think she enjoyed teasing me. Deep down, though, I knew I depended on Carmel to maintain some semblance of reality in the all-female community.

Whether it was my long conversation with the priest, or Carmel's common sense take on things, I can't say, but I felt a lot easier in myself as we answered the bell for evening prayers. That night in the chapel, I made a silent pledge to God and my dead mother to persevere in my vocation.

Though I imagined my decision was final, I was far too young and inexperienced to understand that the only thing in life that's truly final is the finality of death.

Three

"You must be dead inside that outfit."

Sheila was a missionary sister and the clothes she wore were hardly different from what any of the girls in the lecture room were wearing. Not at all like the heavy robes I had to drag around.

"You're still in the Dark Ages, Susan. It's nineteen seventy-seven, for heaven's sake!" She gave me a playful jab as the professor swept into the room, black gown floating in his wake.

I found it hard to concentrate on the lecture as Watson-Bates waffled on for the best part of an hour on the less than riveting topic of Manley Hopkins and his inventive rhythms. It intrigued me that Sheila could get away in a knee length blue skirt with white buttoned up blouse. Nothing to identify her as a nun except the small silver cross she wore on a chain about her neck. In my all-embracing black, I stuck out among other students like a penguin that had strayed into the monkey enclosure at the zoo.

The moment the lecture ended, I was onto it again, how she'd escaped wearing the heavy habit.

"The Vatican Council," she said.

"That was years ago when I was just a child."

"Years ago, exactly. So why don't you bring it up with your superior?"

"Mercy? Well now, she's something else altogether."

"It's up to you, but I know what I'd do if someone tried to make me wear gear like that."

I raised my hand to feel the black veil which hid my head, leaving only my face exposed. I decided to bite the bullet and make the case in person to my superior.

~ * ~

"Most other convents have switched over," I informed her.

She sat behind the barricade of a vast mahogany desk as always when she gave audience up there on the top floor. Somehow I'd overcome my fear of facing the lioness in her den.

"Really? I can see you've been conducting some exhaustive research, Sister."

"I see it all around me, Mother. Twelve years have gone by since the council. The reforms are finally percolating down."

"Clearly you're not aware that Vatican Two left it up to each religious order to make their own decisions. Our Mother Provincial is in favour of holding to the old traditions and so, as it happens, am I."

"But don't you think the habit is a barrier between us and the ordinary people?"

"Ah, now, Sister, isn't that just the point? Our habit is *intended* to be a barrier. Surely you can see that? It sets us apart, apart from the world. It shows the world we live by different values. It's a public declaration of what we stand for."

"But all the other religious congregations..."

"Whatever decision they take is a matter for them. As far as I'm concerned, this is a topic on which there will be no further discussion."

And that was that as far as Mother Mercy was concerned. It was a brief encounter but then Mother Superior's time was precious and not to be wasted on trivialities. Not that I'd expected a sympathetic hearing. Any suggestion coming from me was bound to be dismissed out of hand. That's not to say I'd given up. In fact, I was tugging at the bit. I'd glimpsed the beginnings of a new age amongst the other nuns around college. That tiny spark of rebellion was to be fanned into flame with the arrival of my sister Josie to take up her new job in Dublin.

~ * ~

A dull, overcast day in late October. A chill easterly airflow funnelled up the Liffey from the Irish Sea, early intimation of approaching winter. Civil servants poured from the anonymous glass and concrete Hawkins House.

"You must be real cosy in there, Sis," she said, poking my heavy habit.

"Can I join you for lunch?"

"There's a lovely wee place in Wicklow Street. Makes a change from that crazy civil service canteen."

We talked as we walked.

"It didn't take you long to find your feet in Dublin, Josie."

"We're all country lads and lasses in there. Won't be long before we take over the capital altogether. How's college?"

"Fine. It's just that I stick out like a sore thumb in this stupid outfit."

"Why don't you do something about it, then?"

"I tried but I didn't get very far." I told her about my futile approach to Mother Mercy.

"And you're going to take it lying down? That doesn't sound like the big sister I used to know. You always told me to stand up for myself, remember?"

"It's easy talking, but what can I do?"

"I'll tell you what you can do. You can try wearing some of my things."

"Are you mad, Josie? I'd never get away with it."

We leaned back in our chairs as the waitress laid steaming bowls of soup in front of us. Josie rummaged in her purse and slid a key across the table.

"It's a spare key to my flat. I'll leave some stuff out for you to try on. If it fits and you like what you see, just take whatever you want. You can always change back into the habit before you go home to the nuns."

~ * ~

I let myself into the empty ground floor apartment in Clonskeagh. Stale grease and leaking gas. Those were the smells I recognised. I made my way to Josie's bedroom at the back where she'd laid out a few things as she said she would.

I stood back and looked in the mirror, amazed by what I saw. Who, I wondered, was this stranger gazing back at me, this green-eyed young woman in the fashionable dress, her short-cropped golden hair and smart figure ready to step out and face the world? If this was the new me, I liked what I saw. In the end, though, I chose something more casual for college.

There was freshness in the light clear morning air. The sun had climbed above the rooftops. Strange how everything seemed so different. The streets, the houses, the people were the same as always. They hadn't changed. I knew the change had to be within myself. Something had transformed my world. I felt free as the flock of sparrows that flurried into the air as I passed. In this new persona, I could go where I wished, do what I wanted. People who passed on the pavement didn't notice my existence. Glorious invisibility! That morning I found my first taste of freedom and the feeling was euphoric.

I found a place at the back where I could take in the whole scene. All those young men and women waiting for their lecture, chatting, laughing, just being alive. For the first time I savoured the atmosphere of the university. Other students need never know they were talking to a nun. The barriers were gone and no need for inhibitions on anyone's part.

In the coffee dock, I spotted Carmel sitting alone in the far corner. She didn't recognise me amongst the milling students. I was about to face her in my lay attire and I wondered how she'd react.

I laid the plastic coffee mug on the table, bent down and moved my open palm in a slow circle before her eyes. Startled, she looked up and sudden recognition flashed in her eyes.

"It's you! Susan, I don't believe it!"

"Well, what you think?" I said, twirling like a model.

"You're different."

"Different?"

"I mean you look different. Where'd you get those duds anyway?"

I looked down in mock disappointment at my denim skirt and loose-fitting woolly top.

"They're a bit shabby, all right. Josie's cast-offs, in fact."

"No, no. You look fine. It's just I've never seen you in anything but the habit. What can I say? You look great. Grab yourself a chair."

"You're not shocked, then?"

"Shocked? Are you kiddin'? To tell you the truth, I'm sorta glad you had the guts to take the plunge. But wait till I tell you. We're starting community experience in a few weeks and I'm thinking it's crazy landing in on some poor family dressed like something out of a horror film."

"Any chance I can come with you?"

"Let's see what Sister Berchmans says. She's bound to say yes. You know the way they don't trust us going anywhere on our own?"

"They don't trust us? Why ever not?"

We both burst out laughing.

~ * ~

"I'm totally lost," I said. "I didn't know this place existed."

"Lost are you? Then let me take you by the hand and lead you through the streets of Dublin. I'll show you something that'll make you change your mind."

We turned into a street of run-down red-brick houses, four storeys high over shallow basements, the whole scene overhung by an air of brokenness and neglect.

"My God, Carmel, I thought they'd done away with places like this ages ago."

"They started clearing the slums in the fifties after a couple of houses collapsed and killed the unfortunate people. This place here is one of the last."

I found myself staring into the wide-open front door of what must once have been a grand Georgian town-house in a distant past of servants and carriages. The fanlight above the doorway was devoid of glass. On the broken front steps, ragged children sat playing, balancing pebbles on the backs of their hands. A skinny girl of ten or eleven jumped up and threw her arms around Carmel. A moment later when the child turned her face to me, I was horrified by what I saw, for the features had been shrivelled and shrunken and covered with a mass of scar tissue. There were no eyebrows on this parody of a face, just a permanent expression of wide-eyed alarm.

"Fell into the fire," Carmel whispered. "Say hello to Susan, Jacinta. Susan's my friend."

Jacinta's disfigured face lit up with a smile which could only be described as angelic.

"Susan." She seemed to savour the sound of the word. Then tugging at my sleeve, "Come on up to Mammy."

Nothing prepared me for what I found here in this back street only a five minute walk from Dublin's fashionable shopping district.

The moment I entered the building, I was assailed by the smell, a disgusting all-pervasive stench. In spite of myself, I placed my hand over my nostrils in a futile attempt to shut out the stink of grease, stale cabbage, sewage, overcrowded humanity, all of these in combination. I felt a retching in my stomach. All that stopped me making a dash for the open air was the insult this would imply for the unfortunates condemned to live their lives here.

We pushed past a rickety pram, bits of broken furniture and other detritus. There were treacherous gaps in the floor where boards were missing. Broken plaster hung from the walls on forlorn strips of scrim. No sign the walls had seen paint for perhaps a hundred years. There were doors opening off the hall, mostly ajar, and judging by noises emanating from behind each door, separate lives played out in separate rooms. Radios blared, babies wailed, angry voices scolded. From a room at the end of the hall came the lone sweet voice of a woman singing.

Little Jacinta led the way up the stairs, all the time pointing out missing balusters to watch for. At every level there were four or five rooms, each one, I guessed, housing an entire family. At the top of the house, we came to a door which was partly open. Inside, voices competed with the sound of a radio. Carmel knocked on the door and a woman's voice shouted, "Come on in, will yiz."

I found myself facing a scrawny woman surrounded by six children ranging from baby to teens. All stopped whatever they were doing to stare in our direction. Then, recognising Carmel, the mother relaxed, the care-lined face melting into a weary smile.

"How're you keeping, Maisie?" Carmel said. "This here's Susan, a friend of mine. Hope you don't mind. "

I stepped towards Maisie and took her hand. I detected a deference in her handshake. She'd guessed I was a nun like Carmel. Was there always going to be this invisible barrier between me and other people?

While Carmel greeted the family in her easy manner, I

took in the scene. A naked toddler crawled between the wheels of a pram where an eight month old baby howled for attention. Two young boys used a couple of stacked mattresses as a wrestling ring, circling a filthy stain which seemed to play some part in their game.

"Will yiz turn down that wireless," Maisie shouted at no one in particular, "and let Betty get on with her homework."

At this, a teenage girl with a sly smirk tried to tear a comic from the hands of a younger brother.

Little Jacinta-with-the-angel's-smile dragged me towards the one and only chair in the room, which I declined to take, preferring to sit with the two older children on the bench by the wall.

"Well, Maisie," said Carmel. "And how are you getting on since I saw you last?"

"Ah, sure, pulling the divil be the tail. Sure, one day's the same as the next. What can you do except make the most of whatever God sends."

"Still no word from Jemser?"

"Ne'er a whisper. I'm worn out from watching the post."

"You never heard if he got work in Liverpool?"

"Six months this week since he got on the boat at the North Wall. The minute he got a job he was goin' to do the divil an' all, he was. If it wasn't for Jackie, God bless him, doin' his paper round and Betty bringin' in a few bob from the chipper, I don't know where we'd be, the Lord help us."

As she spoke, I couldn't help but wonder if people who came across little disfigured Jacinta in the busy streets might be moved to toss her a couple of coins and if the child dutifully handed this money over to her mother to help her pay the rent and feed the family.

"And the Vincent de Paul?"

"Oh, yeah, they've been up here a couple of times. They don't have an awful lot to give out nowadays and I suppose there's always them that's more deserving." She shrugged in a gesture of despair and resignation. "There's always someone worse off, isn't there?"

Standing there in that smelly room at the top of a depressing tenement building, I could feel nothing but shame that we had little to offer but words and sympathy. For the first time, I felt something of a hypocrite. I looked down at my clean white blouse and smart navy skirt and I compared the Poverty I professed to practice with the grinding hardship faced by human beings in such hideous conditions.

Maisie begged us to stay for a cup of tea but I said no, we had other visits to make. Carmel knew it wasn't true, but took the hint. We shook hands with each of the children and their mother. They seemed grateful for the visit.

An easterly breeze wafted in from the sea and I filled my lungs with the welcome air. We walked awhile in silence.

"Maybe that was a bit too much for a first visit." Carmel was apologetic.

"I never guessed such a world existed."

"Not much longer," she said. "These tenements will soon be gone. There'll be blocks of flats in their place."

"Will they ever get rid of the poverty, d'you think?"

"Will the Liffey run dry? There's one more family I could take you to see before we finish. Do you feel up to it?"

"Right now, I'm dying for a cup of coffee."

She hesitated, debating, I thought, to come with me for the coffee. She came with me.

That's when she confided her dream of launching a journal for social workers.

"But where will you find the time? You said yourself you're put to the pin of your collar to get your college project written up."

"I thought you might give me a hand with the first edition. I can handle the advertising and stuff. What you think?"

I saw her pleading eyes and yielded without a struggle. This kind of thing was more in my line than the hands-on approach I'd just witnessed. Carmel was a people's person while I was much more at home in the world of words.

"Okay, you're on," I said. "Let's bring out a first issue and see where it goes from there."

I paid the young waitress and we stood up to go, Carmel to finish her social work, I to snatch a quick visit to the National Gallery. There I might find in the solitude and in the paintings some meaning, something to help me make sense of life.

Four

El Greco. I stood transfixed in front of this masterpiece, mesmerised by the bleeding puncture holes in the hands of the saint. St. Francis in ecstasy, sharing the suffering of his Saviour.

I became aware of someone beside me and moved to one side in an unconscious gesture of civility. A youngish man in blue jeans and short-sleeved open-neck shirt murmured something and stepped in closer for a better view.

"You like it? The painting?" he said.

I gave an involuntary jump. People didn't usually talk to strangers in the hushed halls of the gallery. Yet something about the voice sounded familiar. It took a while before it hit me. That voice! The deep resonant voice of the convent chaplain! I turned right round to face him and found I wasn't mistaken, I was staring at the features of Father Gray.

"You're Father Gray!" It sounds foolish, but that's how it came out.

"And you're Sister Susan from the convent!" His eyes glinted with a roguish twinkle.

"But where's your...? You're not dressed like a priest, Father…Finbarr, I mean."

"You're not dressed like a nun, Sister...Susan I mean." He was teasing me.

I looked down at myself and became acutely aware of the outline of my breasts in the tightness of my knitted sweater. I blushed.

"I didn't know you without your priest's collar and things." I'd never seen him without the full outfit.

"I was just about to head for the coffee shop. Will you come?"

"Sure. Why not?"

We talked about El Greco and Goya. At least he talked about El Greco and Goya while I tried to hide my ignorance.

"Any favourites yourself?" he said.

"Artists you mean? No. Not particularly. Who's yours?"

"Velasquez. Now there's a genius if ever there was one. He influenced all the others, did you know that? Murillo, Corot, Manet. Whistler even."

He went on in this vein, blinding me with his knowledge. Then it was all about his fondness for abstract painting and sculpture. I'd be less than honest if I said I wasn't awestruck. So much stuff in one priest's head! I was to find out soon enough there was nothing accidental about this. That's for later, but for now it's enough to say there was something going on there that was a thousand miles from whatever confessor and penitent contact I'd had with Father Finbarr Gray back in the convent. It's hard to pin it down, but I can say I felt relaxed sitting there listening to him, putting in my own tuppence worth every now and then. When he smiled, I smiled in spite of myself. It was a new, and I have to admit, agreeable experience, for my thoughts up to now were more or less confined to the affairs of the soul.

Glancing at the clock, I saw it was already past four.

"My God," I said, "will you look at the time."

He took my hand for a moment and said, "There's a little gallery in Anne Street. There's something I'd love to show you there. Is there any chance… would you be free this time next week?"

I thought quickly. I'd have to find some excuse to get away from the convent for an afternoon. I was sure I could depend on Carmel to help me out. I'd no idea what it was he wanted to show me, but it had to be something worth looking at. On another level, I knew it could turn out to be a pleasant afternoon in his company.

"Where'll we meet?" I said.

"Bewley"s Café. How about two-thirty?"

"Two-thirty it is then."

~ * ~

A snarl of buses forcing a passage down the narrow ravine that's Grafton Street. Pedestrians who found walking on the roadway easier than elbowing the crowds on the pavement. Bewley's coffee-house was a haven for tired feet.

The rich dark aroma of roasting coffee. I spotted Finbarr beneath a Harry Clarke window, beatified by the stained-glass light that fell across the white cotton of his shirt. As he caught sight of me, his expression was one of mild surprise, as though he hadn't really expected me to show up.

He stood as I took the chair facing him.

"I see you managed to escape. I was half afraid you wouldn't make it."

His conspiratorial tone made it seem safe to bring him into my confidence.

"To tell the truth, they think I'm in Belfield. I told Berchmans I'd a lot of reading to do and needed an afternoon in the college library. Poor Berchmans. A trusting dear soul."

A waitress in white apron and lacy cap placed coffee and scones on the table.

"Where's your conscience?" He seemed amused. "Deliberate deception and all that."

"It wasn't that big a lie. I do have lots of reading to catch up on, English and French. I use the National Library a lot. It's what I like about my course. The reading. It really broadens your mind."

"In what way?"

"You know what I mean."

"How does it broaden your mind?"

"Okay. What I'm trying to say is...we're living on this little island. Where I grew up, it was all about going to religious devotions. I never heard mention of Joyce or Beckett, but I heard a lot of giving out about dirty books. All the best literature was on the banned list. Hard to believe that, isn't it?"

"So you admire Joyce and Beckett?"

"Have you read Ibsen? He lets you see behind the facade. That's the sort of thing I'm talking about."

"You sound pretty passionate about it."

"How about yourself, Finbarr? You like to read?" I'd

lost whatever inhibitions I had about using his first name.

"Mostly arcane tracts on theology. Worlds away from your stuff. But absorbing in its own way, I have to say."

Two middle-aged women took the chairs beside us, all excited about the bargain one of them had just picked up, a faux fur coat at a mere eighty-nine ninety-nine.

"Art's your secret passion, I suspect. I'd say you didn't pick that up in the seminary."

"Nothing secret about it."

"So where did it come from then?"

"I suspect you'll have the answer to that question before the day is out."

"You're coming across all mysterious. What was it you wanted to show me anyway?"

"It's just around the corner from here. A little private gallery called Impressions. There's a painting there I think's a real gem. I see you're finished your coffee. Why don't we get a move on and go over right away?"

~ * ~

We stepped down into the long narrow space that was *Impressions* and as the door squealed shut behind us, it took my eyes a while to adjust to the low lighting in the gallery. I stumbled against a stack of framed pictures blocking the passage and felt Finbarr's firm touch as he grasped my arm to steady me. I felt his fingers grip my elbow. It was the first time he'd ever touched me apart from the priestly blessing in confession. The sensation that coursed through my body at the touch of his hand was new and unfamiliar, but at the same time warm and pleasing. I tried to push it out of my mind but whatever it was that had been ignited was not so easily quenched.

"Hold onto me and watch your step," he whispered.

There were paintings all over the place. On the walls, on the floor, every inch was occupied. My overall impression was one of clutter. A stocky grey-haired man in his sixties sat at a desk near the back engrossed in paperwork.

Finbarr cleared his throat and the man looked up. He blinked at us for a few moments before recognition lit his face.

"Ah, Finbarr! Great to see you. How're you doin'?"

He gave Finbarr a warm handshake while gripping him with his free hand above the elbow.

"And tell me, who's this young lady?"

"Forgive me," said Finbarr. "Let me introduce you two. Susan's a friend of mine. I wanted to show her some of the paintings. Susan, meet my Uncle John."

Uncle John pumped my hand with vigour. The grip of his fingers exuded warmth and affection. I fell under his spell from the first moment. I did notice, though, that Finbarr had introduced me as a friend without saying I was a nun.

"Is there any particular painting you want to look at?" said Uncle John, addressing me.

"Well, no…I just thought…"

Finbarr came to my rescue.

"Susan would like to see the Kernoff. She heard it was something special."

"I can tell the young lady has taste. Poor old Harry Kernoff, I knew him, you know. I still can't believe he's gone. He used to drop in here for the chat. Whenever he was stuck for a few bob, he'd arrive in here with a sketch he'd just dashed off." His arm crooked about my waist guided me right in front of the picture.

The Harry Kernoff painting hung in the more secure area at the back. Lit by a pair of spotlights, it stood out among the rest of the paintings. I stared at the picture, intrigued by its simple, straightforward realism. The painting managed to capture a fleeting moment of commerce in a fast-changing quarter of old Dublin. Prominent in the picture were some fruit stalls by the side of a busy street. The scene was populated by women in black shawls, men in peaked caps, horse-drawn wagons weighed down with merchandise and a cart pulled by a young man striding between the parallel shafts. It could have been Meath Street, but who's to say? Kernoff was clearly trying to capture and record a Dublin still alive in the memory of many Dubliners.

"Nice one, isn't it?" His words were barely a whisper. "Would you be for buying it? I can do a special deal, seeing as you're a friend of Finbarr's."

"How much are you looking for?" said Finbarr.

"Four hundred, maybe. Poor old Harry's barely in his grave and they're knocking the door down for his stuff. Soon you won't get your hands on a Kernoff for love or money."

"In a few years, it'll be worth four grand," said Finbarr."

I was starting to like his quirky sense of humour.

"There y'are now," said Uncle John, winking at me. "He'd have made a canny businessman, Finbarr would, if he hadn't set his heart on the Church."

"What's it's called?" said Finbarr.

"The painting? The fellow who brought it in said he'd no notion what it was called. Whoever buys it will have to christen it."

"I know what I'd call it," I blurted and then wished I'd kept my mouth shut.

"You want to buy it, then?"

"Sorry," I said, "but I didn't tell you I'm a religious sister. We don't have two pennies to rub together."

"A nun you mean?" He looked at me with renewed interest and his gaze shifted from me to Finbarr and back again.

"So, tell me this, Sister Susan, what were you going to call it, then?"

Let me take you by the hand and lead you through the streets of Dublin...

"The Streets of Dublin," I said.

I knew I could never aspire to own that painting. The vow of poverty put all that kind of thing beyond my imagining. But things can change and sometimes change comes in unexpected ways.

We sat with Uncle John sipping strong tea from black pottery mugs in a pokey kitchenette at the back of the gallery. I felt his eyes on me before he spoke.

"D'you remember, sister, the nuns going around in long black habits with the funny white things around their faces and them always in pairs? Tell me is all that gone now?"

Finbarr was taking an inordinate interest in some blemish on the ceiling.

"I'll bet it's the first time you've seen a holy nun in blue jeans," I said, laughing. "There's big changes going on."

"D'ye know something, Rose was so proud of Finbarr and him saying his first Mass up there in Terenure. Always wanted her son to be a priest, she did. D'ye remember that, Finbarr? I can see her still, your mother, and her kneeling at the altar steps to receive your first blessing. Proud as punch she was, in front of everyone, the mother of the new priest."

Finbarr didn't seem to hear a word as Uncle John went on in the same vein.

"We're proud to have a priest in the family, Sister. I don't have to tell you what a big thing that is."

Finbarr looked at his watch and made a noise with his chair.

"I have to be getting back," he said.

We thanked Uncle John for the tea and as we stood up to go, he said, "That was a grand visit, Sister. Don't you forget now, anytime you're passing, you'll have to drop in for a bit of a chat."

I was about to say not Sister, call me Susan, but felt Finbarr's grip on my arm urging me away.

~ * ~

Instinctively we must have thought it was better to keep this whole thing to ourselves. In religious institutions, there's a horror of what they call particular friendships. So imagine what they've make of this if they ever found out.

From time to time, I'd drop into Uncle John's to see if the Harry Kernoff had been sold. Then at the end of July it was gone. I missed it in an odd kind of way, like the death of an old friend. Uncle John spotted me there and threw a friendly look in my direction, but since he was dealing with a customer I decided to leave him alone. I mentioned my sadness to Finbarr as we sat in the Green on a balmy August day. Mothers with their broods were making the most of the early autumn sunshine. We sat on a park bench near the edge of the pond. We watched a toddler throw a crust of bread under his mother's watchful eye and we laughed as ducks of all shapes and sizes came crashing across the surface to shower the terrified child with muddy pond water.

"We've never gone back to Uncle John's," I said. "Together, I mean. How's that?"

He seemed to be mulling it over.

"Finbarr?"

"Yeah?"

"I'm asking how come we've never gone back to your uncle's gallery. Maybe you don't want him to see us together. Why's that?"

"Oh, it's not that."

"What is it, then?"

"Ah, you know the way he goes on. Finbarr's first Mass. Finbarr's first blessing. There's only so much of that I can take."

"I can't see any harm in that," I said. "It's obvious he's very fond of your mother. They must be real close."

"Yeah, I suppose you could say. There were just the two of them and Mam was the little sister. John never married. Typical Irish Catholic upbringing. You know the scene."

"She's very devout, your mother?"

"Don't talk to me. Daily Mass. Just try and stop her!"

"She wanted you to be a priest?"

"It never left her mind."

"And, of course, you couldn't let her down?"

He didn't answer and I thought maybe I was pushing him too much. When he spoke again, he sounded reflective.

"I was little more than a boy when I entered the seminary. Straight out of school. It's a funny thing, but once you're in there you kind of get carried along with the tide. You don't feel the years going and suddenly it's ordination time. I saw a lot of lads pulling out along the way. One morning you'd go down to breakfast and you'd have an empty chair at the table. Next morning the chair was gone. But I stuck it out."

"Because of your mother?"

"Maybe, I don't know. The study I liked. Theology became my big interest. Still is, as a matter of fact."

He fell silent. I turned to look at his face, but he avoided my glance and I began to regret my intrusion. I placed my hand on his hand and gave a little squeeze. He didn't reject my touch and we sat there indistinguishable from other couples enjoying the quiet seclusion of the Green. The afternoon sky was cloudless as I lifted my face to the heat of the sun and closed my eyes. A new contentment filled my soul. It was a good place to be.

Five

"First class honours! You've done us proud, Susan. Mother Superior will be delighted to see you bringing home the laurels."

Berchman's words were nice, but the Mother Superior she was talking about wasn't the same one I knew. I wondered if that old fig was capable of a kind thought for anyone, least of all for me.

"Have you given any thought to a Master's? Wouldn't it be a shame not to make the most of your talents?"

"Oh, Sister! I'd be…I mean yes, I'd love to."

"Think about what you'd like to study, then. I've some ideas of my own but I want to hear what you come up with."

I'd an urge to dash around spreading the news, but you don't do that sort of thing in a convent. After supper, I'd see Carmel and she'd be delighted for me. Probably tease me with "Sister Einstein." But there was someone else. I couldn't get away from the need to share my news with someone who was already more friend than priest. The problem was he was taking part in a sit-in at Wood Quay protesting at the corporation's plans to build on the site of the earliest Viking settlement in Dublin. 1979 was the year the plain people were waking up to the vandalism of the developers.

I hoped to see him on Friday evening for confession. This had developed into a regular catch-up time, our chance to be together without intrusion.

Finbarr's face shone when he heard my exam results.

"We're going to celebrate," he said.

"Don't tell me you've got a hip flask hidden in your pocket?"

His eyes twinkled. He enjoyed it when I adopted that familiar tone.

"I meant go out for a meal."

"Are you mad or something? In full public view? No way, I say."

"How about a picnic then?"

"Well now, that might fit the bill okay."

"Tell you what then. I'll borrow my old man's car tomorrow and we'll head for the hills."

"What about the food?"

"You can leave the catering to me," he said.

~ * ~

He turned the car onto the road going south towards Wexford and Rosslare.

"So where are we off to?"

"Like I said...we're heading for the hills."

The early afternoon sun was high in the June sky and it was towards the sun that Finbarr steered his father's Rover.

"Tell me something," he said. "What would you be doing if you weren't here in this car with me?"

"I'd be buried under a pile of books in the library."

"Doing what, exactly?"

"Searching for a topic for my masters. Which reminds me. I wanted to tap your brain for ideas."

"Funny you should ask. I've just been reading The Crock of Gold. You know it?"

"I read it as a child. You're surely not suggesting..."

"We're all children at heart. You should read it again. I'll lend it to you."

"You want me to do my thesis on James Stephens?"

"It's only a suggestion. And you did ask. Anyway, think about it. Ask the Spirit to guide you."

"God! You go on like a priest sometimes."

"But I am a priest."

"So what are you doing with a woman in your car?"

We both laughed.

"Don't be hard on me," he said.

We turned off the main road and the narrow country lane followed the twists and turns of a mountain river rushing through a narrow gorge. Beyond Enniskerry, we took the snaking road that climbs into the hills on the northern flanks of the Wicklow Mountains. We came out onto a peaty plateau Finbarr called the Featherbed. He started to talk about his parents taking him up here as a child. He seemed to know the place like his own back yard. He told me why this was called the Military Road. It was put there by the authorities to supress insurgencies of the eighteenth century.

No traffic, just pure silence. I broke away and trotted off down an overgrown path. At a bend in the track, I found myself staring at a small circular lake with the blackest of still, icy water. The word bottomless popped into my mind. I turned around at the cracking of a twig and he was right there behind me. I put a finger on his lips lest he break the magic silence. The quietness was broken though by myriad insects, birds and shy darting creatures suddenly aware of the intrusive trespass of humankind. There we stood, silent both of us, for words didn't seem right in a place like that, the way lovers might be when a benign sun stills the air and the only sounds are the sonorous hum of honeybees and the twittering of skylarks in the blue above. It was a space more fit for meditation than communication.

I know it might seem silly to some ears, but everything I needed to say to him and he to me was transmitted by the movement of a finger or the glance of an eye. Is this what he was thinking when, without a word, he slipped his arm around my waist? I moved away, disengaging myself. It was an instinctive reaction on my part, for even such an innocuous gesture threatened all I held dear. I mean the whole chastity thing I had committed myself to in the convent.

We stayed there for how long I don't know, absorbing the peace of the place until sated with the stillness of the glacial lake, we retraced our steps along the grassy path back to the where we'd left the car.

We retrieved the picnic basket from the car boot, climbed a locked gate and found a secluded corner in which to spread a Foxford rug. We had an uninterrupted view along the Glencree Valley to a hazy point in the south where I could see a line of mountains punctuated by peaks and rounded summits.

"That sharp point sticking up above the rest?" I pointed.

His eyes followed the direction of my finger.

"Like a woman's nipple pointing to the sky?"

This coming from a priest. I was mildly surprised.

"What's it called anyway?"

"The Sugarloaf. The one to the left, like the woman's face, that's the Little Sugarloaf and to the right you can see her knees bent upwards, that's Djouce."

"You've some imagination."

It was my first sight of this landscape and already I'd fallen in love with it.

"You've nothing like this where Cavan meets Fermanagh?" he said, as if County Wicklow were his personal demesne.

"We have our drumlins." I felt defensive about my birthplace.

"Hand me that wine. We're here to celebrate, remember."

I'd never in my life and especially since entering the convent had wine with a meal. It was a new experience. It tasted bitter. Yet it was a challenge, like a ritual step into independence and maturity. But after the first glass, I became reckless and allowed him to fill it again.

There wasn't much talk, just a sense of contentment as we ate in the open. The food and wine he had cajoled from the college chef.

We finished the bottle and the wine began to have its effect. Meal eaten, we stretched our relaxed bodies on the soft rug. Heat was starting to build in the moisture-laden air.

Finbarr peeled off his shirt and I opened the buttons of

my blouse to soak up the summer sunshine. Innocent enough. All around us tall ripe grasses swayed beneath the weight of their bursting seed heads and wild flowers raised golden cups for the approval of the sun-god.

I lay back with my eyes closed and felt Finbarr lean in to place a kiss on my cheek. A kiss that was gentle, tentative and respectful. I didn't pull away as I'd done by the lake. Instead I turned towards him so that he could kiss me again. That kiss was the smouldering ember that needed just the faintest draught to coax it into flame.

There was struggling with clothing. I scarcely knew what I was doing. At that moment, all I knew was I wanted him to love me. I wanted to give myself and have him give himself to me. A consuming, irresistible desire beyond my control.

So when he drew me into his embrace, I did nothing to resist. Whatever was happening I wanted it to happen. I felt my whole being dissolve and flow as I melted in his arms. There was no part of my body that wasn't a part of this experience. My toes, my fingertips. Two became one. One body, one mind, one spirit. The fulfilment of it went to every cell of my receptive body. My very soul glowed with the joy of it. And as we lay back in exquisite exhaustion, I wished only that such joy would last forever. I wanted it never to fade.

Oddly, we didn't talk afterwards about what had happened. Maybe to have scrutinized it would have dispelled the magic. One thing I did know. A bond had been fastened, a link forged between two souls. How strong a link in face of vicissitude only the passing of time would tell.

The sky darkened. A splatter of large drops thudded into the dust and unlocked that smell of rain on earth so evocative of my youth. Our lovely day had come to a sultry end.

Windscreen wipers sloshed from side to side as he drove in silence, his attention on the tricky bends. I remained lost in my own thoughts. Thoughts that had to do with the transgression of sacred commitments and the niggling realisation that I'd crossed a line and there would be no stepping back.

I couldn't bring myself to share any of this with Finbarr, so when he asked me what I was thinking, I said, "The Garden of Ireland. It's what they call this place, isn't it?"

"Yes," he said. "And well named."

"I'll remember it as the garden of love."

"Are you happy?"

"Happy and sad."

"Why sad?"

"I've been conditioned to live by the rules."

"God is forgiving."

"Confession on Friday evening."

"I've no doubt the priest will understand."

"I wish I could understand the way I feel right now."

"Like what?"

"The Sugarloaf and the way it seemed to warn me about something."

"Magic mountains don't fit in with the glum humdrum of life as we know it."

"Is that how you see it?"

"Let's face it, Susan. We're both tied into a system

where someone else calls the shots. We go where we're told, live where we're told and do what we're told. That's the grim reality for both of us."

"It's called the religious life," I said.

I wanted to say more. I wanted to try to explain how everything had changed. How I was going to find it harder to allow anything or anyone get in the way of my longing for freedom and self-assertion. How could I begin to explain that uneasy sense of warning from the mountain? The Sugarloaf telling me the day I made love with a priest was the day I signed myself up for a life of anguish and disappointment?

Six

Magnificat anima mea Dominum.

I join with the other sisters as we chant in unison the Virgin's *Magnificat.* My soul praises the Lord and my spirit has rejoiced in God my Saviour.

Evening vespers, our way of winding down the day's activities. English and Latin on each facing page. I find myself flicking back to the Song of Songs, the only love song to have found its way into the Sacred Scripture.

Let him kiss me with the kisses of his mouth: for his love is sweeter than wine.

The words leaped out. I'd read these verses many times before, but now for the first time I could see what they really meant. These were words of love, the human kind of love that most people, if they're lucky, will experience at some point in their lives. Of course we'd always been told something else. We were meant to understand this psalm as a symbol of Christ's love for his Church.

His left hand beneath my head, his right arm embraces me.

For the first time, I could see these words for what they really were, the longing of a young girl for her lover, a clear expression of erotic love.

By night on my bed I sought him whom my soul loves...I sought him, but I found him not.

As the sacred music rose around me, it celebrated a joy known to me alone. I floated free, away from the chapel, away from that convent to a place that existed only in the secrecy of my soul. Since our lovemaking high in the hills, I'd been consumed with thoughts of Finbarr, with a love sweeter than wine.

For days now, ever since we had lain together, my thoughts had been possessed by him. I couldn't, even if I wanted to, banish from my mind the image of his face or the sound of his voice. I could no longer deny it to myself, I was lost in love.

Salve Regina, the final hymn and we shuffled off to our separate rooms to settle down for the night. I sat at my little table beside the window and struggled to put words on paper. Mid-summer's night, which meant there was still enough daylight for me to work. Sisters in their cells were setting themselves to collecting their thoughts around spiritual things while I in my lovelorn confusion fought to come to grips with emotions that were a long way from the denial of the self and union with God I'd been taught to pursue.

My thoughts began to crystallise in verse as though verse were the only medium to express my emotions. I crumpled page after page until the last wisp of mid-summer light had faded. I wondered what Finbarr would think when he read my effort, because naturally these words were for his eyes alone.

Bless me, Father, for I have sinned.
How long since your last confession?
One week, Father
...one sweet, sweet week...
You've offended your God
In this past week?
Grievous is my sin.
...sin with me, sin with me...
And what was the nature
Of your sin, my child?
I violated my sacred vows.
...violate, violate me, again and again...
In thought or in deed?
In deed have I sinned,
In thought, word and deed.
...indeed, in deed, in thought, word and deed...
A priest of God it was
Who led you to sin?
My soul's desire.
...a willing sacrifice in holy hands...
Go on your knees
And beg for His mercy.
I will beg for his love.
...forgive me, my love, who denied you so long...

In His infinite mercy
May he pardon the pain
Inflicted on His sacred heart.
Take up your beads and ask the Virgin
To grant the virtue of holy purity.
I absolve you
In the name of the Father, Son and Holy Spirit.
You may go in peace, my child.

~ * ~

A million specks of dust danced in the shaft of sunlight that lit the top corridor from the narrow window at its western end. I gave a timid, hesitant knock on the heavy oak door. Previous confrontations with my superior didn't augur well for whatever it was she wanted to say to me now.

I could only assume I was here to be reprimanded. Last time it was that little pocket radio Josie had given me as a gift, something I'd held onto instead of handing it up. What possible harm could there be in that, tuning in to a little Irish dance music in my bed at night, to remind me of neighbours gathered in the kitchen at home for music and dancing? At any rate, someone must have reported me because I was forced to hand over my radio and told to live without frivolity, to think instead about the sufferings of Jesus.

Mother Mercy, behind her desk, wore an expression of quiet calm. She'd the air of someone in full control of the world around her. Someone who had all the cards stacked on her side. She pointed to a chair on the other side of the desk.

"Sit down, Sister."

"Thank you, Mother."

Once I was seated, she opened a folder and drew out a single sheet of paper. What struck me at once was that the page had been crumpled and someone had done their best to straighten it out. All her movements were slow and deliberate. She'd a way of dragging things out to invest them with the utmost gravity.

"No doubt you are wondering, Sister, why I summoned you here?"

She looked at me with penetrating eyes, but since I said nothing she went on.

"I'm trying to trace the owner of this...this document. It's obviously been mislaid by its author. This page was found and handed to me yesterday by one of the sisters and I've been attempting to find the rightful owner, so far, I confess, without success. Nobody is aware of having mislaid any such manuscript. I was wondering if you might be able cast any light on its ownership. You don't by any chance happen to recognise it?"

The way she made use of words like author and manuscript intrigued me. After all, it wasn't a page from the Book of Kells we were talking about here. Her tone remained relaxed, casual almost, as though it were merely a minor matter that could be disposed of quickly.

As she turned the crumpled paper around to face me, I recognised it straight away. My mouth went dry as I saw my own writing and knew it was the poem I'd been preparing to pass to Finbarr, a crumpled copy I'd flung in the basket to go out with the rest of the convent refuse. Questions flooded my mind. How had a scrap of paper I thought I'd thrown away come into the possession of my superior? Had Mercy already guessed I was the one who'd written it? But of course she had. It was all so obvious.

"You recognise it, Sister? Can I take it this is your writing?"

The thought that someone, anyone, had been reading my private correspondence was almost too much to take in. But the realisation that a very personal communication of mine had fallen into the hands of this harridan was just beyond belief. She'd manoeuvred me into the position of having to answer her probing, of having to defend myself and justify my actions. She was, you might say, putting me on trial. I struggled to compose myself.

"I was asking if this is your writing, Sister."

"Yes, Mother, it's mine. That note belongs to me."

I reached across the desk and drew the page towards me and began to smooth and fold the paper in a slow deliberate way. I wanted her to see I was taking possession of what was mine and at the same time taking ownership of my actions. She should know I was no longer the frightened little novice, glad to take any humiliation, grateful for her motherly guidance. Things had changed. I was determined not to be bested by someone for whom I'd lost the last vestige of respect. The gall of this woman to have set her spies on me even to the point of rummaging through my discarded papers!

Mercy was speaking.

"I found a somewhat bizarre perspective coming through in those lines of yours, Sister. I hesitate to say this, but it comes across as a mockery of the sacrament of penance. Not what I'd expect from a soul dedicated to the service of Our Lord."

Her gaze never left me as she spoke but I was determined not to be browbeaten. Time to take my courage in my hands and speak out for myself.

"I'd like you to understand, Mother, that these are my own private notes, for my own private use, never intended to be seen, much less discussed, by anyone else."

I marvelled at my own bravery. I'd no idea where my courage was coming from.

"As a matter of fact," she said, "That's just the point I

was about to raise with you, Sister. Despite what you say, your lines were clearly intended to be read by someone else. You'll see it there at the top of the page, To my beloved F. That tells me it was intended to be read by the recipient, wouldn't you agree?"

The blood rushed to my cheeks and I couldn't think of an answer. After what she must have considered a suitably dramatic pause, she went on.

"I was wondering if you might like to throw any light on the identity of this person, the "F" it's written for?"

It goes without saying I'd no notion of satisfying the voyeuristic curiosity of this woman. My initial feelings of shock gave way to a rising wave of anger. I had to make her understand this last question went well beyond the bounds.

"I take full responsibility for my own actions, Mother. I feel no need to explain or apologise to anyone. I've no intention of saying anything to involve another person. That's something I'm not prepared to do."

"So you won't tell me who this… F is?"

The pause before the F showed me how she relished the moment. Like a cat with its prey, she was intent on playing this little drama to the limit for her own prurient pleasure. In the absence of any answer from me, she spoke again.

"Very well, then, I shall not force you to betray anyone. I'm in no position to judge you nor would I wish to do so. I'd ask you, though, to reflect on your position as a professed sister and give careful thought to the meaning of your vows and your commitment to Christ whose bride you became on the day you made your solemn promises."

For the first time, I noticed an unusual patch of color high on the otherwise deathly cheeks of the older woman. But I lost interest in this detail when the conversation took a new twist.

"There's just one other thing I'd like to ask you before you go. I've been asking the same question of the other sisters." Her eyes were on me. "It's about Father Gray. What is your assessment of Father Gray? As a chaplain, I mean? I'd just like your honest opinion. Confidentially, of course. It's important, you'll agree, that we have someone who is totally suitable as chaplain in a religious community."

An involuntary gasp escaped my lips. She'd held this card till last so as to play it with devastating effect. Either she knew a lot more than she was letting on or she'd done some very astute guesswork. The cunning old shrew.

"I don't think I understand your question, Mother."

If they were spying on me inside the convent, who's to say I wasn't being watched on the outside as well? Did she have a network of informers? Anything was possible.

"I'm simply asking if you know anything about Father Gray that might make his position here, shall we say, inappropriate."

It was too clear where this was heading. I struggled to keep my anger in check.

"I'm quite sure, Mother, you don't need my help in your prying. You have your cronies and they seem to be doing a good job of keeping you informed. As for Father Gray, or anyone else for that matter, I'm afraid you've come to the wrong person."

"Sister!" Shock and hurt showed on her face. The smug look had deserted her.

I understood at that moment there was no going back and the time had come for some straight talk.

"If you've something to say," I said, "why don't you just say it straight out? There's been enough beating around the bush. Or maybe this is how you get your kicks, inflicting distress on subordinates who can't answer back. It's not the first time I've noticed a sadistic streak."

"You will control your tongue, girl. I have never had to endure anything like this. Don't you realise who you're speaking to? You're not dealing now with some down-and-out in the slums. As your religious superior, I am due a modicum of respect."

"Respect?" I laughed in her face. "Tell me about respect!"

She didn't answer. Like a wounded animal in no condition to fight on. Her breathing was fast and audible. For my part, I'd run out of invective and decided it was time to get out of there. I hadn't planned to go so far, to say the things I said. But they were said now and there was no going back. I'd put Mercy in her place and felt the better for it. Things could never be the same between us again. As I stood to go, my superior watched, like a cornered vixen, not knowing if the attack was over or if there was more to come. It was only as I opened the door to let myself out that she spoke.

"You can expect to hear more about this, Sister."

"I don't have a lot of time to waste on this kind of nonsense."

As I walked away from her room, I knew that although I might have won that particular battle, the tide of the war was not in my favour.

Seven

I'd no wish to talk to anyone, no desire to listen to empty chatter. I needed to be alone, alone with my thoughts and my fears. I'd lain awake during the night wondering if the convent was really the place for me. It occurred to me during morning meditation that even if I didn't decide to leave, I might be given no choice. Mercy's words sounded ominous. You can expect to hear more about this. She had more than enough reasons to get rid of me, gross insubordination being the main one. There was also the possibility she'd heard whispers about me and Finbarr.

If I were to begin again on the outside, I wanted it to be my own decision. It would mean throwing up everything I believed in and writing off the past five years of my life. I still had a certain fondness for the sisters and their way of life. However, I couldn't dodge the question much longer.

I wished Finbarr were around so I could talk to him. On Friday evening, a strange priest had shown up for confessions. Finbarr must be ill, but I'd no way of finding out. I prayed to my guardian angel, Guide me, Michael, tell me what to do.

"You found a nice spot for yourself here under the trees."

I looked up to see Sister Consolata towering over me. A woman in her mid-thirties, Consolata had acted as novice mistress for me and Carmel, but since no more novices had joined she'd found a new role for herself as a counsellor in the outside world.

"Mind if I sit down?"

I moved over on the wooden bench as she sat down beside me. A tall ash tree provided some shade from the overhead sun. I relaxed a little. Consolata wasn't the worst. As my novice mistress, she had opened up new insights into life's meaning, something she couldn't have done if she weren't herself a deeply reflective person. When the two years of induction were over, she shed the strict persona and emerged as a warm friendly personality. She revealed an unexpected knack of talking to us in our own language. That's how it was now as she leaned back on the seat and stretched her legs in front of her.

"I don't blame you wanting to steer clear of that crowd," she laughed.

I didn't answer. I couldn't alter my mood like the throw of a switch. She made another attempt.

"I was talking to Mercy this morning. It seems you two had a bit of a spat."

"You mean you two were talking about me? What did she say?"

"She seems anxious to patch things up."

"What sort of things?"

"Things were said that might have been better not said."

I turned around to face her.

"Things were said that should have been said long ago. It's about time she heard it like it is. Has no one ever told her what a cow she is? I can't be the only one who's had it up to here with her."

Consolata didn't seem too shocked by my outburst.

"Listen to me, Susan. In any community, you're going to have the odd personality clash. It doesn't mean one's right, the other's wrong. It's just the way things are." She spoke quietly, reasonably. "Going through a bad patch right now?"

"Why is it suddenly all about me?"

"I'm only trying to help, Susan. Mercy's in a mood for mending bridges. She wants to make up. If you're facing some kind of crisis, she may be the one to help you sort it out. She's on your side, believe me."

"Oh, for Heaven's sake!"

"She thinks she knows a way to help."

"Are you having me on?"

"She suggested counselling."

"Counselling? For whom, may I ask?"

"For you."

I stared at her, incredulous.

"And you went along with this insane notion?"

She looked shamefaced and immediately I regretted my attack.

"It's no big deal," she said. "I go for counselling myself as part of my training."

"So why not give Mercy the benefit of your training and tell her she's the one who needs the shrink. She's a madwoman, Connie, I'm telling you."

She leaned towards me and put her hand on my forearm.

"Okay, but remember I'm here for you if you need someone to talk to."

The bell sounded for the end of recreation and the sisters made their way in silence to their separate duties. I stayed where I was. I needed to think. Sitting alone in the convent garden in the late June sunshine, I finally decided I no longer wanted to be part of a religious community. It was a decision that had been gestating within me, taking silent shape for some time. I'd looked for meaning within those walls. I'd sought and failed to find it.

But when that decision finally emerged into the daylight, it was as sharp and clear as the ray of sunlight that cut a path through the leaves above my head to illuminate the rounded pebbles at my feet. It wasn't without a tinge of sadness that I made my way to my cell to begin drafting a letter that would wind its way along labyrinthine paths to end at last on the desk of some official in the Vatican. A letter in which I'd beg for release from the solemn vows I'd made to the virgin mother of God a few short years before.

~ * ~

On Friday there was still no sign of Finbarr. This time it was a balding man who kept his head bowed as I whispered my sins in his ear. Afterwards the word went around the convent that Father Gray had been transferred. What this meant no one seemed to know. He just dropped out of sight.

When Berchmans called me to her office to say she'd arranged with college for my masters, it was obvious she knew nothing about my decision to leave the convent. Consolata knew and she'd warned me to keep it to myself. It would be too unsettling for the others. I put off telling Carmel because I knew she'd cry. But all the time I thought of the day fast approaching when that letter of dispensation would arrive from Rome and I'd find myself cut adrift to make my own way in the world, alone for the first time and forced to fall back on my own resources.

"Open it. Go on, look inside the front cover. What's it say there?"

Carmel handed me the first issue of Slán and there in the list of credits I saw my own name, Advisory Editor, Susan Enfield.

"Oh, Carmel, you rascal. I did nothing to deserve that."

"Go on out of that. What about the front cover with the kids on a swing…whose idea was that? Not to mention the proofreading and the layout. I don't know what I'd have done without you."

In the half year since I'd left the convent, I'd kept up my friendship with Carmel. Belfield was convenient to the convent and from my point of view I was reluctant to let her anywhere near my dingy bedsit in Rathmines. She kept me up to date with developments. Consolata had confided in her that Mercy wasn't going be there much longer. Her behaviour had become more erratic and there were moves going on behind the scenes to have her shifted.

She told me about the new chaplain, a bearded priest in a long brown habit, toes peeping out from leather sandals and a rope around his waist. He walked with eyes on the ground and never spoke to anyone except in confession.

"You never heard what happened that other one?" I said. "Father Gray."

"Finbarr, you mean?" Her eyes twinkled. "You keep on asking about him. I'd swear you had a crush on him or something."

I think I blushed, but she didn't seem to notice.

"Who knows where he is? Off out on the missions, if you ask me."

That evening as I tried to keep warm beside a single-bar electric fire, the window jammed shut against the traffic on Rathmines Road, I mulled over Carmel's throw-away remark that Finbarr might be on the missions. I couldn't believe he'd go off like that without attempting to contact me. He'd surely have got a message to me one way or another. Not knowing anything was the worst part. You don't stop being in love with someone just because they disappear without a word. Especially if they disappear without a word. I hated to think he'd treat me like that.

I felt abandoned. To be honest, I felt betrayed. We'd entered into the closest intimacy possible between two human beings. Such a bond, I believed, neither heaven nor earth could sunder. Yet months had gone by with no word from him. I found myself doing meaningless things, futile things like wandering into little art galleries, places I'd discovered in his company. Maybe I hoped to surprise him in earnest discussion with some gallery owner or hear his name dropped casually in conversation. It was all a foolish dream. Without him, those same galleries had lost their magic.

The one place I might have found the answer I didn't go near. What was it held me back from calling on Uncle

John? Probably I didn't want him to know I harboured amorous designs on his celibate nephew. I remembered him explaining at length what a privilege it was to have a priest in the family. The very last thing I wanted to do was ruin his admiration for his nephew.

My only hope of escape was to lose myself in research. Study might help me get over my childish infatuation. I'd managed without male company during most of my time in the convent and I could manage without it now. So the National Library became a sort of second home where I spent hours plundering the vast pile of source material around my subject.

"Dad has a new pep in his step since you left the convent," Josie said when we met for coffee. She'd told me before that he'd viewed my entering the convent as a profound loss to the family and something of a wasted life.

"He keeps on sending me cheques. I hate being a drag on him."

"Well maybe you should have stayed put, then. You'd no money problems in the convent, had you?"

"I'm on the lookout for some bit of part-time work. Something that won't cut into my study time."

"I wish you luck."

It was going to take a lot more than luck to rid myself of the futile longings that haunted my days and nights and find fulfilment in intellectual pursuits.

Eight

I'd only been home three times since leaving the convent. The first a flying visit soon after I came out. That's when I felt the eyes of the neighbours on me. I knew what they were thinking. There's the wee lassie that jumped over the wall.

"Don't leave it too long, Sue. Dad misses you."

I noticed this about Josie since I came out of the convent, a not so subtle change in the way she related to me. I'd ceded my position as big sister. A sort of role reversal, that's how I saw it. And this would now be sealed by the fact that she'd found herself a boyfriend and was talking as if marriage were just around the corner.

My mind went back to Josie's first day at boarding school. A timid little first-year girl, it had to be as frightening for her as it had been for me three years before. Away from home and family for the first time, it would have been like a kind of bereavement. I'd been there and I knew. Alone and bewildered, she'd have been mystified by weird figures in black who appeared to glide instead of walk and possessed the strange ability to materialise out of nowhere.

That first day she'd clung to me and I'd kept her with me for as long as I could, to make the break from home as painless as possible. When the time came for night prayers, we were corralled into separate seats in the chapel and afterwards led away to different parts of the building.

I'd lain awake thinking of my lonely little sister, knowing she was sobbing silently like all the rest of the first-years between their cold white linen sheets. Then in the darkness I felt a tugging at my blanket and could just about make out in the dim light of the Sacred Heart lamp a plump little figure trying to climb in beside me. I threw back the covers and helped her into my bed. There were no words between us as Josie snuggled up and buried her curly brown head in my breast. How she found her way to my dormitory, much less my bed, I still have no idea. Like a homing pigeon, some primal instinct brought her unerringly to where she knew she'd find comfort and solace.

In the morning, I smuggled Josie back to her rightful place without anyone being any the wiser and from then on she settled down to the new regime with little fuss. What happened that night was a rerun of many, many nights at home when to Josie I was a second mother, the one she ran to when she was anxious or afraid.

"What are you thinking about?" Josie interrupted my reverie. "Maybe you're thinking it's time you found a man of your own, am I right?"

"There'll be time enough for all that kind of thing when I've got the master's out of the way."

"It'd take you out of yourself and stop you moping around."

"Don't you think I'm old enough to take charge of my own life?"

All this talk of boyfriends unsettled me. The rational side of my brain told me to concentrate on the thesis and put everything else to one side. Josie's excitement and her attempts to translate it into some kind of message for me dragged the whole thing up again, that sense of loss, of something missing, that horrible vacuum within.

~ * ~

I walked through the Green on my way to the National Library. I spotted the seat where we sat, Finbarr and I, one warm September afternoon. I stopped. Stood there alone. I thought of that day two years ago when I'd experienced the first faint the stirrings of love. So much had happened since. Everything changed.

He seemed to have vanished from the very face of the earth. I remembered the day he'd brought me to a dusty little art gallery on South Anne Street and introduced me to his affable uncle. With something of a shock, I realised I hadn't seen Uncle John for over a year. He must have wondered why I stopped dropping in to swap a few words and share a cup of tea. I felt guilty. Then I thought why not now? No time like the present. It wouldn't kill me to take a few minutes to renew an old friendship. And who knows? I might pick up some hint as to the whereabouts of his priestly nephew.

The door tinkled as I went in. Uncle John came towards me and a look of recognition flashed across his face. A welcoming hand shot out in a warm friendly gesture. The same old Uncle John, nothing had changed.

"Well, well, well, if it isn't yourself, Sister Susan.

What a pleasure! And tell me this, where on earth have you been all this time? I haven't seen you in ages."

"I know, I know. It's been a while, what with one thing and another. I've been up to my eyes with study and exams and the Lord knows what. But tell me, what about yourself? How've you been keeping? How's business?"

"Business, is it? Don't talk to me about business. You're the first one to darken me doorstep since I opened up this morning. The country's going down the tubes, I'm tellin' you and we have government ministers going on TV to tell us we're living beyond our means. They can talk but the ordinary worker is forced to make his protest on the streets. No one's got a penny in his pocket any more. Not to spend on paintings anyway."

"I never got around to telling you," I said.

He looked at me, puzzled.

"I left the convent."

"That's a big move and there's no doubt about it." He was smiling. "To tell you the truth, I always knew there was something…different about you, as a nun if you know what I mean. You just didn't seem the type. That lovely golden head of yours was never meant to be hidden from human eyes."

"Cut the blarney now!"

"I mean it. A fine young woman like yourself deserves a good man to look after you."

"Last thing on my mind right now."

"Well, well, well! I'll have to let Finbarr know about this. But then, I'm the worst in the world for writing letters. I keep putting it on the long finger, you know how it goes."

"Maybe I could drop him a line myself. You wouldn't happen to have his address handy, would you?"

He reached for a torn envelope on the shelf above his desk and handed it to me. "You can hold onto that. I've copied it down."

The School of Philosophy and Theology, University of Fribourg.

I didn't hear what he said next. Everything became a blur as facts fell into place. Finbarr had gone abroad, not to the missions but to a Swiss university. At last I knew the truth but I needed to know more.

"He's in Fribourg, I see. Studying or teaching, I wonder?"

"A bit of both. He's doing a doctorate in theology. I always knew he was bright, that fella. He's going to end up a professor somewhere. Mind you, Susan, I used to hope he'd take over this place one day. I spent years building it up for him, but then he ups and enters the Church and that's that."

He'd a way of leaving people with their shattered dreams.

I needed somewhere quiet to sit and think, to sort out in my head where I stood with this capricious priest. Had I really believed he'd give up his priesthood, risk his future to humour the foolish fantasies of a silly little nun he'd briefly known in a Dublin convent?

I said goodbye to Uncle John and headed for the National Library.

~ * ~

A blank page beckoned me to write. I began randomly but soon my pen drew up memories of Finbarr. I sat with him in the magic light of memory and saw again the ducks make random turns on the ruffled surface of the pond. In a warm glow of contentment I reached again for his hand and felt for the pulse of his inexpressible loneliness. Now I was high in the sun-drenched valley of Glencree, dissolved in his embrace, believing that such bliss could never end.

But end it did and now was gone, faded like the vapour mists that rise from the tops of the Wicklow pines with the passing of each warm sultry shower. I felt empty and wanted to cry. I scrabbled for words to express the weight of loss that crushed my soul. No matter how I tortured the question, I was forced to accept I was lost in love for the man. In love with Finbarr. In love with a missing priest.

It was so clear to me now that my feelings hadn't been reciprocated. I'd just found out he was in Switzerland, absorbed in his studies. Did he retain any memory at all of the young nun he'd tried to help through a difficult patch? Probably not. I was abandoned, cast aside like yesterday's paper. I longed for someone I could talk to. But who? Carmel, still in the convent, living in a world far removed from the one in which I now found myself. How could she begin to understand my torment?

As for Josie, I was hardly going to reveal to her that I had passionate feelings for a priest. I knew my younger sister well enough to realise how scandalised and hurt she'd be to hear such an admission. Respectable Catholic girls didn't go around ensnaring priests, tempting them to betray their calling. That's how she'd see it. That's how any of my family or, for that matter, the wider community would see it.

Sitting at a lonely library table I took out my journal and started to write.

I gave you my heart and you threw it away...
I gave you my soul and you thought it a jest...
I gave you my love and you laughed at my folly.

In the Me Book I could open my heart without fear of judgement or criticism. I wrote about a young woman who had followed a mirage and for whom the mirage had faded in the shimmering sands even as she reached its quenching fountain.

That night I typed up my story for a magazine. For public consumption, the priest became a lawyer and in the end, the object of the woman's yearning reappeared, repenting of his bad behaviour, to give her at last the love she deserved and thus allow her broken heart to heal. I decided on this ending, not because it reflected any faint expectations of my own but in the hope it would go down well with an audience who expected nothing less from life than that all their dreams should have a blessed outcome.

Nine

The phone rang and rang and would have gone on ringing if the fellow in the room downstairs hadn't picked it up and shouted my name. I hurried down to find the receiver dangling at the end of a frayed cord. I put the phone to my ear.

"Susan Enfield?" I didn't recognise the cultivated female voice.

"Speaking."

"Hello, Susan. Sarah Langford here, from Maeve magazine."

"Maeve? Oh yes, of course! Hello, Sarah."

"Hello, Susan. I hope I haven't caught you at an awkward time or anything. I just wanted to let you know I've been reading your story and I like it, I really do. It's nicely crafted, well thought out. We think it'll strike a chord with the readers. I thought you might be pleased to hear we've decided to run it."

"Oh, yes... thank you… I'm delighted. I'm glad you like it. When can I expect to see it in print?"

"December edition. We plan every issue months in advance. But there's another reason I rang. I wonder if you could call around to the office. I'd like to meet you for a little chat. Maybe we could go for a coffee and have a quiet talk. You know where the office is, don't you? Just ask for me, Sarah. You're sure you're free? Say about half ten? Tomorrow?"

"I think I can make it. Yes, that's okay, I'll call by at half ten in the morning."

I couldn't help wondering what this was all about. It was certainly not for a friendly chat. That much I knew. However, I was free in any case, so there was nothing to lose by making the short bus journey to Grafton Street.

~ * ~

A young girl with red cheeks and over-sized glasses pointed me upstairs to a cluttered office on the first floor. Sarah Langford looked up from her work and smiled at me across her desk. I began to introduce myself, but she'd already been apprised of my approach. We crossed over to Bewleys on the opposite side of the street. An attractive woman in her early forties, she wore a smart dark office suit, her brown hair cut tight about her head. She was, she said, involved in every aspect of the magazine, mainly responsible for overall planning, supervising sub-editors and other staff and bearing ultimate responsibility for the commercial success of the publication. All of this she explained in a friendly, matter of fact tone of voice. I was left in no doubt she was the one with the final say on everything that appeared from month to month. I imagine she felt it appropriate to fill me in on her own position before proceeding to ask me anything about myself.

"You're a good writer, Susan, but I presume you're not depending on writing stories for a living. You must have something else, you know, to keep a crust…"

"I'm a post-grad student. I have to confess I'm still living off my family. Spent five years in a convent, you see. I'm not that long out and still trying to find my feet."

"And what are you researching, may I ask?"

"James Stephens. Fascinating character. The more I learn about the man, the more interesting he gets. Have you read any of his books?"

"As a matter of fact, we ran an article on him a couple of years back. He was a big hit in the first half of the century. It often struck me he invented magical realism before the term was heard of."

"I prefer to call it Celtic fantasy, since he drew so heavily on the Irish folklore and mythology."

Sarah held her cup between her wide open hands, pressing it against her chin while she studied me over the rim.

"You wouldn't happen to be the Susan Enfield associated with that new publication, Slán?"

"You know about it? We're really only getting it off the ground. Lord knows if it'll ever come to anything."

"You're listed as Advisory Editor. Impressive. Anyway, it brings me to the reason I wanted to talk to you. No doubt you've been wondering. Here's the situation. I'm in a bit of a bind at the moment. Molly English is out on maternity leave. My fiction editor. I badly need somebody to fill the gap. I loved that story of yours. I'd have sworn it was your own story if you hadn't told me you spent the past five years in a convent. For an ex-nun you've a pretty good grasp of elemental human emotions. More important, though, you seem to have a clear idea what a magazine like ours is looking for. So, what do you say? Will you do it?"

She sat looking at me with that final question mark fixed on her face. In truth I didn't need to think about this. I'd known all along I was going to have to find a job. I'd always dreamt of finding a position where I could continue my love affair with the English language.

"There's just one small problem," I said.

"Oh?"

"I've promised to stick with Slán till we get it firmly established."

"That's hardly taking up all your time, is it?"

"I don't suppose so. For the moment, we're happy to keep it as a quarterly."

"You're talking about a few days a month. That settles it then. You'll come and work with me for the rest of the time. You'll be free to take whatever time you need for your quarterly."

~ * ~

My work involved wading through piles of material sent in on spec by hopeful writers. I soon discovered I rarely had to read beyond the opening lines before deciding whether to consign the whole effort to the waste basket. But it was all worth it for the occasional piece of prose which told me I'd found an exciting new talent to be cultivated and encouraged. That's what made the job such a joy.

I didn't go home that Christmas. Carmel and I were working to put some shape on the next edition of Slán. This, on top of my regular work at Maeve, and research for my thesis which I couldn't afford to neglect.

When I phoned home on Christmas day, there was no mistaking the tone of disappointment and rebuke in my father's voice.

"We were hoping we'd see you, Sue. There's an empty place at the table."

"Dad, you wouldn't believe how busy I am. I'm run off my feet with the new job. But at least I'm earning some money for a change. You won't feel it now till Josie's wedding. Then we'll have a great old chat and I'll fill you in on all the news."

"I suppose I'll have to wait."

~ * ~

February was approaching fast and Josie was on the phone telling me about her problems.

"It'll be a small wedding," she said. "Martin's their best apprentice and still he only gets the same pittance as all the rest."

Martin had a few months to go before he was a fully qualified accountant.

"There's no reason you can't hold onto your job," I said. "Your civil service salary should be enough to keep you going."

"I'm not complaining. A pal of Martin has got us fixed up with a wee cottage in Harold's Cross."

A week later, Josie came up with the inspired idea of digging out our mother's 1951 wedding dress and using it herself.

"You're sure it'll fit you?" I said.

"Mae Gibson's a wizard at that kind of thing. She'll let it out at the waist and do something about the bust. Plus, she'll get a great kick out of fussing around."

~ * ~

I arrived at the old place two days before the wedding. The locals had got used to me by now, the one-time nun blatantly parading around in the open as if there was nothing to hide. Maybe that accounts for why my sister had a packed congregation in church for her wedding.

Valentine's Day. That idea must have come from Josie, since Martin was far too staid to come up with such a romantic notion. Mae Gibson had worked wonders on the dress and Josie looked very pretty in the formal ballerina length grey satin evening gown.

After the ceremony, the four of us stood on the steps of the church while the photographer fussed over his tripod and camera. He motioned us to the right, then back a little to the left. Martin fiddled with his tie. Just as the shutter clicked, it caught Josie fussing with the flowers she'd pinned to her hair. She'd disdained to wear the little black velvet hat with ostrich feather Mam had worn in her own wedding photo.

The onlookers gathered on the street behind the photographer. They stood about in little knots and turned their faces away whenever they wanted to make some comment. There weren't too many distractions to enliven the dull routine of daily life in a small country town.

Dad booked an upper room in the Shamrock Hotel where we all headed after the ceremony. In the early afternoon, Josie and Martin made a dash to the bus for the first part of their trip to West Cork for the honeymoon.

Most of the guests stayed on for music and dancing. I hated dancing, so I spent the time renewing acquaintance with friends and relations I hadn't seen since I was a girl. I could see Dad was tired. Maybe he'd drunk a little more beer than he was used to, but it gave me the excuse I needed to get away. We sat by the range in the kitchen. We had the house to ourselves and we were able to have our first real conversation in years. I saw he was stiffer in his movements.

"There's wee Josie gone off now," he said in a dreamy sort of way.

"You feel sad?"

"Sad her Mammy wasn't here to see her off."

"A loss for both of us, Dad."

"Aye, indeed." He turned to me and said, "There's nothing I'd like more than to see yourself settled down."

I took his hand in mine I told him I'd always be there when he needed me.

"I never doubted that, Sue, but you've to look after yourself number one."

~ * ~

I'd time on my hands before catching the bus. I took a walk out along the narrow road to the spot where my grandmother had lived alone after my grandfather passed away. On that smallholding, she'd managed to scratch a living for herself with her chickens, pigs, goat, cow and potato patch. I met nobody along the road where the night's frost still glistened and the stillness and peace of the morning made a welcome change from the partying of the previous day. I was glad to be shut of all those tedious remarks about it being my turn next to give them a day out.

I leaned on the same old iron gate to gaze across the old farmyard to where a dozen dappled cattle grazed the side of the drumlin. They raised their heads to stare and we stood gaping at each other till they lost interest and went back to searching out the last surviving stems in the winter pasture.

Memories of my mother and father helping out with the harvest. Memories of the pungent smell of manure as my brothers mucked out the sheds while my little sister and I looked on. I mulled over all that had come to pass in the years that followed. My time in the convent, my decision to quit, the way my dream job had landed in my lap. I should have been happy. But no. All I was aware of was the same irrational, inexplicable, utterly futile longing for a man who had deliberately and callously cut me out.

Someone I'd no reason to believe would ever enter my life again.

Ten

"Listen, Carmel, I should have said it to you before, but I'm not going to be able to keep it up."

Disappointed showed on her face. I hated myself for doing this. The autumn edition of Slán was ready to go to press. I'd put in a lot of evenings in a cramped top-floor room in Baggot Street getting the final touches in place for the printers. This was our sixth edition. I'd been spending far too much of my time on something I was getting nothing out of but the satisfaction of helping a friend. All that hassle of trying to coax articles out of people and having to chase them up to get their copy in on time. I could no longer make bits of myself.

"Will you be able to find someone else?" I said.

"Don't you worry about a thing, Susan; you've done Trojan work here. I'd never have got to where we are now without you. I'll advertise for someone."

"Have you time to come next door for a bite to eat?" We were locking up for the night.

It was warm and welcoming in the little café, the perfect spot to catch up on each other's news.

"I can't wait to hear all the latest," she said.

"I got a raise," I said. "I've never felt so rich in my life. I've been out in Donnybrook looking at a place for rent. I just can't wait to get out of that dive in Rathmines."

"Made any new friends?" Her way of asking was there any romance in the offing.

"Are you joking me? I'm way too busy for that sort of thing. Where's the rush? All in its own time, I say. But tell me something, how are things out there in the convent? Any changes?"

"Mercy's gone and Consolata's ruling the roost."

"That's big news. You still have that barefoot monk coming to hear confessions?"

"I thought you might get around to that. As a matter of fact there's been a sighting of your heart-throb, your Father Finbarr."

My heart missed a beat.

"What d'you mean, a sighting? Tell me."

"One of our sisters spotted him the other day at some kind of conference, something to do with theology."

"But I thought he'd gone abroad, no?" I hoped my interest wasn't too obvious.

"She was pretty certain it was him, even in civvies."

My mind was in turmoil. Finbarr back in Dublin? Questions raced through my brain. How long had he been here? Was he home for good? Where was he living? Had he been asking about me? Did he even remember me?

I said goodnight to Carmel and we headed off in different directions.

~ * ~

In the morning I sat at my desk and tried to pull myself together. A letter lay open in front of me saying how much a reader had enjoyed a recent story and asking for more of the same. I threw it in a drawer because I couldn't think straight. I'd slept badly. In my dreams I'd seen a band of dancing demons. They chanted and jeered, Finbarr's back. Finbarr's back. Finbarr's back in town. I'd cried out in the night, "Stop! Stop! Please stop it. You're driving me insane."

I needed to think, to get a grip on things. If I wanted to find him, it wouldn't be too hard to do so. Dublin was a small place, a town where everyone knew everyone. But how was it going to look if I were the one to go running after him? Surely it was up to him? If he wanted to find me, that is.

Sitting there at my desk, I began to feel foolish. Where was that independent young woman who'd outgrown all that dreamy nonsense? The more I thought about it, the more my better sense prevailed and I saw how downright silly I was. What's gone is gone. Silly to imagine there could be anything left of what was little more than a fleeting liaison. All in the past, consigned to history. Pull yourself together, woman. Time to look to the future, forget the foolish fantasies, let go those girlish dreams.

And yet. Supposing, just supposing, our paths should ever cross. What would I say to him? A lover who left without warning or explanation, without even bothering to say goodbye? He who corresponded with his Uncle John and God knows who else, yet never thought to send me as much as a postcard? Ignore him. That's what I'd do. I knew now. I'd look through him like he didn't exist. Turn on my heel, walk away as he had walked out of my life. Maybe he'd see the enormity of what he'd done and maybe, just maybe, he'd suffer some slight pang of remorse for the way he'd treated me.

~ * ~

She greeted me with a friendly smile. "I can take you to the conservatory," she said with the air of someone who'd lived here all her life.

Annie sat in a wheelchair in the far corner of a large ward. Around the room were empty beds, their occupants having taken themselves to the dayroom or out into the grounds. Annie was a slim girl with shoulder-length fair hair and blue eyes that shone when she looked at you. She showed no hint of shyness or reserve.

It was warm in the conservatory, whether from the pale October sunshine or the central heating I couldn't say. A man in his thirties wheeled himself out as we came in and we had the place to ourselves.

"So what you want to talk about?" She exuded a kind of bubbly excitement.

"Do you mind if I leave the tape running while we talk?" I'd grown used to the routine in the past few months, since Sarah had asked me to take on this project.

"How would you feel about trying something new?" she'd said. "A chance to get away from that desk for a while?"

I was to visit hospitals, talk to patients and write up the interviews in a way which would take Maeve in a different direction, exploring things that affect real people, real lives. Today I'd arranged to meet a young woman with catastrophic injuries from a car crash.

"You just fire ahead, Susan. I'm real excited about this."

"Tell me about your family."

She was, she said, the youngest and the only girl in a family of four.

"One or other of the lads tries to get up to Dublin at the weekend. I love when they can make it. Some girls from the camogie club as well. It breaks the monotony, you know. It stops you thinking. You'd go mad in a place like this. Too much time to think."

"How long's it been? Since the accident, I mean?

"Six months. No, seven."

"What's it like in here, Annie? They look after you?"

"Like the Ritz. All mod cons. Room service at the press of a button. Just press that button there beside you. Go on, press it and see what happens."

"I'll take your word for it."

She laughed. A smiling young woman without a care in the world. Until you saw how she was strapped into the chair. How could she joke about her situation, struck down in the blossom of her young womanhood, faced with the prospect of never being able to stand or walk again?

The way she told it, the physiotherapy sessions were hilarious.

"I wish you could see them trying to stand me up between them bars, the two of them holding onto me, John on one side and the nurse on the other. I don't know whether to laugh or cry."

No direct questions about the accident. I'd been warned. Her boyfriend had been driving. He never stood a chance when the car ended up against a tree. In any case, my instincts prevented me intruding where trained counsellors must tread with caution.

"You try to keep the best side out, Annie, but it can't be fun all the time, can it? There must be times…d'you ever feel even the tiniest bit depressed?"

"Just take a look at me, will you."

"How bad is it really? You can tell me."

She thought for a moment.

"In this place, there's always someone else who's worse than yourself. Like that chap who came in last week. A clean C2 cut off."

"What's that?"

"Everything's gone below the neck. At least I can move my fingers…look."

"I'll bet there's times you feel depressed all the same."

"I'm never going to be fixed. They know it, I know it, we all know it. I wish they'd all just go away and let me alone."

"Is there no one you can talk to when you're feeling that way?"

"You mean a shoulder to cry on?"

"Something like that."

A dreamy look came into her eyes.

"There's this guy, a sort of chaplain, I suppose you'd call him. Good looking guy. Kinda knows where you're coming from. Feels your pain, if you know what I mean. I saw him this morning and he was real upset he was. You probably heard what happened."

"Heard what?"

"That girl from the lower ward."

"What happened to her?"

"The whole place is in bits over it. It happened

yesterday. She was hit by a truck. Her wheelchair ended up under the driver's cab. She's below in the mortuary."

"You're saying she went out on her own?"

"I guess she wanted to be independent. You know how it is."

"That chaplain you were talking about, was he here when it happened?"

"Oh, he's in and out most of the time. Lives in the bungalow. That's where he does his writing. You'd like him."

"I've no doubt." Suddenly I wanted to leave, to get away from the place. "Listen Annie, why don't we call it a day? I'll send you a draft of the interview. Remember, you'll have the last say in what appears. Thanks for taking the time. I have to say I really enjoyed meeting you."

"See ya."

I called by the matron's office to say I was leaving.

"How did you two get on?" The round cheeks gave her a jolly looking expression. "Great resilience, that girl. She won't let it get her down. I'm delighted we'll be getting a bit of publicity into the bargain. Great for the hospital."

"That's what I'm hoping, too."

"Oh, I nearly forgot. The chaplain would like a quick word with you before you go. I'll give him a ring and say you're here with me now."

Words went back and forth over the phone.

"He's actually down in the bungalow at the moment, Miss Enfield. He was wondering if you might like to walk down and he'll talk to you there. It's not far."

My pulse began to race. What had young Annie said? Chaplain. Good looking guy. Could it possibly? Not

Finbarr surely? Just too much of a coincidence, the sort of coincidence you'd get in a romantic novel. But this was real life and there was still time to turn about and head for home. But then how would I ever know for sure unless I went and met him? Most probably it was someone else entirely. Yet I felt distinctly apprehensive

I couldn't shake the sense of foreboding as I walked slowly along the narrow tarmacadam path that ran through the hospital grounds. I could see the bungalow just beyond the trees.

Eleven

The sound of the doorbell was a low, dull, distant reverberation. I noticed a patch of peeling paint and resisted the urge to prize it off with my fingernail. Noises like shifting furniture. Then the door was drawn inwards, dragging against the worn carpet. He looked as though he'd been sleeping in his knitted pullover and shabby slippers. Yet there could be no doubt that this was he, the very man, the candle-flame around whom my thoughts had fluttered for two years and more. The same old grin attempted to mask the eyes red with weeping. Neither of us said anything. As if each were testing the reality of the situation, waiting for mirage to resolve into meaning.

He spoke first.

"It had to be you. There can't be too many Susan Enfields floating around this city."

I didn't answer. This man had a lot of explaining to do.

"Don't stand there, Susan. Come in. I wondered was I ever going to see you again. Step in out of the cold. I've a fire going in there."

He sank heavily onto the sofa while I sat down where he'd indicated, though slowly, under protest.

"I suppose you're wondering…" he began.

"You're bloody right I'm wondering. I'm wondering how anyone could be so damn selfish, so…so totally lacking in basic decency. Oh yes, I'm wondering all right. Wondering how you led me to believe I meant something to you, something special. Pretending to love me when all you were doing was using me. Do you hear? Using me for your own satisfaction."

"No, Susan, it's not like that. Just let me explain. I want to explain."

"Explain? Explain to me how you cleared off to Fribourg without a word. No goodbye, no letter, no nothing. Try explaining that. On second thoughts, don't bother. I can do without your explanations. I've grown up in your absence, in case you haven't noticed. I'm a big girl now, not some innocent to be played around with and thrown on the rubbish heap."

"So what do you want me to do? Just tell me and I'll do it."

"I'll tell you what not to do. Never ever treat another woman the way you treated me. Never think that women are there for your selfish gratification. Don't imagine for a moment I'm going to come crawling back asking for more of the same. And one more thing, will you for Christ sake make up your mind whether you're a priest or not a priest. You're either one thing or the other. You can't be both. Face up to it, man. If you want a woman, get yourself a woman, but forget about playing chaplain around those unfortunate patients who could teach you a thing or two about life."

What stopped me there was the sight of him burying

his face in his hands and starting to sob. As I watched his shoulders shake, the impulse to attack gave way to a more motherly instinct. In any event, I'd said what I wanted to say. It had needed to be said. Give it time to sink in. I watched and waited.

He must have realised the tirade had stopped, that I was sitting there watching him, for he looked at me and began to massage his face with the heels of his hands.

"You'll have to forgive me, Susan. I've had a rough time over the past twenty four hours."

A spark shot out of the fire onto the carpet. He stretched out his leg and crushed it under his heel leaving a black smudge where the spark had glowed.

"Something terrible happened in the hospital," he said.

"Yeah, I heard."

"You heard?"

"Poor girl killed outside the front gate. Awful thing to happen."

"I could have stopped it, d'you know that? She could still be alive today."

"Don't talk nonsense. There's nothing you or anyone else could have done. The girl made a stupid mistake trying to cross that road on her own. An accident, pure and simple."

"No accident. She told me she'd had enough. She saw her whole life stretching out ahead of her. She was really depressed about it."

"You're saying she killed herself?"

"I'm there to spot the signals, bring people back from the brink, give them some spark of hope. I wanted to have a long session with her yesterday but I left it too late. I didn't realise the urgency."

"Who's to know what's going on inside anyone's mind?"

"I let her die when I could have stopped it. I'm going to live with this for the rest of my days."

I moved across and sat beside him. Fate had landed me on his doorstep in his time of torment. He needed someone at this moment and I was glad I was there.

"I could have stopped her." He muttered the words over and over, flailing himself pointlessly.

I took his hand between my two hands and squeezed it gently. I wanted to pour balm on his tortured soul. When he settled his head on my shoulder, I ran my fingers through his hair and he seemed more at ease. An orange flame shot upwards from the glowing embers. I felt Finbarr melt into a warm comfortable position and I heard his long soft sigh.

I tussled with the contradictions. On the one hand, there was the callous disregard he'd shown me in taking himself off without a word. On the other hand, the gentle, humane Finbarr, who took it on himself to be there for those patients, to be their friend, to comfort and console and help them face their fears.

How to reconcile these contrasting sides of the same man? How could it be possible to live with someone like that? Should I not simply cut my losses and put clear ground between us before I was hurt even more? What I had beside me at this moment was a raw exposed creature, vulnerable and seemingly consoled by my presence. Somewhere in the deepest recesses of my mind, I knew I couldn't just abandon him.

When the fire had died down to a peaceful glow, I knew the time had come to ask him. I had to know every minute detail of what had happened that fateful week when he went missing from his post at the convent. The same week I had gone through my own crisis of vocation. The very week I had needed him most.

"Why, Finbarr? Tell me why you did it."

"They gave me no option."

"Who gave you no option? And why so sudden?"

~ * ~

"I got a call to go to the Provincial's office. I'd no idea what it was about. I walked into that room and saw him sitting there with his back to me. In a swivel chair. He swung around to face me as I came in."

"'Ah, Finbarr!' he says. 'Good to see you,' he says. 'How's it goin'?'"

Though Michael Drummond had risen to the highest position in the Irish Province, he wanted to hold onto the image of the common man and liked to be on first name terms with all his priests.

"Sit down there and make yourself comfortable. Evening's starting to close in. Summer on the way out. You are, let me see, more than twelve months ordained, now. You don't feel the time slipping by, do you?"

Finbarr knew full well he hadn't been summoned to discuss the passage of the seasons. The Provincial was still talking.

"How have you been getting on, tell me? I believe you've got your Final Theology coming up in a week or two, but then exams were never any bother to you. When

God was handing out the brains, you grabbed a double helping, right?"

He laughed at his own joke. Mike Drummond believed in keeping his ear close to the ground. There was little going on in his bailiwick that escaped his attention.

"You're still going over to that convent for Mass and confessions, am I right? There's nothing like the bit of pastoral experience to remind us what it's really all about. Keeps your two feet on the ground, I always say. Tell me, how do you find those nuns? Funny lot, nuns, wouldn't you say? You've got to tread very carefully around the nuns, I can tell you that. It's like they're watching every move you make. Only too ready to go running with tales, some of them."

"Running with tales? What are you saying, Mike? You're not suggesting…?"

"No, no, no, Finbarr, not at all. I'm not suggesting anything. I never give them the slightest bit of credence. Not for a minute I don't. It seems there's an old mother hen there watching over her clutch with a beady eye. She passed on a couple of complaints. Something about young novices she doesn't trust. And your name came up. That's the thing. As I said, I don't take any of this stuff too seriously. I know as well as anyone how the most innocent actions can be given the wrong slant. Words can be twisted and taken out of context. I'm just saying you can't be too careful. That's really all I'm saying."

"So what are you telling me? Not to talk to them?"

"You can't afford to be too familiar with any of them, Finbarr. Especially the younger ones. They might easily get the wrong idea. Do you follow my meaning?"

Finbarr had said nothing but his mind was racing. How much did the Reverend Mother know of his relationship with Susan and how much of what she knew had she passed on to Mike Drummond? He was well aware he'd flouted the strict rules of conduct expected of a priest, but had managed to square his actions with his conscience.

"You're a young man, Finbarr, and I'm speaking from many years of experience. You and me are committed to this thing called celibacy. It's going to be a struggle, believe me. It doesn't get any easier. Just one word of advice, though. You've got to be careful around women. Women are wily, it's in their nature. Many a good priest was led astray by the machinations of a woman."

"Thanks for the advice, Mike. I appreciate it. I really do. I don't think you need have any worries about me, though. I've got my eyes wide open. I can handle the situation."

"That's what I wanted to talk to you about. You won't be asked to handle this particular situation. I told the convent you're being transferred."

"Transferred? What's transferred mean? Transferred to where?"

"I want you to go to Fribourg."

"You mean the university? But when?"

"I'm sorry to spring it on you like this. I know it's very short notice. A post-grad position has come up there and we've managed to secure it for you. I had to pull some strings, mind you. But it's the perfect opportunity for you to complete your doctorate. It's too good an opportunity to pass up. Your flight's booked for the day after tomorrow. That'll give you a couple of nights at home with your parents before you go."

"I don't know what to say, Mike. It's all a bit rushed, isn't it? I can't even think straight."

"You won't regret it, Finbarr. It's the chance of a lifetime. Top university… their school of theology is second to none. It'll be a whole new scene over there. No, you won't regret it. Oh, just one more thing. No contact with that convent. A clean break, if you know what I mean. No need to communicate with them at all. It's the only way. They'll have a new chaplain and you'll soon be a distant memory. That's the way you want it, isn't it?"

"I guess you're right, Mike. I guess you know best."

~ * ~

I'd listened to Finbarr's account of events in silence and when he finished, we sat staring into the dying embers. I now had a clear picture of the circumstances surrounding his sudden disappearance. He'd no idea I'd left the convent. I wondered what would have happened had he known. Would things have been different? Would he have tried to make contact? I didn't ask him. He'd told me what had happened and for now that was enough.

"I know what you're thinking." He reached for two fresh sods to throw on the fire. "You're thinking I'm a selfish bastard."

"You could have written."

"I was afraid your letters would be opened by the convent. I began to believe it might be better for both of us to forget and move on. My commitment to the priesthood was shaky but I wanted to give it a chance and I thought a complete break was the best way. I filled my days with study, research, preparing lectures. That way I thought I could put the past to rest."

"Seems to me you made a good job of it."

"Think what you like, I never forgot you. You were always there. When things went well for me, I'd find myself wondering would you be proud of me if you knew. And when things went against me I'd catch myself looking to you for support. When a permanent post came up, I faced a difficult decision. Was I to become an anonymous part of an academic community and fade into a grey existence of dusty books and lecture halls? That's when I decided to come back to Ireland."

"What did your superiors think about that?"

"I made it clear I was taking orders from no one. Then I heard about this chaplaincy and thought it would keep me out of trouble and put a crust on the table."

"I find it odd you made no attempt to contact me."

"I ran into one of your former sisters. She said she heard you were working for some magazine or other. I knew we'd meet again and we did."

The tension lifted. We sat on the settee and as he talked, I leaned in against his body. Daylight faded to dusk and through the uncurtained window I could see traffic passing on the busy road. Anyone going by had a clear view of the room where we sat.

"There's no privacy here," I said.

I took both his hands and dragged him to his feet. He allowed me lead him like a lap dog as I sought the bedroom at the back of the house.

"It's quieter here," I said.

The bed was unmade, the curtains still drawn, yet the sinking sun had contrived to find a crevice through which to send a slender shaft of light which placed a spot of gold on the wall above the headboard.

I helped him undress and lay beside him and drew him into my embrace. I felt the strength of his arms about me, his unshaven face against my cheek as we lay at ease with each other, imbibing the peace and tranquility of the moment. I divined that he had in the end found the place he'd been searching for, a place where he belonged. I too was finally at ease, repossessed of what I believed had been lost to me forever. There was peace there in the darkened room at the back of the little bungalow, an immense distance from the hustle and bustle of the hospital with all its pain, its sorrow, its hope and despair.

Here there was no hurry, no pressure, just all the time in the world. I allowed things to take their course. I didn't rush him and when the time was right, with a gentle touch I helped to awaken him. The fantasies I'd harboured in the secrecy of my soul were coming to fulfillment. It wasn't the first time we'd made love, but it was different. Only the coolness of a white linen sheet caressed our bodies. There was total freedom.

No living being knew where we were at this moment. The rest of humanity had ceased to exist. In the world there were but two, cut off, cast away on a distant isle. Pent up passion demanded release. This was the lovemaking of two people who in the darkness of the night had dreamt of the moment they would again come together. Two people, man and woman, who existed only for each other, who believed with unshakable conviction in the destiny of their belonging. Here was a love that had built behind a yielding dam, awaiting release, unstoppable now, a bursting cascade where there was nothing to constrain it. We gave ourselves to each other with an abandoned giving. How else could it be? And as we lay together, our bodies fused, I was permeated by intense feelings of fulfilment, reaching to every point of me, to every corner of my being.

I wanted only that it would never end.

Twelve

The hospital interviews proved a success, and Sarah showed her gratitude the best way she could. She offered me the vacant post of Deputy Editor-in-chief.

With my new place in Donnybrook, the salary was going to come in handy. Plus, my new job title wasn't going to hurt my future in Maeve or wherever I might find myself. In deference to my new status, Sarah began to consult me on matters of editorial policy and I began to feel I had a personal stake in the future of the magazine.

I shared all this with Josie.

"Still, Sue, you can't let your work be the be-all and end-all of your existence. You need to get out more and enjoy yourself."

I'd never mentioned Finbarr to my sister. She knew nothing of his existence, which explained her constant going on about the need for me to get out and meet people. I wasn't going to be able to keep it from her much longer.

"You don't think I'm enjoying myself as it is?"

"Get out to a few dances. Meet a nice fella. You know what I'm talking about."

"Bossy!"

"I don't want to see you turning into an old maid, Sue. There's more to life than work."

I braced myself to tell her. Like a nervous penitent before confession. She'd want to know every detail, who he was, what he did, the breed and seed of him. There was no way in the world I was going to be able to hide the fact he was a priest.

"I'll be seeing Finbarr at the weekend."

"Finbarr?" A look of surprise mingled with curiosity. "I never heard you mention any Finbarr. Fill me in, Sue, I want to hear more." She leant forward across the table, all eager.

"I'm going out with this guy."

"Well you're the smooth operator if ever there was. So go on, tell me all about him. Is it serious?"

"We've been seeing each other for the past few months."

"And you never said a word! Keep going, I'm dying to hear. Give me the whole works. What's the big secret? You don't have to hide anything from your little sister, you know. Haven't I been saying all along you need a man in your life? What does he do anyway?"

"He's sort of ..."

"Sort of what?"

"He's sort of a priest."

I watched the colour drain from her cheeks.

"What do you mean, sort of a priest? There's no such thing as sort of a priest."

"He doesn't practise as a priest any more. He works as a hospital chaplain. It's not important. He's just such a nice guy. I'd love you to meet him."

"You must be out of your mind. God knows the world is full of men. Surely to God you didn't have to go and get yourself involved with a priest?"

I reached across the table to press her hand, but she pulled away.

"Listen here to me, Josie. It's all right. I love him. We love each other. What does it matter whether he's a priest or not? I know I've found the right man. Don't ask me to turn my back on him now. Please. I've never been so happy. You've no idea what it means for me. I'm telling you, I've never been so sure of anything in my whole life."

"I only wish you could hear yourself. We were brought up to have some respect for religion. Think of Mam lying in the cold clay. She prayed all her life her children would turn out right. How could you do this to her now? As for Dad, it'll break his heart. Kill him altogether."

"Don't think I haven't thought of all that. I lie awake at night thinking about it. The last thing in the world I want to do is hurt anyone. But it's my life, Josie. My life."

She rummaged in her bag for a tissue. "It's the shame of it, Susan," she sobbed. "We'll never be able to hold our heads up again."

We stood to leave with most of the food still on the plates. We emerged into the wan winter sun to hear the sound of carol singers somewhere near the bottom of Grafton Street. I wrapped my arms around my sister and drew her towards me. She was barely holding back the tears. I thought of the many times when she was a tiny thing and I allowed her to cry herself to sleep on my shoulder.

"You must trust me, Josie. I'm old enough to know what I'm doing. I promise you I'll do nothing to bring disgrace on the family. Still, I have to take responsibility for my own decisions, my own life."

"It's you I'm thinking of, Sue, you must know that. I'd hate to see you bring any kind of trouble on yourself. Don't make a mess of your life, that's all I'm saying."

The words of a Christmas carol came drifting on the air. The shepherds had an angel, the wise men had a star, but what have I, a little child, to guide me from afar?

Make a mess of my life? What could possibly go wrong? Ridiculous idea. Yet before heading north for Christmas, I told Finbarr two things. I said if he was serious about our relationship, he'd have to cut his ties with the church. I told him too it was time to be open with his parents and let them know the truth, that he was no longer a practising priest.

"We'll see how it goes," he said.

~ * ~

"Deputy Editor-in-chief." Dad read the words aloud with a mixture of awe and admiration. He said the words over as if imbibing them and savouring the taste. I'd brought him a copy of Maeve and pointed out my thumbnail photo on the inside cover.

"Amn't I the proud man this day?" he said, puffing on his pipe while he pondered the wonder of it all. "I hear tell there's something else stirring."

He opened his lips to allow a ball of pale smoke float free. "A wee bird was whispering in me ear."

"I haven't a notion what you're on about."

"Oh haven't you, now? There wouldn't be any young

man in the offing now, would there?"

So Josie had been talking! I'd always been close to my father and I knew I held a special place in his affections. It had broken his heart when he'd left me on the steps of the convent and I'd heard from Josie he could hardly hide his relief when I left. So there was no reason why I should ever want to hide anything from him. He'd shown himself to be on my side at every twist and turn.

"Your sources are impeccable," I said.

"Plain language, if you please."

"It's true, I'm doing a line."

"Well, go on then and let me have it. Why would you want to be keeping your old man in the dark?"

"Dad, he's an ex-priest." I kept my voice down. My brother Johnny and Bridie his wife were in the front part of the house.

He drew meditatively on his pipe.

"And you're an ex-nun! Divil the bit of harm in that."

I threw my arms around his neck and hugged him. It was such a relief to know nothing was ever going to shake his faith in his favourite daughter. I could count on him to stand by me through thick and thin.

In the morning, I drew back the curtains in the spare room overlooking the orchard. I could see the sun's wintry rays glistening on the still surface of the lake beyond Reilly's field. A small boat with a single bent figure lay motionless on the water.

At dinner my sister broke her news.

"I'm expecting," she said.

She held the corner of a linen napkin to her mouth and waited for congratulations to flow.

"Great stuff, Sis," said Johnny.

"Brilliant," said Bridie, his bubbly wife.

"Look after yourself, Josie," said Dad.

"I guess this is what it's all about," said the proud Martin.

"I'm so happy for both of you," I said.

"We didn't want to tell anyone till we were dead certain," said Josie.

"When's it due?" asked Bridie.

"Six months," said Josie. "We're over the moon."

"You won't feel it passing," said Bridie. She'd two of her own at this stage.

"You'll take maternity leave?" I said.

Josie looked at Martin. *Why, oh why, did she need his permission to answer a simple question?*

"She'll take her full entitlement and we'll decide what to do after that," said Martin.

"You'll be flush with money," said Johnny, "now that you've got yourself permanent in that accountancy place."

"We'll see how it goes," said Martin. It was typical of Martin to steer clear of any talk of his finances.

~ * ~

We held hands as we walked the West Pier, glad to be back in each other's company. I told him how reassured I was by Dad's support.

"You told him I'm a priest?"

"It didn't take a feather out of him."

"He sounds a good sort."

"How'd it go with your own folks?"

"Not great. In fact the whole thing was a shambles. My mother asking me what kind of a priest would refuse to say Mass on Christmas night. She sulked right through Christmas day."

"That was your chance to tell her you've packed it in."

"Are you out of your mind? She'd have had a seizure on the spot."

"Something else you're going to have to tell them."

"What's that?"

"You have a lady friend."

He went silent.

"You can't keep running away from things. They'll have to come to terms with reality sooner or later."

"Damn it, Susan, you've no idea how obstinate my mother can be. A priest with a girl-friend is a total no-no. I need time to figure this out."

"She calls herself a Christian?"

"My mother's not the most tolerant of Christians."

We reached the lighthouse at the end of the pier and stopped to watch a brave little boat that had ventured beyond the smooth waters of the harbour.

"Choppy seas ahead," I said.

"Do you think you could take a week off?"

We had turned to retrace our steps along the pier.

"What did you have in mind?"

"Let's get away for a week together. We must do something to celebrate."

"What's to celebrate?"

"Your promotion and my windfall."

I stopped in my tracks and turned to look at him.

"Do you mean money?"

"I found a publisher in the States who's willing to take the book. They sent me an advance to keep me motivated."

"Brilliant, but who's going to read it? Most folks leave the esoterics to the clerics."

"The hope is that colleges and universities will want to have it in their libraries."

We headed back to the bungalow to be greeted by a warm, welcoming aroma. He'd left something simmering on the stove. I lifted a spoonful and sipped.

"For an absent-minded professor, you do a neat line in soup."

"I'm full of surprises."

And so he was. Full of surprises, I mean. It's just I'd no idea how big the next surprise was going to be.

Thirteen

The cottage was high up on a rocky slope, overlooking a tropical cove. I remembered then that he'd lived abroad, had seen places I'd never heard of. He'd be good at finding a place like this.

We swam early in the cool of the ocean and afterwards walked for miles along the water's edge, treading the frothing sand deserted by a retreating sea. We crossed a minor headland at the southern end of the island and came to stand above an inlet whose water wore the colour of olives, translucent in a magical green. We stood transfixed as the breakers spent themselves on a bed of ancient lava reaching far out beyond the shoreline.

Later we found ourselves drawn by the tantalising odours of al fresco cooking and sat gazing out over the ocean, lunching on toasted sardines and cool Spanish beer and chatting idly, more at ease with each other than ever before and possibly ever since.

Arriving back, we bumped into Kirstin, the owner of the cottage.

"From Cesar Manrique," she said, handing Finbarr a pink sealed envelope. "When he found out where you were staying, he sent his driver down here with this message. It wouldn't surprise me a bit if it's tickets for the concert."

Finbarr tore open the envelope and found a neatly written note.

"How sad that John's friends arrive from Ireland to find me gone from my secret hideaway. Such sadness alas is the way of the gods.

Since I cannot be here to make you welcome, I'd be pleased for you to accept my invitation to the Gala Performance. Then, perhaps, you will let me know what you think of my concert chamber in the underworld and tell me if the sound is as heavenly as they say. Welcome to Lanzarote, the most beautiful island in the world.

Cesar Manrique."

Kirstin listened with obvious excitement as Finbarr read the note aloud before producing the tickets from the envelope. "Saturday night in the Jameos del Agua," she said. "You two don't know how honoured you are."

In bed Finbarr told me a lot about Uncle John, things I hadn't known. How he'd gone to Paris to study art and gave it up in favour of art dealing. Uncle John must have written to Cesar Manrique to say we were on the island. They'd met in Paris and remained good friends ever since.

"Just like him to do something like that," Finbarr said. "He wanted it to be a surprise."

~ * ~

The girl at the entrance to the cave pointed us down the stone steps that led to the first level, a brightly lit underground chamber fitted out as reception area and lounge bar. With drinks in our hands, we crossed to a wooden balcony and found ourselves peering down into a space whose main feature was an elongated pool filled with crystal clear water.

"Let's go down," I said. The light playing on the water made me want to get close and see what lay beneath the surface.

"Come on," said Finbarr, "I'll show you the crabs."

"Crabs?"

He grabbed my arm and led me down the wooden steps onto the stone walkway skirting the water's edge.

"I don't see any crabs."

"See those tiny white pebbles on the bottom?"

"I do. What are they?"

"Keep watching."

As I looked, I began to notice the little white pebbles were moving about.

"You're not telling me they're crabs? But they're tiny."

"Tiny albinos. Completely blind. How they got here no one knows."

"Wonders will never cease!"

I spent a fair amount of time staring at those tiny white creatures who couldn't stare back. I was intrigued. They came into the world without eyes, to live and die in total darkness. How, I wondered, could they find and bond with a mate with nothing to guide them but some irresistible instinct? They must live a magic existence in this magical cave beneath the earth.

"Deep in thought, love? Come on or we'll miss the concert."

I allowed him to drag me away and we headed for the auditorium, a larger cave with a vaulted roof hewn from solidified lava. The floor sloped down to the performance area, seats arranged on each side of a central aisle. Our tickets placed us near the front with a clear view of the stage.

Finbarr had enough Spanish to understand the gist of what was going on. Tonight's performance was to be the Concierto de Aranjuez by Rodrigo. Musicians were tuning up when an elderly man was led in and guided up the steps onto the stage, his eyes shielded by dark glasses.

"Ladies and Gentlemen, it is our great privilege to have here tonight the distinguished composer, Joaquin Rodrigo Vidre."

We looked at each other in astonishment. In our wildest dreams we'd never expected to find ourselves in the presence of this man, blind from childhood, whose music had given immense enjoyment to generations of admirers. Rodrigo, here to listen to his own composition performed in a setting unique in the universe. The soloist was a classical guitarist from Seville whose interpretation of the guitar parts was something I'd never before experienced. His phrasing was slow, the very spaces between the notes left floating, invoking a rare sense of suspension. This was music that lifted you onto another plane.

Towards the end of the second movement, the Adagio, I felt Finbarr take my left hand and something was slipped onto my finger. Holding my hand up to the light, I caught the flash of a diamond. I turned towards him and glared but he put a finger to his lips and directed my attention back to the orchestra. On my finger a diamond ring which could only have one meaning. Why had he chosen a moment when I couldn't respond or speak?

My thoughts were in turmoil. If this was his way of proposing marriage, it looked like he was making some extraordinary assumptions. No doubt he'd chosen the most romantic setting possible. But my head was churning with questions. Was I going to marry a man with no reliable source of income? Whose work as a hospital chaplain could end at a moment's notice? Whose parents were likely to write him off as soon as they heard he planned to marry?

Mainly, though, I didn't want to be taken for granted. We'd never really talked about marriage, though I'd been pushing him to apply for a dispensation. Yes, I'd dreamed of settling down with him someday, but it was always sometime in the future. A vague, distant, safe sort of future. The final movement passed over my head as I wrestled with these doubts. Was I being bought with a diamond ring or was I being valued for what I was, for who I was?

Was I a blind crab in a dark underground pool, entering a mating bond with no vision of what the future might hold? Surely not. I had it in me to make something wonderful of our relationship. Like the blind composer who overcame incredible obstacles to bring forth creations which only God could have inspired?

The music came to an end. The conductor acknowledged the applause of a rapturous audience and called the soloist forward to take his bow.

Finbarr brought his face close to mine.

"Well?" he said. "Will you or won't you?"

"I will," I said. "I will."

~ * ~

As Finbarr pushed open the door of the cottage, I picked a scrap of paper from the floor.

Phone call from Finbarr's father. Uncle is ill. Ring home. Kirstin.

Kirstin must have been waiting up, because at that moment she came around to offer us the use of her phone. We followed her to her house at the top of the steps.

"How serious is it, Dad?"

I came close to the phone, straining to hear.

"A stroke?" Finbarr turned to look at me. "How bad?"

"Too soon to say." I could barely make out the faint crackle of his father's voice.

"How's Ma?"

"Too upset to talk. No need to come rushing home. Stay there with your pals. I'll keep you posted."

"Dad, we were to fly home tomorrow anyway."

I'd a real fondness for the cheery little gentleman who'd made me welcome whenever I dropped in for a quick visit. He always made you feel like a long lost friend. Now I worried about his chances of survival. I'd always hoped he'd be the one to smooth the path for us when the time came for Finbarr to introduce me to his strait-laced family. If anything happened to him, I'd have lost a friend in court.

On the flight home, Finbarr was withdrawn and I left him alone with his thoughts. I could understand his fears, not just the prospect of losing his uncle, but the added fear of facing his family with the announcement of his engagement.

A straight dash from airport to hospital. Finbarr asked me to wait while he went in. Through the open door, I glimpsed a tall spare woman in her fifties, her pale face betraying signs of grief and anxiety. Before the door had fully closed, I saw them embrace.

I sat in the glass-fronted dayroom and waited. The only other occupant was a young man attached to a portable drip who picked up a tabloid paper and after less than a minute threw it down and shuffled out without a glance in my direction. Like the Grays, I thought, oblivious of my existence. When I saw Finbarr embrace his mother, I knew I was an outsider. Shut out. At a time like this, a time of crisis, they would close ranks, withdraw into their close family unit, barriers up. Within that tight little circle, there could be no room for interlopers. This was the cell I had to penetrate and it would be Finbarr's job to prepare the ground.

He arrived back to say the news was not good. His uncle wasn't expected to make it.

Uncle John survived two more days.

~ * ~

When we'd laid Uncle John in his grave in Glasnevin, Finbarr's father invited everyone back to the pub where his manager had set aside a room for the mourners. Somehow we became separated so Finbarr sat close to his parents at one end of the table while I found myself among the cousins. Whether he intended this or not, I could see how it saved him from embarrassing introductions. Finbarr had asked me not to wear the ring. This was not the time. Not yet.

I was saved from having to talk about myself by the sound of the father's voice from the other end of the table. When Paschal Gray spoke, his eyes circled his audience to make sure he had everyone's full attention. He regaled us with the story of his own success. He'd arrived in Dublin with nothing but a five-pound note in his hip pocket. He'd served his time as barman and by dint of long hours and watching the pennies, he'd come to acquire his own pub. As for education, degrees were a waste of time seeing as he himself had learned everything he knew in the university of life.

"You want the key to success?" said Gray senior. "One man works for the money while the smart man makes the money work for him."

I heard later from Finbarr this was a well-rehearsed and oft-repeated story. His father had made his millions in property speculation and only held onto the pub for nostalgic reasons. As for all that talk about the folly of education, the truth was he'd spared no expense to give his own son the best schooling money could buy. He was more than happy to see the young Finbarr rubbing shoulders with the future leaders of society at one of Dublin's top schools.

I went in search of Finbarr and came face to face with Rose Gray.

"I didn't get a chance to offer my condolences, Mrs Gray. I'm truly sorry about your brother."

She stood back and studied me a moment before things appeared to fall in place for her.

"You're the young woman I saw at the graveyard. I'm sorry, I didn't catch your name."

"Susan Enfield. I was very fond of your brother, Mrs Gray. Such a lovely, warm-hearted man. He'll be a terrible loss to all of us. To you especially."

"We'll miss him a lot. Especially Father Finbarr. John had a big influence on him since he was this high. John should have been a priest himself, you know that? Very devout as a boy. A missed vocation, I always thought. We were meant to have a priest in the family and thank God my prayers were answered. Father Finbarr is the finest priest a mother could ever wish to see."

"You can be proud of him."

"You hear about so many priests going astray these days. We're living in terrible times with religion under attack on all sides. So sad. But so long as we have priests like Father Finbarr, the church has nothing to fear."

"I'm afraid I can't stay, Mrs Gray. I'm sorry I didn't get a chance to talk to your husband. Hopefully we can meet up on a happier occasion."

"I'd better be getting back to Paschal before he sends out a search party."

With that she was gone. Someone was going to be faced with the task of shattering that woman's illusions and I hoped I wouldn't be around when Finbarr faced his responsibility, faced the daunting task of informing his parents he was engaged to be married.

Fourteen

There's something about the smell of burning peat that calms the soul and conjures up images of more innocent times. I sank into a mood of wistful nostalgia as I watched the wisps of light blue smoke spiral upwards from the glowing sods. I thought about Finbarr as a little boy and wondered about his relationship with his Uncle John.

"Your mother told me John had a big influence on you as a child."

He was relaxed now that we were alone together at last.

"He was always there in our house, or that's how it seemed to me at the time. With no kids of his own, I guess he sort of adopted me. Dad was far too busy making money to have much time left for his son. John took me under his wing. Took me everywhere with him."

"What sort of places?"

"I remember a big exhibition of modern art at the RDS. He was trying to make me understand how Ireland was being dragged kicking and screaming into the world of abstract art. I was far too young to know what he was going on about but it left me with a feel for Impressionism, Cubism and all the other isms of modern art."

"The gallery! What's going to happen it now?"

"Dad's muttering about wanting the will read as quickly as possible. He can't wait to get Uncle John's affairs sorted out."

"I hope he doesn't try to get rid of it."

"The gallery? I'd hate to see it go."

"Did your folks say anything about me?"

"Dad did say at one point, is there someone looking after your friend?"

"And your mother? Did she mention I spoke to her?"

"She just said 'that woman was looking for you.' "

"You're going have to tell them. You can't let it go much longer."

"They still don't know I'm leaving the priesthood, but they're not fools. They must know there's something going on."

"Have you made any moves with your superiors?"

"I talked to the Provincial and put my cards on the table. Mind you, he didn't seem all that surprised, but he warned me there could be problems ahead. The new pope is determined to stop the rush for the exit."

"What do you mean?"

"Priests have been leaving in droves and John Paul the Second is determined to stem the exodus."

This was my first inkling that anything might get in the way of Finbarr's freedom.

~ * ~

I listened as Finbarr described the expressions on his parents' faces as John's will was read in the solicitor's office on Merrion Square. Not only had he money in the bank but he'd been able to buy out the leasehold of the whole building. Art dealing, it seemed, could be a neat little money-spinner.

A few valuable paintings he left 'to my sister Rose,' other bits and pieces to named individuals. The big surprise came at the end when the solicitor said the main beneficiary was to be…'my nephew, Finbarr Gray.'

Finbarr said his father's features remained impassive with the merest hint of worry lines creasing his expansive forehead. His mother's lips tightened like a string purse and seemed to say, 'I'm keeping my thoughts to myself on this one.'

The post-mortem, as Finbarr liked to call it, was held in the front lounge of the Shelbourne where he and his parents went to eat afterwards.

"Start at the start, I want to hear."

"Dad was all on for putting a manager in to keep the gallery going. I said that wouldn't be necessary, that I'd look after it myself. Mam comes in with 'a priest shouldn't be mixed up in business, you know that, Finbarr,' it wouldn't be right. That's when I had to tell them. I said 'I won't be a priest much longer.'

"Oops!"

"Mam's face went white. Then the hysterics. Tears, the lot. Why was I tormenting them with a sick joke? That sort of thing."

"And your dad?"

"Dad? He had to take her side, of course. 'Can't you see what this is doing to your mother? It's never too late to change your mind, you know.' "

"What did you say?"

"I said there was no turning back. My application was gone in."

"All that's left now is to tell them we're getting married."

"One thing at a time. Let the dust settle for now."

~ * ~

When Finbarr took over at the gallery, he had to give up the chaplaincy and with it went the bungalow. He installed himself in the storeroom at the back.

Now I listened to excited accounts of what he'd bought, what he'd sold, what new artists had appeared on the scene.

"It's a shame some of these young people are not getting the exposure they deserve. I'd love to put on a special exhibition just to showcase the new artists."

"You're getting a great buzz out of this."

"I find it fascinating."

Finally Finbarr had found his vocation. I found him dealing with a customer, a well-dressed type who wanted something to hang where it would make an impression. Within seconds, Finbarr led him to a painting by Roderic O'Conor. In this particular case, money didn't seem to matter and I could see Finbarr had that rare combination of finely honed artistic sense and keen business mind.

The family on the floor above moved out and this was the opportunity Finbarr had waited for. He brought me up the narrow stairs to let me see how work was progressing. The furniture and floors were covered in paint-spattered sheets.

"A step up from that pigsty of a storeroom you're sleeping in at the moment," I said.

"It's for both of us."

"What do you mean both of us?" I'd never even

thought of moving in with him until we were married. This was only two years after the people of Ireland had turned out in their millions to give a rapturous greeting to the Polish pope. Traditional mores were alive and well in 1981.

"There's a few things we need to get sorted first," I said.

"Like what?"

"Like you cutting your ties with the church so we're free to get married."

"Oh, I meant to tell you, there's been a hitch."

"What kind of hitch?"

"The whole thing's stalled. The new pope's just put a German cardinal in charge of that side of things. Since Ratzinger took over, the word is out that there are no more dispensations."

I was stunned to think some change in distant Rome could have such an immediate effect on our marriage plans. I was ready to cry.

He sat beside me on a sheet-covered settee, tins of paint around our feet. He put his arm around me.

"Ratzinger's office used to be called the Roman Inquisition. A copy of my book found its way onto his desk and he didn't like what he saw. I questioned papal infallibility and a few other things. I'm in danger of being burned at the stake. But I've no intention of rolling over and letting them mess us around like this."

"What can we do?"

"Ignore them. Just go ahead and do our own thing. We can't allow a bunch of bureaucrats in Rome to get in our way."

"I want to be married in church. I want the full ritual, a proper blessing, the whole works."

"If the church won't marry us, I know someone who will."

"Who've you got in mind?"

"An old pal of mine in Switzerland. Ulrich's a Lutheran priest. He'll do it, all right. If you're happy to go along with it, I'll ask him straight away."

"Just as long as we're married in church I don't mind."

Ulrich in Switzerland was more than willing to facilitate us and we decided on a June wedding. There was still the tricky question of Finbarr's parents. This was going to take some explaining.

I nagged Finbarr into making that fateful visit to his parents' home. It was time to come clean and tell them everything. While he was at it, he could invite them to attend the wedding of their priest son to a renegade nun in a protestant church in Switzerland.

He looked to me for courage and my heart went out to him, a grown man in awe of his parents, visibly pale, terrified I'd say, as he set out alone on that fateful visit to the house in Terenure.

Fifteen

"Beautiful, beautiful. *Sie ist so schön!"* Anneke let out a squeal of approval as she buttoned up my dress, an ivory silk-satin organza gown I'd found in a little boutique in Dublin.

In the absence of my sister, Ulrich's wife agreed to be my bridesmaid and now she was taking great pains to present me at my best. She placed in my hand a single red rose to carry as a symbol of my love. Finbarr dressed in another room and emerged in a sober charcoal-grey suit and pale-blue silk tie.

"You sure look the part," I said.

"And you! You look stunning, my love!"

By noon we were ready to set off. Ulrich drove Finbarr to the hamlet near the Swiss-French border where he was pastor. Anneke and I followed in her car. A church bell resonated across the valley. The quaint stone church had a small open belfry directly above the entrance. Lifting my eyes, I noticed an inscription carved into the stone lintel.

Wenn der Herr nicht das Haus baut, so arbeiten umsonst, die daran bauen.

I nudged Finbarr. "What's it say?"

"If the Lord's not on our side, we're wasting our time."

"Is he on our side today?"

"Just believe our marriage is made in heaven."

"Oh I'm happy, believe me, so happy."

Inside the little church, the oak panelling on the wall made everything seem dark. The guests were mostly colleagues and friends of Ulrich and Anneke. One or two from Fribourg. No one from Ireland. Albrecht, another friend of Finbarr's Fribourg days, had flown in from Salzburg to act as his witness. The loyalty of these people impressed me.

The assembled guests were in full voice, belting out a hymn with Germanic enthusiasm. We sat side by side in front of the altar and listened while Ulrich, standing on the altar step, delivered a brief discourse in English. A lot of what he said I've since forgotten but some of his remarks stayed with me over the years. In particular a quote from Nietzsche to the effect that there's always some madness in love, but also some reason in madness. And then, as if to explain, he said something I found strange and a little disturbing.

"You take one another for better or for worse. An interesting phrase, that. What exactly do you mean when you say for worse? How much worse are you prepared to accept? At what point do you draw the line and say God does not expect me to take any more?

"You promise to stick by your partner in sickness, in health, in prosperity, in poverty. How about fidelity and infidelity? What if your spouse comes to you and says I have found another love? What then? Are you surprised by this question? Have I shocked you? I simply ask you to reflect on the full implications of the contract you are about to enter into."

"What was he on about?" I whispered as we retraced our steps down the aisle, out through the doors onto the porch, into the bright afternoon sunshine.

"You better ask him that," Finbarr said. "Where are they taking us now?"

"No idea. We just do as we're told."

Even as he spoke, it became clear that the central part of the ceremony, the exchange of vows, was about to take place in the open beneath scudding wisps of white in a blue sky. Ulrich in long white surplice and scarlet stole spoke in measured tones.

"Susan, are you prepared to take Finbarr to be your man and remain faithful to him whatever the trials the Lord might send?"

"Yes, I am prepared to take him."

"And remain faithful?"

"And remain faithful."

I listened as Finbarr gave the self-same commitment. He placed a gold ring on my finger and I placed one on his.

"I hereby pronounce you man and wife."

Now two children stepped forward, a boy of about ten in lederhosen and a girl, younger, in a white puffy blouse. The girl carried a box loosely tied with red ribbon. The boy undid the ribbon and swung back the lid. For a few moments nothing happened. Then from the box two butterflies emerged into the air, fluttered around for a while in a bewildered dance before taking off towards the sun, eager to reclaim the freedom of their natural environment.

A tall slim woman stepped forward and looking directly at the two of us she recited a short verse from memory.

"See the flowers,
They are but butterflies chained to the earth.
See the butterflies,
They are the flowers by the cosmos finally made free."

Ulrich spoke.

"The butterfly emerges from the chrysalis to begin again in a new manifestation. In marriage, your life takes on a new form, different from anything that has gone before. Like butterflies, you will take to the air, tasting the freedom of the sky but never straying far, always drawn back each to the other. Freedom and attraction. These are the forces which will balance each other to keep your marriage in harmony and equilibrium."

Back in the gloom of the church, we placed our names in an ancient leather-bound book alongside the records of the generations who lived out their lives in these valleys and hills. Everyone was invited back to the house for the barbeque. No formalities. Neighbours and friends kept dropping in throughout the afternoon to partake of the steaks and sausages coming off the open grill.

Weissbier flowed from a cask propped on the end of a long trestle table. Men and women drank from glass tankards. And when at last the sun decided to take his leave and began to slide away below the long ridge of hills to the northwest, music started up and the party glowed with new life. Wrapped in warm jackets against the sudden chill, people began to sing and the rousing songs they sang demanded the participation of many voices. Folk dances arose from nowhere, dances which gained momentum as more and more joined in with abandon and delight. Who could ever forget a wedding like this?

Dominique was the tall woman with curls in her hair who'd composed and recited the poem at our wedding and it was her children, Patrice and Sophie, who released the butterflies during the ceremony.

"Au'voir," she said as she was leaving.

"Au revoir, Dominique, et merci beaucoup."

"Do not forget, Susan, when you reach Lausanne you come to see us. You will meet René."

The scenic shore of Lac de la Gruyère, with the sun falling away from us in the west. I walked with Finbarr along the water's edge and sat on a rock to drink in the stillness of evening. Timber houses dotted the distant shore. Out of the silence, my husband was moved to confide how he had sat here years before, wrestling with the question of his vocation. I listened as he spoke for the first time of the anguish and guilt he'd suffered at the thought of giving up his priesthood to pursue what might easily be selfish human desire. "Help me, God!" At this very spot, he'd heard his cry bounce across the still waters to die amidst the wooded slopes on the opposite side.

"Why did you never tell me this before?" I'd always felt there were places within him I wasn't able to reach.

"God, or this lake, helped me make the right decision."

I'd never heard him talk like this. Was he too haunted by the same sense of guilt that made me fear the divine anger? For when I walked out of the convent, I'd reneged on a solemn commitment to devote my life to God. Finbarr had renounced his priesthood to be with me. Only now did I know how torn he'd been in making that choice.

Yet all I said to him as we undressed in the log-style chalet was that he need never again keep anything from me. In the nuptial bed, I sought to banish forever the guilt that beset him. Yet in the days that followed, I wasn't able to free myself from the thought that I'd married an enigma. There would always be deep waters I couldn't quite fathom.

~ * ~

On the drive south, something young in me thrilled to the glint of a plucky little steam train clinging like a silver lizard to the side of a steep slope on its arduous climb into the mountains. This is how it ought to be on one's honeymoon, for the joy is short-lived, however we might wish for it to be otherwise.

We found our friends' spacious villa in a winding lane amongst the apples and plums on the south facing slopes above Lake Geneva.

While Finbarr parked the car around the side, I went to the front door and rang the bell. Something like a Tibetan gong sounded deep in the heart of the house and when Dominique opened the front door, she embraced me warmly before calling out to her husband, *René, c'est la femme du prêtre. Priest's wife!*

Dominique lived with René and their two children at the edge of a village with breath-taking views across the lake and they took pains to point out for us the snow-capped peak of Mont Blanc in the south. After breakfast, Finbarr and René headed into Lausanne to view a little gallery where local artists were attempting to create something based on the Secession in Vienna.

"What did you make of Ulrich's sermon?" she said, quite out of the blue. Dominique switched easily between French and English. We were in the remains of a Roman villa near the lake and had sat to watch the ferry arriving from Geneva.

"About fidelity and infidelity? I was taken aback, now that you ask. What was he thinking about?"

"Who knows? Men are strange. You never know what's going on in their heads, do you? I wonder was he ever tempted himself."

"Ulrich? I couldn't imagine it."

"Ulrich's a man, Susan. A priest maybe, but a man all the same. You've married a priest yourself. How does it feel to be a priest's wife?"

"Ask me that in a year or two, Dominique. But you're right, I'm beginning to think men are a mystery."

She laughed.

"You're a quick learner, Susan, but I think you'll cope, no matter what life throws at you."

Sixteen

They waited till Josie was back on her feet before bringing her "wee flower" to be christened Blaithín in the old church on Francis Street with me and Martin's brother, Eamon, as the child's sponsors. I had the privilege and the pleasure of holding little Blaithín in my arms. This was no formality. I wanted to take my role seriously, to be a real godmother to the child as she grew. But something in Martin's attitude told me my influence on the child would be carefully controlled.

I caught Finbarr looking at me and I wondered if he was thinking what I was thinking, that we wouldn't be fully a couple until we were presenting a little child of our own at the baptismal font.

My first intimation this might be about to happen came a month or so later, but I waited another month before I felt confident enough to mention it to Finbarr.

"I think there's something happening," I said as we sat down to a late Sunday morning breakfast.

He looked puzzled. I wondered how an intelligent man could be so slow on the uptake.

"Something happening in here." I put my hand on my

belly and made a circular motion.

A wave of understanding washed across his face.

"You mean …you think ...?"

"I'm pretty certain."

It was obvious to me then that he'd longed for this moment. He jumped up, threw his arms about me and kissed my head, nose, ears and lips before going on his knees and pressing his face in my belly. We started to make plans.

"Are we going to stay here, over the gallery?" I asked him.

"I thought you were happy here."

The busy shopping area around Grafton Street wasn't my idea of the best place to raise a child. Finbarr seemed content, though. He'd lived his earliest years above a pub in the shadow of Christ Church before his family had moved to a fine Victorian house whose garden reached down to the banks of the Dodder.

Finbarr only had to trot down the stairs to open up for the day's business while I walked the hundred paces or so to my office in Grafton Street. Now there was a third individual to be considered. I dreamed dreams of some idyllic setting in the countryside. Or by the sea. Or high in the hills. One way or another, I knew that living over the gallery wasn't how I wanted to spend the rest of my days. Yet when I told him I couldn't see myself bringing up a family in all the hustle and bustle, he looked desperately disappointed.

"We spent a fortune on this place. Are you saying now it's not up to your expectations?"

"It's fine, don't get me wrong. I'm thinking about the

baby. I only want what's best for the baby. Okay, we're tight for money, but it won't be that way forever. There's no harm planning for the future, is there?"

"Nothing wrong with dreaming, just so long as we don't get carried away."

I'd never noticed him being tight with money, but I suppose things had to be different now if he wanted to keep the business going and provide a living for a wife and young family. I couldn't fault him for that, but it didn't stop me nursing a secret dream of bringing up my children in the fresh air of the countryside outside the city. On weekend drives, I'd admire some house as we passed and ask Finbarr how he'd like to live in a place like that. Just my way of keeping the dream alive and a little reminder for him of what I longed for.

~ * ~

"Blaithín will soon have a little cousin to play with."

A gasp from Josie at the other end of the line.

"Yes, Josie, I'm expecting."

"Time to give up work, Susan. You need to conserve your energy. You're working far too hard in that place. They'll just have to get by without you."

My sister was always free with the advice.

"Give up work? I'd go nuts with nothing to do. I'm better off out there meeting people and getting on with life."

~ * ~

The fact was, I was faced with the task of coming up with a strategy to build circulation at Maeve. Sales figures had stalled. Recession or no recession, Maeve had something to offer and I saw this as a personal challenge.

The task was to retain our loyal readers while attracting a new following. I'd discussed my ideas with Finbarr.

"We need to brighten it up with more pictures, more empty space. Change the layout."

"You mean less for the hoity-toity and more for the hoi polloi?" He'd a way with words, Finbarr.

"I certainly don't want would-be celebrities and nameless models scrambling to push their image. That's not what Maeve is about," I said.

He came up with some helpful suggestions. Interviews with personalities from the arts, or business or politics. I listened to his advice and the board saw merit in the idea. Sarah gave me her full support and cooperation. Eventually we got the green light from above and the revamp began.

Yet pregnancy was taking its toll and there were mornings I arrived in the office feeling wretched. When you're there on the spot, you're expected to perform. People will show great solicitude and ask are you sure you're feeling all right but the next minute they'll hand you a bundle of paperwork. So long as you're at your desk, you get on with it. I tired more easily and was fit to collapse when I arrived home in the evenings.

I began to consider who'd best handle the work in my absence. Ingrid had come to us from Stockholm on a work placement and showed no eagerness to go home. I began grooming her to take over my routine duties while Sarah would continue to implement the revamp in my absence.

~ * ~

"You look pale. What did he say?" Finbarr leaned across to open the passenger door from the inside and studied my face as I flopped in beside him.

"The blood pressure's high. He wants me to stop work right away."

"Well, Sue, you'd better do whatever he says. No point having the top doc if we're not going to listen to what he says."

"There was never any mention of blood pressure when Josie was expecting."

"Stop worrying. You're in good hands with Fitzgibbon-Raye."

~ * ~

The following morning I told Sarah I wanted to take maternity leave. "The doctor says I'm to stop work. It's got something to do with high blood pressure. He's insisting I have to take it easy. Luckily I've got Ingrid well briefed, so she'll be able to handle things in my absence."

Sarah wished me well and sent me home. I filled Ingrid in on a few last minute details before slipping out of the office without making any fuss. I wandered aimlessly down Grafton Street feeling empty and useless. I passed a human statue motionless on an upturned box, its hand stuffed inside its jacket. Napoleon gave a wink as I passed, but he failed to lift my spirits. In Switzers I poked through the gowns on the maternity rails and wondered how on earth I'd fill my days while I awaited the arrival of my baby.

~ * ~

Finbarr was amused when I told him where I'd been…in the college library leafing through all the gynaecological texts and medical journals I could bluff the librarian into handing me. Earlier as I sat in the little park at the heart of Merrion Square having handed in a sample of urine at the hospital, it occurred to me I could make very good use of this unaccustomed freedom by doing a little research of my own. I wanted to pin down every possible angle.

"We've one of the top men looking after you. Why not leave it in his hands?"

"I had to know more about this blood pressure thing."

"So what did you find out?"

"It's usually not a problem, though it can affect the baby and cause it to develop more slowly."

"Anything else?"

"Toxaemia in the mother. It shows up as protein in the urine."

"That explains why he asked for a specimen!"

"At least I'll know the right questions to ask next time I see him."

~ * ~

Finbarr suggested I take a week at home in the country. The break would do me good, he said. I suspected he had other motives, since I knew he was putting together an exhibition of the young artists, working all hours, day and night, to get this project up and running. No matter. I grabbed at his suggestion and took myself off to my brother and sister-in-law in Annagopple, leaving my husband all the space and time he needed.

It was my first time away from Finbarr since my pregnancy, since our wedding in fact, and I rang him several times that first day just to assure myself he was coping. He was so busy, he said, he didn't have time to think. I was lonely, though, and hadn't expected to miss him so much. Next day I confined myself to a single call. Better let him get on with his preparations for the exhibition which seemed so important to him.

Dad was especially glad to have me there all to himself, if only for a short week or so. But all was not as it seemed at first. I couldn't help but notice how he'd started to go downhill.

"The oul' arthritis is giving me hell," he said, as he tried to raise himself from the wooden armchair in his favourite spot near the fire.

"Well, there's nothing wrong with your brain and that's for sure." I was lying. The number of times he paused in the middle of a story and forgot what he'd been saying was too obvious to be ignored.

Johnny's wife had noticed as well.

"Old age," she said. "Sure it's ahead of us all, the Lord save us."

Bridie possessed that solid homespun philosophy that helps some people face life's inexplicable trials with a level of stoic resignation.

"Set your mind at ease, Susan. Sure he's happy as the day is long with the children to keep him company and not a care in the world on him. There's no harm can come to him as long as he has us here to look after him."

She and Johnny were doing all they could for Dad but there was no escaping the fact that a time was coming when my brother and sister-in-law could not, in all fairness, be expected to shoulder the burden of looking after a feeble and senile old man.

Seventeen

"How's your energy since I saw you last?" Fitzgibbon-Raye had my file open in front of him, obviously doing a quick recap of my details.

"My energy? It's okay. Well, no. To be honest it's not okay. I'm pretty tired most of the time."

"Step up here a moment and we'll check your weight."

I stepped on the platform of what looked like a Victorian weighing mechanism while he manipulated the weights until at last the apparatus was in balance and he gave a grunt of satisfaction.

"Perfect." One of those non-committal words beloved of the medical profession.

After my weight, my blood pressure. Reading the blood pressure, he said fine. I wanted to ask him what fine meant but he cut across me.

"Any trouble walking?"

"Not really, apart from some pain around the knees and ankles."

"Okay, let's take a look. Hop up here."

I climbed onto the couch and as I lay back he did a quick examination of my arms and legs.

"I can see you've got some swelling here around the ankles."

"Is that bad?"

"It ties in with what I got back from the lab. High protein level, some swelling of the limbs. What it points to is you're very likely in the early stage of pre-eclampsia."

"I'm getting toxaemia?"

He shot me a quick look as if I wasn't supposed to know anything about such things.

"Let me see." He picked up my file. "You're at twenty-one weeks gestation. We're lucky to have picked it up at this point."

"How serious is this, Doctor? Should I be starting to worry?"

"Worry won't get us anywhere."

"But what about the baby?"

"The scan shows your baby developing well, so you've nothing to worry about on that score. You're both important, mother and baby. I'm not about to take any chances with either of you."

"What does it all mean? I mean, what are you proposing to do?"

"I'll continue to see you every two weeks to keep a close eye on you. Any change for the worse and I'll have to take you in."

As he said the words take you in, I suddenly got that odd sensation when voices, your own included, seem to echo from a distance.

"Take me in...to hospital, you mean?"

"Only if it becomes necessary and we're nowhere near that stage yet." He must have sensed my panic." Whatever steps we take will be for the safety of your baby and your own health."

Arriving home, I went straight upstairs without looking in at Finbarr. I wanted to be on my own. I needed time to take it all in. The thought of going into hospital to lie on my back, immobile, useless, just existing, was too much to contemplate. Yet I knew I must heed his advice and do nothing to make things worse. I was to rest, take things easy, maintain calm, avoid all forms of excitement.

When Finbarr closed up shop for the day, I heard his footsteps on the stairs. As he flung open the apartment door, I saw he was excited about something and it was obvious he'd forgotten all about my visit to the doctor.

"There's great news," he said, "just wait till I tell you."

"What news?"

"It's all set. I've settled on a date and title for the exhibition."

"Really? It looks like your baby's coming along nicely, then."

"Yeah, that's a good way to put it."

"So you won't have to worry about my baby anymore."

A look of horror transfixed his face.

"Oh, my God. Your appointment. I clean forgot."

"This is our baby, Finbarr, not Susan's baby. Ours. Yours and mine."

"I know, I know. I'm sorry. I want to hear how you got on." He sat on the arm of the settee. "Tell me what he said, the doctor. Everything okay?"

"He might have to take me in. That's how bad it is."

"Oh God." He stood up, straightened himself, walked to the window and stared at the street below. Then he turned to face me. "Well, if that's what you've to do, then that's what you've to do. Sorry for annoying you with this exhibition thing. I just got carried away, that's all."

"The last thing I want is to find myself stuck in a hospital bed for the next few months."

"You're going to have to take it real easy from now on."

"You'll excuse me if I don't get involved in your exhibition?"

"No question of it. There's only one thing matters now."

~ * ~

Promises are easily forgotten and events can overtake the most resolute of intentions. The New Artists Exhibition was scheduled to run for two weeks from the end of November. I found there were forces dragging me in opposite directions, one warning me to steer clear of excitement, the other urging me to help my husband in any way I could. So when he talked about lining up publicity for the opening, I felt here's one area I can be of use. Apart from Maeve, I'd a network of contacts in most of the papers. I prepared a press release which tried to convey some of the excitement of giving a platform to up and coming artists.

I climbed the rickety stairs to Sarah's office.

"I know the deadline's passed, Sarah, but I'd be thrilled if you could stick this in before you go to press."

Sarah took the A4 sheets from me and skimmed through what I'd written.

"I wouldn't do this for anyone else, Susan. Not if the President came calling in person. Of course we'll run it."

She rummaged in a file and pulled out a printed card.

"Take this. It's a notice from the Arts Council about a press conference."

~ * ~

The press conference was something of an eye-opener. There was the Arts Council press officer delivering his plea for more generous state funding while the newspaper people he depended on to bring his message to the public were attending to more serious business in the bar. I saw I was wasting my time pretending to scribble down a few notes and slipped away to where the real action was.

"Hi, I'm Jack. Jack Cardiff."

"I'm Susan Enfield. Maeve magazine."

"What can I get you to drink, Susan?"

"Sorry, I'm not allowed touch a drop." I indicated my distended abdomen. "I'll tell you what, though, I'll have a tonic water."

"No gin?"

"No gin."

"You were in there?" He pointed in the direction of the on-going press conference. "Did you take any notes? What was the gist of it?"

"They're worried sick about the cutbacks. They think the arts should be the last sector to be hit."

"I know, I know, every lobby fights its own corner. How about a press conference to plead for the print media, what d'you think?"

He laughed at his own joke and when his eyes screwed up, I saw the mole at the side of his nose, black with a single hair. It must have been airbrushed from his picture in the Sunday paper.

"I owe you, Susan. You've given me enough to write up an impassioned piece about the place of the arts in the life of the nation."

I handed him a copy of the Arts Council press release which he stuffed into a baggy pocket of his jacket. Then I remembered the real reason I was here. I delved into my bag.

"For you," I said. "A personal invitation to the opening of the New Artists Exhibition. My hubby and I'd love to see you there. There'll be extra drinks for the press guys. And of course the more publicity it gets, the better."

He grabbed my arm and guided me to a corner where a cluster of hacks sat nursing pints of beer and laughing uproariously at each other's jokes.

"Allow me, lads. This here's Susan from that posh magazine none of you guys would be literate enough to read."

You could tell they were well used to his banter and took it in good part. They pushed up along the wall seat to make room for me. I was ready to put myself through anything to help Finbarr, even if it meant sitting in all-male company, listening to all-male jokes and mopping spilled Guinness with my elbow.

~ * ~

I learned a lot about Finbarr as he plunged himself into the preparations for that pre-Christmas exhibition. Single-minded and determined barely describes him. Nothing was allowed get in his way. Result, everything fell into place on the night, all the right people turned up and the young artists were there savouring the excitement of having their work on view for the general public. I was there, needless to say, for he needed me to be the gracious hostess making everyone welcome and keeping an eye on how people reacted to what they saw displayed.

Finbarr himself, suave and professional, circulating through the room, interrupting conversations with a firm handshake or a complimentary comment on someone's dress. Always he seemed to have just the right word to make a guest feel important. In a room full of strangers, he could make any individual feel the focus of his special attention.

This wasn't the man I knew at home, so often silent, introspective, lost in his thoughts. Tonight's sociable, genial Finbarr was possessed of an easy affability reminiscent of his Uncle John before him. I stood and smiled sweetly as he bestowed a kiss on each cheek of each gorgeous female.

"I'm so glad you were able to come. Have you had a chance to look at the paintings? Did you like anything? Oh, this is Susan. My wife Susan. My pregnant wife, Susan."

Looks of gentle concern for me and admiration for him. I excused myself and moved towards the end of the gallery where some of the artists stood chatting and comparing notes. Young men and women starting out on a tenuous career, relaxing in their own familiar company.

"I see you've got a red sticker," I said to Carl, a long-haired student-looking fellow with an incipient ginger beard. "Someone likes your work."

"Yeah, I'm blown away."

"You always work in charcoal?"

"I usually blend in a bit of pastel. I sort of experiment a bit."

"This is your girlfriend?" I turned to face the young girl who stood beside him.

"No. Céline's got a couple of paintings hanging." He laughed at my mistake.

She just smiled. When she smiled, her mouth turned upwards at the sides with an imp-like kind of expression.

Embarrassed at my faux pas, I offered her my hand. "Céline? I haven't seen any of your paintings."

She pointed towards a corner of the gallery near the entrance.

"Camille," she said. Her accent told me she wasn't Irish, probably French.

"Camille?"

"My art name. It's how I like to be known."

I'd seen that painting inside the door. So this must be the artist Finbarr had talked about, the woman who created those strange paintings in mixed media.

"Ah, now I remember. Collage? Is that how you'd describe it?"

"Junk on canvas," said Carl, "is how I'd describe it."

Céline's smile faded. You could tell she was furious.

"You stick to your charcoal, Carl. You wouldn't know good art if it jumped off the wall and bit your backside."

The young Frenchwoman seemed to have a pretty good grasp of the vernacular.

"People appreciate original work." I wanted to smooth over her wounded pride.

"Who cares?" she said. "Most of them don't deserve it."

Before I could answer, Finbarr drew me aside.

"See if you can find the press people," he whispered.

"Try and find out what they think."

A moment later he was standing on a box calling for silence.

"Those of you who have already had time to look around must be hugely impressed by the sheer wealth of talent on display. The wide range of styles and the diversity of the media employed will surely leave you lost in admiration.

"These young artists deserve all the support we can give them and that's why I'm so pleased to see how many of the paintings have already been snapped up. To those of you who've been fortunate to have got your hands on one of these works, I can only say you've made an investment I've no doubt will pay handsome dividends in time to come. The future of art in Ireland lies here in this gallery tonight."

Some dignitary from the Academy then made a few remarks in a similar strain before proceeding to declare the exhibition open. Quite a coup, I thought, on Finbarr's part to have got someone like that when you considered the conservative reputation of the RHA. He'd put a lot of effort into this and his network of contacts was growing by the day.

"Over here, Susan."

I turned to see who was calling me.

It was Jack Cardiff, my journalist friend, a glass of spirits in one hand while he beckoned me with the other.

"Come and meet the press," he said. The press people were having a private little party of their own. Finbarr hadn't stinted on the hospitality. In this corner of the gallery it was a matter of 'help yourself.'

"Come on, Susan, give us the lowdown on these artists. Any juicy bits? You know the sort of thing we're looking for. We have to keep the readers happy."

"Look here, guys. You're here to write about the art. Forget the tittle-tattle."

"What about the human angle, Susan? That's what the public wants. We try to give them what they want. You know that."

"It's all here." I held up a catalogue. "A biographical note on each artist. You'll have lots to work on. Or go and talk to the artists themselves. They'll be thrilled with the attention. They'll tell you all you want to know."

"Are you trying to kid us or something?" This was Sam from one of the Sundays. "I tried talking to that Frenchwoman. She said if I couldn't understand her paintings, it's time I got another job. Would you believe that? She's some lassie, I can tell you."

The others laughed. Composing copy in their heads.

"That's her over there talking to your husband."

I followed his gaze to where Finbarr was absorbed in conversation with the girl with the French accent, the one who wanted to be known as Camille.

One of the things I'd noticed, especially as the evening wore on, was how vibrant Finbarr seemed to become in the presence of the opposite sex. He blossomed in female company. This is his party personality, I thought. Yet I was riveted by what I saw. I guessed he probably had a few drinks inside him at this stage, for his attitude towards the young Frenchwoman was positively flirtatious.

"No need for jealousy, Susan. He'll be glad enough to climb in beside you when this is all over."

I resented Sam's snide remark.

"He's putting everything he can into this," I said. "He's determined to foster new talent. "

"A good eye for talent. I can see that."

The fatigue hit me and I wished I could push everyone out on the street and pull down the shutters on the whole thing.

"I'll say goodnight, gentlemen, and don't forget we're depending on the reviews. I know I can rely on you guys to do the right thing."

As I edged my way towards the door, I saw Finbarr still engrossed in conversation with the pretty young French brunette.

~ * ~

It must have been the rain that woke me. The insistent drumming against the windows. My fingers felt for Finbarr, but his side of the bed was empty. I was unsteady on my feet as I went to the windows to let up the blinds. A steady downpour descended from a leaden sky. On the pavement opposite a sputtering stream erupted from a broken downpipe. Hopeful but lonely Christmas lights blinked sadly against the furious onslaught. A few brave souls out and about this late November morning were well wrapped against the weather or hidden beneath great multi-coloured umbrellas.

I was weighed down by the exhaustion of the night before and the growing bulk of the baby within me. End of second trimester is how the doctor had put it. Baby about two pounds weight, he'd said. Ten inches from crown to posterior.

Finbarr, I guessed, was downstairs clearing up after the night before. I made myself a cup of coffee, aware that I'd stayed too long at the launch when I should have been in my bed, yet hopeful the whole thing had been a success for the sake of Finbarr who'd invested so much of himself in his project.

I was still in my dressing gown when he came in carrying a bundle of newspapers which he scattered across the table.

"Everything tidied up below?" I said.

He managed a tired smile.

"Larry came in early to give me a hand. Between us, we've got things back in shape. He's holding the fort to let me get some lunch."

"Larry's a brick. I hope you told him that. Have you looked at the reviews?"

"They're not bad. You seem to have a way with the press." He put a hand to his head.

"Headache?"

"I shouldn't have mixed my drinks."

He opened out the papers and I saw where he'd circled one passage in red.

…Take a stroll down South Anne Street and get a peek at what is likely to hit the art scene in the not too distant future... a brave and ambitious attempt to give emerging young artists a deserved opportunity to display their work in the full scrutiny of the public gaze...

…young artists who can look to a beckoning future, if the depth of talent on display here is anything to go by...

"I call that faint praise," said Finbarr. He read aloud from another paper.

…Much credit is due to the promoter, Finbarr Gray, for showcasing an exciting young French painter, Camille, whose canvases reveal a flair and originality too long lacking on the Irish scene. If there are those who find her work in any way shocking, it should be remembered that a fundamental function of art has always been to raise questions about the status quo, to shake the world from its complacency…

Finbarr was smiling. His judgement had been vindicated.

"Interesting they picked out the Frenchwoman," I said.

"You saw her paintings," said Finbarr. "What did you think? Would you say they were shocking?"

"All that impasto with pieces of torn photos stuck into the paint. As if she's trying to say something, though it beats me what it is."

"How do you mean, trying to say something?"

"It's like there's an inner rage or something. Did you not get any of that? You had a long conversation with her. What did you pick up?"

"I thought she was more interested in discussing the future than the past."

"What's this Camille notion? She must have a surname."

"Céline Dubois. She's from Brittany originally, although she came here from Paris."

"So you managed to find out something?"

He winced and his hand went to his head once again.

Eighteen

"Relax. It's purely precautionary. As soon as I can arrange a bed, we'll get you in. Nothing at all to worry about. I want you where I can keep an eye on you. Your baby's fine. I've looked at the scans and he's perfectly formed and well positioned."

"He? Did you say it's a he, Doctor?"

"I'm fairly certain it's a boy. He's a little bit on the small side, but otherwise a perfectly healthy little fellow." He began to scribble something on a printed form.

I placed my hands on my abdomen to cradle my son. In the secret sanctum of my mind I spoke to him. I love you, my little son. Nothing bad is going to happen. We're both in this together and together we'll see it through. If that means lying in a hospital bed, if that's what it takes, then so be it."

Tears filled my eyes. The doctor looked at me a moment and without a word proffered a fistful of tissues. Then he went back to updating the notes in his files. I could see it made perfect sense to go into hospital where I could be kept under constant observation. I knew that. And yet the prospect appalled me, the thought of long days and weeks of inactivity.

As he let me out, the doctor said, "I'll be in touch just as soon as I can make the arrangements. Keep your chin up and when you're feeling down, say a little prayer to Our Lady."

~ * ~

Holy Joe. That's what Finbarr told me the other doctors called him.

"He should stick to what he knows best and leave the preaching to the priests."

I began making preparations. I packed my things into a holdall and kept checking to make sure I'd forgotten nothing. Finbarr came upstairs several times to ask if there anything he could do to help. I suppose he was just as upset as I was at this turn of events and that he was going to miss my company as much as I'd miss his. He kept reminding me Holles Street wasn't a thousand miles away.

"If you need anything, just give me a ring. I can be there in five minutes."

For most of that last day, I was on my own. I'd nobody to talk to but my son and the more we talked, the more we got to understand each other. Instead of words he used his own Morse of tiny movements, a system of jolts and nudges which I had no difficulty interpreting. It wasn't my imagination. When I asked him a question, I got an answer on the spot. That was the kind of bond we had. It was a beautiful relationship for we understood each other intimately. He was a plucky little fellow, my son. He just couldn't understand what I was so worried about. Already I could recognise his father's determination and stubbornness, for he made it clear he was going to be no pushover for anyone.

The phone call came at five-fifteen that evening. Fitzgibbon-Raye's secretary to say the bed would be available the following morning and they wanted me in before eleven. This evening was to be my last at home with Finbarr before the birth.

~ * ~

"Why Kevin?"

We sat in the room which overlooked the street below as the sinking sun disappeared below the ridge of the rooftops. Finbarr eased me forward to adjust the cushion behind my back and then worked himself in beside me. I felt a distinct sense of comfort in his closeness.

"Kevin's a Wicklow saint."

"What's special about Wicklow?"

"Are you letting on you don't remember!"

He snuggled his head into my shoulder and took my hand. He remembered all right. Our very first lovemaking beneath the cloudless Wicklow sky, with the Great Sugarloaf Mountain at the far end of the valley bestowing a benediction on our bonding. Finbarr sighed. I sensed his deep down contentment. Little Kevin snuggled down too and went fast asleep. For the first time, I had a sense that we were a family. A moment like this is unique and should be cherished, for nothing is lasting, nothing permanent and the more intense the joy, the more surely fated it is to pass.

"How does it feel to be a father?" I said.

I wanted to get inside his head, to hear what he really wanted. He thought a minute before he spoke and then there was this sad look in his eyes as he said, "All the things my father was too busy to do with me."

I took his hand and placed it on my bulge. "He's asleep," I said.

"We'll be the best of pals." His face had a dreamy look. "As for education, we'll teach him to think for himself. We'll give him the tools to beat his way through the jungle. In thrall to no one. You and I will be proud to be his parents."

I placed my hand on his, where it cradled the tiny creature deep in an amniotic dream. Had our baby heard the plans being laid out for his future? And if so, did he know something only he could know? For now though, he seemed happy and relaxed and to that extent he fitted with the mood of his contented Mum and Dad.

Tomorrow I leave the comfort of my home for a bleak bed in a bleak ward. But for this brief period when we sat together, an embryonic family, I dared to hope that things would turn out right after all.

~ * ~

I must have slept because when I opened my eyes Josie was gone. The bunch of flowers lay in their cellophane waiting for a nurse to stick them in life-giving water. Josie with her staccato questioning spattered with adulation of her ineffective husband. After four weeks stuck in that bed on the top floor of Holles Street, I'd no wish to sleep my life away, but the nurses seemed to think there was nothing like it. The great panacea. Sleep would solve all my problems. They knew nothing of those bad dreams. Monster baby with mocking eyes and leering lips. Doctors with heads of wolves tearing at my body and I powerless to prevent them. While I screamed in terror, they laughed at my helplessness.

Finbarr arrived with more books.

"A few copybooks is what I need right now," I said.

"You want to write?"

"Something to show him when he's old enough to read it. Let him know what his poor mother had to go through. Anyhow, it'll keep the time from dragging."

"Try to be patient, love. Another few weeks and it'll all be over. I'll have you back home, yourself and the baby."

~ * ~

"Is the wee devil behaving himself?"

I could smell the starch of her uniform as she leaned across the bed to straighten the covers.

"Begob, but you're doing a fierce amount of writing altogether." She gave a tug at the under sheet to straighten it. "You'll end up with a book written before you know it."

"I'll be gone out of here long before that."

Mary Jane was in her element. She was the ray of sunshine sweeping into the ward countless times a day with a mission to put a smile on every face. Humour was her weapon of choice in the fight against fear.

"Watch how you talk or you'll find yourself in the book," I said.

"Sure wouldn't that be a grand thing altogether."

I understood the sudden rush to straighten my bed when Fitzgibbon-Raye breezed into the ward and marched over to where I sat propped against a yielding pile of pillows. At his heels, the ward sister positioned herself slightly behind and to his left at the end of the bed. He ran a practised eye over my charts.

"Good morning, Doctor," I said.

"Everything all right today, Susan?"

"So far as I can tell. Do you think I'll go full term?"

The whole ward listened for his reply. He made no effort to keep his voice down.

"Everything's still on track, yes. Just as long as you do your bit and keep nice and calm. Your baby's due in..." He glanced again at the chart. "You're due in three weeks, but we have to be prepared for any eventuality. Mother Nature is unpredictable. Things could start to happen at any moment. Your job is to stop worrying and relax."

"But what if I go into labour?"

"I'll be here the minute I get the word things are moving. You don't have to worry about a thing."

He glanced at the ward sister and she nodded as if to confirm she'd noted everything he said.

"Happier now, Susan?"

"I'm in your hands, Doctor."

He managed a little smile of encouragement before they strode out as briskly as they'd arrived…doctor, ward sister and a trailing intern. The consultant gynaecologist was a busy man.

The deep silence in the room after his departure was a futile pretence that everyone had been so occupied with their own thoughts that not a word of this doctor patient consultation had been overheard. In the silence, I rummaged for my diary, found a pen and started to write, adding yet another episode of my epic confinement to those already recorded.

A nurse wheeled a small trolley into the room with an assortment of little dark bottles. The daily routine had resumed and soon everything was back to normal.

Nineteen

It wasn't a pain really. More like a tightening somewhere in my middle. I said nothing to anyone because I'd had something like this a few times. Anyway it was gone in a minute, so it must have been what Josie had been telling me about, false labour. Everyone gets those.

But two or three hours later, it came again. It seemed to last a little longer this time, maybe up to two minutes.

After the third time, I called a nurse.

"Braxton Hicks," she said. Jennings was a woman in her forties and had that experienced look that ought to inspire confidence.

"Braxton what?"

"Like false contractions. Means nothing really."

"Can you be sure?"

"If it happens again, you just call me, right?" Then she was gone.

I tried the breathing exercises. As the contractions became more frequent, each was stronger than the last. I called her again.

"Here, let me help you out of the bed."

No-nonsense-Jennings told me to walk around for a while.

"You've been too long in that bed, that's your problem. A good long walk down the corridor should do the trick."

Two giggling nurses went silent and waited for me to pass the nurses' station. The corridor seemed a mile long. I came to an elevator. A sudden urge to play truant. To escape the confines of the floor which had been like a prison for the past two months. A bell pinged and the elevator doors slid open. A bed with a comatose patient manoeuvred into the corridor. I pressed a button, the doors slid closed and I was moving down, down, down.

I stepped out close to the main entrance where the workaday world met the quiet solemnity of the hospital. People coming and going, noise, conversation. A young woman waited with her days-old baby in her arms, both of them wrapped up against the cold air that swept in every time the doors swung open. A couple of smiling nurses stood beside her. As I watched, a man I presumed to be the husband arrived to escort them out. One of the nurses took the baby and led the way through the double doors and out onto the pavement and I found myself caught up in their joy and excitement. Through the glass I saw the solicitous husband settle his young wife into the back seat before the nurse handed the precious bundle into her tender care.

In a couple of weeks, if God is good, that same movie will play again, this time with Susan Enfield and her newborn son in the lead roles.

A gust of cold air swept through the swinging doors. I drew my flimsy dressing gown about me and turned to make my way back. Too long out of my warm bed. Better get back before I catch pneumonia. That's the last clear thought I can remember passing through my mind.

It was like someone had driven a sword into my gut. It went right through my abdomen and out through my back. I clawed the wall for support as I slid onto my knees. I bent forward, doubled up, but nothing I did made any difference. Worse than the pain was the fear. A cold sweat drenched my head since I'd no idea what was happening, could only believe my life was in mortal danger. I thought of God and prayed for mercy.

A hand on my shoulder. Then more hands, under my sticky armpits and about my waist. I was too dazed to know who was trying to lift me. Strong arms hauled me into a wheelchair. The next thing I knew I was in bed and a voice was saying, "You'll be fine. You're back where we can keep an eye on you." The ward was quiet, the other women had settled for the night. I must have been sedated.

I knew without being told that my labour had well and truly commenced. Contractions continued into the night, coming more regularly, every fifteen minutes or so. As well as the acute discomfort in my pelvis, there was a sharp pain in my back. The night nurse hovered around, never far away.

"How long is this going to go on?" I said to her.

"I'll ask the doctor to take a look at you as soon as possible."

"Get him now. I can't bear this. I'm frightened."

"Stop your worrying, Susan. Everything's going to be just fine."

"Get my husband."

"He was here earlier on but we didn't want to wake you."

"Get him. I need him now."

"It's three in the morning."

"I don't care. I want him now."

No Finbarr. Instead a young doctor appeared with white coat swinging open. Too young for my liking. Solemn expression. He took my pulse and put a stethoscope to my belly. He took a look at the sticky discharge reddening the sheets and went into a whispering session with the nurse, his Asiatic features contrasting with her pasty white. The grave expression on his face spread to hers.

"What did you find, Doctor?"

He looked at me as if the sound of my voice was the last thing in the world he'd expected to hear.

"How long will this go on?" I said.

"Everything depends. Who's your consultant?" Then glancing at my chart, he said, "Fitzgibbon-Raye. I'll give him a call and see what he says. In the meantime, Nurse is here if you need her."

"Did anyone ring my husband?"

"In the morning," the nurse said. "We'll ring him in the morning."

"Does he know how bad I am?"

"We'll ring him the morning."

~ * ~

He hadn't arrived when my waters broke. The membrane ruptured and fluid gushed like someone had turned a tap. The bed was soaked. They got me out on the floor to strip off the wet sheets and spread some fresh ones. My consultant arrived before my husband.

A blur of people coming and going. Whispered conversations, options being considered, decisions being made. People peering at my chart with mortal gravity. Fitzgibbon-Raye nodded at a nurse who leaned over the bed to peel back the covers and pull my night-dress up under my breasts. The consultant leaned in for a closer look, ran an exploratory hand across my abdomen before gently prising my legs apart to check for developments. He spoke in an undertone to the young doctor at his elbow and they both turned to the ward sister in urgent consultation. I attempted to read the message in the furrowed brows, strained to hear the earnest responses. In vain.

Fitzgibbon-Raye's voice was gentle and concerned.

"Susan, we've decided to do a section."

"Section?"

"A Caesarean. It's really our only option. We can't risk waiting."

"Risk?" The first time anyone had used that word.

"If we wait for nature to take its course, we'll be placing the baby at risk. You don't want that."

"You're saying the baby's in danger?"

"You're going to have to trust me. Believe me, I know what I'm doing."

"I want you to save my baby. That's all that matters."

"Good girl. I'll see you in the theatre, then. Now try to get some rest."

Moments later, Finbarr was leaning over me. He kissed my forehead and placed his cheek alongside mine.

"He told you what's happening, Finbarr?"

"Yes, they're going for a Caesarean."

"What else did he say?"

"If labour is allowed to drag out, the baby could be deprived of oxygen. He won't risk that, he said."

"Oh, Finbarr." I tried to restrain my sobs. "I don't know what to think. It's all so sudden I can't take it in."

"Let's leave it to the doctors. They know what they're doing."

"Stay with me, Finbarr. Don't go. I'm terrified to be on my own. It's just you and me now. And little Kevin."

He leaned over so his face was touching mine. He spoke into my ear and his words were comforting, reassuring.

"Nothing bad is going to happen to our son. In a few hours it'll all be over and we've a lifetime to look forward to, you and me and him, the three of us."

I so wanted to believe him.

I've a vague recollection of being shunted along the corridor on that long lonely journey down labyrinthine passages to the theatre. Somebody was walking alongside, holding my hand. Was it Finbarr? Was it a nurse? I've no idea.

The wide doors of the theatre swung open, swallowed me whole like the gates of Hades and spoke to me of abandoned hope. I was in a world of green acolytes in weird masks, whose ritualised movements and semaphoric eyes yielded no clue to their inner thoughts or intentions.

I heard the word epidural and was powerless to resist as someone inserted a slender needle in my lower back. I existed in some strange abstract representation of reality, aware only of the mystery rites being played out on my sacrificial body. The screen before my face saved me having to play eyewitness to the bloody ravishing of my integrity.

A muffled voice urged me to look. I looked and saw blood. I looked harder and saw a bloody manikin in the hands of a green-robed figure.

"Smile, Susan, it's your newborn son. Let him see you smile."

The blood-streaked blob they called my son was whisked out of sight before I could get my head around the reality that I'd just had a glimpse of my longed-for child. I did manage a weak, tired smile of acknowledgement before the screen went up again.

I wasn't aware of anything else until I woke to find myself in a regular hospital bed in what must have been the recovery unit. The gentle touch of a nurse feeling for my pulse. A dull persistent ache in my abdomen. My mind swam as I struggled to reconstruct my memory, trying to piece everything together from scattered fragments. It was a hopeless struggle against that pain.

Twenty

"Where's my baby?"

"Susan! You're awake! Take it easy now, just lie back there and relax."

"My baby! I want to see my baby. Where is he?"

"It's okay. We'll take you down to see your baby when you've rested a bit. It's way too soon to exert yourself. Here, put this pillow behind your head. You'll be more comfortable that way."

She leaned over me, smiling into my face and brushing my hair back from my brow as a mother would with a fevered child.

When I woke again, Finbarr was there holding my hand.

"Where's the baby?" I said.

"He's in the incubation unit."

"Have you seen him?"

"I've been down with him a few times."

"How is he? Does he look all right?"

"There's a nurse there watching him all the time."

"What does he look like? Tell me."

"Tiny. He looks tiny. He's on oxygen and there's some

sort of monitor attached to his foot. They wouldn't let me touch him."

"Why? Why not?" The first stirring of fear within me.

"It seems he's not yet out of the woods." He took my hand and held it. "He barely made it and the odds are not on his side."

It was something I didn't want to hear and what I was hearing I didn't want to believe.

"I have to see him. I'm his mother. He needs his mother."

He went to the door and whispered to the nurse. Meanwhile I waited. I was too overcome by fear to speak and Finbarr had no words to reassure me. Instead he gripped my left hand in both his hands, maybe to inject whatever faltering courage he could find within himself, maybe to seek from me the courage that failed him. After what seemed like a lifetime of waiting, the nurse came back with someone more senior who asked if I felt strong enough to use a wheelchair.

"All I want is to see my baby."

After much to-ing and fro-ing my tubes were disconnected and two nurses eased me out of the bed and into the wheelchair. I tried to ignore the acute pain that shot across my middle and around to my back.

A row of transparent boxes rested on tables along one side of the neonatal unit. Inside each container a tiny being clinging to a feeble life.

Finbarr led the way to the end of the row and placed his hand on the very last incubator. Inside lay our most precious little child. He looked very different from the blood-soaked creature lifted out of my open belly and held up for me to see in the middle of the night. Cleaned up now and lying naked on a soft white piece of fabric, to my eyes he was a thing of extraordinary beauty. I was overwhelmed by an all-consuming feeling of love, difficult to describe except to say I related to him as a part of myself, an extension of my own very being.

"He's so tiny, Finbarr."

I had an overwhelming urge to take him and press him to my body. One of the nurses noticed me fondling the outside of the incubator. She exchanged glances with her colleague before she leaned down and whispered, "I can let you hold him for one short minute but then we'll have to put him back inside for his own good."

"One minute. If I could hold him even for a minute."

While her companion held open the lid, she leaned in and with two hands and infinite care brought him out, the lifelines still attached. She handed him to me to hold. Finbarr crouched down beside me, his face close to mine. It was a moment that would stay with me for as long as I lived. The features in the tiny face were perfectly formed and beautiful. As I stroked his cheek with my little finger, the eyelids seemed to flicker for a brief moment. Then I pressed him to my flesh where my nightdress was open at the neck and I could feel the heat from the little body as I am sure he must have felt mine. For those precious seconds, he and I renewed and strengthened the bond already formed between us as he grew in my womb.

"Kevin," I whispered, "Kevin, it's your mama. I love you forever. Fight on, little love, you've so much to live for. We're both here with you, your mam and dad."

A pair of hands tried to take him away from me, but I

wanted to hold onto him. I wanted this moment to last, but firm, insistent hands took him from my grasp and returned him to his oxygenated cocoon. So cruel. Bathed in oxygen but cut off from the oxygen of his mother's love that no machine could replicate.

We stayed watching our little son engage in his lonely silent struggle, unable to help other than by wishing and willing. I prayed. I prayed then as I never prayed before. I prayed to the angel Michael, who was supposed to be on my side in every crisis. Save him, Michael. Let him grow up to be big and healthy. Don't let us down in our time of need.

Weak and tired, I realised there was no more I could do. I kissed the hard, uncaring sides of the plastic container and Finbarr wheeled me back to my bed. A great wave of exhaustion swept over me.

~ * ~

"I warned everyone off. I told them you're having no visitors today."

"Thanks, love." I gave a weak smile of gratitude. I wanted no one to see me in my state of mental torment. Not to speak of the physical pain. The slightest movement shot flames through my inside.

"I can ask the nurse to give you a stronger painkiller if you think you want it," he said.

"I could do with something stronger."

The nurse arrived with some tablets and a glass of water.

"Thanks, Nurse. I usually try to avoid this stuff. But right now..."

"Cathy. Call me Cathy."

"Thanks, Cathy."

"Swallow them down. They'll help you get some sleep."

"How can I sleep when my son is down there fighting for his life?"

"You need to rest, Susan. You've been through a lot."

~ * ~

I must have dozed off because when I looked around, Finbarr was gone and the clock said it was just after four in the afternoon. I'd slept in spite of myself. They probably had me full of drugs. Drugs to kill pain, drugs to make me sleep. But no drug yet devised was going to change reality and that reality was lying in an incubator in the neonatal unit fighting a pathetically unequal struggle with the forces of life and death.

Where was Finbarr? Gone to grab some lunch, I imagined. Or maybe he went back to take another look at Kevin. When Nurse Cathy saw me stirring, she slipped out of the room. Something odd about that. A minute later, Finbarr came in.

"You've been down to see Kevin?"

He pulled a chair close to the bed and sat down but said nothing. There was something about his demeanour that caused me to look straight into his face, but he didn't meet my gaze. His look was distant and obscure as though a veil had descended. Why couldn't he bring himself to meet my eyes?

"Finbarr! What is it? What's wrong? Tell me."

Did I need to ask? The answer cried aloud from his expression of doom. I leaned toward him, trying to reach his face and make him look at me.

"What, Finbarr? What?"

"I've just been down there. It's not looking good, Susan. Not good."

"Not good? Not good!" Already my tears were flowing. Already I knew but I had to hear it. The primal scream built silently in my soul. "Tell me, Finbarr. Tell me. I need to know."

"He's gone, love. Our little son is gone."

The scream came. I screamed without restraint. The feral, futile scream of the animal in the jaws of the predator.

He threw himself on the bed beside me. Our tears blended. We wept together, knowing in the certainty of the moment that nothing could ever console us for our loss.

How long we remained there I know not, riven by our individual pain while joined to each other's, yet powerless to assuage either. In time the tears ran dry, but even then I knew that each of us had suffered a wound which would forever leave its mark, a searing scar on each of our souls.

There was a knock on the room door and, after a respectful pause, Cathy came in. She hugged me and said she understood. Her words were sincere and I appreciated her kindness. I believed she meant it, that she did understand and feel my grief. She took Finbarr's hand and pressed it in silent commiseration.

"You won't have to leave the bed, Susan. I'm going to bring him up so you can hold him."

I wept again, this time for the kindness and understanding of a virtual stranger. Doubtless it wasn't the first time she'd faced such a situation. She knew in her heart what to do. When she left to collect my baby,

Finbarr helped me into a sitting position and propped me up with pillows. He dabbed my face with a towel. Minutes later Cathy was back with Kevin. She placed him with extraordinary gentleness in my arms and I pressed him to my body in an aching, despairing embrace. The little body was still warm. Now that I had him again, I never wanted to let him go. With finger and thumb I rubbed the golden wisps of hair from his forehead. The eyes were closed and I thought how I'd never looked into those eyes, never had the joy, the privilege of exchanging a glance, never that chance to see into his soul.

Cathy produced a Polaroid camera.

"Something for you to remember him by," she said.

Kevin's little face was towards the camera and in that moment he looked so peaceful you'd think he might wake at any moment.

Later, when I reluctantly let him go, they took away his tiny body and Finbarr and I were alone. We didn't talk much. There wasn't anything either of us could say. For the moment, I'd cried myself out. There were no more tears to call on. But the ache, the terrible emptiness remained. I glanced at Finbarr. I wondered what he was going through. I'd seen his grief as our tears had mingled, but now he seemed more composed, more like the stereotype of stoic fortitude.

"I'll have to talk to someone here about the normal procedures," he said.

"Procedures?"

"You know what I mean. Death cert, burial and so on."

"Could you just leave it, please? Anyway, I'm not going to be rushed into any decisions."

I realised afterwards he used those practicalities to displace the emotions, the bitter disappointment, the sense of helplessness he must have felt. I know now that's how men deal with their grief.

He fell silent, his eyes fixed on a spot that wasn't in the room. I wanted him here with me, to comfort and be comforted. I searched for something to say.

"It's not the end, love," I said. "I know nothing will ever take his place, but with the help of God we'll have other little ones to love and cherish and we'll do for them all the things we had planned for him."

I wanted to allow Finbarr that tiny ray of hope. Strange that I should be the one attempting to console my husband. Or was it that I felt some responsibility for what had happened?

"We'll try for another child," I said.

"Child?" He repeated the word in a distant, puzzled sort of way.

"You and me. It's not the end."

"Susan..."

"What? What is it? What are you trying to say?"

"Susan, you're not going to have another baby. They had to operate."

A wave of panic swept over me and swamped my brain.

"Finbarr! Tell me what you're saying. What operation? What are you talking about?"

He took my hand between his hands and his grip hurt.

"They had to take your womb to save your life."

Twenty-one

It was the only night he would lie there with us in our bedroom. Tomorrow we'd put him in the cold, damp earth. I got out of bed to sit beside the open box and rest my hand on the tiny cold body. I wanted to warm him, a futile thought.

"You're sure you want to do it this way?" Finbarr was awake.

"I thought you agreed."

"We can still do it the official way."

"He's our son. He has a name. He's somebody. He'll have his own special spot." No way did I want our son to share a plot with all the other little angels who never got a chance to live. "He'd be lost in that place. No, we'll take him where we decided last night."

"There's probably some law against this."

"You know what it means to me."

"Exposed to wind and rain?"

"In the shadow of the mountain."

"If it's what you really want, I'm not going to stop you."

"It is what I want."

We were eating breakfast when the phone rang. His mother. I knew they've been in contact right through the crisis. The death of her grandson brought some softening in her attitude to her son, but it remained to be seen how far the thaw extended to her daughter-in-law.

He held the phone facing me so I could follow the conversation.

"You've had a terrible time, Finbarr."

"Imagine how it must be for Susan."

"Time is a great healer. And there'll be other babies. All in the Lord's good time."

She didn't know my chance of a family had been cruelly whipped away from me. Before he could answer, though, she was onto a new tack. She wanted to know had we made arrangements for a funeral.

"I'll let you know the minute we decide."

"Your father and I want to be there."

"Of course, Mam."

~ * ~

Good Friday morning and the Bray road was veiled in a holy quiet. On an afternoon in September, we'd travelled this same road and I'd remarked to Finbarr how individual the houses were, spaced apart with no two alike. The world had seemed so different then, so full of hope. Now our hopes and dreams lay shattered like shards of a priceless vase.

Were the same thoughts going through Finbarr's mind? No hope now of a family. No little man to protect and guide on his first tentative steps in the world.

"How are you feeling?" I broke into his reverie.

I sat beside him, the miniature casket on my lap, the

baby's face exposed, the tiny eyelids closed. Finbarr hadn't said a lot in these past few days. He seemed to have suppressed the horror of what had happened. His composed exterior must be hiding an ocean of hurt.

"How am I feeling?" He seemed puzzled by the question.

"You must feel I've let you down."

"What makes you say that?"

"I need to hear you say it. How you really feel."

"A million times worse for you."

"I'm sorry I let you down."

"Oh my God, Susan, don't keep saying that. You did everything you were supposed to do. It's one of those things. No reason. No meaning. Don't blame yourself. Blame God. Blame fate. When all's said and done, we're playthings for the gods. Nothing we say or do will make the blindest bit of difference. Blame solves nothing. We're just going to have to live with it and cope whatever way we can."

"Cope you say? I can't believe it'll ever get easier. You think it'll get easier?"

He took his hand off the steering wheel and put it on the back of my neck. I felt his fingers caress my skin. That was his only answer but for now it was enough.

Beyond Bray we left the main road and began to climb through a steep-sided valley with rocky outcrops on each side.

"Where are we now?"

"Rocky Valley it's called."

"Where will it take us?"

"Onto the plateau at Calary."

"I'm leaving it to you. You know these parts."

The old Ford Consul struggled against the gradient. Ahead of us lay the mountains and behind us the sea. I caught a fleeting glimpse of Bray Head planting a bold foot in the Irish Sea. We emerged on a broad plateau ringed by the summits of North Wicklow. One peak I recognised immediately and at that moment I knew why Finbarr had brought us to this place. The southern base of the Sugarloaf Mountain was instantly recognisable from its pointed cone. This was my mountain, the one who had placed his seal on our first love.

"Here, Finbarr, down this side road."

The place was deserted. A half mile away, a solitary car glistened a moment in the morning sunlight. We crawled along, scanning the terrain on either side.

"Stop!" I said. "Right here."

He reversed onto the grassy verge. He came around to my side and took the casket which I'd been nursing on my lap.

He stood staring at a covering of green gorse that stretched to the base of the scree spills radiating from the peak.

"Over there." I pointed.

I scrambled over the rough ditch and he passed the box over to me before going back to the car for a spade.

I found an area of short spongy grass, close-cropped by sheep. A lark shot straight into the air, its alarm call breaking the silence of the spring morning.

"Right here, beside this boulder," I said.

He placed the box where I pointed and I knelt on the soft grass to say my last goodbye to our baby son. I looked with love and longing at the little face I knew I'd never see again. With my finger, I gathered a tear from my eye and used it to moisten his eyes and lips. I said no prayer. There was too much bitterness in my heart to involve any deity. Nor would I have known what to say, what to ask for. His soul was out there somewhere in the April air wafting the mountain perfume across the peaty uplands of Wicklow. His body would find safe haven here beneath the protective presence of my adopted Sugarloaf.

While Finbarr dug, I looked around to assure myself there was no one watching. Only a mother sheep standing over her lambs kept a watchful eye from a safe distance.

I lifted my baby's body from the box and pressed it to my breast. That's how we spent our last moments together, Kevin and I, lost in a last heartbreaking farewell. I never wanted to let him go, yet when the hole was deep enough, Finbarr turned to me and his eyes said now's the time. I gave Kevin a final kiss and handed him to Finbarr, who kissed him before placing him back in the casket and screwing down the lid. No mark or inscription of any kind. Inscriptions are there to be read but no human eye would ever find the secret grave which enfolded Kevin's remains.

We fixed the sods in place to make the site invisible. We alone would find the lump of granite jutting from the ground, destined to mark forever the final resting place of our infant son.

"We'll go back through Enniskerry," he said.

"Whatever you say."

Occasional shady conifers alternated with bud-bursting branches displaying their shy translucent greens. They all took meaning from the presence on the slopes above of my infant son whose eternal destiny was to lie in this most beautiful corner of Ireland's garden.

"Why are we stopping?"

"I just spotted something. A house for sale."

"Leave me alone. Please Finbarr, some other time."

"I'll just walk back for a quick look."

He left my door swinging and a gust of scented air left me a little more relaxed. At that moment, I'd no interest in looking at houses but I followed him. A gravel driveway curved down the slope to the house. Finbarr pointed.

"Across the valley. Move your eyes up the slope on the far side. See that field with the furze and the sheep?"

I made out the specks of white which had to be distant sheep.

"So what are you telling me?"

"That's where we buried little Kevin. With binoculars I'd swear you could find the exact spot."

We walked back to the car, silent each of us in our own thoughts.

~ * ~

It hit me a week after we buried Kevin. Out of nowhere it struck. Guilt and remorse took up residence in my brain, my body burdened with a weight which threatened to stifle my very breath. An invisible giant sat on my chest, determined to shut down my heart and lungs. I tried massaging my heart with slow circular strokes. I gasped for mouthfuls of air. The pressure seldom left me. I found some relief in sleep but knew I couldn't afford to sleep my life away. There had to be some way out of my torment but the possibility of escape seemed a forlorn hope.

De profundis clamavi ad te, Domine. From the depths of my despair I cried to the Lord to release me from my pain, but not knowing what was wrong with me, I couldn't see from what direction any relief might appear.

The worst part was the conviction that I deserved to suffer, that somehow I didn't merit a moment's happiness ever again. It was a punishment for neglecting my newborn baby left to die motherless while I lay asleep in another part of the hospital. I felt too my first faint inklings of God's anger at my decision to turn aside from His path when I'd left the religious life.

"Are you sure you're okay, love?" Finbarr looked concerned.

"I'll be all right."

"You've hardly stopped crying. There must be something I can do."

"Nothing." He'd have to experience it himself to know.

"Remember that nurse in the recovery room? Cathy, wasn't it? I'm going to give her a ring."

"What would she know?"

"She must have dealt with the same thing before. I mean mothers who lost their babies."

"I think you're wasting your time."

Next day he had a piece of information.

"I talked to Cathy, you know, that nurse."

"Oh?" I was apprehensive.

"My hunch was right. She's had other mothers in the same situation."

"Is that supposed to make it any easier?"

"She knows what you're going through."

"How could anyone know what I'm going through?" I

almost spat the words.

"She said if you could share with someone...you know, talk."

"Talk?"

"How would you feel about talking to a therapist?"

"In the name of God!"

"She gave me a name and a number. A Miss Hamilton. Very good, she said, especially in...what did she call it...perinatal bereavement."

"Look Finbarr, I'm sorry for snapping at you. I'm just not ready for…"

"Think about it."

I did think about it. In all that darkness, a part of me retained a tiny spark. That part of me that was a fighter. The part that had refused to be walked on by an overbearing Mother Superior. Even in my worst despair, I knew I'd have to act. It was that or crack up completely.

Yet still I hesitated. Was I ready to trot along to some know-all shrink and admit to her I was on the point of going mad? My whole being shrank from making such an admission, exposing my weakness to a total stranger.

I sat staring at the receiver in my hand. I don't know how long I remained like that, wallowing in self-pity, drowning in despair.

I toyed with the idea of finishing it all off. I thought that death might be the only way out. That way at least I could be with my son and we'd find peace together in another place. Yet some tiny thing inside me was reluctant to let myself go under and not grasp the lifeline that had been flung in my direction.

I dialled the number. A recorded voice. "Ms Hamilton is not available to come to the phone...If you wish to leave a message..."

There was something familiar about that voice, yet the name Hamilton meant nothing to me. I gave my name as Susan and left my number. I could always pull back from the whole thing if I changed my mind. As I put down the phone, it was in the desperate expectation that I'd taken a first small but decisive step in my own recovery.

Twenty-two

"I think you're expecting me, my name's Susan Enfield." I spoke before the door was fully open.

A woman in navy skirt, white blouse buttoned to the neck, her left hand still on the latch, peered at me through the opening. Greying hair brushed back and tied behind her neck. As she studied my face, a slow smile crept up from the corners of her mouth to blossom in her eyes, a smile that signalled the dawning of recognition. She flung back the door and threw her arms around me.

"Susan! Have I changed so much that you don't know me? The one who taught you everything you ever knew about being a good little nun?"

It all came together then. The voice, the face, the manner. Unmistakable.

"Connie! Consolata. I'd never have known you without the...without the, you know, the habit."

"You too, Susan. You're totally different. Your hair's lovely, by the way. The length suits you. I'd forgotten you were golden blonde. I'm Jennifer now, by the way." The granny hairstyle, the strands of grey shining through, combined to make her older than her years. There was still something nunnish about the skirt, the blouse, her whole demeanour.

"Jennifer? So you've left the order?"

"Lock, stock and barrel." She seemed to relish my surprise.

"Last I heard they'd made you Mother Superior! I thought you were perfect for the job."

"Not everyone thought so. Someday I'll tell you all about it."

My former novice mistress put her arm around me and ushered me inside. We were in the garden flat, the basement of a red-brick Victorian house outside the gates of Phoenix Park. She led me into a low-ceilinged room and put me sitting in a well-worn armchair near the fireplace where an electric fire stood in for the natural flame of coal or wood. This place, I thought, was probably prone to damp and cold. I knew myself how grim it could be for someone leaving the security of the convent to make their way in the outside world. I'd been through all that.

Now I felt the familiar sense of ease in Jennifer's presence that I'd known during my final days in the convent. The mature friend who, despite the decade or so that separated us, I could rely on to understand me. She'd proved herself a respectful confidante when I was in the throes of leaving.

"Jennifer! Where did that come from?"

"I was christened Anna Jane but I grew up as Jenny. Skinny Jenny, the other kids called me. It's why I never really liked Jenny. When I left the convent, I decided on Jennifer. Think it suits me?"

"Like a glove." I laughed and she laughed with me.

I hadn't laughed in weeks. For a brief moment, I forgot the sadness and pain that had brought me here. I was back in the comforting familiarity of someone who'd always understood me.

An odd thing happened. One minute I was laughing, and the next I was crying. How is that possible? Like a summer shower from a cloudless sky.

She made no attempt to hush or comfort me, just sat quietly, watching, relating. Great sobs heaved in my breast so that at one point I feared I'd become hysterical, lose all control.

I looked in embarrassment at Jennifer, my watery eyes attempting to convey apologies and shame. She met my glance with a look of infinite understanding and acceptance. Take your time, her eyes seemed to say. You need to do this. There's no shame in venting your suffering. You're in a safe place now. You're with me.

Then with infinite skill, she led me to open my soul.

"Tell me about your husband."

"I want to talk about my baby."

"Yes, tell me about your baby."

"My baby's dead."

"Oh, no!"

"He's dead, Jennifer, dead. My little baby's dead."

"I'm so sorry."

"How can I go on living when my baby is dead?"

"You're very hurt. That I can see."

She didn't rush me or interrupt as I started to tell her my story. I began with Finbarr. She hid any surprise she might have felt about my marrying the convent chaplain.

"Your baby, Susan. Tell me about him. What did you call him?"

"His name's Kevin. We buried him in Wicklow."

"What happened to little Kevin?"

"Under the Sugarloaf."

"Talk to me about him. Was he a beautiful baby?" At last someone who seemed to understand.

"Beautiful. Twelve short hours. That's all he got."

"When was this?"

"Almost a month ago." March 26th would be forever engraved in my memory.

"And you've suffered on your own all this time?"

"I hoped it would pass, but instead of getting better, it's getting worse. I'm close to breaking point. I thought if I could find someone to..."

"What about Finbarr?"

"I don't want to worry him. He's up to his eyes with work. Anyway, I know he feels as bad as I do."

I sobbed into a tissue. She waited.

"It's worse, Jennifer, a lot worse than that. Oh, Jesus." I couldn't voice it. "I had a hysterectomy."

"No!"

"I'm never going to have a child, Jennifer. Never. Never."

We talked a long time. In reality, Jennifer did very little of the talking, just enough to help me pour out the blackness inside. Here was someone to whom I could open my heart, secure with her when I hadn't been able to confide to another living soul. So it was that I told her how I came to loathe myself and cover myself in blame for what had happened. Even the unspeakable shame and guilt that I feared would lead me to destroy myself.

Only her eyes spoke and the message they conveyed was one of empathy and understanding, as if she herself could feel the depths of my despair. Only when she was sure I'd no more to add, did she say anything.

"You've been brave, Susan, to bring it all out into the open. That's the first step. Between us, we'll look for a way out of your despair."

I sensed she could see into my soul and I was glad I'd opened up to her as I had, given expression to the inexpressible, given voice to the unspeakable.

"How has Finbarr taken all this?"

"I've let him down badly."

"Has he said that?"

"He doesn't say anything. He's too much on his plate right now."

"Have you told him how you're hurting?"

"He was the one who came up with the idea of counselling. I'm the one who's been locking him out."

"Do you talk to each other?"

"Men don't talk about feelings." I'd no desire to criticise Finbarr.

"Some men don't. Show him you need him, Susan. And show him you know he's hurt too. You may be surprised. Tell me this. Do you have any kind of memento of Kevin?"

A subtle change of direction. Perhaps she sensed my reluctance to talk about my relationship with my husband.

"I have a photo," I said.

I drew it out, as though it were a sacred relic. I passed it to Jenny and studied her face. I saw an expression of immense pity and sorrow.

"He's beautiful, Susan, just like you said. It's no wonder your heart is broken."

"In little bits."

She leaned across and put her hand on mine.

"Stabat mater, dolorosa," she whispered.

"Juxta crucem lacrimosa." I responded in the words of the Latin hymn. Our years in a religious order had left us a common language to express the insupportable sorrow of the grieving mother.

~ * ~

As I boarded the no.10 bus that would take me through rush-hour Phibsboro towards the city centre, I was conscious of a lightening of the load that had weighed so heavily on my soul in the past few weeks. In Jennifer I knew I'd found a friend, a soul mate who'd be there for me in times of stress.

Twenty-three

"I'd a visit from that young French artist. You remember her." He hung his jacket on the back of the door and tugged at his tie.

"Camille, she called herself. Am I right?'

"Céline Dubois. She's pushing me to do another exhibition."

"Some cheek. I hope you told her where to go."

"You wouldn't believe how persistent she is. Kept going on about it. Then I thought, well okay, if she's willing to do the work..."

"You're not telling me..."

"I thought I'd call her bluff. I said what about a one-woman show?"

"Good thinking."

"She jumped at the idea. I said if her work wasn't up to scratch, she could just forget it. I'm not going to show any old trash."

"Don't tell me you gave in just like that. How do you know she's not just using you?"

"Of course she's using me. I'm using her. That's business. But the girl's got something. Something special.

I think it's more than talent. If it turns out I'm right, I want to be the one who discovers her."

"You know more about this kind of thing than I do. Maybe I should let you follow your instinct. I have to trust you."

He never ceased to surprise me, Finbarr. Theologian turned art connoisseur. Priest turned businessman.

"How did you get on with that therapist?" He had a way of changing the subject when he thought he was ahead. "Tell me, what's she like?"

"You're never going to believe this. She knows both of us."

"Seriously? How come?"

"Does the name Consolata mean anything to you?"

"Of course! She was with you in the convent. That must have been awkward."

"Far from it. I was delighted."

"Did you find her any help? What's her approach?"

"She said what I really need is someone I can talk to."

"Isn't that why you went to her? To talk it through with a professional?"

"I think she meant someone else."

"A friend like?"

"Or even a husband."

For a moment he looked startled.

"What about your sister? Some things women understand better than men."

"That reminds me, I haven't talked to Josie in weeks. She'll be wondering what's become of me."

"Just don't make it tomorrow."

"Why not tomorrow?"

"We're going for a drive, you and me."

"What's this all about?"

"Remember that house we spotted in Rocky Valley?"

"I'd forgotten all about it."

"I've been talking to the agent. We can just about manage the asking price."

"When did all this happen?"

"I was meeting a customer in Bray and spotted the estate agent's office. He asked me if I'd like to take a dekko. I said why not and he took me up there. I'd love you to see it."

"Well, I suppose there's no harm looking."

~ * ~

Whether it was the sheep with their little lambs or the crispness of the April air I wasn't sure, but already my mood was lifting. Up here in the hills, away from the city, away from everything, I forgot the blackness that had dragged me down. The place had the same deserted look as before, the padlock on the gate, the empty driveway, the absence of life.

"Who'll show us around?"

"Don't worry, love, I have the keys. They'll trust us not to steal anything."

Like he was already in possession, he opened the door leading into the old fashioned porch, slotted keys into two separate locks and pushed the heavy front door inwards. Inside I found it very different to what I'd expected.

On the outside, a single storey farm worker's cottage built a hundred years ago. Once inside I could see it had been radically renovated. Perhaps a previous owner had been an architect. All the windows had been enlarged to give an atmosphere of light and space. I opened a door and found myself in the sitting room, which extended almost the full width of the house from front to back. Facing the fireplace, a bookshelf lined with books. A few minutes browsing would tell a lot about the reading tastes of the owners. The remains of the last fire still in the grate, spilt ashes on the marble tiles. A book lay open on a low table. I felt a guilty sense of intrusion. It was as if the family had just stepped outside and would be back at any moment.

Finbarr arrived back from his own tour of inspection.

"You've got to see the conservatory," he said.

He ushered me through a door which had once opened to the outside and we stood in a sun-room enclosed on three sides by glass, about half the length of the house.

"Well, what do you think?" He made a gesture like a magician producing something from thin air.

"Fabulous."

That sun-room had been created with one clear vision, to form part of the extraordinary vista stretching down into the valley below before sweeping upwards on the far side, up onto the facing slopes dominated by the distinctive cone of the Sugarloaf to the east. I had a sense of standing before a vast canvas on which a divine artist had worked his magic. There stood my beloved mountain…about his head a misty turban of low-lying stratus, a sure indicator of impending rain. Here at last was a place I might find peace.

In the kitchen, I found a cast iron stove which took me back to the old place in Annagopple. I pictured myself keeping that fire going with logs from the nearby plantations. There was a homely feel to the place.

"Well, my little love, what do you think?" He stood behind me and wound his arms around me, resting his chin on my shoulder. Through an open door, I caught a glimpse of yellow gorse on a distant slope.

"It's too beautiful for words."

"Open your hand." He pressed something into my hand.

A bunch of keys.

"Only say the word and all this is yours."

"We need time to think. To talk about it."

"You don't like it then?"

"Oh yes! Yes, it's what I've always dreamed of."

"So what's there to discuss?"

"Well for one thing, there's the small matter of money. We can't rush into something with our heads down."

"I talked to the bank manager. He knows my old man well. It's a simple matter of taking out a mortgage on South Anne Street. With bricks and mortar, we can't go wrong."

"I need time to think."

"You've been pining for a place in the country, but it's your decision. You decide."

~ * ~

"Are you mad? It's way down in Wicklow, for God's sake. People would give their right arm to live around the corner from their work."

"Rocky Valley is not the South Pole, Josie. Besides, living in the city centre isn't my cup of tea. Finbarr's getting a new car and I can hold onto the old one."

"We can't afford one car, never mind two."

I couldn't imagine Martin losing much sleep if he never saw us again.

"I can assure you it's putting Finbarr to the pin of his collar to scrape up the deposit. Plus the car loan on top of everything."

"Didn't you tell me his folks have millions?"

"They don't throw any of it in our direction."

"When you're driving home to Wicklow in your car, don't forget your sister queuing for a bus in the rain.

I decided to change the subject.

"Blaithín can come and stay with us for a while after we settle in. It'll give yourself and Martin a break and we'd both love to have her."

"I don't know what Martin would say to that."

"Jesus, Josie, why don't you stand up to him for a change? Start making your own decisions."

Her wounded expression made me regret having said anything. Any slight on Martin cut her to the quick. Again I switched topic.

"Did I tell you I went to see a therapist?"

"A therapist? What's this about?"

"I thought you knew. I've been down in the dumps lately."

"So you're depressed? Who wouldn't be after what happened? But running to a therapist? From what I hear, they only make you worse."

"Are you saying I should do nothing and it'll just go away?"

"I didn't say do nothing. As a matter of fact, that might be your problem."

"What you mean?"

"I'd have thought that's obvious. When are you going back to your work?"

"I just can't face back. You've no idea how bad it is. Times I think I'm headed for the loony bin."

"Spend all your time moping at home and that's where you'll end up. It's time you pulled yourself together. Go back to work, Sue. It'll take you out of yourself, get your mind off things."

"I'll think about it."

Josie's suggestion about going back to work did make me think. It was something I would decide in my own good time.

Twenty-four

I stood in the conservatory and looked across at the magnificent sweep of hills and valleys. A strange destiny had brought me to this part of Wicklow. On the slopes opposite there lay a secret grave with a little body, blood of my blood, flesh of my flesh, fruit of my being. This was a place that had beckoned me over the years, biding its time until destiny should bring the dream to realisation. I felt an affinity with the mountain reaching for the sky on the far side of the valley.

"Do I smell cooking?" Finbarr had arrived home early from work as though he too had fallen for the charm of our cottage in the hills.

"It's Wicklow lamb."

"Caught it yourself in our neighbours' field?"

"Not much chance of that. Whenever I step outside, I see this odd character watching me."

"He probably lives around here. Just curious to know who's moved in. We really should make an effort to get to know the locals."

Next morning I began to tear away the ivy around the front gates and found a metal plaque cemented into the stone.

GILTSPUR. There it was, the name of the house, revealed at last, having lain hidden under years of accumulated ivy.

I wondered about that name, where it came from. I stepped into the centre of the road to view the name against the backdrop of the hills and decide if it was a fitting name for our new abode.

I turned and saw the figure of a man farther up the road staring in my direction. The same character I'd seen before, always watching, always too far away to address. I raised my hand to wave but he stepped back out of sight, hidden by the trees which came right to the road's edge. I waited a few minutes but he didn't reappear. I found it hard to imagine there could be a dwelling on that side of the road with its continuous cover of spruce and pine. I resolved to do a little exploring later, but right then I'd some phone calls to make. First, my boss, Sarah.

"Susan! How are you bearing up? I can't imagine what you've been through."

"I'm only just beginning to come to terms with it. I suppose everyone has some cross to bear. If it weren't this, it'd be something else." Platitudes have their place in the way we relate to each other.

"You're a brave woman to be able to cope the way you have. I wish there was something I could do."

There was empathy there, a woman's understanding of a woman's pain. But soon she was bringing me up to speed on office gossip. Who'd got engaged, who'd left for pastures new, new ideas she had in mind for the magazine.

"Sounds like I'm going to find big changes."

"Nothing like what's coming down the tracks."

"Oh? Am I allowed to ask?"

"I'll fill you in when you're back. So when are we going to see you, then?"

"I'm just about ready to face the fray."

"Why don't you start with a few hours a day till you get back in the swing of it?"

I'd been out of the office for half a year, since the day the consultant had ordered me to stop work and I'd lain in a hospital bed for several months. And what did any of it avail me or my baby son?

These were my last few days of freedom. I set off to explore my surroundings. In the top branches of a mountain ash, a lone blackbird proclaimed his territorial rights. A car with a single occupant slowed as it passed and as the sound of its engine faded away an extraordinary peace descended in its wake. I walked at a leisurely pace up the slope. The conifers jostled for space right up to the road's edge where an old stone wall looked as though a breath of air would be enough to bring it down.

On the other side, there was mountain pasture, dotted with grazing sheep. Looking back, I could see farm buildings nestled in the valley and distant cattle foraging in the fields. I came to a gap in the forest where an unpaved path snaked between the trees. I caught the aroma of burning peat. Turf smoke meant human habitation, a living hearth. I followed the rough track where a lively mountain stream ran splashing and sparkling on its mad, excited dash for the sea. Suddenly I caught sight of the slow wispy spiral of white smoke in the clear morning air.

"Good day to you, ma'am."

I jumped as a man emerged from the trees beside me, the same man I'd seen spying on me since we moved in. He carried a bundle of twigs bound with ragged rope. His trousers, held up by an old neck-tie pressed into service as a belt.

"Good morning." I tried to hide my nerves. "Collecting sticks for the fire, I see."

"All on your own, are you? Himself must be out trying to make a few pounds. These is hard times to be trying to make a crust, there's no doubt about it."

I got that feeling he knew a lot about our movements. Maybe he'd little else to occupy his mind. He seemed open and guileless enough.

"You live around here?"

"Just round the bend. That's what I tell them all. Chaser Cambridge, just round the bend."

Just then I saw his cabin, a low building of rough stone to which a coating of lime wash had been applied. A bit like the cabins I'd seen in remote parts of the west.

"Come on inside, wouldn't you? Herself will give us a cup o' tay."

Finbarr had talked about getting to know the locals. Well, here was my chance. A chance to meet the Cambridges and try to figure out how much they already knew about us.

I found myself in a room so full of smoke it was hard to see anything. I made out the figure of a woman staring at me. She was wrapped in a blue overall covered with floral spots and tied about the middle with white tape. Her expression hovered between apprehension and suspicion. She looked towards her husband as if for explanation.

"Missus down the road wants to meet you, Mona. Them new folks in Cassidy's house."

He pointed at the stained pottery teapot, reminding his wife of her duty.

"God bless us and save us, Chaser." Mona wiped her hand down the front of her smock and offered it to me to shake. "Are you telling me you're after moving into that place and all that happened them poor people?"

"It's a lovely spot."

We sat at an old pine table whose grain rose in ridges from years of vigorous scrubbing. My mug had a chip on the edge nearest my mouth. Smoke from the open grate gave a sooty feel to the surroundings.

"You musta got a great bargain," said Chaser, "with them having to sell up so quick."

I said nothing.

"It's that oul thorn bush, I'm always telling you," Mona said, scolding.

"Thorn bush, me eye. He was a ravin' madman and that's all there is to it."

"Th'oul thorn bush never brought a bit of luck on that house and you know that yourself."

"Now that your man's locked up for good, that poor woman and her wee ones will be safe."

"They started out happy enough," said Mona. "But you could hear the shoutin' and roarin' a mile away. You often said you could hear the wee ones crying their wee hearts out."

"I wonder where they went," said Chaser.

"A troubled marriage is a woeful thing," said Mona.

"A great place to live," I said. "I love the view across the valley."

"Wait till I tell you something," said Chaser. "The antiquity man arrived one day and him lookin' for old stories. And d'you know what he told me? He said the Sugarloaf Mountain there used to be called O Cualann. Would you ever believe that now? And the other one, the Little Sugarloaf, used to be called Giltspur."

"Giltspur? Why Giltspur?"

"There's a story there. Hundreds of years ago, all the land hereabouts was leased to one man and d'you know what the rent was? For thousands of acres of fine mountains, rivers and valleys? Well, let me tell you then. A pair of gilt spurs, and that's the God's truth."

"You're not telling me!" So that's where our house got its name!

"There's lots more I could be telling you. I could be telling you about graves up there on Glencap Commons. Graves that few knows about."

"Stop it, Chaser, will you. The woman doesn't want to be hearin' tell of graves on the side of the mountain." Her protest sounded a little half-hearted.

A shiver ran through me. I felt uneasy at the morbid twist the conversation had taken. It was time to go. I stepped out into the bright daylight, then remembered something. I turned and ducked back inside.

"Would either of you happen to know someone who'd be willing to do a small bit of housekeeping? Hoovering, dusting, that kind of thing. I'm going to be out all day and too tired to do anything when I come home. You know how it is."

Chaser and Mona exchanged glances and it was he who answered.

"Mona here will give you a hand. Till you get yourself sorted out, like. To get you out of a hole, like."

I did some quick thinking. I definitely needed someone. The house was a mess. I hadn't even made the bed. Why not give her a try? I could always get rid of her if it didn't work out.

"Next Thursday all right?"

I'd need a few days to sort through my stuff and lock away anything personal or confidential. I hoped I'd have no reason to regret bringing this nosy woman into the privacy of my home.

Twenty-five

"I remember you liked it black, Susan. I haven't put any sugar in."

She carried her own cup around to her side of the desk.

"Any developments in my absence?" I said. "Anything I need to know?"

"I've been waiting to tell you." Sarah walked to the door and turned the key. "Now this is very hush-hush at the moment."

She told me the board had received a bid for the magazine, a London-based publishing house on the acquisitions trail.

"That's flattering," I said.

"Frightening is how I'd put it. If it happens, none of our jobs are safe."

"Tell me what you know, Sarah. You're close to the action."

"Can you spare a half hour? Let's take a stroll in the Green."

It was dry and crisp in the May sunshine. Sarah wasted no time getting to the point.

"The Board's already discussed the takeover bid.

There's a majority in favour of acceptance. But the buyers have made it clear they'll be looking for redundancies."

"Oh my God. I don't like that at all."

"Some of us are looking into it."

"What do you mean, looking into it?"

"Some of us are thinking of mounting a counterbid. JB, myself and one or two others."

"You're talking about a management buy-out?" I looked at her in amazement. "That's a huge step, Sarah. I presume you don't have that kind of money lying around?"

"Some investment bankers might want to come on board. That's the hope, anyway. By the way, keep all this to yourself."

"I won't breathe a word."

"How about yourself?"

"What do you mean?"

"Do you want to be part of it? It could be in your own interest."

I didn't answer for a few moments. I'd never thought of myself as a businesswoman, yet I didn't want to say no straight out.

"Let me talk to Finbarr. I'd like to hear what he thinks."

I dropped into the gallery. A single browser moved from painting to painting. Finbarr was in the little office at the back from which he had a clear view of everything.

"What was it like, your first morning back?"

"I never went near my desk. I'd a long conversation with Sarah, though."

"Any news?"

"Quite a lot." I told him about the takeover bid for Maeve and the counteroffer being prepared by senior management. "Sarah's in on it."

"Are you serious?"

"And she wants me to come on board."

"Financially, you mean?"

"She thinks it's in my own interest."

"Don't think about it. There's no room for the small operator any more. The big boys are taking over. You'd be pouring your money down the drain."

"My money? I don't have any money."

"Oh, well, that solves that then, doesn't it?"

I trusted his judgement in these things. In the event the MBO fell through, Sarah and the others couldn't match the deep pockets of the predators and so it was that Maeve fell into the hands of RJK Worldwide.

~ * ~

In due course an executive arrived from London and installed himself on the first floor. His first task was to oversee the transition and he applied himself with single-minded dedication. One by one, people made the lonely journey to the office which bore the nameplate Charles S.W. Allgood. Journalists, artists, editors, office staff. No one was exempt. They went to face their fate. Some emerged relieved and smiling, others with ashen faces and barely suppressed tears.

Then it was my turn. I was resigned to whatever was coming. Finbarr's words had given me courage. "If these people are stupid enough to let you go, you'll move on to something better."

"Susan Enfield? Good to see you." He was smiling. A

gold crest on his blue tie. Signifying something prestigious, no doubt.

"Good afternoon, Mr Allgood."

He was clean shaven and younger than I expected. The hair showed grey at the temples but I thought he might still be early to mid-forties. His expression was open, intelligent and not at all unfriendly. He stood up and extended his hand across the desk. He indicated a chair and I sat facing him.

"Susan Enfield! Deputy editor-in-chief. I've been looking forward to meeting you, Susan."

I sat upright with my hands joined on my lap and waited.

"Now that I've assumed control of Maeve, I shall be implementing a number of reforms." Educated accent. Public school, no doubt. "Number one priority is to make this a leaner, fitter machine. Therefore the first item on the agenda has to be numbers. The journal is hopelessly over-staffed, as I'm sure you're aware."

"This is the first time I've heard Maeve described as a machine. I've always seen it as a vehicle for creativity and talent."

"Vehicle, yes. An excellent metaphor. A vehicle with too many passengers inevitably grinds to a halt. I'm sure you can see that."

"Here's what I see, Mr Allgood. I see a cabal of wealthy tycoons whose sole aim is to wring the last drop of blood and the last penny of profit out of this enterprise."

He looked surprised and then amused.

"Shall I tell you what I see? I see a woman with

strongly held views who's not afraid to express them with conviction. That's a thing I admire."

"Just how do you see me fitting into your programme of reform?"

"Okay, Susan. Let's not waste any more time on generalities. We're losing our editor-in-chief. Miss Langford is no longer with us."

"Sarah?"

"Sarah Langford and the company are going their separate ways. We're minus an editor-in-chief."

This information came as a shock. I'd seen Sarah in her office this morning but got no chance to speak to her. If he'd told Sarah she'd lost her job, did it mean I was next in line for the dole queue?

"We're going to need a replacement." He flicked through papers in a spiral binder. "I've looked through the due diligence reports. Your name comes up more than once."

"Oh? And how do I rate in your reports?"

"Impressive. You pioneered the whole fiction project. You established Maeve as a launch-pad for new writing careers. That in itself is no mean achievement, but more to the point, readership figures have been turned around during your time here. The circulation, I'm pleased to note, continues its upward trajectory."

"It was a team effort."

"When Maeve was headed for the wall, you were first to spot the warning signs. You devised a life-saving strategy. And you did this almost single-handed."

"That's some praise!"

"And deserved. Listen Susan, I want you to take over

as editor-in-chief. The position comes with an improved financial package including bonuses. Take your time to think about it and if you see fit to accept, you'll have a voice at the board table."

Passing Sarah's office, I glanced in through the glass door. The office was empty, the desk cleared and no sign of Sarah. My exhilaration evaporated. At that moment, I knew that my gain had been my friend's loss. My advancement had come at the expense of her job. I knew her involvement in the attempted management buy-out hadn't done her any favours, yet I couldn't escape a sense of having stabbed her in the back as I seated myself at Sarah's desk. I tried to tell myself it wasn't my doing. Sarah was gone and I now sat in her seat. Nothing ever stays the same.

~ * ~

I congratulated Finbarr on the poster.

"She designed it herself."

"So I figured."

His desk was covered with invitations and envelopes, the addresses handwritten.

"Does your young French lassie realise the trouble you're going to?" I said. "I wouldn't want her to take any of this for granted, like it was her due."

He laughed.

"Self-doubt's not her weak point."

"Personally, I think you're mad."

"If she scores with the critics, we'll all be on the pig's back."

"That's where your wife is right this minute."

He screwed up his eyes in puzzlement.

"I've just been promoted," I said.

He jumped up, grabbed me in a bear-hug and rocked my body from side to side. There could be no doubting his pleasure in my success or his faith in my ability.

"I'm taking the rest of the day off," I said. I want to go home and collect my energy for tomorrow."

"Oh, just one thing. I suppose I can depend on you to whip up a bit of interest among your friends in the press."

"I'll do what I can. But I'm doing it for you, not the Frenchwoman."

He just smiled.

~ * ~

I drove at a relaxed leisurely pace, my mood rising with the rise of the road above Kilmacanogue. Tomorrow I'd face the problem of producing the magazine to the same high standard with a much-reduced staff. A challenge I was determined to put out of my mind for the moment.

The rains of the past few days had moved away, leaving in their wake a glistening freshness which infused the whole place with a born-again joy. Stepping out of the car, I was treated to the cheeky song of a robin hidden in the branches of our rowan tree.

I walked around the side of the house, across the terracotta patio into the garden at the back. I took in details I'd barely seen before. I noticed the children's swing over to my left, near the shed and close to the dry stone wall of the boundary, its little red plastic seat moving in the gentle updraft that rose from the valley floor. I wondered about the children who'd lived and played here. I puzzled over those cryptic remarks of

Chaser and Mona's. They must have been happy here, those children, before whatever awful events had rent the family asunder. All that was left now was an empty swing swaying in the breeze. The empty swing found an echo in the emptiness of my heart. I looked away, needing no reminders of my childless state. If we got rid of the swing, there'd be nothing to speak to Finbarr of the barrenness of his wife or the sterility of his life.

Then I remembered the thorn bush that was supposed to have brought bad luck on the previous occupants. I knew about the old folk beliefs. Anyone who dared to interfere with the hawthorn tree was asking for trouble. People and animals would be cursed, get sick and die.

Finbarr laughed at this kind of thing.

"I'm surprised anyone still believes that silly nonsense. A relic of pre-Christian paganism."

I was curious to see that tree. I followed the curved line of the flagstones across the lawn and between the old fruit trees whose delicate pink blossoms attracted the attention of a thousand bees.

Beyond the orchard, the slope was more pronounced and I was out of sight of the house. The ground here was rough, reverting to nature. Scratchy branches of bramble and furze struggled to claim their rightful space. Tufted mountain grass fought for a foothold between lumps of granite protruding from the bedrock below.

Then I saw it. At the very end, where the garden narrowed to a point, a gnarled and twisted old tree, its twiggy stems laden with pink and white blossom. The ancient trunk grew out of the broken stone-wall ditch and leaned at a crazy angle into the garden. Six or seven feet up, a sinewy branch extended its horizontal reach. Low enough for a child to climb onto and explore its length. Sad that people should harbour such fear of a tree which produced so wonderful a display of flowers, May after May, year after year, through a hundred years.

Before going back inside, I went to inspect the swing. Perhaps Josie and Martin would see their way to allow Blaithín come and spend some time with us when she was a little older. Then the place would resound again to the excited chatter of a happy child. In the absence of a child of my own, I felt motherly towards my little niece. For consolation, I could still play the kind, interested, generous aunty, the only role I would ever fill.

I thought of Finbarr. Did he sometimes long for the noisy presence of children? Had he not confided in me his hopes and plans for a family of his own? Perhaps it went some way to explaining his dedication to the cause of the young artists. Were they his surrogate children? And that young Frenchwoman for whose sake he was putting in all those hours of effort? Did he see her as a child in need of his fatherly support to launch her on the path to artistic success?

The phone rang. Finbarr.

"What's it like up there in the mountains, love?"

"Beautiful. Sun's shining, birds singing, bees buzzing and a lovely mild breeze to top it off."

"It's hot here in town. I had to prise open that old window to let some air in."

"Why don't you just close up and come on home? I'd love you to be here with me, my last day of freedom. There's still time for a walk on the moor and afterwards who knows what we might do, you and I?"

"It sure sounds enticing. That's what I wanted to tell you. I won't be home for dinner. I'm really up to my eyes with this Camille exhibition. We've decided on the third of June for the opening, which gives us very little time."

"We've decided? Who's decided?"

"Oh, Céline's been here. She wants to push ahead before the holiday season kicks in."

"Looks like she gets what she wants, that lady. My concern is that you don't overdo it. Your health comes before any youngster's ambitions."

"I love to have something to get stuck into. It's what keeps me going."

"Don't be too late home. I've an early start in the morning."

"Don't wait up for me."

My journal entry for that evening alludes to loneliness.

> *It's very quiet, very still. The only sound a blackbird spilling his heart out in a solitary song. The sun has already slipped behind Djouce and the Sugarloaf has closed his eyes on the long summer day. I feel a chill run through me. I wish Finbarr were here with me to keep me warm. I will wait for him in my lonely bed.*

Twenty-six

"Well, now that you ask," he said, "I am worried. We've less than three weeks to go and now this."

The 'this' he was talking about was Céline's imminent eviction.

"She says the landlord's on her back for the rent. Not just that. Apparently he doesn't like having the whole place cluttered with paintings. Her stuff is all over the place, on the landing, everywhere. Seems he's had enough and he's handed her her walking papers."

"I can't say I blame him. That kind of thing would drive me mad."

"It couldn't have come at a worse time. She's nowhere near ready."

"So where'll she go?"

"We have to go ahead regardless. Invitations have gone out and I've posters up everywhere."

"So what's she going to do?"

"I've got an idea. It's just an idea, mind. I've said nothing to Céline about it. Not till I talk to you first."

"I don't see where I come into it."

"How about we bring her here?"

I didn't answer. Just sat and stared at him.

"Look, Susan, I know it's a huge thing to ask, but it is a bit of an emergency. She needs somewhere to work and somewhere to store the finished pieces. She won't find anywhere at such short notice. I thought the conservatory would make a perfect..."

"The conservatory?" I glared at him. "The one place in this house I go to relax? To look across at the Sugarloaf and think about my dead child? The reason we bought this house, if you remember. And now you want to turn it into some kind of artist's digs. Are you out of your mind? No way, I say."

"There's no need to get worked up over it. I'd have offered her our old apartment over the gallery except I just signed it to a young couple and they're moving in next week."

"It's her problem."

"She's being turfed out of Portobello. She's no money, nowhere to go, nowhere to work. She's in dire straits, I'm telling you."

"She seems to have confided a lot of her problems. What do we know about her, anyway?"

"Her mother's Irish. Father was French, died when she was a kid. She's alone in this country and finding it hard to make out. I'm only trying to give her a break."

"Why should I bring a total stranger into my house?"

"Take time to think about it. It's only for a few short weeks. Then everything will be back to normal."

~ * ~

I broached my theory to Jennifer.

"He always wanted a child. Now he's on the lookout

for some young person he can foster."

Talking things over with my friend helped me sort my thoughts.

"You mean he sees himself in loco parentis, taking the young French girl under his wing?"

"That's the kind he is."

"Have you met her, this girl?"

"At the exhibition, but I'd only time for a few words."

"If I were you, I'd try to meet her. A chance to suss her out for yourself."

"You've just given me an idea," I said. "I do an interview, write it up in Maeve and bingo, she gets publicity beyond her wildest dreams."

"And you get to do a little probing of your own." Jennifer looked mildly amused.

"If I'm going to allow a stranger into my home, I might be allowed ask a few questions, what do you think?"

She just laughed.

~ * ~

I was greeted by Chaser's dog which hurtled through the door and ran straight at me. It stopped just short of my feet and the barking reached a crescendo.

"Don't be scared." Chaser was framed in the doorway. "She won't bother you. Her bark's worse than her bite."

"She never barked at me before."

"She's got a litter inside be the fireplace."

The dog gave me a distrustful glare before retreating inside to check on her progeny.

"Well, I won't bother her. I'm just taking advantage of the good weather for a stroll."

"I'd be careful, if I was you. There do be funny types

up around here. Next week's mid-summer. That's when you do see them."

"Mid-summer?"

"Mid-summer, aye. Funny goings on, I can tell you that."

As I resumed my stroll up the track, I heard Chaser call after me.

"Collie sheepdogs like the mother. I'll keep one for you."

I turned and looked back.

"You couldn't go wrong with one of them lads. Great guard dogs they do be."

"I'll have to talk to my husband. We're out all day, the two of us."

"Then you need a dog," he said.

How would Finbarr feel about having a dog? Something to take his mind off business matters. And way better than sitting with his nose stuck in a book of theology.

~ * ~

This was a pub frequented by writers and artists, so she didn't look at all out of place in her loose denim jacket and torn jeans. As I came through the double doors, she raised a hand above her head to show where she was sitting. She acknowledged me with a confident smile.

"Hi, Susan." As if she'd known me all her life.

"Hi, Céline. Something to drink?"

"G an' T". Just the hint of a French accent.

"Finbarr told me your mother's Irish."

I tried to catch the attention of the lounge boy.

"He told you? Yeah, she's Irish. Irish as they come.

She's from Barna. You know Barna? Just outside Galway. I spent a summer there as a child. Like the Breton landscape in some ways."

Her sentences ran together like a tumbling mountain torrent. When she spoke, her eyes glistened with life. Her rounded face was framed by the dark brown hair reaching just to the shoulders. A few stray strands fell across her forehead. I wondered whether it was the hazel eyes or the full lips that made her so attractive.

"You must have relations there. In Barna I mean."

She ran the fingers of both hands through her hair and raised her shoulders in a shrug.

"They know I'm in Ireland. I've written but heard nothing back. Talk about Ireland of the welcomes! That's not very welcoming now, is it? Well, it's their loss, not mine. I've survived on my own for a long time now."

"Who's there now in your mother's old place?"

"My grandparents are gone. Uncle Bartley's there with his family. I remember him and Aunty Biddy when Maman took me to Galway as a child. I remember them looking at me as if they didn't really approve of me. And the cousins would talk Irish when they didn't want me to know what they were saying.

"Why d'you think they haven't answered your letters?"

"My mother lost touch long ago. I'd say there was a falling out somewhere along the line. I was never told the ins and outs of it. Papa told me they were all a bit mad, though he never said it when Maman was listening. Maybe he was right. About the madness, I mean. Anyway, I tried to make contact and all I got was total silence. I suppose they just don't want to know me."

I studied her as she spoke. If anything, she looked prettier than I remembered from the night of the exhibition, yet she wore no makeup and the large punk earrings gave her a distinctly bohemian look.

"Have you told your mother?"

"She knows nothing about it."

The shutters came down here as if she felt she'd already said enough. Up to this moment, she'd been much more forthcoming than I'd expected. Not that I knew what to expect. Now I felt I'd touched on a topic she didn't want to pursue. When I'd asked for the interview, she'd no hesitation in accepting. Almost as if she expected it, as if the public would naturally want to know about her, to hear about the next big name on the art scene.

"I hope you don't put this stuff in the magazine. All this family stuff. It wouldn't go down too well in Galway."

"Nothing personal gets into print, I promise you that. I'm curious, though, to hear how your mother came to marry your father."

"She met him in Galway. He was over on business. He was a wine exporter, see, and she worked for wine merchants in Galway. He took her back with him to Lorient."

"And they ended up married?"

"They married and a year later my sister arrived. Then there was a gap of six years before I appeared. Papa passed on when I was only seven. And my sister followed him a year later."

"God, that's terrible. What happened your sister?"

"Meningitis. In the space of a year, there's no one left but me and Maman. Yeah, that was tough, all right. I lost

Papa when I most needed a father. I really missed him. I still do. Petite Ange, he called me. He carried me around on his shoulders. I was just a little kid when he took me to Pont Aven. Told me all about the artists who came there. Paul Gauguin, Roderic O'Conor. I often wonder what he'd have thought if he'd known I'd end up in Ireland trying to follow their footsteps."

"Proud as punch, I'd say."

"Yes, he would. Then, suddenly, he was gone. Can you imagine that?"

The large brown eyes had a distant look as if she saw again some sun-filled scene tinged with a hidden sadness.

"Why did you come to Ireland?"

"I got to know this guy in Giverny. You know? Claude Monet's place? Anyway I met Seán there. He was doing a stint, a sort of internship. He kept saying what a great place Ireland was for artists. How he was going to come back here and make his name in portraits. I wanted to believe him, being half Irish myself. I suppose I sort of fancied him. He seemed so genuine. Gave me his phone number and said he'd see me right."

"You looked him up?"

She gave a sardonic laugh.

"I rang the number. He didn't live there and no one could remember him." A faraway look and a wistful expression. "Anyway I'm here now. I might as well try to make a go of it, what you think?"

"And no boyfriend?"

"Free as the wind, as they say."

A waitress arrived to collect the empty glasses. Céline declined another drink.

"Your paintings mystified a lot of people."

"You're slipping seamlessly into your journalistic role, Susan." Céline was in control of this interview.

"I have to give the readers something to chew on. Besides, it can't hurt your career."

"So people are mystified? What's their problem? Where have they been, for Christ sake?"

"Do you really have to disfigure and rip the photos before using them?"

"What artist can explain what drives them? You can translate a novel, but you can't translate a painting. When I paint, I give free expression to something inside me. There are forces there I can't explain."

From there, the conversation moved to her school days, her scholarship to the Beaux Arts, her student life in Paris. Of her family she spoke very little.

"Your hopes for the future?" A useful one to round off an interview.

"Oh, that?" The question seemed to take her by surprise.

"Are you planning on staying here? I mean living and working in Ireland?"

"Who knows where I'll be tomorrow, the day after, or the day after that? My future is out of my hands. The future, like the past, is best not thought about."

I was sufficiently impressed by that answer to write it down. Words so perceptive in the mouth of one so young, and so prescient in the way things were to turn out.

Twenty-seven

As I wrote up the interview, I began to understand why Finbarr would want to nurture and promote this new talent. All he wanted to do was take her in until the exhibition was over and she could find somewhere to live. Céline had answered my questions, filled me in on her background, yet I'd detected a certain guardedness there, especially in relation to her mother.

I heard a rustling noise out back. I peered through the window but there was nothing to be seen in the garden. I went out the front door, walked up to the gate and out onto the road. In the bright moonlight, I could see the figure of a man. At the end of a rope he dragged a reluctant young animal. I guessed it was Chaser attempting to train one of the puppies. But why so late? What was it about the night-time that he found so agreeable?

"They sound like a weird couple, the pair of them," Finbarr said when I told him. "You wouldn't want to give them too much latitude."

I told him Chaser had offered me a pup.

"This is no place for a dog. Who'd look after it?"

"You're right. We're out all day."

"You were talking to Céline?" he said.

"Yes. Some girl!"

"What makes you say that?"

"Well, for one thing, she's not short on self-belief. I get the impression she learned to depend on her own resources from an early age."

"Did she mention her mother?"

"Much more inclined to talk about Papa. Do you think she's hiding something?"

"I get this sense she's something of an orphan. I'm sure we'll hear the full story in due course, but right now I'm more curious to see what she comes up with for the exhibition. The few pieces I've seen so far look promising. Avant garde in the main. You can tell a lot about someone from the kind of art they create."

"Has she found somewhere to live?" I said. "It wasn't mentioned today."

"She'll be out on the road in days. She can't afford anywhere decent."

That was the moment I caved in.

"Maybe it won't kill us to let her work here until the exhibition is over. We have the space. As long as she understands it's only for a few weeks. When her work starts to sell, she'll be able to find somewhere suitable and I presume she'll want to be independent."

"We'll be out at work all day, so she shouldn't bother us too much." A clear look of relief on his face.

Had I given in too easily? She seemed a well-adjusted twenty-three year old, somewhat alone in the world. I hoped I wouldn't have cause to regret my decision.

~ * ~

Finbarr spent most of Saturday helping Céline shift her things from Portobello to Giltspur. He made several round trips while I made ready her bed in the north room. Seeing this selfless side of Finbarr, I was glad I hadn't been so mean-spirited as to refuse to help them both in a time of crisis.

She moved in that evening. She cleared every scrap of food I put in front of her. Not that I'd gone to any trouble, opening a tin of salmon and serving it up with lettuce and scallions from the garden. The bread I'd baked myself, Saturday being my baking day. No wine, just a big pot of tea. Start as you mean to continue. We made courteous if strained conversation, feeling our way in tentative exploratory forays.

"You should have plenty of room out there in the conservatory," I said.

"Yeah, and the east light's perfect."

"East light? I hadn't thought of that."

I'd no idea how this was going to work out, a virtual stranger moving in to occupy our space. Her clothing and personal effects had gone to the room which would be hers for the duration of her stay. Her working equipment, easel, canvases, brushes, paints, the entire artist's paraphernalia, were installed in the conservatory.

"I'm sure you're well used to looking after yourself," I said. "I'll show you the washing machine and you can take it from there."

Nobody would be playing skivvy to her. There'd be no special treatment. As I laid down the ground rules, her intelligent eyes told me she knew exactly what I was getting at.

The weak signal from Kippure carried wavy images of some earnest-looking people discussing abortion. A law professor said the law went back to 1861 and needed updating. An animated young woman said the law couldn't be more explicit, abortion was a crime and we ought to leave well enough alone. Céline turned to face Finbarr and me. On her face a look of perplexity.

"Am I to take it abortion's still a crime in this country?" she said. "It's nineteen eighty-three, for heaven's sake."

"Of course," said Finbarr. "It's a Catholic country."

"And you allow the Church to dictate your laws? But that's mad. We got rid of all that nonsense in the Revolution."

"On the contrary," said Finbarr. "You were still hanging women during the Vichy regime. You've only had legal abortion for the past eight years."

She didn't answer, just switched off the TV, picked up the current issue of Maeve from the coffee table and flicked listlessly through the pages. Finbarr buried his face in a theological journal while I caught up with the Saturday papers.

~ * ~

It can only be pure coincidence that our guest's arrival in Giltspur coincided with the appearance on our doorstep of Kandinsky. We were in bed with all lights out when the rain began in earnest. I woke to the pounding of massive raindrops on the roof of the conservatory. A flash lit the bedroom, flickered and flashed again. I lay there listening to the downpour and marvelled as the room lit again and again with brilliant light. Thunder rumbled in the distance and I knew it was coming closer. I envied Finbarr his ability to sleep through the commotion. The conservatory is the place to enjoy a spectacular storm and that's where I went for a grandstand view. I found a space among the paints and paintings where I could sit and watch. With only glass between me and the elemental fury, I was right at its heart.

I watched lightning bolts forge channels of fire between heaven and earth, each incandescent flash followed by the rumble of rolling barrels reverberating from side to side of the valley. As each spike scorched the ground, I heard the crackle of burning air and the house seemed to shake in sympathy with the suffering earth. Celestial pyrotechnics held me hypnotized for a good half hour before the last of the lightning moved away from the valley, eastwards towards the sea.

Just when I thought the show was over came the culmination, a climactic strike at the cone of the Sugarloaf. Quartzite crackled and sparkled for half a minute. As fire played about his head, the mountain glowed with a fierce pride. Heroic warrior indomitable in the midst of his enemies.

I felt a movement behind me and looked around to see a pale figure in white night-dress standing just inside the door.

"Céline! What's the matter? Is the storm keeping you awake?"

"I heard something outside."

"Like what?"

"A kind of whining outside the window."

I went back with her to her room, opened the window

and leaned out, scanning the bushes in the dripping darkness. It took a couple of minutes for my eyes to adjust, but when they did I saw a creature crouching beneath a leafy shrub. An animal whimpering.

"Looks like a dog. We can't leave him there in the rain. Wait till I throw on a coat and bring him inside."

I knelt on the mucky ground to undo the knotted rope that secured the shivering creature to a shrub.

"Poor little fellow. Let me take you in out of this awful rain."

The terrified pup shivered in my arms as I carried him into the house. I'd no doubt it was one of the litter I'd seen in Chaser's kitchen. We used towels to dry him out on the kitchen floor and left him lying beside a hot water bottle wrapped in an old pullover.

Finbarr was amazed to find an animal in the kitchen. The creature had recovered well and the moment Finbarr came in bounded at him like an old friend. Finbarr stepped back to avoid the assault and the pup sat looking up at him, head leaning sideways, the hairy tail slapping the tiles.

"What's this?" Finbarr said.

"It's a pup," I said.

"Where did it come from?"

"It's one of Chaser's pups. I can tell from the markings."

"It must have escaped and ended up down here," he said.

"Escaped my foot. The poor thing was tied to a bush."

"Well then, the sooner we get him back where he belongs, the better."

"Dead right. We don't want to be landed with two guests instead of one."

He motioned me to hush as a sleepy looking Céline appeared in a pale pink dressing gown. For a moment it seemed she'd forgotten about the pup, but soon she was crouched on the floor, allowing him to lick her face. As she sat sipping coffee, she lifted him onto her lap and fondled his ears.

"Any plans for today?" said Finbarr.

"I have to get some work done," she said.

"Don't you take Sunday off?"

"There's a painting I have to finish. But first there's all that stuff to be unpacked." She nodded in the direction of the conservatory.

"You just go right ahead, then," I said. "We won't disturb you. We're going to visit my sister in hospital."

"Is she all right?"

"Nothing serious. Just some tests."

I wasn't quite as relaxed as I let on. Josie had admitted to feeling off-colour in the past few months. I kept at her to get it checked out and now that she was doing just that, I couldn't rest in my mind until I knew it was nothing.

~ * ~

The hospital concourse reminded me of a busy mall. The shop was doing a brisk business in sweets, fruit and magazines. I was alarmed when I saw my sister. The spirit seemed to have gone out of her. I stood at the side of the bed where she was propped in a sitting position. She blinked to focus her eyes.

"How are you, feeling, Josie?"

"Okay."

"Any tests yet?"

"Every test under the sun."

"Any results?"

"They found a lump."

"A lump?" I wondered had I heard her right.

"Here." She placed a hand on her left breast.

I took her hand.

"It's not the end of the world," I said. "We just have to be grateful they found it in time."

"I suppose." Probably contemplating the loss of her breast.

"They're coming up with new discoveries all the time," I said.

"I'm too sick to even think about it."

"I'm sorry, Josie. Pray and put your trust in God. And don't forget, Ma is up there in heaven looking after you." It was the best I could offer.

"I wish I had your faith."

So did I. These words and phrases were little more than wishful thinking.

For a long time, she sat staring into space, her pale drawn features betraying her inner despair.

"Is Martin managing on his own?"

"He's taken a few days off to look after Blaithín. After that, Maureen will take her until I'm home again."

I felt a pang of jealousy that it fell to Martin's sister to be the caring aunt for my godchild.

Finbarr was waiting outside in the car and we talked as we drove.

"If she has to have a mastectomy," he said, "the sooner they do it the better. Most people go on to have a full and normal life after the operation."

"We can only pray."

We arrived home to find the dog had been sitting for his portrait.

The moment Finbarr inserted the key in the front door, we were assailed by a spate of high-pitched yelping. The pup had assumed guardianship of our house. Finbarr was almost knocked off balance by an excited animal throwing itself at his legs.

Céline's voice called from the conservatory. She'd something to show us. On the easel was a fresh painting. In her spattered smock, she pointed to the glistening canvas and stood back to await our comments. I looked closely and wondered what I was meant to see. I could see thick streaks in primary colours but nothing recognisable.

"What's it meant to be?" I said.

"Isn't he gorgeous?" said Céline.

I screwed up my eyes but saw only a jumble of shapes in a multitude of colours.

"Kandinsky," she said.

"Kandinsky?"

"Kandinsky. The dog."

"You mean that's him? In the painting?"

"That's him. What you think?"

I burst out laughing.

"Well, so long as he's happy with his picture, I suppose that's all that matters."

I looked at the pup stretched on the floor and wondered if he was pleased with his portrait. He gave a noncommittal stroke of his wispy tail against the tiles.

Kandinsky, for the name stuck, was never to return to his original home. When I tried to take him back where he belonged, Chaser trotted out some rigmarole about being out for a walk when the storm broke and the dog refusing to budge another step. He had chosen our front lawn as the safest place to leave him, he said. He even tried to suggest the dog had chosen us as his adoptive family. He showed no desire to have the dog back and so Kandinsky came to live with us by default.

It should have been obvious, of course. Céline and Kandinsky, two homeless waifs turning up on the same day. Two unwanted strays depending on the hospitality of strangers to give them a roof over their heads. Two who had formed an instant attachment to each other and one at least of whom was not about to go anywhere anytime soon.

Twenty-eight

I stayed away from the launch. It was Finbarr's baby. And Céline's of course. Her big debut in the world of art. And his paternal concern that the fruit of her labour would arrive in the world squealing for recognition.

In any case, I'd seen enough of Céline's paintings to provide nightmares for a lifetime. If the forlorn figures splashed across her canvases shared any one thing in common, it was despair. Disintegration might be a better word to describe it. A world coming apart.

So let the arty people make what they would of her work. I'd my own problems. Problems to do with Maeve. Publications were folding left, right and centre and I'd no intention of allowing mine to join the heap.

And on top of all that, there was Josie. She'd just had her mastectomy and I phoned Martin several times to see how she got on. She was still sleeping, he said, and wouldn't be up to visitors until tomorrow at the earliest.

That was the day of the opening, so instead of pestering Martin with any more calls I settled down for an early night. It was going to be late when Finbarr and Céline got home. That was to be expected.

I heard the crunch of his car on the gravel and opened my eyes to squint at the clock. Six in the morning. A few minutes later he slid into bed beside me.

"Things go well?" I said.

"I'm fagged." He was asleep in seconds.

~ * ~

"Well?" I said. "What do the papers say?"

I'd just come out on the patio and was trying to make room on the table to put down the tray. Finbarr pushed aside some of the papers but was far more interested in reading the reviews than bothering with toast and coffee.

"Have a listen to this:

"…The religious experience is a constantly recurring theme in the oeuvre of this artist with recognisable echoes of mediaeval church imagery..."

He raised his eyes to heaven in an expression of impatience.

"…The relationship between art and religion is, of course, well established, each interrogating the universe in its own unique search for answers to the age-old questions..."

"What sort of claptrap is that?" I said.

He looked at me for an instant before reading on.

"…here we find a robust rejection of the old certainties. One is reminded of Francis Bacon's Three Studies for Figures at the Base of a Crucifixion…some fine examples of Expressionism at its most poignant, the same restless quest for meaning one associates with the work of Edvard Munch..."

"Call it claptrap and maybe it is, but it can't be at all bad to be mentioned in the same breath as Bacon and Munch."

"Any bad ones?"

"This one sounds a bit grudging. Listen,

"…a compelling desire to force us to share in her troubled dreams emphasised in one exhibit by the depiction of the torn bodies of the lost in hell."

Listen to how the bastard sums it up.

"… too much of the angst, too much of the silent scream, something that has been done before and I dare say better."

I couldn't help wondering how Céline would take the mixed reviews. No sound from her room. She was probably out for the count with exhaustion. It must have been a hectic night.

"You were late getting home last night. Or should I say this morning?"

"It went on till all hours. A lot of drink. She probably had more than she's used to."

There was something about the two of them out enjoying themselves till the early hours that gave me a frisson of unease. But I banished the thought and let the subject drop.

Finbarr went back to his papers and Céline still hadn't appeared when I left for the hospital.

~ * ~

Josie was propped against a wall of pillows. When she tried to straighten herself, she winced in pain. Martin had just left.

"You're looking a lot better than I expected," I said.

"I'm up to me eyeballs with pain-killers."

I filled a vase with water and rearranged the flowers on the window ledge.

"The operation," I said, "have they told you anything?"

"Martin was talking to the doctors. They got it all." She put her right hand where her left breast should have been. "I was terrified it could have spread, you know, into the glands." The pain showed in her face.

"Well, you can relax now. It's all behind you. Here's a few grapes. Oh, a copy of Maeve. You can look through it later."

"Still as busy as ever?"

"Run off my feet. We've got this new super-efficient English chappie calling the shots. Not a bad sort, really, when you get to know him. He comes over two or three times a week. Otherwise he leaves the whole running of it to me."

Josie's eyes closed. I sat with her and dabbed her face with a moist towel from time to time. A chain around her neck carried a miraculous medal. She'd put herself in the hands of the Immaculate Conception. Well, there's no harm in praying. Like I prayed when my little son's life hung on a thread. And all to no avail.

I thought about this. I'd made no conscious decision to abandon religion. I still believed in something. But what exactly? Well, for one thing, I was aware of my feelings of awe in the presence of the mountain. For spiritual solace, I'd go into my garden and look to O Cualann, the Sugarloaf Mountain, to maintain his endless watch for my welfare as he cradled within his bosom the pitiful bones of my only son.

And Finbarr? Finbarr believed in business. Business, yes, but he hadn't entirely abandoned his grounding in religious matters. He kept up a sort of scholarly interest in the field of theology, which every now and then prompted him to take up his pen and fire off an article to some learned journal or other.

~ * ~

It was Finbarr's idea. The Camille exhibition had excited such interest that he wanted to make the most of it. And so it was he came up with the whole Kilkenny thing and Céline for her part raised no objections. Why would she? She'd already made sales in Dublin and there was every chance she could build on her success.

Her solo exhibition would transfer to Kilkenny to coincide with the opening of Finbarr's new gallery. He'd filled her in on Kilkenny's reputation as a centre for the arts, somewhere she could expect to achieve proper recognition. He was determined to push her career any way he could.

I have to say I didn't see it quite like that. What I saw was the inevitable delay in Céline finding a place of her own and getting all her goods and chattels out of my house. I longed for the day when I'd regain my cherished conservatory, where I might be go to be alone, to stare across the valley at my mountain, to meditate on the ebb and flow of life's fortunes.

"We have to be patient," he said. "Another few weeks, a month or two at the most and it'll be all over. A few more sales and she'll be solvent, able to pay her way. She'll dash off some more paintings to replace the ones she's sold."

Whenever he put it like that, I'd ask myself if I was the one who was being unreasonable. I suppose she didn't impinge on our lives all that much. I worked long hours and I'd arrive home to find Finbarr and Céline had eaten and seemed at ease in each other's company. They both seemed happy with the set-up. Which might explain why I didn't feel all that bad leaving Finbarr with Céline while I took myself off to London on a business trip with Charles Allgood, my affable boss.

But the night before I left for London, for some strange reason, it popped into my mind, something I'd said to Finbarr's mother when the Grays had paid us their first visit. I'd said it just to annoy her. I'd said, 'he's very fond of her. Quite likes having her around, in fact.'

Now my own words came back to haunt me. Finbarr betrayed no hint of jealousy at my skiving off to London with my boss, though you could never be sure how he really felt. But suddenly it occurred to me that he might welcome the chance to have time alone with Céline. An irrational fear which I immediately dismissed as unworthy. Unworthy of Finbarr and even more unworthy of me to entertain it.

~ * ~

RJK Worldwide. London headquarters. Charles Allgood, my boss, delivering his presentation. You couldn't help but admire the way he handled it. All the usual business jargon, the Irish operation, the current state of play, future prospects and so on. Smooth and polished, that was my main impression as I sat and listened. Towards the end, he credited me as the one who had done most to lift the magazine out of the doldrums. He went so far as to say I was in the best position 'to take things forward,' to guide Maeve into the future. I'd no idea anything like this was coming up. Except that coming over on the plane he'd handed me an unexpected compliment.

"You're a highly intelligent woman, Susan. Your one shortcoming is you don't realise how intelligent you are."

I wanted to make the best possible case for the journal's survival. They ought to hear this, I thought. If there was anyone who understood Maeve and what it was all about, I was the one. So I tried to inject a bit of passion as I explained the philosophy that had moulded Maeve since its early days. Things they wouldn't have known. Couldn't have known. All the values I felt committed to and which I'd slaved to preserve in the years since I achieved a position of responsibility at the journal. I took pains to project the future in as optimistic a light as possible.

Maybe until that moment I hadn't realised just how I felt about Maeve or fully realised the position it occupied in my heart. Their questions, though, showed they'd missed the point entirely. They wanted to know if I saw Maeve as a financially viable proposition. There it was again. Money topped everything.

"Some performance there, Susan," Charles said

afterwards. "I'm impressed. You made a super case for your magazine."

My magazine! I liked the sound of that. And I liked Charles even more for saying it.

"We're expecting you down for dinner on Saturday evening. Emily's heard me talking so much about you she'll be delighted to meet you."

Charles' home in the Cotswolds was two hours from London. Emily made me feel welcome.

"I've been hearing a lot about you, Susan. Seems you're his most valuable asset over there. Indispensable is what he says."

We walked where the river widened to make a pond in the centre of the village. A clutch of ducks scrambled to catch scraps thrown to them by excited children. The houses and shops facing each other across the pond were in Tudor style, many dating back four hundred years. All, said Charles, subject to preservation orders.

"You can't even drive a nail in the wall without planning permission."

"Not that we'd ever want to," said Emily. "It's a privilege to live here."

On the plane home, Charles talked about himself and his family. He came from Devon, from an idyllic little hamlet near Totnes. He'd met Emily at Cambridge where she read Mediaeval History while he took Economics. He surprised me by mentioning her chronic heart condition which forced her to stay at home, avoid stress and take care not to overdo the physical activity.

"I don't know what I'd do if anything ever happened her," he said.

~ * ~

Finbarr's preparations for Kilkenny were a shambles. The building turned out to be completely unsuitable. Huge expense involved to put things right. Everything—the opening of the gallery and Céline's solo exhibition—held up until the engineer came up with a solution involving steel beams to carry the load of the upper storey.

"The good news," said Finbarr, "is we can now power ahead."

"The bad news," I said, "is the expense. How long is all this going to take?"

"I don't know. Months maybe."

"Months?" I heard my voice going shrill.

"There's nothing I can do about it. We've just got to relax, else we get stressed out of our minds."

"What'll happen about the exhibition?"

"We'll still open with Céline's work."

"Will you listen to me for a minute? She should be out of here by now, lock, stock and barrel."

"She's getting to you?"

"Can you not see? The house is no longer our own. How long was she supposed to be here? A week? A couple of weeks? A month at the most. What's going on, will you tell me?"

At that moment I heard Kandinsky's excited yelp. Céline was back from walking the dog. I looked at Finbarr and he looked at me and we were forced to park the issue for another day.

~ * ~

I took a few days away from the office and headed north. They'd phoned from home to say Dad was paralysed on the right side and his speech was slurred. Things turned out to be even worse than I expected. The doctor told me there was always the danger of a more devastating stroke.

The implications were huge. There was no question of Johnny and Bridie being saddled with this burden. We'd have to find somewhere suitable for Dad not too far from home. Everyone could chip in according to their means.

Josie was upset at the thought of Dad going into a nursing home.

"Have you ever been inside one of them places? The smell of piss is enough to make you sick."

"It's okay, Johnny's found a place near Killeshandra. He says you could eat your dinner off the floor."

"To think it's come to this." Tears showed in her eyes.

"It's a funny old world," I said. "When we were kids, our father called the shots. Now his children make his decisions for him. He's got no say in his own destiny."

"I hate the thought, Sue, of shunting him off somewhere."

"I'll drive up at the weekend and suss out that place Johnny found."

"Is Finbarr going with you?"

"He's got things to do."

"You're leaving him on his own, up in the mountains?"

"He'll be okay. Céline's there most of the time."

"Who?"

"Didn't I tell you? We have a lodger. An artist."

"No, you didn't tell me. How long's she been there?"

"A couple of months. It's just till she gets somewhere to live."

"Hold on. Let me get this straight, Sue. You're leaving your husband alone in the house with a strange woman. What age is she?"

"About twenty-three and she's not a strange woman. More like a family friend. You could be paranoid about things like that. You clearly don't know Finbarr. I trust him."

"Take my advice and get rid of her."

I was about to object when Blaithín woke, disturbed by the voices. She moved to the safety of her mother's knee and eyed me up and down. I made some cooing noises at my niece before it was time to go. As I was leaving, Josie gave me another dose of unasked for advice.

"Listen to what I'm saying, Sue. I wouldn't be taking too much for granted with a young one like that around the place."

"I'm afraid you've got Finbarr all wrong, Josie. He treats Céline like a daughter. I've seen it with my own eyes, the way he's taken her under his wing."

"I only hope you're right."

"Of course I'm right."

Afterwards I was sorry I'd argued with my sister. She was still recuperating from serious surgery. I'd even forgotten to admire her new breast and say she never looked better, that you'd never tell the difference. Maybe the fact I hadn't noticed would make her feel good about her shape.

~ * ~

I wheeled Dad's chair down to the edge of the lake and along the bumpy track that followed the lapping shoreline. The surface of the water was placid in the pale light of a low hanging November sun. Five swans at rest among the reeds near a narrow headland.

"Look Dad, the Children of Lir. Remember? You told me that story."

Would he remember how I climbed on his lap to hear him read for me the story of Fionnuala and her brothers, turned to swans by a wicked stepmother and condemned to wander the wild waters of Ireland for nine hundred years? I'm sure he remembered. His eyes were smiling. The earliest memories are last to fade. He made an effort to say something and I pretended to understand.

"They're still here, Dad, waiting for the sound of a Christian bell to release them from their spell."

He gripped my fingers tight. A tear glistened in his eye. The sad-sweet tear that afflicts us all at the memory of vanished days. Thoughts of little ones, now grown and gone, of happy innocent times lost in the labyrinth of time.

"I owe you so much, Dad. I owe you everything. I want you to know that. I don't think I've ever said it before, but I say it now."

How often we regret the things we should have said but never quite got around to saying until it's far too late to make a difference. His face brightened as he struggled to say something and I turned his wheelchair around to take him back towards the grand Palladian entrance of the home.

~ * ~

A marble fireplace dominated the dayroom. Logs and peat had burned down to a warm glow. Around the room residents sat and gazed into space or just dozed the day away. There was no conversation. Each appeared oblivious of the existence of the others. I imagined when they first arrived here they'd made brave, cheery efforts to engage in conversation. But when at last it dawned on them that their efforts were doomed to failure they too must have lapsed into the silence of those who have lost all hope, locked within their own brains with only their dreams and imaginings to engage them.

I couldn't avoid the thought that once in here there was only one way out. There was a grim inevitability about it.

"Goodbye, Dad. Someone will be in to see you tomorrow. Take it easy and don't worry about a thing. If you need anything, Matron here will give me a ring."

Twisting his body about, he grasped my hand in his good hand and the arthritic fingers gave a little squeeze. That feeble gesture attempted to convey some message. Maybe it said, this mightn't be such a bad place to see out my days. Or maybe, I can't fight the inevitable. I'm lost and helpless and I have to trust you to do what's best for me.

A decisive moment had been reached, a critical point in his life, in mine, in all our lives. The tide was now on the way out for my dear, dear father.

As I negotiated the road home with its interminable twists and turns, and kept a wary eye out for farm tractors, my thoughts drifted back to another day nine years before. I was a girl of nineteen when my father drove me along these same twisty roads from Annagopple to Dublin. He took me to a convent in the southern suburbs to yield me up to a life of contemplation and charitable works. As we stood on the granite steps, surrounded by black-robed nuns, he had said goodbye in choked tones that told me his heart was broken by loss.

Today, that scene had played out once more, except that this time the principal actors had swapped roles. Now it was I who drove away with a heavy heart. I was the one who had abandoned him, helpless, into the care of strangers.

It's the nature of things. Sad when you think about it. That there is no such thing as permanence. Nothing ever stays the same.

Twenty-nine

I found them relaxing in the glow of the log fire each with glass in hand. A whiskey bottle stood half empty on the floor beside Finbarr while she was helping herself to the contents of the gin bottle on the low table beside her. A cosy scene.

"Come in near the fire," Finbarr said. "I'll pour you a drink."

I threw my coat on a chair, too tired to hang it up.

"You two celebrating something?"

"You tell her, Céline."

"I got a commission."

"She's landed a commission," said Finbarr. He smiled the proud smile of a father for the achievements of his child.

"How big is it?"

"Real big. An insurance company needs art for their new headquarters."

"Insurance? They're the only ones with money to spend right now."

"We're not complaining, are we, Céline?" said Finbarr.

"Well done, Céline," I said. "That should put a few

pennies in your pocket." It was a pointed rub, but I couldn't resist the opportunity.

"They want something for the entrance lobby. Something to dominate the whole area. I'm thinking of doing a triptych. I'll sketch out a few ideas and see how it goes."

"How long is it going to take, d'you think?"

"Forever." A nervous little laugh. "I've all the time in the world. And they're letting me have an advance payment. Imagine!"

We talked about it in bed.

"When she gets going on that triptych she's not going to budge out of here till it's finished. You know that as well as I do."

"I know, Susan, I know. But this is just what she's been waiting for. How could we throw her out now?"

My thoughts were in a muddle. I knew he was right. It would be callous to force her out right now. Besides, I'd grown used to her presence about the place. If she was going to be around for another few months or so, well what of it? She wasn't going to kill me. Besides, she should now be in a position to make some contribution towards her keep.

"I suppose we can let her stay," I said.

"Of course we can."

"I'm not saying forever."

"No, not forever."

I put my arm around him and tried without success to turn his body towards me. I slid my hand down his thigh to tell him I needed him. He turned his face to me and made a kissing sound. "Good night, love."

"I want you to hold me."

"I'm really tired."

"You're always tired. When's the last time we made love?"

"Not tonight, Sue. Tomorrow."

Céline was in the money. A vanload of canvas, paint tubes and brushes of all kinds and sizes delivered to the door. She set herself to work, sketching out drawings on sheets of paper spread across the conservatory floor.

She must have had cash left over to explain what happened next. Saturday morning she took the bus to Dublin. She was all got up in bohemian style, multi-coloured gypsy headscarf with lots of cheap jewellery. Who she hung around with was anybody's guess. The last remnants of the hippy community, I'd have said.

In the afternoon we sat outside, Finbarr and I. It was unseasonably mild for November. Finbarr's new manager looked after the business on Saturdays, which gave him leisure time to browse his books. We talked about Kilkenny. Things were starting to come together and he was excited about his plan to open in December with an exhibition of Céline's work.

"She's been working up some new pieces. She wants to push the boundaries, she says. Mind you I haven't seen the new pictures so I can't tell you how far the boundaries have been pushed."

We lapsed into silence. Kandinsky had taken up his usual position, crouched motionless on the gravel, eyes fixed on the gate. In guard-dog pose, he seemed ready to drive off any intruders. Of course, if the truth were known, he was simply awaiting Céline's return. Happy to lie there, ears alert, eyes glued to the gate for however long it took. Such singular devotion can only be wondered at.

She'd take the St. Kevin's bus from St Stephen's Green, get off at the foot of the hill and walk the rest of the way. Not strenuous for the young and fit. If the weather was bad, she'd use the pay phone in the village and one of us would pick her up.

The peace of the countryside was shattered by the noisy exhaust of a car approaching. We looked at each other as it skidded to a stop outside our gate. Kandinsky raised a din with his frantic barking. We could hear someone pushing open both sides of the wooden gate, hidden from view by the variegated holly. The car door slammed and the engine revved into life.

With a crunch of gravel, the car came into view and drew to a halt close to where we sat. The black leather hood was pushed back in the open position and behind the wheel sat a proud young woman wearing a look of achievement on her face. Kandinsky's barking came to an abrupt halt as he recognised Céline waving at him. She looked every bit the part…dark brown wavy hair in careless disarray and about her neck a red and yellow silk scarf adding to the effect.

"Nice wheels," Finbarr called over as the car door clunked behind her. "Whose car?"

"C'est la mienne! My own, of course. You like it?"

"You bought it?"

"It didn't break the bank. She's an old banger. Nineteen seventy-two."

"An eleven year old MG! I have to say you're a fast mover!"

Fast all right. Not one to miss an opportunity, I thought.

With a set of wheels under her, she no longer depended on either of us to drive her anywhere. Perhaps she had Kilkenny in mind. She could travel up and down, come and go as she chose. And that's exactly how it worked out. She made daily trips with her exhibits. Finbarr took some of the larger canvasses in his car. She was quite assertive, he told me, about the placing of her paintings. She knew what she wanted and stuck to her guns to get it. It was her exhibition, her paintings, so he was happy to stand back. Or so he said.

She'd talked about pushing the boundaries and, if she was trying to stoke up controversy, she certainly succeeded. The town was divided over one particular painting. Most of the citizens had nothing but praise for Finbarr's initiative in bringing them this young avant-garde artist. But not everyone saw it that way. The first hint of anything amiss came on the Monday morning with an urgent call from Paul. Finbarr had asked his manager to stay in Kilkenny for the first couple of weeks till he got things established on an even keel.

"What kind of protest?" I heard Finbarr say.

I picked up the kitchen phone to catch Paul's excited voice. "They're threatening to picket the place if I don't take it down."

"No sign of Céline? No? Maybe it's just as well. I'll be there as quick as I can."

"What's all that about?" I said.

"Probably nothing at all. I'll deal with it. I'll ring you later, love."

A quick kiss and he was gone.

~ * ~

Later Finbarr told me the whole story.

He told me he found his manager in an agitated state. Paul pointed out a picture in a prominent position just inside the door. La Danse Macabre was easily visible from the street but Finbarr had to stand back a little before the heavy impasto resolved itself into recognisably human forms. He could make out wild dancing figures, skeletons with grinning skulls. One of the dancers stood out, not a skeleton but a naked male figure wearing a bishop's mitre and on its face a vulgar smirk. And right at the centre of the painting, in among the dancers, Céline had pasted a black and white photo of a little girl in long white communion dress. The head was missing where she'd roughly torn the print across the top.

Finbarr was convinced the painting was designed to shock, otherwise why had she hung it where it would have maximum impact on passers-by?

"Take it down, Paul. We'll decide what to do with it when things calm down."

Paul went to remove the painting while Finbarr stepped outside to address the crowd.

"You never can trust these artists, can you?" He smiled jovially, setting himself firmly on the side of the common man.

He was happy to announce the painting had been removed and to show his gratitude for their interest, he was asking them to accept a hot cup of coffee with his compliments. When some hesitated to step across the threshold, he told them he had inspected the pictures personally and could assure them that nothing offensive remained.

Those bold enough to accept his invitation cast cautious glances at the exhibits but relaxed when they found nothing else to offend their sensibilities. Paul came back with a tray of pastries and the protest movement disbanded on the very day it had formed.

This wasn't the end of the affair however. A local radio station had picked up on reports of a blasphemous painting. All through the rest of the day, there was a steady stream of curious patrons demanding to see 'the bishop painting.' Finbarr thought that when the fuss had died down, he'd hang 'La Danse Macabre' in a less conspicuous spot near the back.

As he told me all this, his face was drawn and his eyes had a tired look. I told him I hadn't seen Céline all day.

"I wonder has that girl any notion of the trouble she stirred up?" he said.

"I don't know. There's something eating her up. Like she wants to stick people's faces in it."

"Controversy for the sake of controversy."

"I wonder. I've a gut feeling it goes deeper than that. Why don't we let her talk about it when she shows up?"

She didn't show up. Finbarr seemed particularly edgy. He couldn't sit in one place for more than a few minutes. He stood up, went out the kitchen door, stood outside in the cold studying the stars. I suspect he walked to the front gate to look up and down the road before coming back indoors and trying to resume his reading.

I was wasn't much better myself. At one point, I went to Céline's room to see was there any sign she'd been home during the day. The unmade bed yielded no clues. As I sat and stared into the fire, I asked myself why I was fretting over this girl. She was nothing to me. All right, she'd been with us since the summer, but in another short while, she'd be gone out of our lives, free as a swallow.

"She's probably gone home to Brittany for Christmas," Finbarr decided.

He couldn't hide a trace of disappointment that she'd take herself off like that without a word to him. He'd been looking forward to her face when he told her most of her paintings had been sold. Maybe she'd been back to the exhibition and seen the flurry of red stickers proclaiming her triumph. Maybe she knew that 'La Danse Macabre' had been switched from the prominent position she'd given it.

~ * ~

On Friday evening the roar of the MG in the driveway told us she was back. It was not for long, though. Just long enough for her to get one or two things off her chest.

I heard the porch door being pushed in with an irritating screech as a jagged chipping scraped the tiles. Then the squeak of her boots on the parquet floor in the direction of her bedroom. The muffled flush of the toilet followed by her bedroom door clicking shut. Then silence. I looked at Finbarr and knew he had noted every one of these telling sounds.

As we ate in silence, I wondered if she'd arrive into the kitchen expecting to join us at the table, but when she appeared it was clear she was dressed for going out. She had on a silk blouse tie-dyed by some previous owner in a range of extravagant colours. Her full-length skirt had a patchwork trim, the colours a muted echo of those on the tie-dye. Over her arm a quilted jacket and in her hand a thick-knitted wool cap with ear-flaps. Just the sort of vintage gear you'd expect to pick up in the charity shop. Her outfit had the merit of being comfortable and warm against the chilly night air.

"Want something to eat?" I said.

"I'm going out." Curt to the point of cutting.

I wondered what I'd said or done to offend her, but it soon became apparent her ire wasn't directed against me but against my hapless husband. She turned to face Finbarr square on, ready to deliver the fury that was pent up within.

"I want my money."

"Your money? The sales money, you mean? I was going to wait till the last of it had come in. Sorry, Céline, it never occurred to me...you're not stuck for cash, are you? Look, I can give you something right now, part payment. How does that sound?"

"How much?"

"A few fifties in my wallet, that's the sum of it."

"I'll take what you've got."

"You upset over something?"

"Ah, you noticed!"

"So why don't you just say it out and then we can deal with it, all right?"

"Make out you don't know what I'm talking about. Do I have to spell it out for you? I got the whole story from Paul. You, Finbarr, the one person I thought I could depend on. You melt before a posse of holy marys. Instead of standing up for me, you run shit scared before the mob."

"Oh that! You're talking about that picture?"

"That picture! I should have known I could depend on no one. Not even you. Looking after my interests my arse. You take down my best work and hide it away in a corner where you hope no one will see it. So tell me, Mr Finbarr Gray, what kind of support is that?"

I saw she was close to tears but restrained myself from getting involved. Between the two of them it was, and I was happy to use this as a learning opportunity. I hoped to get a glimpse of what lay beneath the surface of our unpredictable guest. At the same time, I was curious to see how my Finbarr would react under fire.

"I've no intention of hiding your art, Céline. It's going to get pride of place in Anne Street. There are connoisseurs in this city who know and appreciate good art when they see it. Believe me, 'La Danse Macabre,' will get the plaudits it deserves."

Céline remained silent, seeming to turn his words over in her mind. When at last she spoke her voice had assumed a more reflective tone.

"That painting means a lot to me," she said. "More than either of you will ever know. I value that painting and I want it appreciated by whoever sees it."

"You can relax," Finbarr answered. "I'll see that it gets due recognition. Take my word for that."

"You're heading off somewhere?" I said.

"I'm going to Tara." She sounded defiant.

"In the middle of winter?" I was intrigued.

"It's the Winter solstice."

"What's going on there?"

"It was a big, big feast in ancient Ireland."

"I'd rather you than me. You could freeze to death on top of that god-forsaken hill."

"We'll light a fire that'll be seen in all four corners of Ireland."

"You'll be back for Christmas?"

"I'll be in Port Aven for Christmas."

"You're going home to see your mother?"

"Of course. I'll take the car-ferry from Rosslare."

We heard her drive off. Finbarr was silent.

I imagine he was as shaken as I was to discover a side of Céline neither of us had guessed existed. Here was a woman who was well able to assert her rights. Not only had she demanded her money before Finbarr had a chance to tot up the takings, but she'd shown she wasn't going to be pushed around by anyone.

This was a new Céline, maybe even the real Céline. I couldn't but notice how readily Finbarr had yielded in the face of her attack, an early insight, given the pressure he was to come under from the same lady in the not too distant future.

Thirty

"What's that you're reading there?"

I gave a guilty jump but I was too tongue-tied to answer the teacher's question.

"I asked what you're reading, Susan."

"1984, Sir."

"Really? So we're into George Orwell now, are we? Moved on from the Brontë sisters, have we?"

"The Brontës are about the past, Sir. This is the future."

I knew the other girls were gawking at me and I could hear the giggles.

"The future?" Mr Shaw's face melted into an indulgent smile. "I dare to hope we have a better future ahead of us than any of your Orwellian fantasies. Just as long as you don't take it for a literal prediction, Susan. It's meant to be read as an allegory. A warning for society. Now put that book away and try to pay attention to what we're doing in the here and now."

~ * ~

The year1984 dawned on a Sunday morning. Funnily enough it came back to me, that distant run-in with my geography teacher at school. I knew I was being irrational, but I went to the conservatory to look across at the Sugarloaf. Everything seemed normal except for the unseasonably mild air. A soft drizzle left precious diamonds to sparkle on the tips of pine needles. It was okay then to take the dog out for a brisk morning walk. Kandinsky tugged at the lead in his hurry to get to the gap in the fence where I'd always let him loose and he would make his mad dash for freedom. Nothing to threaten or frighten. Just the start of another year. 1984. A year like any other year.

Céline was back from France. How she got on in Brittany, where she stayed, who she met, what she did, none of this did she mention. That didn't stop me asking about her mother. It was only then she told me for the first time her mother was in long term care. However, she made no effort to take it any further, so we were left to ponder the precise nature of her mother's condition. You couldn't help feeling that for her the past was the past and was best left in the past.

Céline was only ever happy when she was immersed in her art. It's where she found release from tension and stress. I saw her throw herself into her project, an outsize triptych to adorn and dominate the foyer of the client's new headquarters. She claimed to feel the ghostly presence of a long dead Gustav Klimt at her elbow in the long hours spent in her studio. At intervals she'd emerge to reward Kandinsky's patience with a well-deserved walk through the heather. And so a sort of strained peace descended on the household.

At weekends she took herself off to hang out with her hippy friends. Then we had the place to ourselves. That's when it fell to me to walk Kandinsky and I learned to trust him to lead me where I hadn't gone before, to share with each other the excitement of discovery.

If I warned him to keep his eyes off the sheep, he would adopt a wounded expression. To give him his due, he didn't see sheep as some kind of quarry to be harassed and chased. True to his breeding, he afforded them an intelligent respect. Yet I never saw myself as having the same relationship with the dog that Céline had achieved from the moment they met and bonded that stormy night of their arrival.

We wandered aimlessly across the moor and I tried to work out where we were. My points of reference were the peak of the Sugarloaf on my left and the listless noonday sun on my right. Then I spotted a bus in the middle distance and knew I was headed towards the Glendalough road. I crossed a gate onto the road and realised I was not very far from where Finbarr had parked the car one June morning when we brought the lifeless body of our son to his resting place in the hills. I'd driven to this spot many times since then, but this was my first time to arrive on foot across the boggy terrain. With a light shower misting against my face I realised how bleak this place could be in mid-winter. Missing now the golden yellow of the furze. Not a trace of the wild flowers hiding in the heath. No fluttering in the undergrowth, no cheery overhead song of the skylark. Only the insistent rain laying a soggy cloak across the landscape.

I knelt like people do at a graveside. Then I stretched out flat on the earth and kissed the damp sod where he lay. I spoke to his little bones beneath the soil. I tried to explain how I missed him on the dark days when clouds of depression threatened my very existence. I reminded him how we'd moved to be near him so he was never out of our sight across the valley.

~ * ~

I told Jennifer about my visits to the grave.

"Talking to him there on the mountainside takes me out of my misery. Do I sound like some kind of crazy?"

She seemed to understand.

"It's only natural to look for release from your despondency. So who better to talk to than your own son? Just remember, it's a slow process. You're not going to get better overnight. You need something else. What else do you to take your mind off things? What about work?"

"You're right, Jennifer. Work's a drug. We launched the new look Maeve in time for Christmas. I brought you a copy. Plus we've turned the corner with the circulation figures. Charles is thrilled.

"Charles? Who's Charles? I thought you told me you were the boss."

"Charles Allgood. He's English. A dream to work with. Gives credit where credit is due."

"Sounds like Allgood can't be at all bad."

"A real gentleman. I've been to his home, met his wife and kids."

"Really? That sounds like a pleasant enough kind of relationship to have with your boss. Speaking of relationships, how's it going with yourself and Finbarr?"

"How d'you mean? No rows worth talking about. He's fully occupied with his business while I'm working all hours on Maeve."

"And weekends?"

"Same thing. He tries to catch up with his reading while I try to do a bit of writing."

"Has he met this Charles chap?"

"Not so far. I'll try to arrange something soon."

"So you're happy in your marriage, then?"

"We get along fine. We talk." I wondered where all this was leading.

"There has to be more to a marriage than just 'getting along.' What about concern, tenderness, affection, that kind of thing. You still have a good sexual relationship?" This was Jennifer cutting to the chase.

"Well, maybe not so often now as we used to. We're usually too tired for anything. You know how it is."

"Who's too tired…you or him?"

"I don't like to pester him."

"Have you talked about it? You've got the whole weekend together, just the two of you. Isn't it time you two sat down and had a long chat?" For a single woman, she seemed pretty clued in.

"By the way," she said, changing direction, "whatever happened to that woman? That artist you had staying with you?"

"Céline, you mean? She's up to her eyes with a big project so we can't just turf her out."

"She's getting to be a permanent fixture?"

"Ah no, she's no trouble. Spends most of the day painting and clears off at the weekends, God alone knows where. We get along okay. Apart from one bit of a blow up with Finbarr. He's like a father to her. He gives her advice, makes suggestions. Whether she appreciates all that is another question."

"His main duty is to his wife. You, Susan, should be his number one priority."

~ * ~

I told Finbarr I was taking the dog for a walk as far as Kevin's grave.

"Would you like to come?" I said.

"I'd love to, honest, but I was hoping to get stuck into this." He held up a brand new edition of Thus Spake Zarathustra. "Why don't you and Kandinsky enjoy your walk? I'll be fine here till you get back."

"I hate to tear you away from old Nietzsche, but I thought it might be nice to walk and talk. It's a year and a half since Kevin died. I don't think you've ever once gone back to his grave. So how about it?"

"I'm happy to sit here with my own thoughts."

"Ever think of Kevin?"

"Of course I think about him. And yes, I miss him."

"What way? What way do you miss him?" I sat down again. This was too important to let it drop.

He seemed to rummage around for an answer.

"Okay, let me tell you. I wanted to show him things. Things like catching minnows in a stream, bringing them home in a jar and watching as they circled for hours and hours in a glass bowl. I'd have watched his face light up with the wonder of it all. Yes, that's what I miss."

I caught the longing, the loss in his voice.

"I'm sorry, Finbarr. I'll never be able to give you a son."

"I wasn't saying that. It's not your fault."

"Can you forgive me?"

"Don't talk like that. You're not to blame. Neither of us asked for this."

"I wish I knew what to say."

"We all have to find our own ways to handle whatever shit life throws at us."

"Is that why we hardly make love anymore?"

He shot me a look.

"Are you trying to analyse me or something? Why don't we leave that kind of thing to your shrink?"

"You don't love me anymore."

"I hate to hear you going on like this. You must know I love you."

"I want you to show me. In bed."

"Forget your walk then and come to bed. See if I don't make up for everything."

I kissed him on the top of the head. The dog saw me stirring and stood up ready to go.

"Kandinsky's waiting. We'll be back in an hour. And don't blow your brain with that philosophy stuff. You're going to need all your energy."

~ * ~

The Sugarloaf was overlain with cloud as though a pair of priestly hands had spread a silken veil over the cone as over a sacred chalice. The ground was too wet to kneel so I stood a few minutes before the grave in silent sorrow and meditation.

My prayer to my son was that his dad would never grow tired of my body, never cease to love me nor seek his solace in the metaphysical meanderings of a nineteenth century philosopher.

There was lightness in my step as I made my way back

to the house and to Finbarr. I couldn't remember when we'd last made love in the daytime. All I knew was that there was a special something about it, maybe to do with our first coming together on the side of a hill on a sunny afternoon in Glencree. An innocent quality we'd never quite managed to recapture since.

I walked in on an animated discussion. Céline had come back early and Finbarr was quizzing her on her association with the druids. He asked her what drew her to the pagan festivals.

"Are you trying to say the druids are mumbo-jumbo?" She was in argumentative mode.

"I'm just trying to make sense of the whole thing. You rubbish Christianity but you've no problem prancing around with a bunch of nuts in their night-shirts. How can you explain that?"

"You're forgetting I grew up in Brittany. All around me I saw traces of Celtic and pre-Celtic people. The druids were here hundreds of years before any Christian priests arrived with their talk of sin and redemption."

"So you're telling me you prefer pagan gods to the God of the Bible?"

"Susan, will you ask your husband to lay off me?"

"Leave the girl alone," I said. "You're hardly an example of orthodoxy yourself. Ignore him, Céline. He got himself in trouble with the Inquisition in Rome, so he's hardly in any position to lecture other people."

He stood up, went over to Céline and ruffled her hair like a reassuring father.

"Don't take it too seriously. I'm curious to know what other people believe, that's all. One way or another, we're all trying to make sense of this mess we call life."

"In that case, let me get on with my own way of making sense. I hate being probed." She turned away from him with a shrug of her shoulders.

"As you wish."

I suspect he was less concerned about her religious beliefs than with the kind of company she chose to hang around with.

Our planned love-making never happened. That night we were both too tired. We were into the first month of 1984 and already the portents were not looking too good. I couldn't shake off an irrational fear of what this year might bring.

Thirty-one

The same dream as always. I lay powerless, circled by masked doctors and nurses wielding knives and scalpels. Fully aware, yet powerless to move a limb as my belly was ripped open. I could only lie there and watch, unable to resist or protest, a silent scream frozen on my lips. The dream climaxed as before with the tearing of a monster from the gaping wound and a pair of bloody hands shoving the hideous features in my face.

I awoke shivering and frightened, yet relieved to find myself in my own bed with the warm familiar feel of my husband's sleeping body beside me. I snuggled closer to smother the dread that tormented me. That recurring dream saw to it that I should never forget, never escape the trauma and loss which lay at the base of my persistent depression. Always the same nagging question…why God had seen fit to deal me a double blow, the loss of my son and the loss of my womanhood in one terrible act of divine fury. Whether the dream and the questioning were part of my recovery or the opposite, I had no way of knowing.

I lay there in the silent morning, with the grey light of a

July dawn penetrating the fabric of the curtains and thought I heard my son calling. Come talk to me in my lonely grave on the side of the hill.

Only there, only at his grave could I seek answers to the questions that besieged me. Finbarr didn't stir as I got up. I knew he planned to finish off an article for some theological review.

I'd be late for the office, yet the urge to visit the grave was irresistible. I swallowed a cup of steaming coffee against the morning chill, peeped in at a sleeping Finbarr and let myself out through the kitchen door.

Stepping out of the car, I stood to admire the grandeur of the mountain in the still summer morning. A light misty cloud clung to the summit. In the natal newness of the day, the eastern sky was streaked with delicate shades of green and orange while a lake of white fog had pooled in the valley below.

The tufted grass on his grave was heavy with dew. I drew my skirt above my knees to feel the moisture as I knelt and made contact with the soil. I asked the same tormenting question I'd asked so often before. Why had he and I been singled out? Why had God betrayed us?

Why me, who had sought always to do His will? Why my baby, pure as the pristine dew that graced the grassy slope? Once again the voice in my head gave the same answers. I'd violated my sacred vows, my solemn promises to God, and chosen instead to go the way of the flesh. I was like the man in the gospel story who'd put his hand to the plough and then turned away. They had warned me in the convent that those who say no to God will not find salvation for their souls. Divine retribution had been visited on me when God snuffed out the life of my baby while destroying my very means of procreation.

In deep despair, I cried aloud the dying words of the Saviour as he hung in torment on a Roman cross, *Eli, Eli, Lamma Sabacthani?* Why, oh why, have you forsaken me? My cry hung in the morning air, heard only by startled creatures in the grass. Why me, oh God, why me? What more can you do to me? What further torments have you in store?

A stillness came over the earth. The birds stopped singing. After some moments, the stillness was broken by a low rumbling within the rock beneath me. Almost immediately the ground shook. At first the pulse was so slight as to be barely felt, but it was followed straight away by a more distinct shudder.

As the ground vibrated beneath my knees, the shockwaves rose through my body. Had I been standing instead of kneeling, I'd have lost my balance. I flung myself forward to lie face down on the earth, my fingers scrabbling for woody stems to fasten onto.

My body was directly aligned with the brooding presence of the quartzite peak in the sky above me. Like a worshipper in an ancient Egyptian rite abasing myself before Horus, Ra, Osiris, whichever of the deities held power over my destiny.

Once more the mountain shook the great bulk of his body with a ferocity that frightened me. I felt and heard his muffled groan deep in the bedrock, like the dying spasm of a mighty beast, mortally wounded, making one last futile effort to rise.

Then there was silence. All was still. After another

minute, a skylark sent out a few tentative notes to test the quiet air.

What was happening? Had the spirit of the mountain awoken, no longer able to stay silent in the face of my anguish? Had he convulsed in sympathy with my suffering?

And yet as my thoughts grew more coherent, I knew it had to be an earthquake. It was the only rational explanation. My thoughts turned to Finbarr and I wondered where he was when the earthquake struck. My watch said it was shortly after eight. Thursday morning he would usually be setting off for the city, but this morning he intended to do some writing. Céline, I expected, would be still in bed.

I had to get back and check they were all right. Driving down off the mountain I came across signs of structural damage. Old walls collapsed. I got to within two hundred yards of Giltspur before I found the way blocked. A couple of large stones had rolled onto the road, making it impossible to get past. I decided to leave the car and walk the short distance to the house.

Two cars stood side by side in front of the house. If they were still in bed they might be unaware of what had happened. I went in through the side door, but the kitchen was empty and the house silent. My coffee cup was upside down on the draining board where I'd left it. It was clear neither of the other two had surfaced.

I stuck my head into the conservatory to see if Céline was at work. It was empty. Likewise the lounge. I went to wake Finbarr and tell him about the quake. In the hallway I heard his voice. He was awake, after all. I headed for our bedroom. Then I heard a tinkling laugh. It was Céline giggling like a teenager and the voices were coming from the room at the end of the corridor. Céline's bedroom. There was something odd about this.

I found her bedroom door partly open, pushed it in and stepped inside.

Finbarr and Céline sitting in the bed, side by side. His right arm was about her naked body, her head cradled against his bare chest. His expression changed from foolish grin to a look of startled surprise and then extreme alarm.

Céline looked at me with a silly expression on her face, like this was the most ordinary state of affairs in the world. She made no attempt to cover her flat breasts.

"Hi, Susan," she said. "Thought you were gone to work. Is everything okay?"

I was speechless. The sheer insolence. What was I to say? No one has ever come up with the words for a situation like this.

"You're in bed with my man! You understand, girl? Finbarr is…my man! That's my husband in your bed. Now get out of there, slut, and get the hell out of my house!"

I caught sight of myself in the mirror, arm outstretched, pointing to the door, like some climactic moment on the Abbey stage. But this was no melodrama. This was real life. And it was tragedy.

Finbarr slid out of the bed, his nakedness repulsive for the first time ever.

"Hold on there, Susan," he said. "Take it easy now."

He moved towards me and I stepped away from him. I hated him.

"There's no need to fly off the handle," he said. "We can talk about this."

"Talk to my arse. And get that hussy out of here. Right now."

He tried to place a placatory hand on me, but I slapped him away.

"I want her out of here. Out. You understand? Out!"

I struggled with the tears that threatened to take the edge off my fury.

"Let's just talk, right?" he said.

"We'll talk when she's gone. Is that clear? Is that clear?"

Céline sat with her feet on the floor, unashamed in her nakedness, a look of amusement playing about her mouth. Fearing the eruption of tears, I made a dash for the back door, seeking refuge in the open air. Out into the garden and on down through the orchard, as far from the house as I could get. Down where the grass is wild and unkempt, where garden blends with wilderness, to a point where there was nowhere else to run. I collapsed in a heap at the base of the old hawthorn, whose white flowers had taken on the withered brown aspect of disappointment and death. Sitting there against the rough trunk I heaved my heart out in a flood of uncontrollable grief and despair.

Several times he came to me in my garden refuge. Each time the same confrontation. Finbarr pleading for calm and reason, always getting the same response. I refused to budge. I would not go back inside the house until she was gone. It was she or I. There was no middle ground.

"If you'll just listen to me, Susan, I can explain everything."

"Stuff your explanations. And don't even talk to me till the little bitch is gone out of my house. I never want to lay eyes on her again. Are you listening? Trust is gone out the window, Finbarr. Your words mean nothing anymore."

Betrayal is a dagger and its wound is deep. It releases a rage that is red like spilt blood.

I imagined them arguing inside the house with him attempting to mollify her and she extracting promises and undertakings.

At last I heard the MG roaring into life, the furious crashing of gears, and I knew she was gone. Even after she drove away, I stayed there in my refuge, too confused and upset to know what I should do next.

Back inside, I shoved a nightdress and personal items into a travel bag. I had to get out of there and while Finbarr looked on distraught, he made no real attempt to stop me.

"Where are you going?"

"Don't pretend you're interested."

"I'm concerned about you, that's all."

"Save your concern for your trollop."

~ * ~

"Stay as long as you want," Jennifer said. "You're going to need some time and space to think things out."

"Thanks, Jen. If I can just stay a night or two, it's enough. I hate to come crashing in on you like this."

"The main thing is not to rush into anything, Susan. You're very hurt. It'll take time before you can start to see things straight."

I hadn't even phoned to say I was coming but one glance at me standing on the doorstep, bag in hand, told her all she wanted to know. Hers was the only place I could think to go. The one place I knew I could be sure of some sympathy and understanding.

I realised from the start I couldn't impose myself on her indefinitely. Apart from the disruption on my friend, I knew I couldn't function away from my base. But a few days with Jennifer would give me time to reflect, a chance to mull things over with someone I trusted.

"You're welcome to stay, Susan, but you need to ask yourself who's the winner and who's the loser in all this? You've gone into voluntary exile while he still has the comfort of his own home. And remember, as long as you're not there, you've no guarantee he's behaving himself."

~ * ~

I dreamt I lay with Finbarr under an azure sky. The sun was warm and its rays played upon our bodies. We made love with all the ardour and excitement of first time lovers. I was suffused with a contentment that flowed through and over me. I was back in a lost time before death and suffering and treachery crept out from the shadows to strike.

In the dream, our happiness was forever, immutable. Nothing in prospect but the promise of undiminished love and lasting commitment. As I came out of that dream, I stretched out my hand for the familiar feel of a body beside me but my hand found only cold empty space. I awoke to an awful reality. On my own, solitary, I'd reached a new low. I sobbed into the pillow, crushed by the hopelessness and futility of my plight.

Back at work, I presented an exterior which gave no

hint of my domestic troubles. My personal life remained my own. I've often thought how you can share space with a colleague and have no idea what is going on in their lives. No one knows who is crying in the depths of their soul. You never know who is losing the struggle to go on living.

~ * ~

Josie didn't spare me. You can never trust a man, surely I knew that? And giving some French doxy the run of my house was asking for trouble. Any fool could see that.

"Go on, rub salt in the wound. Feel free. I thought I might get some tiny grain of sympathy from my own sister."

"What are you going to do?"

"I have to straighten things out with Finbarr."

"A waste of time. Give him his walking papers."

"What? That sounds a bit over the top."

"You're not going back as if nothing happened, to make dirt of yourself? Talk sense, girl."

"I'll make it clear he's on his last chance."

"Tell it to him straight. Any more of more of his tricks and he's gone. From now on, you make the rules, Sue. Don't let yourself to be kicked around. And first off, he has to cut out the French lassie. No ifs or buts about it."

On the street outside, builders had sealed off a demolition site with crude hoardings. Someone had grabbed their chance to scrawl a messianic message to the world. 'They stole away your happiness. Now steal it back.'

~ * ~

Paul was with a customer at the front of the gallery. I walked right through to where Finbarr sat in his office.

"We need to talk," I said.

"It's about time."

"Don't you think it's a bit rich?" I said. "I mean, I'm the one who ends up being driven out of my own home."

He went to close the office door.

"I've been begging you to come back."

"On whose terms?"

"Any terms you like. There's nothing that can't be sorted out."

"You're sure the bitch is gone?"

"Céline? There's been no sign of her since."

"I should bloody well hope not. I'm going home now. We'll talk later."

Everything reminded me of her. The conservatory cluttered with her art stuff. The usual mess. I could barely bring myself to look in her bedroom, but when I did I found everything exactly as it was that awful morning, the sheets in disarray, dirty knickers on the floor. Just like it always was. Like she was due back any minute. I turned my back on the scene of my betrayal, pulled the door behind me and waited for my husband to arrive.

I saw the beam of his car lights cross the window and heard the sound of the wheels on the driveway. I waited.

Thirty-two

"I owe you an apology, Susan.

Silence.

"If you'll just listen to me I'll try to…I want to explain."

"Spare me your whimpering, for Christ sake."

After a few more efforts, he gave up and retreated into a book.

I clattered around the kitchen trying to restore some sort of order. I slammed presses, banged saucepans, a dismal attempt to express any way I could the devastation that devoured me.

I told him he was welcome to use the bed in the box room. Sullen and silent, he complied. Alone in my bed, I longed for the warmth of another body. What is it about love and loathing? How fine the line that separates the two!

We barely grunted at each other in the morning and slept apart again the following night. Yet I knew in my heart I couldn't hold out forever. I was making him suffer and the sight of his suffering appeased me and to the extent that it appeased me, it softened my soul a little.

And still I could not forgive. We must have gone for weeks like this, my freeze-him-out tactic and his stoic forbearance. I could not see that it was getting me nowhere, the standoff. All attempts on his part to raise the core issue came up against my stony silence. At some point, though, he must have decided on a different approach.

"You'll never guess what I found today." There was a chirpy note in Finbarr's voice as he came in through the front door one evening.

I tried to hide my curiosity.

"Hang on," he said, "I'll go get it from the car."

I heard the car boot slam shut. He came into the kitchen, arms extended, gripping what was clearly a framed picture wrapped in brown paper. He laid it flat on the table and began to undo the wrapping.

The moment I saw it, my heart jumped. Five years had passed since I'd laid eyes on this picture and now I gazed at it like a long lost friend. Harry Kernoff's oil on canvas depicting a Dublin street with market stalls and bustling shoppers.

It all came flooding back. A summer's day in 1979. Finbarr introducing me to Uncle John and forgetting to mention I was a nun. Uncle John saying the first one to own the painting would have the privilege of naming it and asking me what I'd call it if it were mine. 'The Streets of Dublin,' I had said.

"I came across this in the storeroom," he said.

"I thought it was sold years ago."

"Maybe the deal fell through. Who knows what happened?"

"So what're you going to do with it? It must be worth an awful lot of money now." I'd forgotten we were supposed to be fighting.

"There's a huge interest in Irish artists nowadays."

"You'll have no trouble selling it then."

"He wanted you to have it. I'm convinced of that."

I didn't know what to think. Our quarrel was nowhere near being resolved. How could I bring myself to accept a gift from Finbarr when we hadn't even begun to talk about his treachery?

"I want nothing from you, Finbarr."

"You don't have to take anything from me. This is Uncle John's gift to you. I don't come into it. Where would you like me to hang it?"

My eyes fell on the blank space where Céline's painting of the Sugarloaf had hung before I took it out back and trashed it.

"Hang it there."

Maybe Uncle John was playing a part in all of this. He'd always had a soft spot in his heart for me. I was finding it harder to hold out against my husband. Clearly he still loved me and to be honest my feelings for him remained.

I sat for a long time looking at my new painting before I said anything.

"Well, are you sorry?" I was desperate now to forgive him.

"Of course I'm sorry. I've been trying to tell you."

"Well?"

"Well, what else can I say?"

"I need to know why you did it."

He beckoned me to sit beside him on the settee but I stayed where I was.

"It's hard to explain."

"You're going to say this was a once off. A moment of weakness, right? I'm not a fool, Finbarr."

"I never said it was a once off."

I stared at him in disbelief. Suspecting is one thing, but hearing him come straight out and say it really struck deep.

"You sit there and tell me you've been screwing that little bitch under my nose, in my own house, whenever you got my back turned. The two of you laughing and sniggering at your gullible fool of a wife. Just how sick is that?"

For a moment he didn't answer, sat with his eyes on the floor. Then he said, "I never intended to hurt you."

"But why? Why? That's all I want to know. You tired of my performance in the sack? Is that it? You wanted something new, was that it? New ways of doing it. What's the technique? You'll have to teach me, Finbarr, teach me the French way. Pass along what you've picked up. You'll find me an avid pupil."

"Stop it, Susan, stop. It's nothing to do with any of that."

"So what is it then? Are you going to tell me you're infatuated with a strip of a girl who lived here as your daughter? Tell me, I want to know."

"Nothing to do with infatuation. It's going to be hard to explain."

"Try. I'm listening."

"I didn't want to hurt you, but you've left me no choice."

"Just spit it out, whatever it is."

"I've always wanted a son."

"So?"

"With Céline I thought I'd found the answer. A child of my own, bearing my own genes."

He'd warned it was going to hurt and boy was he right. Like when a grenade explodes in your brain. A million fragments. Here he was telling me I was less than a woman, could never give him the one thing he craved, a child of his own.

"Ah! So you found a woman with a womb!"

"Susan, please don't."

"Now I know where I stand. I ought to be grateful to you for putting me in the picture. You're right, of course. I'm no better than a dried up fig. No, no, don't worry about my feelings. I can take it. And if there's anything else you want to fling, just feel free."

For a long time there was silence. He'd forced me to face the impossible truth that I'd failed him in the one area that mattered most to him. It wasn't anger I felt now so much as a hopeless sense of grief.

Finbarr sat opposite me, his hands covering his face, fingers splayed. In spite of my own hurt I felt a sneaking sympathy for him.

~ * ~

We ate in silence. I tidied away the dishes while he returned to his spot in the sitting room. A book lay open on his knee but I could tell his thoughts were elsewhere. I sat facing him. I needed more answers.

"Did she go along with your grand scheme?"

"Scheme?"

"To give you a child. It's what you wanted, isn't it?"

"She'd no idea. She thought it was all a bit of a lark."

"So how do you know she wasn't taking precautions?"

"You're asking me was she on the pill? I don't think so."

"You never asked her?"

"No."

"You're not making any sense, man. Make her pregnant and to hell with the consequences. What a way to use a young girl. You're even more disgusting than I thought."

Bedtime came and we went to our separate beds. I lay there, cold and miserable trying to make sense of all he'd said. He was telling the truth. I never doubted that. The galling thing was I'd often encouraged him to be open with me. Instead he'd kept it buried inside, gnawing away like a worm in his belly. Then he'd dreamed up this madcap notion of using Céline to achieve his dream.

I wished things were back the way they were before. But that was impossible. Something precious had been broken. I pulled the blanket tight about me.

I felt a movement in the room. He stood there in his pyjamas.

"I can't get warm," he said. "How about you?"

"Get in."

He slid under the covers and gave an involuntary shiver. I put my arm around him to heat his body. I'd missed him in bed. Maybe we could find a way out of the mess. Now that he'd come clean. Maybe...maybe...I drifted into sleep and slept more soundly than I had for many nights.

~ * ~

He worked to repair the damage. He admitted his affair with Céline had been an aberration, over and done with. He began to express an interest in my work. How I was getting along with Charles, my boss. He asked about circulation figures, outgoings, advertising revenue and so on. I could almost see the financial calculations flashing in his brain.

Just as well I hadn't listened to my sister's advice to send him packing. How could I throw away all the good things we had shared, all the memories? What we had was worth saving and rightly or wrongly I was going to make the effort.

Céline's stuff continued to clutter the conservatory. As long as her things were still lying around, I couldn't shake off the brooding sense of her presence. Things weren't helped by Kandinsky's whining and pining, snuffling around in the sunroom in search of his mistress. We'd have to get her to come and take her belongings. I handed Finbarr the job of trying to track her down.

"Find where she is and get her to move her stuff out of here. Look at the conservatory. You can hardly get inside the door."

He said he'd had no contact with her since she drove away that awful morning. I chose to believe him, because if I chose otherwise, I'd have to believe my marriage was a sham. And that would be too unbearable.

When he did track her down, she was sharing a house with an artist friend in one of the little streets around Stoneybatter. Whether she got his note or not I can't say, but she walked into the gallery one Wednesday afternoon when things were quiet. He took her to a café down the street for privacy. Only when they were sitting did he notice the pallor in her cheeks.

I'm completely dependent on Finbarr's account of what passed between them but I've no reason to doubt the substance of what he told me.

He suggested she hire a van to take away her belongings.

She sat looking into the distance as though she hadn't heard a word he said.

"You don't look too good, Céline. Are you sure everything's okay?"

"What's it to you?"

"Are you sure you're not ill?"

"If you're asking about me dragging myself out of the bed and vomiting my guts out in the lavatory bowl, well yes, I'm ill. If you're asking am I sick, yes, I'm sick. Sick of the day I ever laid eyes on you."

"You're going to have to get yourself checked out."

"Oh, I've been checked all right and I know exactly what the problem is."

"That's a first step. I'm sure something can be done…"

She managed a sarcastic laugh. "How thick can you get? Something can be done all right. And I've made arrangements to do it."

It hit Finbarr like a hammer blow. She was pregnant and she'd already booked herself in for a termination. He tried to say something, but couldn't find his voice.

"What have you to say now?" Her eyes blazed.

"I don't know what to say. This whole thing's taken me..."

"You're the one who planted this thing inside me. You might display some interest in the outcome."

"I need time to take it all in, that's all. We need to work out the best way to handle it."

"You won't have to bother your intellectual brain about anything. It's all arranged. I've been asking around and I've found a respectable clinic in Manchester that'll look after everything."

~ * ~

"So your little slut is pregnant? Is that what I'm hearing, Finbarr?"

"She's in a bad way, Susan."

"My heart bleeds. She got herself into this, now let her deal with it. She needn't come running to me for sympathy."

"She never dreamed it could happen to her."

"Oh come on. She's been around. If she didn't want to get pregnant, she knew how to avoid it. I haven't a shred of sympathy for her."

"Right now she's scared and confused."

"You talk like you had no hand, act or part in the whole saga."

"The baby's mine. She left me in no doubt about that."

"I suppose congratulations are in order?"

"Don't be like that, Susan. I'm going through hell. I've no idea how to stop her."

"What do you mean, stop her?"

"She's made arrangements for an abortion."

"Oh my God!"

~ * ~

I tossed and turned all night. Even if there were anything I could do about it, why should I help him out of his dilemma? Spurned by my husband and scorned by his mistress, why should I be the one to pick up the pieces?

Even if I tried to stop her, what chance was there Céline would listen to the woman who had ordered her out of the house? And why should I make dirt of myself by going on my knees before her?

I dug my elbow into his kidney to wake him.

"Can't you sleep?" he mumbled.

"We have to stop it," I said.

"What?"

"We've got to make her to change her mind."

"Nothing's going to change her mind."

"I'll talk to her."

Silence from his side of the bed.

"Get me her number," I said, "and let me do the talking."

"What'll you say to her?"

"Leave that to me."

From what he'd said, I knew this was an impossible task. Yet the thought of the baby being aborted horrified me. How could I ever rest easy again if I allowed it to happen? Not after the loss of my own helpless baby before he ever got to experience the love of caring parents.

I might well fail in my mission but I was damn well going to make the attempt.

Thirty-three

The scent of roses floated on the August air as Jennifer threw open the French windows. Across the city to the south, the outline of the Dublin Mountains guided my eyes to the distant cone of the Sugarloaf in whose shadow the source of my concern had been conceived.

"I can tell there's something on your mind," she said as she poured tea and pushed a plate of biscuits in my direction.

"Céline," I said.

"I thought she was gone."

"Gone, yes. But just when I thought we'd heard the last of her we get word she's pregnant."

"Céline? Pregnant? You're not telling me it's...?"

"It's Finbarr's all right."

"Can you be sure?"

"He's in no doubt about it."

"You must be shattered."

"It's even worse. She's talking about an abortion."

She pursed her lips.

"Abortion's illegal in Ireland. She must know that."

"She's found a clinic in Manchester. She's waiting to be given a date."

"And why do you want to stop her?"

Her question shocked me. My Catholic upbringing had moulded my way of thinking about things. My years of conditioning in the convent made me abhor the very notion of terminating an innocent life. Jennifer had been my novice mistress. I'd taken my lead from her in everything.

"Jennifer! 'A human being from the moment of conception,' that's what you used to say."

"We're not in the convent any longer and things aren't as black and white as I used to think. Okay, so we know what she wants. Do we know what Finbarr wants?"

"That's the whole point. This is his chance to replace the child he lost, the only chance he'll ever have. It's eating him up inside, I can see it. It's for his sake I want to stop her. If she does this to him, I can't see how he'll ever get over it. He depends on me to do something."

"What does he think you can do?"

"He says only a woman can understand a woman. He's probably right."

"Some would say he got himself into this, let him get himself out of it."

"Listen, Jennifer. I know he did the dirty me and all that, but I still don't think he deserves to go through what he's going through."

"So tell me, Susan, what are you going to do?"

"There's only one thing I can do. I'm going to have to talk to her."

"You could have your work cut out."

"Still, I have to try."

"Well, since you're determined, I'll wish you the best. I'm behind you all the way, Susan."

"The only problem is I don't have her address. Somewhere near here by all accounts. Finbarr's working on it."

~ * ~

A nice day for walking. I turned into Oxmantown Road. Children playing those age-old street games. Little girls swung a skipping rope while their companions lined up to jump through the loop in time to a chanted song. Other children in a circle, hands joined, a five year old in the centre. 'Ring a ring o' roses, Pockets full of posies.' All their cares in a far off future.

What Jennifer seemed to be saying was this was Finbarr's problem and if anyone was to approach Céline, he was the one to do it. On the other hand, she hated him. She'd made that plain. And the chances were she hated me as much.

I was still mulling this over as I walked down Stoneybatter. If I followed the slope, it would take me to the river which would point me to the city centre. The sun had begun its descent over Islandbridge towards its touching down point in Phoenix Park.

A woman emerged from a little grocery shop clutching to her chest a brown paper bag. Something about her walk made me look again. From thirty yards away she looked like Céline. As she started across the road, I felt impelled to follow. If it was indeed she, I was curious to see where exactly she was living. We were in a maze of little streets which bore the names of Norse gods and Viking warriors.

Names like Thor and Sitric and Olaf.

She stopped in front of the red painted front door of a terrace cottage and began to fumble for her key. As I came closer, I saw that it was indeed she. She glanced up and recognised me. A startled look was replaced by a weak smile.

"Quelle surprise! How'd you manage to find me?"

"I spotted you in the distance and wanted to say hello."

"You better come in, then."

The tiny space where we sat served as dining and sitting room combined. I sat on an upright wooden chair beside the Formica table as she went to leave her shopping in the scullery. Cold cinders in the fireplace looked like they'd lain there forever. An air of untidiness pervaded the place. The wallpaper was covered with garish murals, in places done over more than once. It wasn't Céline's work. I'd have known it. There must be a deranged artist in residence. She came back and caught me gazing around.

"All Freddie's work," she said. "He uses every available surface. Canvas is expensive, you know."

"Where do you paint?"

"Out there." She pointed through the scullery towards the extension at the back. From what I could see through the open door, it was a ramshackle, thrown-together construction.

"Finbarr says you're expecting a baby."

Her only answer was a tired sigh. Her skin looked pallid beneath the unkempt dark brown hair.

"I gather you're not too happy about it."

"Your husband's the one who left me like this." She glared at me as if I shared some responsibility.

"Finbarr? I don't blame you one bit for being pissed off with him."

"Pissed off. Now you said it. But then why should you care? Why should anyone care?"

"Will you believe me if I say I do care?"

"You hate me. Hate my guts. You made that bloody clear when you threw me out. Just don't come trotting along pretending to be concerned. Anyway, you'll be delighted to hear it's taken care of. I've got it all arranged."

"What's arranged?"

"I've been onto the clinic and they've given me a date. I'm going over next week to get shut of this thing. I'll be free to get on with my life. There'll be nothing left to remind me of either you or your husband."

"Don't do it, Céline."

"What are you talking about, don't do it?"

"The abortion. Cancel it."

"Are you mad or something? Do you know what you're saying? Just look around you, for Jesus sake. I can barely survive as it is without having to drag up a child in this dive. No way. It's decided. I'm putting an end to this nightmare."

"Céline, I'm begging you. Please don't do it."

She stared at me and her face registered total incomprehension.

"I can't figure you out. This baby means nothing to you except to remind you your husband was shagging another woman every time you took your eye off the ball."

Her words cut me but I wasn't about to give up now.

"We both want you to have the baby and we're ready

to do anything we can to help."

"Like what?"

"Like…well, for one thing you won't be short of money."

"So I'll be living on your hand-outs? Is that what you're saying?"

"It's not a question of hand-outs. It's about us facing our responsibilities."

She seemed to turn this over in her mind and what she said next showed she might be wavering.

"And just supposing I decide to keep it, where do you propose I live and work?"

It took a few seconds for me to see where this was going. I swung my arm in an arc to indicate her present accommodation. This brought a scornful laugh.

"Stay here? Not on your life. You know damn well there's only one place I can work. You should know that by now."

"No. I don't know."

"I presume my atelier is still the way I left it?"

It was clear what she was driving at and the sheer brazenness of it took my breath away. One wrong word now and I'd lost.

"We can talk about it. I'm not ruling anything out."

"It's that or nothing."

An image of her boarding the boat for Holyhead flashed before my eyes. I knew she was serious. I had to think fast. Maybe we could let her stay in Giltspur until things sorted themselves out.

"And you'll cancel the abortion?"

"You drive a hard bargain," she said.

"Ring them now and I'll see to it you get whatever you ask for."

The phone was mounted on the wall by the front door. I watched as her finger scrolled through the mish-mash of numbers scrawled on the wallpaper.

"Is that the Wellness Clinic?" Her voice was calm and composed.

~ * ~

Finbarr accepted I'd little option but to allow her back in the house.

"All this is for you, never forget that," I told him.

"You must hate her guts," he said.

"Nothing would do her but to come back to live and work here. She's one tough cookie, all right."

"It won't be easy for either of us."

"Pretty awkward for you, I imagine, your wife and your mistress under the same roof. Whose bed to honour with your presence." It was cruel, but I couldn't resist the swipe.

"You need have no worries. The past is the past, fini. It's you and me from now on."

"Don't think I'm nagging but some things need to be said."

"I told you, I've learned my lesson."

Maybe he'd learned his lesson, but he was a man like any other man. And just like any other man, full of the best intentions.

"Just as long as we're clear on one thing," I said. "If I get even a whiff of dishonesty or cheating, that's it, you're out. Is that clear?"

"Absolutely."

"I hope so."

~ * ~

Kandinsky ran a slobbery tongue over Céline's face. His antics helped ease the awkwardness of her return. I wondered what was going through Finbarr's mind as he carried her bag to her old bedroom and put it by her bed. He knew and I knew that the next seven months would be defined by a single overriding reality, the as yet hidden presence of Finbarr's child slowly growing to term inside a moody and unpredictable Céline.

~ * ~

I knew I couldn't keep this news from my sister for long. Céline's pregnancy and the fact that it was Finbarr's child. That much I'd have to tell her, but the full story I decided would be just too much for her to take.

"Am I hearing you straight? This is not your idea of a joke?" She applied the back of her hand to her forehead like someone on the verge of fainting. "It's beyond belief. You catch your husband in bed with another woman and what do you do about it? You treat him like nothing's happened. He's the fair haired boy, kiss and make up, all palzy-walzy. And now you tell me he has his doxy back under your roof."

"You're surely not suggesting I should walk away from my marriage because my husband makes one stupid mistake? Let me tell you, Josie, I happen to believe a marriage is worth fighting for. And I'm ready to do whatever it takes."

"Get rid of that woman, Susan. Use whatever grain of sense God gave you and show her the door."

"I can't do that, Josie."

"You can't?"

"I can't."

"In the name of God!"

"She's expecting."

A look of incredulity crept across Josie's face.

"She's pregnant with Finbarr's child."

She moved her head in a sad sweep from side to side.

"It's all decided," I said. "This baby means a lot to Finbarr. She'll stay with us till the child is born."

I said nothing about an abortion. She didn't have to know everything.

"I worry about you, Sue. I hate to see you being treated like shit." Her parting words as we hugged and said goodbye.

I wanted as much privacy for Céline as possible. But there was always Mona and her husband Chaser. I left a note for Mona to say Céline would be staying in the guest room for the time being and that I knew I could depend on her to look after things. I hadn't the slightest doubt she retailed all our comings and goings to her husband to become the subject of gossipy speculation within his fertile imagination.

I took to reminding Céline when Mona was coming for the cleaning, suggesting she take the dog for a long walk in order to stay out of her way. But sooner or later, Céline's bump would start to show and I wondered what the strange couple in the forest would make of that.

Thirty-four

A public holiday. The nation celebrates the driving out of the snakes. For me the chance of a long lazy lie-in. But if that was my hope, it wasn't to be. At half past eight, the phone was hopping off its stand.

I woke to the news that Céline's daughter had made her grand entrance less than one hour before. A sleepy Finbarr wasn't sufficiently stirred to leave a warm bed, though it was he who'd driven Céline the day before to the private nursing home he'd arranged for her. He gave not the slightest hint of disappointment that the longed for son had turned out to be a girl. Leaving him there to absorb the full impact of the news, I got dressed and drove to the nursing home in Ballsbridge.

Surprised by a sudden shower of hail, I made a dash for the porch. I was shown to Céline's room by a matronly nurse in uniform.

Céline sitting up in the bed was surprisingly fresh looking for a woman who'd just given birth, while the baby, asleep in a cradle beside the bed, was the picture of comfort and contentment.

"I'm sure you're relieved it went so well," I said.

"Yourself and himself can be happy now and I'm free at last to get on with my life. The sooner I get out of here, the better."

"Where's your rush? Why don't you take it easy for a few days? Have a good rest. Make the most of it."

"I've no intention of lying around when there's work to be done. There's that new Clew Bay project I must get stuck into. I just want a normal existence, nothing more."

A normal existence! When did the setup in our house come anywhere close to normality? Couldn't she see nothing would ever be the same again?

"Finbarr says he'll try to get here in the afternoon," I said.

Her silence gave no clue what she thought of that news.

"Can I hold her?" I said, suddenly remembering the sleeping infant beside me.

I lifted the child carefully from her cradle and when I held her up to my face I experienced an unexpected wave of emotion. The feel of her, the soft warm smell of her, the immediacy, the barely perceptible breathing, her total helplessness. At that moment I was back in that lovely terrible time when I held my infant son for a few brief seconds before they took him away from me to put him in an incubator from which he would never again emerge alive.

"You'll get plenty of chances to hold her," she said.

I didn't quite know what to make of that remark but it did remind me I'd have to start looking around for someone to mind the baby in a household where all the adults had their own full time jobs.

"Have you given any thought to a name?" I said. "What d'you want to call her?"

"Aline."

"Aline? It's got a lovely feel to it. Are you calling her after somebody?"

"My sister."

"Your sister was Aline, was she?"

"She was only fourteen."

"It's too terrible. Especially since your mother had no more children. Just you."

"It finished her off, really. So soon after Papa. She never got over it. I'd say it was the start of her problems."

"She's not in good health, I take it?"

"Locked up in a mental home. Completely out of it. Now you know why I don't go to see her anymore."

"God, I'm really sorry. It can't be easy for you or her."

"I try not to think about it and I really don't want to talk about it."

"Well, now we have a new Aline. A new beginning as they say. A chance to start over."

"Yeah, well."

Seeing her there in the bed, half sitting, half lying, her face lacking any glimmer of interest or excitement, I searched for something cheerful to say.

"At least you've no worries about the future."

"How d'you mean?"

"I mean you can to stay with us in Rocky Valley as long as you want."

"You're not going to throw me out in the wind and rain, then?"

There was no missing the irony in the question. Yet I

couldn't believe it would ever again come to the point where I was driven to get rid of her. Just so long as she behaved herself.

When I told Finbarr the baby was fine, his face lit up. He asked about Céline.

"She seems mighty relieved it's over. Don't forget she's gone through with the pregnancy and given birth to this baby purely to please you and me."

"I know that, but what more can we do?"

"We're going to have to find someone reliable to mind the baby."

~ * ~

I spotted a hand-written note on a used envelope stuck in the Post Office window and wasted no time ringing the number. Margo seemed to fit the bill. A widow with her own children almost reared. When I told her we were offering shelter to an unmarried mother and her baby, she oozed interest. The job, she said, would suit her down to the ground. She'd be there at nine every weekday morning to take complete care of little Aline for the day.

Aline changed everything. This tiny new arrival was determined to make her presence known. From then on, everything would centre on Aline's needs.

Credit must be given to Céline who prepared the feeds before she went to bed and had to drag herself to the kitchen to reheat them to satisfy Aline's nocturnal needs. Yet she was up before Margo arrived to take the child off her hands in the morning. She took her coffee with her to the conservatory so she could get straight into her work. Sooner or later all this would take its toll on an already fragile personality.

More and more, I noticed themes of violence cropping up in her paintings. I wondered if it was all down to the stress of the new baby or something deeper, something in her own past maybe. I was less and less inclined to look at her work when I came home in the evenings. It was just a little too unsettling.

~ * ~

The first real row following Aline's birth happened after I found the tablets. Mona had left the rubbish from Céline's room right next to the garbage at the back of the house. I saw it there and picked out a little brown plastic container. It rattled. The label said Prozac. I felt the sort of guilty feeling you get from going through someone else's things. I emptied the waste basket into the bin, hoping she'd notice nothing out of the way.

Yet I couldn't shake off this new knowledge that Céline was medicating herself for depression. How long had it been going on and why on earth did she feel the need to fall back on this drug? We'd done all we could to accommodate her in every sense of that word. But then I remembered my own postnatal depression and straight away I felt a surge of sympathy. I'd had my own struggle with the evil monster, had come close to suicide, in fact. I knew from experience how helpless, how hopeless she must be feeling.

I was in the kitchen knocking up something for the evening meal. Aline was sound asleep in her cradle, Kandinsky stretched full length on the floor beside her, chin resting on fore-paws, vigilant and protective of his new charge. I heard Céline go to her bedroom after she finished up in her studio. As things turned out, it was just as well Finbarr hadn't come home yet, because there's no knowing how he would have handled the scene that followed.

I heard Céline's door slam, heard her steps striding towards the kitchen. She burst in and when I turned to face her I saw her eyes blazing in an ashen face.

"You've been going through my things." A vindictive fury in her voice.

"No."

"Who told you to open my presses and mess with my things?"

I felt nervous. I'd never seen her like this.

"Just hang on a second, Céline. Are you saying I opened your presses?"

"Well, if it wasn't you I want to know who the hell was in my room. Whoever it was I don't like it. Do you hear me? I don't like it."

"No need to shout. If you'll just calm down a minute. I'm not long in from work. I didn't go near your room. I'm tired and I'm trying to get a bit of food ready. Now, can you just take it slowly and tell me what all this is about?"

She strode right over to where I stood facing her.

"My tablets are missing and I want to know who's been snooping around my room."

"Mona was here. You must have heard her. She'd have cleaned your room as usual."

"I want no Mona snooping around. Tell her to keep the hell out of my room. I expect a bit of privacy or is that too much to ask? Will you tell them all to keep away from me? No snoopers, I said."

She turned and strode out of the kitchen, slamming the door behind her. Seconds later I heard her own room door slam and there was silence. I found Kandinsky sitting on his haunches with his head slightly to one side, puzzled, looking at the hysterical Aline who had been frightened out of her sleep. The dog showed more concern than her own mother. I lifted her from her cot and walked her up and down with little bouncy movements.

"Aline allana. Aline aroon."

Then as peace settled over the house, I placed her back in her cradle and moved it to where she could see me moving about. My crooning to the child had had the effect of soothing my own nerves.

Later I could hear the sound of rummaging in the bins at the back of the house. Céline must have been trying to retrieve whatever it was she was missing.

I told Finbarr the whole story when he came in.

"You've never seen the likes of it," I whispered. "She went berserk. Like a… like I don't know what."

"It's obvious she wants no one to know she's on medication."

His voice had a conciliatory note. He almost certainly thought I was exaggerating. I asked him to call Céline for her meal and wondered what kind of reception he'd get. I heard her raised voice. I waited till he came back and closed the door behind him. I caught the look of shock on his face.

"Well?" I said.

He just looked at me.

"Well? Is she going to eat or isn't she?"

"It doesn't look like it."

"What did she say?"

"She said to leave her the fuck alone."

"She used that word?"

"What's for dinner anyway?"

"T-bone steak. There's a bottle of red in the cabinet. We could both do with something."

"Give her time," he said. "She'll cool off. She'll soon get over it." He eased the cork from the neck of the bottle with accustomed skill, ending the operation with a satisfying pop.

"I hope for her sake it's not postnatal," I said.

"What makes you say that?"

"I was lucky to get over it. Some women never get over it. I worry we could have a real problem on our hands."

I spoke through Céline's closed door to say Aline was in her cradle in the kitchen. There was no answer, but after a while I heard her take her daughter to her bedroom.

There was still no sign of Céline as we got ready for work the following morning. No sign except for a single unwashed coffee mug left in the kitchen sink and some biscuit crumbs on the kitchen table.

Thirty-five

Who did little Aline imagine to be her mother? Of the three possible candidates, Céline, myself and Margo, there can be little doubt that the one offering her consistent motherly attention was her minder. Margo fussed over her like a hen whose brood is reared and who is left with the one little chick on whom to load all her motherly attention.

"My heart goes out to the poor little mite. The little thing'll never know who her father was." Margo had bought into the story of the single mother abandoned by a reckless father. Neither Margo nor Mona seemed to question this version, which we hoped was the one that would gain currency.

As for Céline, she was going to let nothing come between her and her painting. She did her mothering stint during the night, sure enough, but for the most part she left it all to others to bring up her child. There remained a conspiracy of silence around Finbarr's relationship to his daughter.

Aline began to recognise and respond to the different faces peering at her and as the weeks became months, she grew more and more alert to the comings and goings in her immediate surroundings. We waited for the day when she'd pronounce her first word.

"Do you want her to call you Daddy?" I said.

Finbarr looked at me with a startled expression.

"I hadn't thought about that"

"Why not? Is she to grow up thinking she has no father?"

"I've nothing to be ashamed of."

"Well, Daddy," I said, "aren't you going to introduce yourself to your daughter?

"Ups-a-daisy." His big hands lifted the child and held her at arm's length just above the level of his eyes. "By God, but you're a pretty little girl. Better looking every day. Why don't you and I go for a little walk outside? You want to see the apple blossoms? And the honeybees? Kandinsky can come, too."

"Hey, tuck this around her shoulders. There's a nip in the air." I handed him a little woollen shawl and helped him wrap her up and when I said 'big smile for Daddy,' I caught his expression of quiet pride.

I was happy to see him play father to his child. Yet I felt torn inside. Was it some sense of inadequacy in that I could never hope to share with him the joy of parenthood? I'd come to love Aline like my own child, so why shouldn't I want her to have a father's love and for that love to come from her natural father, the only male figure in her young life? And why should I deny him the joy of fatherhood for which he'd waited so long?

Let's face it. I was wife to the father of another woman's child. It's a role I'd have to get used to, ignoring any feelings of resentment, loving that child as if she were my own. Having spent years in a convent seeking my vocation in a life of sacrifice I was about to find the true vocation for which I was destined from the start.

~ * ~

It seemed to suit Céline, this arrangement, three adults and one child, as long as she herself remained on the margins. I arrived home one evening to find Aline crying in her playpen, looking for attention, uncomfortable. Margo had gone. I wondered where Céline was. I stuck my head into the conservatory and found her sitting on a chair, staring at a canvas.

"Are you all right, Céline? Is there anything wrong?"

"Should there be?"

"It's Aline. She was crying when I came in. You might want to take a look at your child."

"There's my child." She pointed at the canvas, erect on its easel, fresh paint glistening.

I'd noticed a change lately. She'd become more distant and moody. I was more and more afraid she was showing signs of depression. I sat down on a dirty chair.

"You don't seem in the best of form, Céline. Are you sure there's nothing getting you down?"

"I'm fine."

"If you need to talk…"

"Right now I just want to be left alone."

~ * ~

Saturday morning I found her in the kitchen making a cup of coffee. She didn't speak as I came in.

"Anything wrong, Céline?"

"Everything's perfect."

"Tell me, are you worried about anything?"

"Look, can we just leave it? I can sort myself out just fine. Can't you just leave me alone?"

"It's lovely outside. Why don't you join us on the patio?"

"Far be it from me to intrude. You two won't want me shoving my nose in."

"Don't be ridiculous. You're a part of the family."

"I don't see too much sign of that. Now, if you'll excuse me."

Finbarr put it down to her workload.

"She's under pressure," he said. "Clients can be damned unreasonable. Some of them think art comes off a conveyor belt. People who know all about making money, nothing about making art."

"It's not that simple. How come we didn't see any of these moods before?"

"Before?"

"Before Aline was born. If it's a bout of depression, she's going to need some kind of help. We can't sit there and hope it'll go away."

Finbarr was finally forced to accept there was something amiss when Margo complained that Céline had screamed at her.

"I don't need this job, Mr Gray. I only took it on to oblige yourself and the missus."

"What exactly did she say, Margo?"

"Words I won't repeat, Mr Gray. I'm a respectable woman and I'm not used to that kind of talk, if you know what I mean."

"She complained about your work, is that it?"

"She said if I couldn't do what I was paid to do, to get myself the...the hell out of here. I've a good mind to do just that."

"Leave it to me, Margo. I'll sort it out. You're doing a terrific job. You've worked wonders with the baby. I don't know what we'd do without you."

I hoped Finbarr would have better luck that I'd had. Any effort I'd made to get to the bottom of what was bugging Céline had come up against a blank wall. He got his chance as we relaxed in the lounge after dinner. The wine was good and the mood was amicable. Aline was asleep in her cot, Kandinsky stretched on the floor. Céline was in one of her sparkling spells. The discussion came around to religion and belief, a hobby horse of Finbarr's. Céline had been brought up a Catholic. While her Breton father had been indifferent towards the Church, her mother was devout, attached to the beliefs and practices of her Galway childhood.

Finbarr was doing a little probing.

"You've lost faith in the church?" he said.

"You don't seem too devout yourself."

"But I want to hear about you. Do you believe in anything?"

"I left all that stuff behind long ago. When Papa died, that's when I began to question the whole thing."

"You blamed God for taking your father?" I said.

"I adored Papa. They told me God had taken him for Himself. I was only seven, remember. I had to blame someone, so I blamed God. It was easy to blame him so I blamed Him for everything. I blamed him when my sister died a year later. And then I saw there was no point. No point cursing God. If he was really there, he wasn't listening. Wasn't God supposed to show some interest, you know, some compassion? Anyway, I decided it was all a sham, one big confidence trick."

There was an awkward silence.

"That's a pretty depressing thought," I said.

"Sure it's depressing, but you get used to it. You learn to live with it."

"Are you depressed now?" Finbarr seized the moment.

She hesitated…seemed tobe struggling to come out with something.

"When's the worst time?" he persisted.

"Like when I see you and Susan playing happy families with Aline."

I tried to make sense of what she'd just said.

"You feel left out?" said Finbarr. "Is that what you mean?"

"Isn't it obvious I'm the outsider?"

"I'd hate you to think that."

"Oh, I have my uses. First you use me to give you a child. Then you keep me hanging around to salve your conscience. But where do I stand, really? A shameful secret to be hushed up and hidden away. Don't try to fool me. I know my place, all right."

This outburst left me shaken. Anger and recrimination mixed with sadness and resignation.

Finbarr saw an opportunity.

"I heard you had some words with Margo. You must have been really at a low ebb?"

"She's been complaining, has she?"

"She gets on really well with Aline. We'd have a job finding someone to replace her."

"Okay, maybe I went too far. Sometimes I just lose it completely and then I wonder why I said what I said." She sounded contrite and unusually candid.

"You'll have to control your temper then." Finbarr spoke quietly. "It doesn't do yourself or anyone else any good. I'm not trying to be critical, just offering friendly advice."

"Advice? I need your advice?"

"We want you to be happy here. Believe me, we only want what's best for you."

"You want what's best for me?" Her voice was heavy with sarcasm.

"I hate to see you down. Whatever you want or need, don't be afraid to ask. I'm ready to…"

"That remains to be seen."

He didn't answer and we were left to our own thoughts. I felt she'd revealed more than she intended when she admitted she wasn't always in control and not always able to explain what was happening. But I suspected there was a lot more we didn't know, psychological baggage from her early days in Brittany.

Later I asked Finbarr what he made of it all.

"Céline? I don't know what to make of it," he said. "All that talk about being excluded. I mean that's absolute nonsense."

"Maybe so, but she doesn't see it like that. I keep asking myself is there anything we can do to make her feel more...more accepted."

"She lives like one of the family. She does her stint at

the cooking, shares our food, relaxes with us in the sitting room. She has the total run of the place. I'm beginning to think nothing will satisfy her."

"There must be something. I'll have to talk to her and see if I can get her to open up."

"If you think it'll do any good."

I reasoned the best way to get Céline to talk about herself was to take her into my confidence more. And so I started to visit her in her studio as she worked. I'd take Aline with me to watch her mother painting.

I began by talking about my own work and then about my family. I reminisced about my childhood, my school, my parents. I told her how my plans to study in Galway were put on hold when my poor mother was diagnosed with cancer. I told her about the effect it had on me, watching her wasting away for the best part of a year. I told her how my mother's death finally decided me to dedicate my life to God.

"But you left the convent. Why?"

"For the love of a man."

"You mean Finbarr?"

"Think 'impressionable young nun falls for convent chaplain.' "

"And you ran off together!"

I laughed.

"If only it were so romantic. The truth is he disappeared and it took me years to find him."

"That's even better. The woman who'll stop at nothing till she gets what she wants."

That last comment of Céline's was about as far as she came to opening up with her own story. She still showed no inclination to go into her early life and neither did she throw any light on where she saw her life going in the future. Some instinct told me my efforts wouldn't go to waste. I'd sown a seed and given time it would bear fruit.

~ * ~

When snow frosted the facing slopes and a single yellow crocus stuck its nose through the frigid earth, that's when Aline decided to utter her first word. Here's how it happened. Finbarr had stoked the range with dry logs and soon the kitchen was the warmest spot in the house.

I watched him lift his daughter from the playpen and bring her closer to the source of heat. He brought her face up close to his.

"Say Daddy." Usually when he said this, all he got was a happy gurgle. Not this time, though.

"Dah...dee." She'd repeated the word. There was absolutely no doubt it.

"She said it, Susan, she said it. Did you hear that?"

An excited Finbarr jumped to his feet, swung the child in a circle repeating the word over and over. Daddy, Daddy. I'd never seen him so animated. Aline giggled with pleasure but in spite of his efforts she refused to give a repeat performance.

Finbarr was still pleading for an encore when I caught sight of Kandinsky bounding down the garden. Céline was back from her walk. As she came in through the patio door, her face glowed from the bracing breeze of the hillside.

"Céline!" I said, "You're never going to believe what happened when you were out."

"Oh? Tell me."

"She said her first word. It's amazing."

"Aline? She's talking already? This I have to hear. So tell me anyway, what did she say?"

"Daddy. Would you believe it? She said Daddy."

A dark cloud crossed Céline's face. She turned to face Finbarr, who stood there holding the child with a triumphant grin on his face.

"So she said Daddy! Well at least she knows her fuckin' Daddy." She spat the words. "You must be real proud of yourself, Daddy. I hope you're happy now. Am I supposed to offer congratulations?"

Neither Finbarr nor I answered. I couldn't think of anything to say.

"Well," she said, "seeing as I'm not needed around here, don't let me disturb the celebrations."

The glass shook as she slammed the patio door after her. The frightened child seemed about to start squalling, so I took her from Finbarr and placed her back in her playpen.

When I turned back, he was slumped in a chair, his face like paper. I put a hand on his shoulder.

"I'm okay," he said. "She'll get over it. She always does."

"It's the worst display I've seen."

"I wish I knew what's bugging her."

"I'm going after her."

"Don't be mad. God knows what she might do."

"Exactly. I don't want to see any harm come to her."

Kandinsky came with me. He'd show me where she'd gone. He led me up the slope till we came to the track that led to Mona and Chaser's cottage. He stopped to raise his nose in the air, as if testing the wind for clues. He decided to stick to the road. I waited while he sniffed the scent trail on every wisp and weed along the wayside. At the spot where the road levelled out and the summits of West Wicklow came into view, we found her. She stood propped against an iron gate, looking across an expanse of rough grass to a line where the land fell away into the valley before rising again to the slopes of bracken on the opposite side.

She didn't move her head or look at me when I stood beside her, but her hand went down to where the dog nuzzled her knee. We stood in silence, side by side, looking towards the crystalline peak of the Sugarloaf. When I broke the silence, it was to talk about the mountain.

"Doesn't it lift your heart to look at it?"

She didn't answer.

"I know it sounds weird, but that mountain has been a friend to me since the first day I set foot in Wicklow."

Still no answer.

"You know I lost my baby. He died the day he came into the world. I got to hold him in my hands for less than a minute. Can you believe that, Céline? Less than a minute to talk to my son before he was taken away to die alone."

"So what has the mountain got to do with any of that?"

"It's where he lies buried. I'm looking right across at his resting place."

She glanced at me and then across at the facing flank of the mountain.

"My baby's over there. I've formed a special bond with

the mountain who took my baby into his bosom."

"Is this some sort of parable or what?"

"In a way you could say so. We all need something to believe in, something to hold onto."

"And you believe in mountains. It takes all kinds."

"When I left the convent, I was lost. Lost for purpose. Lost for meaning. I started my search for a new meaning. Kevin became that meaning. But when he was taken from me, my life again lost its meaning. I'd nothing left to live for. That mountain over there helped me find a new meaning."

"You want to tell me?"

She was beginning to engage. Maybe this was the moment I could get through to her.

"My life's meaning has only begun to come clear. My marriage. Finbarr."

"Surprise, surprise."

"But it's more than that. There's Finbarr's baby and there's the mother of Finbarr's baby. All part of my meaning."

She swung around to face me.

"In the name of Christ, how can you keep going on like this? You know damn well what a shagging mess my life is in. I'm living a half-life in that house of yours. I'm a nobody. Barely tolerated. And the best you can do is talk about meaning. You can stick your meaning, Susan."

"You're Aline's mother. You carried Finbarr's child. That means an awful lot. It's why we've made you one of the family. I thought you knew that. I've racked my brains for what more we can possibly do."

"Don't kid yourself, Susan. And don't try to fool me.

How many people know she's Finbarr's child? What have you told your family? Or his family? What do the locals believe? They think you've given shelter to a fallen woman. That's the official story, isn't it? Don't take me for a fool. In your mind, I'll always be the loose woman who seduced your man."

She was putting it up to me to bring everything out in the open. I couldn't see myself agreeing to that and certainly Finbarr would never do it.

"We're not France, Céline. In this country, men don't flaunt their mistresses."

"So that's what I am now, the mistress? You're the respectable wife while I'm just the bit on the side."

I wasn't winning here.

"There has to be a way around this," I said. "The three of us need to talk. I'm certain if we talk it out, we'll come up with an answer."

The fire was gone out of her as we walked back down in silence.

~ * ~

Later, alone with Finbarr, I filled him in on the conversation. When I told him she was looking to have her status as the mother of his child fully out in the open, his annoyance showed.

"So that's what this is all about. Well, at last we know what's been eating her. But you can tell her from me it's never going to happen."

"Margo doesn't know, Mona doesn't know," I said. "And they don't need to know anything. As for the neighbours, not a single one of them has ever crossed our doorstep since we arrived here."

"None of your colleagues or my business acquaintances knows anything and that's the way I want to keep it. Can you imagine the gossip if the tabloids ever got wind of it?" He touched the tips of his fingers to his forehead as though massaging an ache.

"Will you tell your parents?"

"No way. They still can't cope with having a married priest for a son. No, we've got to make her face reality, the damage it could do to our reputations. I'm sure she'll see sense."

"That lassie's not going to be fobbed off so easily."

So this is the impossible situation we were faced with. Céline wanted everything out in the open. While everyone knew she was Aline's mother, no one knew Finbarr was the father. What she wanted was for him to come out and acknowledge her as the mother of his child.

But maybe the problem wasn't as intractable as it seemed. Already there was growing in my mind the germ of an idea, an idea so preposterous and wild I couldn't bring myself to mention it to Finbarr. Yet the more I mulled it over, the more convinced I was that it was the only way Céline's demands could be met.

Thirty-six

I was the only one who would really suffer. The other two might protest, raise objections, throw shapes, but the big sacrifice was always going to be mine, no doubt about that. And yet the plan I'd come up with was solely designed to make life easier for Finbarr and Céline, to put an end to the squabbling and sniping.

But if I'd learnt anything from the events of the past few years, it was that I was born to suffer. I'd been slowly, painfully, coming to terms with the loss of my baby son. Then, just as I thought life was becoming bearable, I'd been dealt another blow, the betrayal of my love by my husband's infidelity.

These two events reminded me that my life from the beginning was bound up with sacrifice. And so we were back to the convent again. My mother's painful death leading me to offer my life as a sacrifice to God. I thought I'd managed to push all this into the background since leaving the convent, but now those notions of suffering and sacrifice were right up there again in the forefront of my consciousness.

I was convinced my plan had a good chance of

working, but instinctively I knew Finbarr would find it impossible to buy into it. As for Céline, well she was unpredictable. Depending on her mood, she might think it the perfect answer to her demands or she might fling it back in my face.

I knew I'd have to test his reaction before broaching it to her. My instinct told me he'd find it a total no-no. Anyway, she wasn't due back from France till sometime in January, so I ended up putting it off and putting it off. But I got my chance sooner than I expected.

It was fortuitous really how it came about. After Christmas, Finbarr closed the gallery to give himself a week's holiday. For him, holiday meant getting stuck into some obscure aspect of religious belief with a view to contributing an article to Studies or some other theological journal. He'd often talk to me about his research. He'd been reading up some scholarly investigations into the beliefs and practices of the ancient Celts and found that women were powerful within those societies. For example, he discovered divorce was a relatively straightforward affair and could be arranged at the request of either the husband or wife.

"They even had provision for trial marriages," he told me. "Give it a go for a year and then decide if it was your cup of tea. There's a lot of eye opening stuff here."

"What about polygamy?" I said.

"Oh yes, they had that too."

Here was my chance and I jumped right in.

"These were purely social contracts, right? Religion had nothing to do with it?"

"Why should it?"

"So what's to stop you telling Céline she can be your wife? Wife number two."

He stared at me. No, glared, at me. The frown told me he didn't like what I'd said. His silence told me he couldn't decide if I was serious.

"It's very simple, Finbarr. She wants to be recognised as the mother of your daughter. Your daughter, Finbarr. That's the whole nub of the matter."

"I don't know what exactly you're suggesting, but in my book there's only one wife in this marriage. That's you, Susan, and that's how it's going to stay."

"You're right. Of course I didn't mean announcing it in the paper or anything. I meant convincing the poor deluded girl that you've finally accepted her. No one else need know a thing about it. Not your parents, not my family, not anyone. Just you, me and her."

"I don't want to hear another word about it. I may be liberal about some things, but here I draw the line."

I made a few half-hearted attempts to get him to listen, but I knew I'd lost. The annoying thing was he didn't even ask me exactly what I had in mind. So I left it there and said no more. But I still hadn't given up on my idea. I just shelved it for another day.

~ * ~

The only explanation I can think of is that Mona must have left Céline's door open when she finished cleaning her room. Neither Finbarr nor I would presume to go near it. Céline was paranoid about her space, so we knew to keep away from there.

The first inkling there was anything wrong was when Mona arrived the following morning in a state of agitation. Chaser had found a bag of notebooks on the side of the road, just up from our gate and taken it back to his house for a closer look.

"Tis some kind of foreign writing, Mrs Gray. I told Chaser it must belong to the French woman. We were wondering would you want to come up and have a look."

"I'll be there in a jiffy."

Just outside our gate, draped like a wet rag on the brambles, I saw a single soaked page. I pealed it off, trying not to tear it. On the way up to Chaser's, I saw more pages and decided I'd come back later to recover as much as I could.

Chaser had a pile of copybooks spread out on the table in his gloomy kitchen. He peered at the writing, trying to make it out. He'd been walking in the rain the previous evening when he came across a dog tearing at something in the ditch. When he shouted, the animal scurried back into our driveway.

"It was that collie of yours, missus, I'd swear to it."

"Kandinsky?"

"Look at that bag, missus, the way he chewed it open. Stuff scattered all over the place, it was."

My eyes were getting used to the darkness and I could see it was the sort of canvas haversack used by children as a schoolbag. It had seen years of use, by the look of it.

I knew from the writing that the bag and copybooks were Céline's. I thanked Mona and Chaser for their diligence.

"You did the right thing to call me."

Back in my own kitchen, I plonked the bag on the kitchen table. Kandinsky lay in the corner, his chin on the ground and in the big round eyes an unmistakable expression of guilt.

Finbarr, in dressing gown and slippers, sat sipping strong coffee.

"What have you found?" he said.

"It's Céline's handwriting all right. Her diaries, by the looks of it, going back years. And there's more of it out there on the bushes."

"Pour yourself a cup of coffee first and then we'll try to collect as much as we can."

Like children in August stripping the brambles of berries, we peeled the papers from the bushes and collected them in a plastic bag. It was foolish to imagine we'd be able to find every scrap.

Back in the house, we spread notebooks and loose pages on the kitchen table and left everything to dry in the heat of the fire.

How was I going to break this to Céline? How was she going to react with her private diaries in full public view? She was a very private person, that we knew. Looking again at the torn pages, I could see they came from a single school copybook. A child's diary written in a childish hand. I found myself starting to sort the pages, to put them in sequence. Who can blame me then if I was drawn into reading some of the entries?

Lundy, 27 Mai
Ma première confession.

Aujourd'hui, je suis allé me confesser pendant la toute première fois...

...today I went to confess my sins for the very

first time. Mlle Marette said we should keep in mind it's not M. le Curé we're talking to but Jesus himself. It's all very strange. She said when I take the host on my tongue next Saturday, I will have Jesus in my mouth. I'm trying to figure it all out. Today M. le Curé was Jesus, on Saturday the host will be Jesus. M. le Curé said Jesus told him to look after me because I have no papa. So I have to let him touch me like a papa and I have to let him do whatever Jesus wants. I don't know why Jesus told him to do that, Papa never did that. I was afraid to say stop to Jesus so I closed my eyes and tried to think about the day Papa took me to see the Atlantic Ocean. The waves started way, way out and as they came closer and closer they got longer and longer and a thin white fringe came on the top and I saw all the long white lines moving towards me and I ran down to the edge of the sea and let the cold water run up to my knees and then the sand was sucked out between my toes and it was a lovely, lovely feeling. I was happy with Papa because he would let nothing bad happen to me. Then M. le Curé took his hand away and said he was going to forgive me and the biggest sin of all is to tell anyone what happens in confession, a big, big sin and I will go to hell if I tell. Jesus is a strange man and I don't think I will ever understand him.

I put the rain-smudged page flat on the table and covered it over with my spread hands as if to blank out the horror it contained. I sat there desolate and helpless like someone who has stolen a rare forbidden glimpse into someone else's private hell.

~ * ~

"It's starting to sleet," Finbarr said as he hauled in Céline's luggage. His head and shoulders glistened with moisture. "It won't surprise me if it turns to snow."

Céline told us she'd left her mother behind in a special unit of the hospital where she hovered between life and death. She'd left her number to be contacted the moment there was any change.

Aline showed no particular excitement at her mother's return.

"Say hello to Mamma," I said.

The child said a dutiful hello and turned her attention to arranging her dolls. Kandinsky made up for Aline's indifference. There was much tail swishing as he brushed himself against her legs. I felt horrid that I was about to betray him, to point the finger of blame in his direction. As Céline sat down to a late supper and answered our enquiries about her mother, there hung over me all the time the question of how to tell her about the diaries. Coward that I was, I opted to wait until she found the bag on her bedroom floor where I'd left it. It was a moment I dreaded.

"You must be worn out after the journey," Finbarr said.

"I can't wait to hit the hay." Her face showed the strain of the past week.

As her door closed behind her, I pictured her finding the bag where I'd left it and wondering how it had got there. While I fretted, Finbarr seemed unconcerned. She'd be thankful we had managed to recover so much of her stuff.

The problem, though, was she'd know I'd seen her diary. That was my dilemma.

I found it impossible to relax as I waited. At last I heard her door opening and her determined footsteps approaching on the parquet tiles. My fears were confirmed the minute I saw her expression. It was one of suppressed fury.

"Someone's been in my room."

I pretended to ponder the question.

"Mona was here as usual on Friday."

"Somebody moved my bag, which means somebody was at my wardrobe. Where I keep my personal stuff."

"Oh, the bag, you mean? I've been meaning to tell you. Why don't you sit down? I'll tell you the whole thing."

She stayed standing while I told her all we knew.

"Are you trying to tell me the dog was able to open the door, go in, open the wardrobe and ransack my personal belongings?"

"All I can think is that Mona must have left the door open and the dog went in looking for you. Maybe Mona left the wardrobe open as well."

"We ought to ask Kandinsky about it," said Finbarr. It was the wrong time for wisecracks.

"So the dog's to blame," she snapped. "You're all agreed on that. Seems everyone else is completely innocent. Well, since we're blaming the dog, he'll have to bear the consequences. It's the only way he'll learn. Now, if you'll excuse me, I'm badly in need of sleep."

We heard her door close behind her.

"What does she mean about consequences for the dog?" I whispered.

"She's exhausted after the journey." He leaned forward with the poker to coax the last bit of heat from the embers. "At least she accepts your explanation. She'll soon get forget the whole thing."

Finbarr was first asleep. He had a wonderful capacity for slotting everything into compartments. Bedtime was for sleeping and nothing would come between him and his night's sleep.

I was woken by a howling sound. It sounded like the banshee of my childhood. The wailing of the Fairy Woman signified an imminent death. I gave Finbarr a vigorous shake.

"Did you hear that?"

"Hear what?"

"A sort of crying somewhere outside. Like an animal in agony."

"Foxes have to eat too, you know."

"It was horrible, almost human."

"I'll check it out in the morning. Try to get some sleep."

I woke again to the sound of Céline's car leaving the driveway. Light streamed between the curtains.

"She gave no hint last night she was going anywhere," I said.

Finbarr yawned.

"She doesn't have to account for all her movements."

I peeped into Aline's room and found her sound asleep in her cot. In the kitchen, Céline's coffee mug stood half empty on the table. The rug where Kandinsky slept was unoccupied. I made porridge for myself and shook out Finbarr's corn flakes while he shaved. When he came into the kitchen, the first thing I said was, "There's no sign of Kandinsky. She must have let him out before she went."

"He always comes straight back in."

"Kandinsky! Here boy!" At the open door, I called him several times with no response. "I'll take a look outside. God knows what kind of mischief he's up to."

"Cover yourself. It's starting to snow."

I scanned the road in both directions. Céline never took him in the car since she couldn't tolerate dog's hairs on the upholstery. With an increasing sense of foreboding, I went to search at the back of the house where Kandinsky liked to seek out the smells of wild creatures that came visiting in the night.

Through the wet snowflakes I slithered down the garden to the scrubby neglected area where the furze and bracken never rest in their battle to reclaim lost territory. Down there you're out of view of the house, screened by shrubs and fruit trees. It's where you can hide from the world if secrecy or privacy is what you crave. A space presided over by an ancient hawthorn sending its twisted branches out from the side of the old stonewall boundary.

That's where I found him. The gnarled old tree put out a horizontal branch about five or six feet above the ground. Someone had fixed a length of rope to this branch so that branch and rope conspired to carry the weight of Kandinsky's rigid body swinging in barely perceptible motion among the drifting snowflakes. The whites of his eyes were revealed in a way I'd never seen, as if the orbs had tried to burst from their sockets. The tongue hung out to an impossible length from the side of his mouth and I pictured the unfortunate legs threshing about in a futile attempt to gain a foothold as the cruel noose tightened around his windpipe. I threw my arms about the stiffened body and struggled to lift him. It mattered to me that he shouldn't be left there dangling. I didn't hear Finbarr approach but he was beside me and between us we managed to loosen the knot and lower the sad, forlorn body to the ground. We stood there looking down at him. Neither of us spoke, each of us, I imagine, struggling to make sense of what we'd found. As for Aline, how were we going to explain the absence of her faithful friend and companion? The loss of Kandinsky was the loss of a part of the family.

We dragged ourselves away, leaving the limp form lying there, to go inside and try to puzzle out why a harmless innocent pet would have to pay such an appalling price for what amounted to no more than harmless curiosity. For on this we were agreed, that there could be no doubt whatever who was responsible. It was an outrageous act of revenge.

Time would pass before we got the opportunity to confront Céline. That morning she went missing as she'd done in the past. She'd a habit of taking off like this and most times we'd be told she'd been with her bohemian friends. However a week went by and there was still no sign of her. The anger and grief we experienced at the brutal slaying of our gentle Kandinsky began to give way to a gnawing worry about what might have happened to Céline herself.

For by this stage, we could be in no doubt whatever that the balance of her mind was more than a little disturbed.

Thirty-seven

It was a male voice asking to speak to Finbarr Gray. I passed the phone to Finbarr and almost immediately he was signalling me to pick up the phone in the kitchen. I recognised the name of the psychiatric hospital and heard him tell Finbarr he had a patient who'd given his name as next-of-kin. Céline Dubois. Céline, he explained, had presented herself ten days ago for voluntary admission. The patient was now ready to be discharged and he wanted to be sure she'd be returning to a safe environment. Finbarr had the presence of mind to ask about her diagnosis.

"Indications of early psychosis…under control. The programme I've prescribed should keep her stable. Needless to say, it's important she keeps to the regime. That's vital."

The call shouldn't have been that big a surprise given the irrational eruptions we'd witnessed and the terrible death she'd inflicted on the defenceless dog. Yet the doctor's words left us shaken. What exactly had we let ourselves in for with this strange girl? Where was it going to end?

I made a point of coming home early Friday afternoon to be alone with her. I thought I detected a new sadness behind her eyes, though when she talked she was perfectly reasonable and rational. Moreover she seemed ready to talk. Don't they teach people with emotional problems the value of talk as therapy?

I wanted to explain how I'd come to read her childhood diary.

"Don't blame yourself," Céline said. "I'm actually relieved someone knows at last. In there, you know, in the hospital, I talked about things I'd bottled up for years. Every morning we sat around in a circle and everyone was given a chance to, you know, let it all out. It opened my eyes that everyone's story as bad as the next. Jesus, I'd no idea there were so many people suffering in silence."

"I'd love you to tell me about it, what happened to you, way back."

"I'm not sure how much you saw in my diary."

"Just enough to let me know your childhood wasn't a barrel of laughs."

"My father died coming up to Christmas, a week after my birthday. I was seven that December.

"He can't have been that old?"

"Mid-fifties. He never really took care of himself. A year later, Aline my older sister died. I told you that. Just me and Maman left and when they dragged Maman away, I was a virtual orphan."

"What do you mean... dragged…?"

"The woman could take no more. She just cracked up and had to be shoved into an asylum."

"She's been there ever since?"

"Ever since. Until she took that turn before Christmas. Funny, isn't it? She only gets out of the madhouse to waste away with the life of a vegetable. Poor Maman. She was dealt a crummy hand."

"Why do bad things happen to good people?"

"When I saw her thrown there in a coma, I cried. I was crying for her and I was crying for myself. I wanted to ask her why she didn't take me to the asylum with her. It couldn't have been worse than what happened."

"Your father and sister dead and your poor mother in the asylum. Where did you go?"

"I went to live with relations thirty kilometres away. I made my first Communion among strangers. I was abused by the priest. Next time he sent for me, I refused to go and they forced me to tell what happened. My aunt called me a dirty-minded little liar. My uncle took full advantage of my situation and started to rape me. I was tainted, he said, so it made no difference what he did."

Her hand felt around for Kandinsky's familiar touch, but there was no Kandinsky there, nothing to ease the pain. I waited for her to go on.

"Then it was Confirmation. I'm all dressed up in my Confirmation outfit and standing in front of the bishop waiting to be made a soldier of Christ. And who do you think was standing right there next to the bishop? The Curé.

"You don't mean the same…?"

"The same abusing bastard. Here's the bishop rubbing oil on my forehead and all I can see is that filthy grin on the Curé's face. At that moment I swore I'd never set foot inside a church again. How could I serve a God who allowed little girls to be violated by His own ministers? It made no sense then and it makes no sense now."

I couldn't answer. Nothing I could've said would have been in any way adequate. After a long pause ,she spoke again.

"I really miss that dog."

"We're all lost without him. Little Aline. I showed her his grave but it doesn't mean anything to her. None of us can make sense of it."

"Me neither. Poor old Kandy. He never judged, never criticised, never wavered."

"Why did you do it, Céline? How could you kill a creature that loved you so much?"

"I've spent the past two weeks trying to figure it out and I still don't know the answer."

"What do you remember about that night?"

"I was fuming at you and Finbarr. I went to bed. I must have slept. I had a dream."

"What did you dream?"

"I was in this dark room. More like a cell really. Maman was there. There were other women and they crowded in around us, grotesque women, mad gibbering women. Maman put a rope around her neck and the end of the rope was tied to the leg of a bed. And all the time she never took her eyes off me. Then she climbed onto the window ledge and she was afraid to jump. She looked at me with pleading eyes. 'Push me, Céline. Push. Just a little push.'

"But I couldn't bring myself to do it. 'I love you too much, Maman.'

"'I'm begging you, mon enfant. In the name of God and His holy mother.'

"And all the women cried in a kind of chorus, 'listen to your poor mother, child, don't turn away.

'I can't, I can't.'

'Don't harden your heart against her, child, just a little push, a little push.'

"When I pushed, the rope ran whirring across the ledge before it snapped taut with a shudder. And the women were laughing, laughing at me with a mocking laugh. And an old hag with no eyes in her sockets and no teeth in her mouth made a cackling sound in my face and her jeering was taken up by all the others closing in about me in a tight circle, pointing their bony fingers in my face. 'You've done for her, child, now you've killed her.'"

"I don't remember leaving my bed. My nightdress clung to my skin in the sleety rain. I knew I had to destroy those demons. I found a rope hanging at the back of the shed and I made a noose around Kandinsky's neck and led him to the thorn tree. I watched the life choking out of him and felt a strange release. The demons were destroyed. At last I'd been able to escape the past.

"Next morning I saw the terrible thing I'd done to Kandinsky and knew it was no dream. I drove to the hospital and begged them to take me in."

"Come here, Céline. Come to me."

She came to me and I embraced her. Tears mingled on our moist cheeks. I resolved then that if there was anything in the world I could do to help this unfortunate child I would not hesitate to do it.

Then I remembered my original plan to bring her into a closer family circle, a step up from where she stood at present as permanent guest and mother of a fatherless child. Finbarr would have to be persuaded, though, and he'd already made it clear he wouldn't go along with it. I said nothing to Céline and decided to wait for the right moment to broach it to him.

~ * ~

Charles gave instructions he wasn't to be disturbed.

"I've just had word from headquarters, Susan. It looks like Maeve is on the market."

"Why on earth would they want to sell out now? We're performing better than ever. We've beaten our sales targets."

"You've got to understand the way these people's minds work. They stand back as we build the magazine to become a leader in the field. Then they move to cash in their gains."

"Where does that leave you and me? Suppose a new owner wants to make a clean sweep and put their own people in place?"

"Anything's possible. Your guess is as good as mine. Anyway, I'm going over to London on Monday to check it out with the top brass. I want you with me. We'll get a better handle on what's going on. As you say, it's important for both of us."

I suspected he had some scheme up his sleeve, but I was happy to wait and see how he'd play it.

~ * ~

"I'll be in England most of the week. I presume you'll be able to take care of Aline?" I said.

Céline used the point of her brush to trace a very fine line across the canvas. She worked with the assurance that comes from years of experience.

"Who's going to look after your husband?"

"He'll look after himself."

"I mean who's going to keep him warm in bed while you're off gallivanting with your boss?"

I looked to see was she joking. Céline seldom joked about anything.

"He can suffer in silence for four or five nights. Remember what they say, absence makes the heart grow fonder."

"Absence, maybe. Abstinence, not so sure. What d'you think it'll do to him?"

"One thing I do know is I'm not about to share my man with anyone."

"I thought you were my friend."

"And that's how I'd like it to stay."

She smiled and took up a brushful of vermilion.

Later I spoke to Finbarr.

"I pray to God she stays on an even keel for a while. Those mood swings of hers!"

"I'll try to keep her happy," he said.

"That could be tricky. She has this notion she's entitled to more than she's getting."

"If she thinks she's going to share my bed, she can forget it."

"I worry she might try to harm herself."

"Hold on a minute. You're not suggesting you'd allow her…"

"Of course not. I just meant she'll need gentle handling. She's vulnerable."

~ * ~

Charles was surprisingly well-versed in Irish politics.

He was predicting the government wouldn't run its term to the end of '87.

"Fitzgerald imagines he's in the driving seat, but I'll tell you something for nothing, Susan, it wouldn't take a lot for Dick Spring to gather his troops and walk out. They're a touchy crowd, those Labour people."

Pretty perceptive as things turned out.

He talked about the budget and the defeat of the divorce referendum. Everything in fact but the reason he and I were on that flight to London. All I knew was that we were to attend a vital meeting on the future of Maeve.

When he grew tired of discussing politics, he began to talk about his concerns for his wife.

"She hasn't been well lately. Emily's never been very strong. I told you before about her heart problem. It's always been there, but it seems to be getting worse. Low energy. The least little thing and she's exhausted. We're getting it checked out. I hope to God it's nothing serious."

"And the children?"

"David and Rachel are good kids. Fingers crossed they stay that way."

~ * ~

We'd eaten on the plane, so we took a taxi straight to the meeting. The chairman left it to the group CEO to do most of the talking. Chambers went on about how delighted they all were with our performance in Dublin and the way we'd succeeded in changing the face of Maeve and driving sales to new levels. Between us, we'd made the Irish operation one of the best performing divisions in the group.

That all turned out to be so much hot air when he went on to explain how they needed cash to fund their new acquisition in South Africa. It was going to mean hiving off some of the smaller divisions. Maeve had been selected as one of those to go. Unfortunately.

"Thank you, Chambers. Now, do we have any questions?" Major Thomas swung his gaze around to where Charles and I sat. "How about our friends from Ireland? We'd like to hear your reaction."

Charles cleared his throat to speak. Audrey, a middle aged woman with her hair tied back and a mole on her chin, waited with pencil poised.

"Would the board be disposed to consider a management buy-out?"

All eyes looked at Charles, then at me and again at Charles. The major's face betrayed no hint of surprise, though his fingers made a little drumming motion on the polished surface of the mahogany table.

"Interested in taking Dublin for yourself, Charles? Now, that could turn out to be a smart move, right enough. Think you can raise the capital?"

"Provided the terms are right. There's a lot to be teased out. I thought I'd declare my interest at an early stage. That's all it is at this point, an expression of interest."

"I understand. I'll bring your proposal to the full board, Charles. Then we'll talk again. As you say, we need to sort out the details and check out your financial backing."

~ * ~

We dined in the Queen's Head near Charles' place in the Cotswolds. Emily had begged us to excuse her. She was suffering an inexplicable lack of energy.

"What's your own view, Susan?" said Charles. "You think I'm mad?"

Charles topped up my glass with the excellent Bordeaux red.

"Not the least bit mad. Maeve has never been healthier. Why not go for it if you can find the funding."

"Maeve's got great potential. You and me, we know the business inside out. We've seen off all the challengers. We've found a formula that works. We understand the market. Between us we can drive our baby forward into the future."

"What exactly are you saying?"

"Isn't it obvious? We're a winning team, you and I. I want it to stay that way."

"Stay what way? I'm afraid you've lost me."

"If you'll agree to join me, Susan, we'll put in an offer for the magazine."

His excitement was almost boyish. For my part, I'd been down this road before and last time around, Finbarr and I had decided it was too big a risk. Could it be different this time, I wondered?

"You're hesitating, Susan."

"I'm hesitating, you're right. You spring this on me and expect an instant answer. Don't you think my husband might have some say?"

"Finbarr's a businessman. He can spot an opportunity. Look how he's been expanding his own business. How many galleries now? Three? Talk to him, Susan. He'll see the sense in it."

Next day the bones of a deal began to take shape. Charles let it be known he'd lined up some interested parties. He also told them I was willing to remain on in an executive role.

That evening we drove over to Evesham. Again Emily was too weak to join us. Charles, I knew, would want to spend the time talking about his business proposition. He came at it in a roundabout way.

"You've been lost in thought, Susan. Bet you're pining for that man of yours!"

I denied it, of course, but Charles was perceptive. Finbarr had indeed been the focus of my thoughts. Finbarr and Céline. Were they, too, at this moment sitting down to a meal and sharing a bottle of wine? And later, in my absence, how would he handle it if she started pressing her demands for more?

"What do you think he'll do, Susan? How will he react?"

Charles dabbed his mouth with the corner of the linen napkin and looked at me with the hint of a smile.

"Finbarr? Oh, he's pretty cagey," I said. "He doesn't make many mistakes. He'll give it a lot of thought before he makes a decision. But I'll say this much. If he decides to back me, he'll commit himself to the hilt. That's the kind he is."

"Do I hear the loyal wife speaking? D'you think he misses you when you leave him on his own like this?"

Charles had just drained his second glass of wine and reached to refill both glasses. He was in a relaxed mood. I too was a little more relaxed but not so relaxed that I was about to reveal to this upright church-going Anglican any anxieties I might have about the evolving situation back home.

"All jokes aside, we do have a good relationship, thank God. I don't have to tell you how important that is."

His intelligent blue eyes studied me as I spoke. I was relieved when he got off that particular topic and spent the rest of the evening outlining his hopes and plans for Maeve.

~ * ~

As I flew back alone across the short stretch of sea separating the two islands, I wanted nothing to spoil the warmth and joy of our reunion. I had no interest in talking about what might or mightn't have happened while I was away. I pushed aside all those questions for another time. For now, I'd be happy to have Finbarr beside me and share with him our cosy bed in the Wicklow hills.

He made love with a blend of tenderness and passion. Afterwards he held me as if he never wished to let me go and I slept sound in the comfort of his arms. It was going to be the following morning before I heard his account of how he'd been tempted and how he'd fought off the assault on his virtue.

Thirty-eight

She was up and dressed and grabbing some coffee with a slice of toast and marmalade. She had on a warm woolly sweater and heavy slacks.

"Heading off this morning, Céline? Looks like we've had a heavy frost last night."

It was something of a routine for Saturday mornings—Céline getting out of the house to spend the day with her friends, leaving Finbarr and me with some welcome space to relax and do our own thing. We'd leave little Aline to wake in her own time.

"Watch the road," I said, "it could be treacherous."

"Might as well go one way as another."

She said this without a hint of a smile. It's all she said. Never the slightest acknowledgement that Finbarr and I were being left to look after Aline. Nor did she show the slightest interest in how I'd got on in London. She's in one of her moods, I thought.

I went back to bed and found Finbarr had been wakened by the sound of her car driving off.

"She didn't seem in the best of form," I said. "How did you two get on when I was away?"

"Crazy. I've never seen anything like it."

"That bad? Tell me."

"Where do I start? You're hardly out of the house when she starts walking around in her nightdress. At first I say nothing. Then next evening same thing. So I ask her if she needs a new dressing gown. I thought I was being tactful."

"What did she say to that?"

"You've no idea. It's like it's all pent up just waiting for something to set off the explosion. Recrimination and tears. I'm accused of treating her like dirt. All that stuff we heard before. I'll leave it to your imagination."

"She'll get over it. She always gets over it."

"No, but it's different. It's the morbid way she's been talking. Like someone who's had enough."

"Like what?"

"The other night she's sitting there after putting Aline to bed. It's like she's brooding and then out of the blue, she says, 'what's the best way to kill yourself, at the end of a rope or under a train?' "

"I'd say that got your attention."

"I just said why on earth would anyone want to do that? And she said, 'when there's nothing to live for, you think about the grave.' "

"And what did you say?"

"What do you say? I said things are never as bad as they seem. I said if you keep thinking like that, things only get worse. And I asked her what would happen to Aline with no mother to look after her."

"Did she say anything to that?"

"'My poor little baby.' She said it over and over like she's talking to herself. It frightened me, I can tell you, to see her like that."

It frightened me too to hear it, this talk about killing herself. I wondered if she was taking her tablets as she was supposed to.

Later in the morning, I noticed Finbarr taking an interest in Aline, going through her books with her, explaining things, the meanings of words. Then taking down one of his own books, he started telling her stories from Greek mythology.

Despite Aline's amusement at the strange tales she was hearing, there was a sense of foreboding hanging about the place, not in the least helped when Finbarr put on an LP of Barber's Adagio for Strings. The mournful lament of the violins spoke to me of immeasurable sorrow. I found myself worrying about Céline's safety.

"Do you think she's okay? What time is it now?"

"Céline? Relax. She's often this late getting home."

Nevertheless we both stayed up until we heard the wheels of her car crunching to its usual spot at the front of the house. We heard her come in and go straight to her room, but I didn't hear the front door closing after her. A few minutes later we heard movement in the corridor and the door to Aline's room squeaking open. I looked at Finbarr and he too was alert to her movements. Aline's sleepy voice told us she'd been taken from her bed. I went out into the passage to see what was happening and saw that Céline had wrapped the child in a woollen shawl and was carrying her towards the front door.

"You're not going out again Céline? Is everything all right?"

I caught the startled expression.

"I can't hang around or I'll miss the train."

"The train? At this hour?"

Without answering she stepped into the freezing night taking Aline with her. The engine revved, a quick reverse, the crunch of the gears and I watched as the car left the drive and roared off down the road.

"What's going on?" Finbarr was beside me at the front door.

"She said something about catching a train. And she's taken Aline with her!"

Finbarr let out a cry of anguish.

"Where's she headed?" he shouted.

"She just said train."

"That could mean either Bray or Greystones. We have to stop her. Get a move on."

"Okay, I'll head for Bray," I said. "You take Greystones. There's no time to lose."

The train would reach Bray around midnight. My old car had nothing like the power of Céline's, so there was little chance of catching her. My only hope was I'd get there before the train arrived. The streets of Bray were empty except for a cluster of men outside the closed doors of a pub, cigarettes glowing in the darkness. I took a shortcut down Novara Avenue and as I got closer to the station, I felt the grip of fear in my throat. My mouth was dry, my heart pounding. Despair at first, then a wild hope. It was all a charade, I told myself, a stunt she'd thought up to frighten us. I tried to convince myself she'd no intention of going through with it. The threat of suicide as a way of getting notice. A desperate cry for help. I begged my angel to get there ahead of me to stop her before it was too late. Saint Michael, I'm begging you, don't let us down.

I saw the red MG with the hood pushed back, the driver's door swinging open, abandoned on the roadway with no regard for other traffic. I pulled in ahead of it, jumped out and started running towards the gates. I heard the creaks and groans of the barrier beginning its descent as the train approached. Warning lights began to flash. The train's siren sounded. But where was Céline?

I caught sight of a woman dragging a child by the hand towards the crossing, a child too sleepy to keep up. There was a purposeful determination in the woman's stride. I strained my eyes in the ghostly light of a full moon and saw it was her. I ran towards the gate. Through the soft fabric of my slipper a sharp pebble cut into my sole. As woman and child reached the narrow gap leading onto the tracks, I screamed.

"Stop her! Stop her! She's going to kill the child!"

People were waiting to meet passengers off the train. They looked at me and then in the direction I was pointing. A young man was quick to react. He ran and grabbed Céline and dragged her back outside the barrier. The train was already slowing but it would have made little difference had she been able to fling herself and the innocent Aline in its path.

Even before I got there, a garda had a hand on Céline's shoulder while his female companion knelt on the ground talking to Aline. I threw my arms around Céline's neck and she melted into my embrace. Tears of relief and shock ran down my cheeks and onto the golden head of little Aline clinging to my legs. Whether Céline's tears were of gratitude or frustration, I'd no way of knowing. What happened after that is all a blur. Aline was handed over to me to bring home while Céline allowed herself to be put in the police car. The female garda promised to take her straight to hospital. I supposed they knew what to do.

Before I collapsed into bed that night, I made the effort to find my diary and scrawl a couple of desperate lines under the date, 14 Mar 1987, just three days before Aline's second birthday.

The second worst night of my life. Two lives almost gone.

What can I do to ensure nothing like this will ever happen again?

~ * ~

"He's very frail, Susan. We must be prepared for whatever happens."

When I'd got the phone call, I sensed things were serious but now standing in Matron's office I knew things were even worse than I'd expected. Dad had had a number of strokes and it was clear what she was trying to tell me. He could be carried off at any time.

That night I slept at Johnny's and spent much of the next day at the home with my father. Though I sat with him for hours, I felt unable to reach him. I tried to chat but couldn't be sure how much was getting through. His face contorted when he tried to speak and his words were garbled. The only consolation was that my being there must reassure him and take the edge off his isolation. I could read the gratitude in his eyes and that in itself meant a lot to me.

That night in my bed my mind was in turmoil. Thoughts of my father alternating with thoughts of Céline. Finbarr had told me on the phone he'd picked her up from the hospital and brought her home. Her second spell in a psychiatric unit had come to an end and we could only hope she'd never have cause to go back there. I prayed she'd settle down and give up the ceaseless taunting of Finbarr about his supposed neglect. It was so unjustified. So undeserved.

When I got back home, she seemed much subdued and we suspected she was heavily medicated.

While Dad lingered, I travelled most weekends to be with him. I owed him that. He'd stood by me when times were tough, had never measured his efforts for any of us. How could I grudge him my time in the short space left to him on earth?

It wasn't easy, though, this pressure coming on top of everything else. Especially since negotiations for the buyout were in full swing.

"I've been onto Dad's bank, he knows about it," Finbarr told me one evening. "They're willing to back us, provided you get an equal stake in the new entity with Charles."

When he and Charles got together to discuss the future of the fledgling company, it was clear Finbarr was already on top of the whole magazine publishing business. He and I were now partners in marriage, partners in business. This extra bond must have helped as we faced the future with an unstable Céline at the heart of the household.

~ * ~

Céline was the focus of conversation when I met my friend and confidante in our usual nook in the Wicklow Hotel.

Jennifer already knew all about Céline's troubled background, her childhood experiences at the hands of her abusers and her mother's incarceration in an asylum for the insane. I filled her in on the suicide attempt. She'd treat anything I told her with absolute confidentiality.

"You're not telling me she'd have killed the little girl as well? She has to be really disturbed to do something like that."

"My mind is addled trying to work it out, but it all seems to stem from some kind of fixation around Finbarr."

"She sees herself as a sort of second wife, this is what I hear you saying."

"I didn't take it seriously for a long time, but then something clicked inside me and I began to think why not?"

"You're joking, Susan?"

"Don't look so shocked, Jen. What I have in mind is pretty harmless really. I came round to thinking why don't we stage a sort of mock-marriage ceremony. It's not going to hurt anyone and if it keeps her happy…"

"But Finbarr? How's he going to take it?"

"I tried to tell him what I had in mind, but he wouldn't listen."

"So that's it, then."

"He'll listen now. She tried to kill herself and Aline. That changes everything."

~ * ~

Actually it was easy in the end. I'd coaxed Finbarr into coming out onto the moor for a walk in the spring air. It was one way of getting away to somewhere we could discuss things.

"Okay, I'm listening," he said. "It sounds mad but I'm listening."

"You know that crowd she hangs around with? Those

hippies or whatever they are. Out all night on the hill of Tara celebrating the solstice. Loonies, but there you go."

"Just tell me what you're getting at."

"Think of them as her extended family. She relates to them. Okay, she's got us, but after us who's she got? She's got that crowd. So why don't we use them to give her what she's looking for?"

"I'm afraid I'm not with you at all."

"All we have to do is set up some kind of ceremony with all her friends present, some way of recognising her position in the family."

He looked doubtful.

"I don't fancy drawing that crowd around here."

"So what's the alternative? I'll tell you. The alternative is she continues to act the she-cat, throwing tantrums without warning or provocation. Not to mention what she might do to herself and Aline if she …"

"Okay, okay. Point taken. I'll go along with it. But this has to be kept strictly in the family, strictly amongst ourselves."

So I'd got Finbarr's grudging agreement. I still hadn't broached it to Céline and I couldn't guess how she might react. Logic told me she should be delighted to be offered what she'd been agitating for. But what if my pretend marriage ceremony didn't measure up to her demands and what she was looking for went way beyond what either Finbarr or I could possibly agree to?

Thirty-nine

"Fred Hay might do it." Her face and eyes were lit with an excitement I hadn't seen in ages.

I'd hardly begun to explain my notion to Céline when she grasped at the idea and ran with it, made it her own.

"Fred who?" I said.

"Fred Hay. He's big, I can tell you that. Founded the whole thing in Cornwall."

I was about to ask her what whole thing but decided it wasn't important.

"Why don't we go ahead and ask him, then?"

Within days Céline was able to tell me this Fred, founder of whatever he founded, had agreed to officiate at a Celtic ritual for Céline and Finbarr.

Finbarr didn't seem very enthused, but was coaxed into taking part. We picked the date, Mayday, the morning of Beltaine, the magic morning when the ancient Irish kindled the Bright Fire of Fertility to invoke the blessing of the gods.

Once the date was decided, things began to take shape. We were going to need robes for the occasion. There were no strict rules about this just so long as we looked like priests and priestesses. Céline had no trouble putting together an outfit from bits and pieces supplied by her bohemian friends. Finbarr dug out a long white mass vestment for me to wear. For himself, he borrowed a monk's outfit from a friar friend of his.

And so we were all geared up. We gave Margo the day off. Aline was to play an important role in the proceedings.

~ * ~

Fred Hay, an Englishman with an interest in all things Celtic, arrived on Sunday afternoon on the eve of the ceremony as we were having brunch on the patio. Céline and I walked him up to the woodland clearing not far from the house and he pronounced it a 'propitious location.' Fred took charge and had us all collecting firewood for the ceremonial fire. I caught Finbarr breaking up a worm-infested chair he'd dug out of the shed. Later that afternoon, a van-load of Céline's friends arrived and were straight away dragooned into carting the sticks to where the fire would be lit.

Luckily I didn't have to provide beds for this pack. Apart from one couple who slept in the minibus, the rest were happy to camp out in the garden.

"Sure you'll be warm enough there?" said Finbarr.

"We'll make out, man." They looked as if they were used to the rough life.

The evening air grew heavy with a pungent sick-sweet smell and I noticed a reefer passing from hand to hand and mouth to mouth. Thus relaxed, they retired to their hard beds on the cold earth beneath the glistening stars. They planned to be up well before sunrise.

Fred Hay, who would sleep indoors, showed no inclination to retire early. By the blazing log fire in the lounge, we relaxed and talked while the wine mellowed our brains. There was little thought of the dawn, only a few hours away, as Fred gave forth on what he called 'pre-Patrician spirituality' and the re-awakening of neo-paganism in recent years. Groups were springing up all over the place to explore the beliefs of the Celtic peoples who lived in these parts long before the arrival of Christianity.

"Neo-pagans?" I said. "You mean like the Wicca?"

"The Wicca's one aspect, sure. People who want to revive the old practices."

"But why would anyone want to go back a couple of thousand years?" I said.

"Why? Our ancestors had a respect for nature, something you don't see much of nowadays. Plus they understood that the spirit world lies at the heart of everything."

I could see Finbarr listening intently, waiting for his moment. There was nothing he loved more than a good argument about religion.

"Okay, Fred," he said. "If I understand you right, there are gods and spirits in every hill, every stream, every tree. All over the place, in fact."

"Now you've got it."

"That's pure, unadulterated animism."

"Spot on. Call it animism, call it pantheism. Christianity would like us to forget that nature is infused with a soul. Every tree, rock and hill is possessed of a spirit. And despite the best efforts of Christianity, those beliefs just won't go away. You've holy wells the length and breadth of your own beautiful country. People go there to beg for favours and cures. You can't deny that."

My interest was aroused. I just had to ask him.

"If that's right, what you just said, then it means the Sugarloaf out there is a living entity."

"But of course. It's a significant feature of the landscape. It casts its influence over the whole locality. I'd be surprised if you never felt it, the spirit of the mountain exercising its power."

This from a man I'd never met before, a stranger who seemed to have divined my spiritual relationship to that mountain. I said nothing, however, content in the warm comforting glow of my secret knowledge.

Finbarr continued to quiz Fred about his activities and Fred began to talk about his efforts to bring the disparate groups of believers together under one umbrella. A number of groves had agreed to affiliate within the 'Brythonic Order of Druids' based in Cornwall.

"Do you believe in a Supreme Being?" Finbarr was determined to pin him down. "Where did all this...I mean the whole of nature…where did it all come from?"

"You're talking about a creator, right? Why do you need a creator? Think of the universe itself as the Supreme Being. The universe has always existed and always will."

Finbarr turned to Céline, who had been listening but silent.

"Well, Céline, what do you think? What's the meaning of life?"

"Meaning? What's meaning? There is no meaning. We live, we fuck, we die. That's all there is."

"How can you talk like that?" I said. "If life has no meaning, where's the point in going on?"

"Exactly," she said. "Where's the point?"

We went to bed when it was almost time to get up. I found it impossible to sleep. Too much going around in my head.

"There's a lot in what he says," I whispered.

Finbarr yawned and turned his back. "Fred's for the birds. Don't fall for any of that shit. The whole thing's daft. Up in the clouds."

~ * ~

There was no one about in the pre-dawn to see the bleary-eyed line of stragglers wind its way along the track that takes you into the shadowland of the spruce forest. Only the laughing mountain stream was there to mock us in its exuberant dash to the sea.

Too sleepy to talk, we padded in silence past the thatched cottage that was home to Chaser and Mona Cambridge. Even the irascible bitch who normally kept watch must have been deep in slumber for she remained oblivious of the passage of the pagans past the bolted door.

When we reached the wood-pile left ready the previous evening, we each took an armful of sticks which we clutched to our chests as we pushed our passage through a barrier of brambles and emerged at last into the open space set to be the place of ritual.

We stood in a clearing where wood felling had taken place in the past but where the inevitable advance of nature brought brambles, ferns and seedling trees struggling to re-assert their need for space. At the centre of all this vibrant growth was a grassy patch wide enough to take our small band.

Under Fred's directions, we built a pile of kindling. We laid out a circle of stones in a ten foot radius about the fire. We removed our warm coats and jackets to reveal our ritual robes. At Fred's command, we formed a circle just inside the ring of stones and stood facing the centre.

I took the opportunity to study how everyone was dressed. An amazing assortment of styles had one thing in common in that everyone's robes reached to the ground. It was the way you might imagine some esoteric order of pagan priests draped for the sacred rituals. While most wore white, a few experimented with red or green.

Amongst the rest, Céline stood out. She'd put some thought into the design of her costume, a full length dress in three vertical strips, the turquoise of the front and back complimented by a wide strip of Capri blue with a broad sweep of gold from the shoulder, over the left breast and down to the bare left foot. She was flushed but smiling. I stood on her right, with Finbarr looking bored and absent on her left. Aline slept in the arms of a middle-aged matron.

Céline's friends seemed well used to these goings on, and one or two made themselves busy collecting drops of dew in a little dish of turned ash.

Fred used a cigarette lighter to get the fire going and I wondered what our bronze-age ancestors would have made of that piece of magic. The fire took hold and flames leapt into the brightening arc of the dawn sky as I waited to see what would happen. Fred stooped to pick a book from the ground and began to read in a language I didn't recognise. We joined hands in an unbroken circle and I wondered if anyone else understood who or what he might be addressing or what blessings he called down on the little group of worshippers.

He read his text at a galloping pace, conscious perhaps of a need to get to the nub of the ceremony. The irreverent thoughts pushing themselves to the front of my mind at that moment had to do with the incongruity of Fred's attire, the monkish white robe mocked by a black felt hat with the crown pushed up in a dome.

He rummaged in his sack for an earthenware bowl into which he poured a buttery liquid. When he spooned some of the liquid into the fire, there was a blazing flash. The bowl was passed around so that we each might cast a golden spoonful on the flames. The same thing happened with handfuls of wheat and barley, each sacrificial offering being followed by a reading from Fred's book of invocations. When we threw grains of aromatic incense on the fire, the air grew heady with a sweet-smelling intoxication.

I knew something was about to happen when the joss-stick in my hand was lit by a young woman called Evelyn, who moved about with a glowing ember from the sacred fire.

Two men used branches to push aside the burning coals, splitting the fire in separate segments with a passage between.

Finbarr was instructed to take Céline by the hand and lead her across the smouldering space between the fires. He himself was wearing shoes but since Céline was barefoot, he had to lift her off the ground, which he did with evident embarrassment.

Then an even more symbolic moment. With Finbarr back on one side of the fire and Céline on the other, she passed little Aline across to him as if to say here is the child I have given you. At least to me that was the clear meaning and I kept telling myself that whatever else this might be, it wasn't a marriage ceremony. Whatever the initiates might be thinking, Finbarr was still married to me. In no sense could he be married to someone else. I'd dreamed up this little piece of make-believe to humour Céline in the hope it would put an end to her persistent demands for attention.

These thoughts were interrupted when Evelyn, in the role of acolyte, came forward with her little wooden bowl of freshly gathered dew. Fred dipped his right thumb in the pristine liquid and used it to anoint the foreheads of Finbarr, Céline and Aline in turn. "In the mystery of the ever renewing dew, I call upon our gracious Brigit, in whose honour we have kindled the sacred fire of Beltaine, powerful patron of healing, fire and fertility, to look with kindness on these her children, to make them loving and fruitful, in tune with the whole of nature. Make fecund the earth, its crops, animals and people that they may flourish and thrive in the hands of the gods."

A bottle of red wine emerged from somewhere and a goblet passed around for everyone to partake. Relaxed and laughing, they took it in turn to shake Finbarr's hand, hug Céline and make clucking noises at Aline, by then wide awake. Finbarr looked uncomfortable. I was bemused to find myself being congratulated, whether on my new relationship with Céline or my old relationship with Finbarr, I couldn't tell. I decided to view the ceremony as marking the creation of a new entity, a combination consisting of me and Finbarr as husband and wife, Finbarr and Céline as father and mother, three adults and a child forming a unique family unit. It was the only way I could rationalise what we had accomplished that morning.

We filed along the stony lane as the sun showed just above Bray Head to the East. As we drew near Mona and Chaser's cottage, the sound of a barking dog came from within and a curtain moved in one corner of a little window.

Back in the house we grilled a mountain of black and white puddings, sausages, tomatoes and sliced potatoes and brewed gallons of tea to wash it all down. Once replenished, our guests showed no desire to hang about and began to pack away tents and bedding in the mini-van. Fred, too, said he had to be hitting the road. We thanked him for the expert way he'd conducted the whole affair. He said he was delighted to be of service and hoped it would bring the blessing of harmony on the household.

"Where's Céline? I'd like a quick word with her before I go."

"She's gone inside to feed Aline," I said.

With Fred gone off in search of Céline, Finbarr drew me aside.

"You really think this charade's going to solve all our problems?"

"Who knows? Just as long as she doesn't get any wrong ideas."

Fred came back.

"I have to head off. Got a ferry to catch." He lowered his voice. "That girl in there, Céline I mean. She's going to need looking after. Lots of love and tender care, if you get my meaning."

"You don't have to worry," Finbarr said. "I think we understand how fragile things are."

Forty

Dad died that December.

"He's very low," Bridie had said on the phone. "He won't last."

I drove like mad, but of course I was too late. Johnny and Bridie were with him when he went and they were still there when I arrived, sitting on upright chairs either side of the bed. Johnny stood up and we offered each other silent commiseration. I suppose it's some consolation he didn't die alone. Still!

We brought him back to be waked in his own house. Right through the night, neighbours and friends kept coming in and taking their turn to keep watch. Someone had threaded a rosary through his fingers, the little crucifix carefully arranged on his breast. The room where his wasted body lay was filled with the hush of murmured prayer. Also keeping vigil was a plain wooden coffin propped upright in a corner of the room, a silent reminder of the grim fate that awaits us all.

In the morning, there was a patina of frost on the street outside as Dad was sealed in his coffin and carried to the church. Finbarr arrived during the Mass and afterwards stood at my side as friends and neighbours lined up to shake my hand or embrace me and say how they were sorry for my loss. They said the exact same words to my siblings and their spouses. I heard hushed remarks about 'happy release' and 'gone to a better place.'

At the head of a straggling procession, six men carried the coffin to the old graveyard outside the town and I watched with aching heart as they lowered my father into the gaping earth to lie beside the wife who'd waited thirteen years for him to join her in the cold earth of eternity.

There were mumbled apologies as people melted away. A sprinkle of friends and neighbours joined us afterwards to share a meal. Finbarr and I went to sit with Josie and Martin. I couldn't help noticing a certain coolness on Josie's part until we were joined by our brother Hughie and his bride. They had flown through the night to be there.

"This is Carmelita," Hughie said. The men half stood to reach across and kiss Carmelita on the Latin-dark skin of both cheeks.

"You must be finding it bitter cold here," said Josie.

"We left the snow behind us at JFK." Carmelita flashed a perfect set of white teeth.

Finbarr quizzed Hughie about opportunities in the States. We learned he was with IBM, making his way up the ladder with a nice home in Jersey and a pool in the backyard.

Hughie asked Josie about little Blaithín. She said they left her with Martin's sister in Navan.

"You're blessed to have Maureen at times like this," I said.

"I don't know how we'd manage without her. Blaithín adores her."

This cut me, the suggestion that Maureen was the favourite aunt. Yet whenever I invited the child to stay, either Josie or Martin found some objection.

Afterwards I took Josie aside.

"What's bugging you and Martin?" I said.

"What d'you mean? Nothing's bugging us."

"Oh, come on, Josie. I've barely got a civil word from you all day."

"Well if you want to know, we're not exactly over the moon with the goings on in your place. Martin thinks it reckless, he does."

"What's reckless? Try to make sense, Josie."

"Martin's upset the way this country's going. The decline in morals. It's creeping in all over the place."

"Oh, grow up, sister. If it's Céline you're talking about, you can take it from me she's a respectable young girl. You don't have to worry your head about her."

"It's a Catholic country, Susan, but nobody gives a damn anymore. Martin hates the whiff of scandal and what's more, he wouldn't allow any child of his to be exposed to shameless immorality."

"I'm so sad, Josie, to hear you going on like this. Bláithín is my godchild and I'd give any money for the chance to mind her once in a while."

"I've said it before, Susan, and I'll say it again. Get rid of that hussy and her brat before she lands you in more trouble than you bargained for."

~ * ~

Céline always headed for France around Christmas and the New Year. That gave us the chance to have the place to ourselves, free from the fear of any fresh outburst from our volatile guest.

She arrived back on the sixth of January, the day Mam used call nollaig na mbán. It means 'The women's Christmas.' I sensed a change the minute she came inside the door. I asked about her mother, to be told she was still the same, but she made no effort to expand on that barest of statements. She came into the living room and sat with us in the warmth of the fire, giving desultory responses to Finbarr's efforts to make conversation. After a while he gave up trying to be sociable and tuned to a TV channel where a straggle-haired man was getting all excited about Byzantine icons, the sort of thing my husband found absorbing. I caught myself yawning. I'd had a busy day at work and had an early start next morning.

"Don't stay up too late," I said to Finbarr. "I'm off to bed."

"Off you go," said Céline. "Nothing's going to happen here for you to lose any sleep over." She didn't smile.

Finbarr glanced at me and then at Céline. Then back at the screen. He said nothing but he probably took it up the same way I did, along the lines of her posing no danger to his virtue or he to hers.

"What do you mean?" I said, "It never crossed my…"

"It never crossed your mind. Of course it didn't. I don't suppose it ever crossed your mind I might have the needs of a woman. Or that I might have any rights at all in this setup."

"Rights? I don't get it, Céline. What rights?"

Finbarr switched off the TV and we both looked at Céline, waiting.

"Don't give me that innocent look, Susan. You know bloody well what I mean. Slip off to your bedroom now and wait for your man to come running to give you what you want." She turned to face Finbarr. "Isn't that right, lover boy?"

"Hold it right there," Finbarr said, "I don't think that's any of your damn business."

"None of my business. Of course not. Who gives a shit if I have to lie awake listening to the two of you going at it hammer and tongs?"

Finbarr exploded.

"That's enough of that, young lady. What the hell is it to you if I take my wife to bed to make love? That, in case you've forgotten, is what marriage is all about. So don't go sticking your nose into what doesn't concern you."

"Screw your wife all you like. Why should I care? But what's to stop you taking your Celtic bride to your bed for a change? We've still to consummate our union, after all. Or could it be you're just not up to it? One woman's all you can manage. You just don't have it in you, do you?" Her laugh was bitter, sardonic.

Finbarr stood up. I was terrified he might strike her. I moved between them.

"That's really low," I said. "Completely uncalled for."

"Leave this to me, Sue," Finbarr said, "I'll handle it."

I waited to see how he would handle it. I could see he was struggling.

"I'm sorry this is how you feel," he said. "We made you welcome from day one. We did all we could for you. You've a special place her as Aline's mother. But there are boundaries. Boundaries, Céline. That's something you've got to understand."

"You hate me, mister. You won't admit it, but deep down you hate me. I let you fuck me and now you hate me for it."

"I've one wife." He put his arm on my shoulder.

"Remember how we did it? Like wild things we were. Your gutsy little goose girl you called me, remember that? You never thought it could be so good, you said. I was electric, you said."

Maybe her arrows were intended for him, maybe for me, I don't know. But they struck deep and by God, they hurt. They brought it all back, the betrayal, the pain, the loss. But she wasn't finished. With one hand on the door handle, she swung around to face us.

"You can shag her all night for all I care. Just close your eyes and pretend it's me. She'll never know. Fantasise Finbarr, fantasise. You've such memories to fall back on."

The slam of the door drove home the depth of her anger and spleen.

~ * ~

In the sullen silence of the next few days, no one made any reference to her vitriolic outburst but it was there all the time, hanging in the air. Things that are once voiced can never be taken back and neither Finbarr nor I were left in any doubt as to what Céline imagined her rights to be. I couldn't shake off the wounding things she'd said nor the impossible demands she'd come up with. She wasn't going to be satisfied till Finbarr took her to his bed to put the final seal on their mystic marriage.

So the whole thing had been a huge miscalculation on my part. I'd thought to keep her happy by allowing her marry Finbarr in a May Day ceremony. That was a big mistake. With Céline, if you conceded on one point, you were only paving the way for the next demand. Far from being satisfied with her status as mystical wife, she'd now come up with the next, for her, logical step. She wanted to share his bed. Nothing less was going to satisfy her.

And yet if Finbarr and I were agreed on anything, it was the need to keep her happy for the sake of Aline. The little girl would soon be three and was already showing the same assertive streak as her mother. I'd heard about a nursery school in the village, but Céline would be the one to make decisions about her daughter. We'd have to watch our step and try not to put a foot wrong.

~ * ~

Easter fell in the first week of April that year. Dancing lambs were everywhere. Through the glass of the conservatory, I could see Céline standing by the swing, Aline enjoying the gentle back and forth, back and forth movement. A new relationship growing between mother and daughter. Céline had fallen in with my idea of booking a place in the village nursery school. I'd been saying that Aline needed to mix with kids her own age. Now Céline was beginning to talk about her vision for the child's future. She'd go to the nuns for a good grounding and after that, well she could make up her own mind, just as long as no one tried to shoe-horn her into their notion of a solid profession.

"There'll always be a place for her in the art business, if that's what she wants," said Finbarr. For him the prospect of a secure income was number one.

"She'll decide for herself when the time comes," Céline said.

"Hold your horses, you two," I said. "She hasn't started nursery school yet."

April made its debut with false promises of sunshine and flowers. It was to end in misery on two separate fronts.

First there was the return of Josie's cancer. I went to see her in the hospital the day after they removed her second breast. What I found there was a woman with all the life, all the vitality, all the hope drained from her. I tried to cheer her with talk of starting out again with a clean slate.

"Don't try to fool me. I've no guarantee of anything."

"But you're in the clear now. Isn't that what they told you?"

"You've had all the luck, you and Finbarr. You two sail through life, not a worry in the world about money or health or anything else."

You have to make allowances, so I just said, "You've lots to be grateful for yourself. You've got your lovely little girl. You can be proud of Blaithín. You'll be back home with her and Martin in no time. You won't look back, you won't."

But the spark was gone out of her and I longed to see some of the old fire even if it was aimed at me and Finbarr.

~ * ~

A month later when I called to her home, Josie was older, more world weary and seemed to have lost all interest in anything to do with Giltspur. Things had moved on for her and she was more concerned about her own future and that of her husband and daughter. I wanted to help her anyway I could.

"If you'd like us to take Blaithín off your hands for a little while..."

She didn't answer. As if she didn't even hear.

Looking at her sitting there with that distant stare in her eyes, I was very aware of the fleeting nature of life. Though I'd decided not to mention it to my sister, I'd just heard the shocking news of the collapse and death of Charles' dear wife, Emily, the lovely gentle Emily who had made me so welcome in her cottage in the Cotswolds. I went over to the funeral but stayed just one night in Charles' home before coming back to Dublin to take care of the business. He needed time with his children. When all the sympathisers had dispersed and the house had gone quiet, he and they would be left to absorb with each other the appalling loss of wife and mother. To see Charles as I'd never seen him before, desolate and bereft, brought home to me our common human frailty in the face of irretrievable loss.

~ * ~

A minor issue you'd have thought and it all blew up on what should have been a special day in the life of little Aline. Her first day in nursery school. Since Céline was 'up to her eyes' trying to get a project finished on time, I said I'd drop Aline off at the school on my way to the city.

The young teacher with braided pigtail reaching to her waist looked like she was straight out of school herself. She held a clipboard on which she wrote in a slow careful hand the names of her new charges.

"Aline Dubois," I said.

She looked at me, her big eyes beseeching me to spell it for her. Aline's name was last on a list of seventeen. When I bent down to say goodbye, the poor little face tensed with apprehension. We had done all we could to prepare her, telling her about the kids she'd be meeting, all the great activities she'd have in school. But when it was time for me to go, she clung to my skirt and cried. I wasn't her mother and yet I felt something, a tug at the heart on reaching this new point in our relationship. Then she was gone, magicked away by the skilful staff, and I climbed back in my car and headed for the office.

That evening Aline was back home having been picked up by her mother. No sign of tears. When I asked her to tell me all about it, she found it hard to contain her contempt for my ignorance and spoke of her classmates with a familiarity that hinted at years of shared experiences.

Céline came through from the conservatory, wiping the paint from her hands with a torn towel.

I straightened up. "That seems to have gone without a hitch."

"Is that how you see it?" There was a distinct edge in her voice.

I searched her face for clues.

"Was there some problem?"

"You could say that."

I waited for her to say more.

"What name did you give?" she said.

"Her own name, of course."

"What name?"

"Aline. Aline Dubois. Why?"

"Ah! Dubois. So she has no father? You want her to go through life with her mother's name, branded as a bastard?"

"Look, Céline, the child has a father. Of course she's got a father. Why don't we wait and talk to Finbarr about this? See what he thinks."

"It's bad enough for me to be treated like shit in this house, but not my daughter, thank you."

She gave the door a sharp bang behind her and went back to her work. I prayed Finbarr wouldn't be too long.

As soon as he arrived, I whispered to him about this latest crisis and begged him to try and sort it out. He was good at this sort of thing, resolving conflict. I went to the kitchen to prepare the food, but left the door open so I could eavesdrop.

"She'll decide herself when she's older," I heard him say. "Maybe she'll use her father's name, maybe her mother's. Let her decide when she's old enough."

"Don't try to give me that. The truth is you're shit scared people will find out about you and your mistress."

"Okay, maybe you're right. This is Ireland, don't forget, an unforgiving little hole of a place. And yes, it's not something I want made public. But remember this, Céline, if it's not in my interest, it's not in yours either. If you didn't have my backing …"

"Oh, so we're onto this again, are we? Without you I'd be nothing, isn't that it? I should be kissing your arse with gratitude. Well, you can hump off with yourself because I'll make bloody sure the world knows the truth about you and your love-child. What have I got to hide? We've nothing to be ashamed of, Aline or me. It's time people knew you for the hypocrite you are."

"Céline, don't do this, I'm begging you. We can work something out. I've something lined up for you. I've been planning something big, something that'll really make your name."

"You've been able to buy me off before, but not this time. This is crunch time, sir, and you're going to have to face your responsibilities before I do it for you."

"Whatever it is you want, just say it. You can't say I've ever refused you anything."

"No?" There was a pause and I can only conjecture the look of triumph in her eyes as she delivered her coup de grace. "So you're ready to make an honest woman of me, then? I've waited a long time to hear you say it. At long last you're ready to consummate our marriage."

Forty-one

Jennifer was unshockable, I knew that, but I'd no idea how she'd react when she heard what I was about to tell her. I wondered could I bring myself to mention it at all.

"Remember what I was telling you," I said, "about Céline and Finbarr? The way she's obsessed with some kind of notion about him."

"I know, but I thought you'd resolved that one. Isn't that why you put yourself through that whole business with the Druids? To keep her off your back. Both your backs really?"

"I thought she'd be satisfied with the idea of mystical wife but no, she's looking for more. A lot more."

"You don't mean the full works?"

"The whole shebang. She keeps on bringing it up and I can tell you it always ends in tears."

"It's an extraordinary demand. You sure she's serious, not just having you on?"

"There's been blazing rows over it. She attacks him, attacks me. Look Jen, there's not a doubt in the world she knows what she's looking for and she's determined to get it."

"It's your house, Susan. You call the shots. She follows the rules and if she doesn't like it, well, you show her the door."

"Oh, Jen, if only it were that easy. Céline's not just a lodger. She's part of the family. Adopted daughter. Aline's mother. A frail, damaged personality. All those things. I could never bring myself to put her out. I did it once but that was different."

"Well, have you thought what you're going to do? I suspect you've given it some thought."

I took a deep breath. I wasn't sure how I was going to put this.

"I've been thinking…I've been thinking maybe it wouldn't be the end of the world."

"What? Share your husband with that girl?" She stared at me with a look of amazement.

"Look, Jen, she's had a horrible childhood. The more I find out, the more I see how she's suffered…I mean it's no wonder she's the way she is. It's like I want to wrap her up and heal her wounds. Am I making any sense?"

"Don't think you'll ever undo the damage. Help her come to terms with it, yes. But inviting her to share your husband's bed is way out."

"The damage goes deep, Jen. Her, you know, sexual development must be a total mess. Interfered with days before her first Communion, raped over and over as a child. No wonder she's psychotic, depressive. Who wouldn't be? You're a therapist, Jen. You must know what I'm talking about."

There was silence as Jennifer sat looking at me. Like I was some sort of puzzle that she found baffling. She left it to me to break the silence.

"When she found Finbarr, she found a father substitute. Her captivation with him developed from there."

"I presume you haven't broached this to Finbarr. How do you think he'll react?"

"As a matter of fact, I have. I begged him to give it some thought. I told him I was going to talk to you about it. I said he ought to run it past his theologian friend."

"And?"

"I think he's nibbling. You see, she's blackmailing him about publicity, threatening to dirty his name. I wouldn't be a bit surprised if he gives in."

"If it's blackmail we're talking about, Susan, you're about to hand her the perfect weapon."

~ * ~

I wouldn't want anyone to imagine Finbarr seized the opportunity like some craven male panting for thrills in his sex life. It wasn't like that. In fact, when I'd first suggested it, he'd had trouble taking it in. He couldn't believe he'd heard me right. He reminded me of the vows we'd exchanged six years before in the Swiss mountains.

"We promised to do nothing behind backs," I said, "something you could never accuse me of doing. This is different. What we're talking about here is an honest, open response to a particular situation."

He launched into a lot of theological jargon about monogamy and Christian principles. It was then I said he should talk to Ulrich, that Ulrich struck me as an open-minded sort of clergyman.

Now we were out on the moor and a balmy June breeze swept the sweetness of furze into our faces.

"I've been talking to Ulrich," Finbarr said. "We'd a long chat on the phone."

"Remember that homily of his at our wedding? All about fidelity and what it means? I couldn't make head nor tail of what he was getting at."

"Anyway I told him the whole story…you know, Céline and the way she carries on. I told him what you'd come up with as a way of keeping her quiet. He said you must be some woman."

"You could take that more ways than one."

"What I like about Ulrich is the way he grasps the problem straight off. Anyway, he started rattling off quotations from all kinds of obscure writers.

"Like what?"

"Commentaries on the Bible, for example. He said there's nothing in the Bible that says one woman for one man. Did you ever realise that?"

"You're joking me, of course."

"Solomon, King David, most of the patriarchs. They all had several wives. Did Yahweh raise any objections? On the contrary, he offered David more wives if he wanted them!"

"You can't be serious."

"Check it out. It's in the First Book of Samuel. Ulrich says you'll find the same thing with Christian writers like Augustine, Aquinas, Luther. One man, two women. None of them condemns it.

"So your friend Ulrich says it's okay? You won't have to force yourself then?"

"There's no moral objection, that's what he said."

"So you're free to bang ahead with two wives."

"He says the two women have to agree to share and they must get equal consideration. I'm only repeating what he told me. He says he knows a family like that in Switzerland and they're a model of peace and harmony."

"Peace and harmony? He doesn't know our Céline."

"So who's going to talk to her, you or me?"

"You stick to your theology and leave the talking to me."

I found it quite funny to see him searching for moral justification for something that must have seemed like a gift on a golden plate. But the odd thing is that I too felt reassured by what he'd found out. I'm not saying I was blind to the pitfalls. For one thing, there was the danger of scandal and gossip if our set-up became public. As well as that I knew I'd experience the tensions of a woman in the presence of a rival, no doubt about that. But I was determined to set all my fears and misgivings aside for the sake of the vulnerable girl I was working to save.

~ * ~

The usual turmoil in her studio. Canvasses lying face up on the floor gave the impression she was working on all of them at the same time. I decided to grab the opportunity and tell her what Finbarr and I had in mind.

"I'm off to Annagopple for the weekend. I'm depending on you to look after Finbarr when I'm gone."

"Can't he look after himself?" She didn't raise her eyes from her work.

"He's going to need someone to keep him warm in bed."

Now she looked up with a sort of startled expression, searching my face for clues to my meaning.

"Did I hear you right? You want me to go to bed with Finbarr? That's kinda new, isn't it?"

"I've been talking to him about it. A long talk really. We're agreed on it now. We both think you're entitled to something more. Your proper rights, if you get my meaning."

"You're talking about sex, is that it?"

I moved a stained towel and eased myself onto a wooden chair.

"It'll bring us closer to each other, Céline, you and me. I'm just trying to see things from your point of view. Finbarr, too. I've convinced him to be more attentive to your needs. You've been getting a raw deal, I can see it now. I know it's hard to take all this in. Just think about it, that's all I'm saying really."

She put down her brushes and led the way into the kitchen. She positioned herself at the corner of the table and I sat so I was able with my right hand to touch her left. Aline sat on the floor with a large book spread wide on her lap.

"I don't know what to say, Susan. You've had a lot to put up with. Both of you. I've caused trouble, I know that. You see I'm not always in control. You took me in and made me part of the family. And now you're telling me I can…"

"At first I thought of you as a daughter. Then as a young sister. Now like a dear friend. We share a house, we share a lovely little girl and now we're ready to share our man."

"You're amazing, Susan. How many women would do it, go that far? I guess it's the sort of person you are."

"It's up to you, Céline. If you're not ready for it, well that's fine. Whatever you decide, it's fine. But I'm going north this evening and whatever happens when I'm away, you have my blessing."

She leaned across and put her arms about me. The feelings which coursed through my veins as our faces touched were a wild mixture of tenderness and affection, sympathy and understanding, fear and apprehension.

I left for Annagopple that evening. Finbarr came out to wave me off. Standing in the porch I took his hand. I gave him a peck on the cheek.

"Best of luck," I said.

As I drove away, there was a gentle stream of contentment flowing through the Rocky Valley and so long as it was there, Céline was welcome to dip her cup in the water.

~ * ~

My mood changed when I found myself trying to get to sleep on my own in Johnny and Bridie's house. I tried hard not to think about it, to shut it out of my mind, the thought that my husband was at that moment having it off with a younger woman. Was he enjoying the experience? Making comparisons even? And if he was, who was to blame? I could hardly fault him for falling in with a plan I'd come up with myself.

Jennifer had stopped short of giving me her blessing, but she'd helped me to analyse my motives. As my mistress of novices, she was the one who'd introduced me to notions of self-denial and self-sacrifice, so she should have had some idea what was driving me. But no. That was then, this is now.

The fact of the matter is I'd never really got rid of the idea that I reneged on my vocation. You could say my life had been a constant effort to make amends. When you look at it like that, Céline was my way of saying sorry to God.

Back home I didn't ask any questions. I couldn't trust myself not to reveal some kind of emotion. Everyone just acted normal and there was no reference to what might or might not have happened in my absence.

In the months that followed, a pattern developed where Céline would wait till I was away at the weekends before taking Finbarr into her bed. I'd my own way of finding out which bed they'd used and I have to admit to a feeling of relief that the marriage bed hadn't been violated.

On the positive side, you couldn't help but notice a more settled atmosphere about the place. My decision to share my husband seemed to be yielding results. Not just that my connection with Céline was smoother, but my relationship with Finbarr grew deeper. An unexpected bonus was a revival in his virility that gave a new energy charge to our coupling. More satisfying and fulfilling than it had been for a long time. Like a couple of new lovers, we walked together across the moor and took outings into the city to enjoy the latest play or film in each other's company.

~ * ~

Céline and I became more relaxed with each other. She was friend, sister, daughter, sharer. I took a new interest in her work. I'd often go to the sunroom to watch as she painted and found her more inclined to explain what she was doing.

"What's that?" I said. A lump of twisted metal lay on the floor.

"It looks like part of a mudguard. I found it on the side of the road."

"And you brought it home? What are you going to do with it?"

"I've no idea. I'm waiting for inspiration."

We laughed at that and Aline came running to see what it was all about. She went straight to her mother and Céline swept her into the air, something I'd never seen her do before. It was as if something had come about that gave her back her maternal instinct. Certainly our house was a happier more relaxed place than at any time since her arrival on our doorstep three years before.

Forty-two

I'm not suggesting for a moment life in Giltspur was a model of peaceful coexistence. We had our ups and downs like anyone else, but by and large the arrangement worked. One man, two women.

Céline was now more like the old Céline, the healthy, sane, creative individual we'd known when she first came to live with us. She threw herself into her work and her output was phenomenal. We were aware she was on high levels of medication since the train incident. Finbarr had a customer, a psychiatrist, who told him an underlying psychosis can flare up at any time and make an apparently normal person engage in sudden unpredictable behaviour. It was vital, this man said, that the sufferer should stick to the medication.

Céline's suicide attempt was never mentioned, but the fact of it was always there, hovering in the ether like a malign ghost. Finbarr and I made the effort to steer clear of all contentious issues. Nothing could be allowed disturb the delicate balance. I encouraged Finbarr to be responsive to her sexual needs in the hope it might be the key to her equilibrium. As he continued sleeping with each of his women in turn, it was inevitable there would be ups and downs in our cross-wired relationship.

It was rare for Céline to fight with me, though she could be moody. I can't say the same about her relationship with Finbarr. I often heard raised voices when they were together. She had a colourful line in obscenities and made no attempt to curb her language in the presence of the child. These outbursts I put down to her mental condition, which was always going to be difficult to manage. I think Finbarr sometimes forgot how ill she was. Once when I heard her taunt him with *prêtre manqué* I thought how truly like husband and wife they'd become. Spoiled priest is an expression I'd never have used. There must have been times when it was a relief for him to return to the consoling embrace of his first love. Though he and I didn't always see eye to eye, we had a way of talking things out and reaching some kind of understanding.

Finbarr's business expanded as the economic gloom lifted at the end of the 80s. There was money floating around and this was good for Céline, too, who was in a position to accept or reject commissions to suit herself. I was able to devote all my attention to Maeve, which had established itself as the leading journal in its own niche.

Josie rang to tell me about something she'd seen in the paper, a newspaper that would never have found its way into our own home. This particular paper was getting all worked up about a case of polygamy they said they'd tracked down in County Wicklow. What worried Josie was that the writer had made some reference to people with connections in the world of art and publishing.

I met Josie in town next day and she handed me the paper.

"You can't say I didn't warn you, Sue. People were bound to talk. That kind of thing has a way of getting out."

"Hold your horses, Josie. It says here 'somewhere in County Wicklow.' Wicklow's a big place and anyway it's got nothing to do with us."

I wasn't as confident as I let on. I took the paper home to show Finbarr. What worried him was not so much the use of lines like 'hidden decadence of the wealthy', 'flouting convention' and so on. What really bothered him was the promise to name names in a followup.

"Who wrote this shit?" Finbarr flung the paper at the burning logs in the fireplace but it fell short and fluttered to the floor. "Their special investigative reporter! He hasn't got the guts to put his name to it. If I get my hands on the little bollix, I'll give him something to report."

He had no doubt whatever the story was about us. The only question was who had tipped them off. Hardly Margo, a woman who was the soul of discretion. Could it have been Mona who had the full run of the house when Finbarr and I were at work? We were convinced she carried every tittle tattle back to Chaser, feeding his morbid interest in anything that smacked of scandal. We'd no contact whatever with the German family next door, apart from occasional sightings of Otto patrolling his boundary, shotgun in hand. As far as we were aware, none of our neighbours knew anything about us. But whoever the source of the story, Finbarr was determined to get to the bottom of it. Someone was going to pay. An angry Finbarr was a man of fierce determination.

I opened the kitchen door and stepped out into the bitter March night. In the moonless sky, the stars glistened with an unbelievable brilliance. The outline of Ursa Major pointed me along its practiced pathways to Polaris, directly above the ridge of our roof yet unreachable in the vastness of the universe. I thought how puny we people are, how trivial our concerns.

A distant rumble grew steadily louder before defining itself as the familiar snarl of Céline's MG heading up the hill to our home.

Céline came into the sitting room and stood with her bottom to the fire.

"It's cold for March," I said.

"What's that?" She'd spotted the paper lying on the floor and stooped to pick it up. "Exposé."

"Read on," I said.

I watched her as she read. Her face tensed.

"I can't believe this."

"What can't you believe?" said Finbarr, who hadn't spoken up to then.

"I just can't believe it. Such a nice young guy. Real friendly, like. He wanted to talk about art."

"Who wanted to talk about art? When did this happen?"

"A young chap drove up here one morning when you two were at work. He wanted an interview, he said. I brought him in to show him the studio. I felt sorry for him, really. So young, so desperate. He said he needed this story to impress his editor and I agreed to talk to him."

"You mean to say you talked to some cheeky little pup, someone you knew nothing about? And you fed him all this stuff? Our private business? My business and Susan's?"

"He seemed to know all about you. He'd been to the gallery in South Anne Street and knew about the exhibitions. He was very well informed, I'll say that."

"Even better informed when you were done blabbing. You didn't by any chance show him your bedroom? And why not? Pictures of unmade beds to spice things up!"

Finbarr was getting worked up and I could see Céline was distressed. It must have been clear to her now she'd been tricked.

"Let's keep calm," I said." Let's talk it out like sensible adults."

"Calm?" He seemed about to burst. "How can you be calm? Anyone with a bit of a brain will know who they're talking about. Next thing we know, we'll have bigots with pickets at the gate. Christ knows where this is going to end."

"Aren't you lucky to have someone to blame?" Céline said. "Well, let me tell you something, mister, I'll be scapegoat for no one. I'll take no shit from you or anyone else. We're all in this together. I've nothing to hide. If you're ashamed of me, that's your problem, not mine."

I hadn't seen her like this for a long time. Furious. We were on the verge of a violent scene. I knew it. I could see it building.

"It's all right," I said. "No one's blaming anyone. You couldn't have known, Céline. They're up to all the tricks, these people. They'll stoop to anything."

"Tell him that." She pointed at Finbarr. "He'll use me when it suits him and shaft me when it suits him. That's the kind of shitty treatment I have to take in this house. Now if you'll both excuse me, I'm tired after a long day. I need some sleep."

"Hold it a minute," said Finbarr. "We need to get something straight here. If you think I..."

But she wasn't listening. She stalked out and headed for her bedroom, past the room where Aline slept, innocent of the angry scene playing out around her.

In this kind of mood, Céline could do anything. I didn't want any repeat of her mad dash to the railway track. I looked at Finbarr and he looked at me. In his eyes I read the unspoken question, what do we do now?

"Go to her," I said, "Use your magic on her."

He knew what I meant. I went to my own bed and lay awake. I tried not to hear their muffled voices and sounds coming from Céline's room at the end of the corridor. I struggled to suppress my woman's feelings of jealousy and exclusion. Finbarr and Céline making love together while I lay alone in another bed. Only when the sounds of sex had finally subsided was I able to find peace in sleep.

In the morning, Finbarr and Céline were back on civil terms and nobody made any reference to the crisis hanging over our heads. But I noticed that Finbarr was pale, and before I left for work I caught him massaging his chest.

At lunchtime I called around to the gallery and we went to a local eatery for soup and sandwiches.

"You looked pale this morning," I said. "Are you sure you're feeling okay?"

"That newspaper thing has me up the wall."

"You were rubbing your chest. What was that all about?"

"It's nothing. I often get that when I'm stressed. Anyway, it's gone now. Nothing to worry about."

"I want you to see the doctor. Get it checked out, you hear me?"

"Okay, okay."

"Do that today and I'll see what I can do about that newspaper nonsense."

Surprisingly he did as I told him and saw the doctor the same day.

~ * ~

"Well," I said when he arrived home, "and what did he say, the doctor?"

"He just said the usual."

"What's 'the usual?' Tell me what he said."

"You know the usual. Eat less fat, ease back on the work, try not to worry. All that nonsense. Oh, and exercise."

"Exercise! When I asked you to walk with me to Kevin's grave on Sunday, you said you weren't up to it."

"I was flaked out."

"You told him about the chest pains?"

"He wanted to know had I been under any stress lately. A little, I said."

"Understatement of the year!"

~ * ~

The same paper which had promised to open up our private lives to public scrutiny now carried lurid accounts of naked dancing in the Wicklow hills around the time of the solar festivals. It described ritual fires, pagan chants and New Age weirdoes.

"They make this stuff up as they go along," was Finbarr's caustic comment.

"No," I said. "Someone's feeding it to them and I have my suspicions who it is."

I hadn't forgotten Chaser regaling me with a story of naked dervishes dancing about a fire on the slopes of the Sugarloaf. The 'Daily Rag' report was just too close for coincidence. If Chaser was the source of the dancing dervishes story, he was must also be the source of the revealing documents they were promising to publish in the coming weeks. I remembered going to collect Céline's diary and finding Chaser poring over the writing in a vain attempt to make out the French. He must have hidden away some pages until he could find someone to read them for him.

We had to stop the paper going ahead with its revelations. The effect on Céline would be too awful to contemplate. Finbarr was all for a court injunction. I said it would only create more publicity.

"Do nothing," I said, "till I talk to the editor."

When I found out the reporter's name, Finbarr wanted to ring him directly.

"I'll tell that nosy little prick to get the hell out of our lives and back in the slurry pit he climbed out of. He can drown in his own shit."

"Calm it," I said. "He'd have your threats recorded on tape."

"So what do you propose?"

"I'll go talk to his editor. As one professional to another. See if I can't sweet-talk him."

~ * ~

Walking into the editor's office I was relieved to find an urbane and intelligent individual who genuinely believed his paper served a vital role in society. Framed on the wall above his head was the quotation, 'News is what people want to keep hidden. Everything else is publicity.'

He argued that these stories were in the public interest as evidenced by the paper's impressive circulation figures. It took all the diplomacy I could muster, but after a lot of cajoling and persuasion I succeeded in convincing him that there was a vulnerable young woman involved who could easily be tipped over the edge if she were dragged into a public scandal. Speaking professionally and confidentially, of course.

It was understood there'd be a quid pro quo. There always is. I'd be more than delighted to give him a glowing write-up in my own publication, something that would raise his paper's profile with a different readership. You might say I sold my soul, but what other option did I have? I left that man's office assured that he'd shelve the subject of dissolute lifestyles in Wicklow and get back to the old reliable staples of politics and corruption.

Forty-three

The way I'd managed to stop the story going any further put everyone in great form. Harmony was restored to the household and you could see it in the way Finbarr was all over Céline. He revelled in her professional success, no doubt putting it down to his own fostering and patronage.

"An exhibition, Céline. A retrospective. It's time you got the recognition you deserve. We'll work on it together. It'll be huge. A cross section of your oeuvre. All your best work on display. It'll be all over the papers. Think of it, Céline, the exhibition of the decade, the Camille Retrospective."

"It'll mean bringing my stuff back from all over the place," she said. Her voice had a new excitement.

"Don't worry a bit. They'll feel privileged, those owners, to be asked."

"How soon can we do it?"

"November. It'll give you time to include some original work. People are in buying mood at the moment. This is big, Céline, real big."

Actually I suspect this whole thing was cooked up by

Finbarr in the hope she might be weaned away from the guerrilla warfare, the sneaky sniping at each of us which still erupted with depressing regularity. I can't say this with any certainty, but I suspect that whenever she was on a high, with her work going well, she didn't bother with the medication which we knew was so vital for her equilibrium.

I could see she was on a high as she threw herself body and soul into preparing for the exhibition. However, I also knew that the higher she went, the greater the collapse when the bubble burst.

What excited her most, she said, was the chance to put on view again her 'Danse Macabre,' the picture that had caused so much controversy when she first showed it. She attached huge significance to this canvas and she'd been waiting for the right time and place to show it again. She was convinced it would sell this time around and she'd decided to give it a higher price tag in anticipation.

Earlier paintings began to arrive back in their secure packing from owners who felt privileged and vindicated to have been asked to participate. Larry Wiseman, who'd worked with Uncle John in the old days, came back to help with the removal of paintings from their crates. It was critically important that nothing was damaged while on the premises. As always, Céline was hands on in the hanging and placing of the pictures as she hovered around, giving firm orders about where each was to go. The dancing demons of 'La Danse Macabre' found themselves in a prominent position towards which all eyes would be drawn. She'd never been afraid of controversy, maybe even revelled in it. Finbarr, on the other hand, expected an open-minded acceptance of experimentation in the nation's capital. He was aware she'd been working frantically to include some fresh pieces, but he was far too busy to give much thought to what she was doing.

I was handed the job of whipping up pre-show publicity and I succeeded in getting the papers that mattered on board. On the opening night, all the broadsheets sent their art critics along to take a peep. The gallery was packed with the leading lights of the art world with various celebrities and a couple of politicians. I stayed away. I was already more than familiar with her way-out themes and, anyway, as I saw it, the evening belonged to Finbarr and Céline, most especially to Céline.

And here's the odd thing about it. The most significant figure in the whole event failed to show up. It was a bad omen.

Finbarr must have felt a sense of unease as he addressed his opening speech to the assembled guests. I'm depending here on what he himself told me afterwards.

He began by apologising for the artist's absence.

"Some of you will already have met this gifted young artist, who unfortunately was called away at the last moment on family business. However, she has asked me to convey her apologies and hopes you will derive as much pleasure from viewing her work as she herself has in creating it."

The place filled with murmurs of approval. With speeches out of the way, a couple of black-suited waiters circulated with wine-filled glasses. Finbarr encouraged the guests to move around and marvel at the avant-garde daring of the works on display. He himself stayed near the front of the gallery chatting up a small number of newspaper people. He fully appreciated the importance of the papers in generating publicity.

The man from The Times kept looking around, distracted by something going on near the back of the gallery. Finbarr followed his gaze and noticed a number of patrons had gravitated to a spot in front of a particular painting. He caught some in the group glancing back in his direction and their expressions were more apprehensive than cheerful. He felt an urge to investigate but didn’t want to make a big thing of it in front of the newsmen.

“I’m going back there to have a look,” said the man from The Times and moved towards the cluster of chattering, laughing, pointing patrons.

“Maybe you should go and investigate,” said the man from The Independent.

“I might just do that.”

As he approached, a hush fell on the group whose numbers had grown. Though some were smirking, most wore pained looks of embarrassment. They split apart to make a passage for the gallery owner.

The moment he saw the painting, he told me, he felt a distinct weakness about the knees. The caption read ‘Se comporter comme un cochon’, behaving like a pig. The biggest of the three pigs was easily recognisable with Finbarr’s features while the two smaller pigs wore the colours of Ireland and France. The largest of the three, the one resembling Finbarr, had mounted the one with the blue, white and red of France. There could be no mistaking the intent of the picture. It was a public depiction of the three-sided marital arrangement prevailing in Giltspur. He read it as a public demeaning of himself.

His first impulse was to tear the offensive thing from the wall and fling it in a corner. He knew all eyes were on him, waiting to see his reaction. In particular he knew he was being watched by the people from the press.

He invoked an incredible presence of mind, calling upon his capacity to cope with the unexpected. He swept the circle of expectant faces with a broad grin.

"Well, I guess that's art, folks. Good art or bad art is for you to decide."

He moved away, taking care to engage anyone he met with friendly relaxed remarks about the versatility of Camille. He knew he had no option but to leave the pigs painting in situ until the gallery closed in the early hours.

It was three in the morning when he arrived home. The pallor of his face told its own story.

"Is she home yet?" he said.

"I haven't seen her all day. You look terrible." My first thought was that his chest pains had returned.

"She's done it again," he said.

I took hold of his hand. It was cold and shaking.

"Céline?"

"She hung an obscene painting when she got my back turned. It'll be all over the papers in the morning. The little bitch. I could wring her neck."

"Come to bed. Try to sleep and we'll talk in the morning."

In the morning I heard the full story. Now I was the one who was angry. I wanted to get my hands on her, make her understand she'd gone too far this time. Apart altogether from decency and good taste, she'd gone out of her way to humiliate the people to whom she owed most. How could she have forgotten that Finbarr had done everything in his power to sponsor and promote her while from me she'd got nothing but love, understanding and acceptance? It was Saturday and I persuaded Finbarr to stay home and let Paul look after the gallery. There was still no sign of Céline and it wasn't until that evening that she showed up. If we'd thought she'd cower in the face of our anger, we were soon disillusioned, for it was she who went on the attack.

"Where's my painting?" she demanded, the moment she came in.

"I took it down," said Finbarr.

"You took down the one piece the customers are fighting to get their hands on. Paul told me there's been several offers already. You've a damn cheek to take it on yourself to decide what I can or cannot sell to the public."

"I decide what's shown in my gallery."

"Well, you just hand me back that painting. I'll sell it to whoever I damn well like."

"You bloody well won't. I'll not have myself or my wife held up to public ridicule."

"Myself or my wife!" Her laugh was laden with contempt. "Your wife! Tell me, mister respectable art dealer, who is your wife? Just who is the priest's wife?"

I stepped in from the kitchen to see Finbarr's face white with fury and Céline's demented eyes preparing to drive home her attack.

"Céline," I said. "You're looking at Finbarr's wife. His

one and only wife. He only ever had…"

"Shut up," she screamed. "I hate you. I hate the two of you. Fucking pigs, that's all you are and now the whole world knows it."

I took a step towards her to try to calm her. She stepped away and her hand found the Waterford crystal lamp on its small table behind her. She half turned and with slow deliberation lifted the globe and launched it in my direction. It flew past my head before shattering in a million pieces against the stone fireplace.

In the strange shocked silence that followed, I stared at the crystals of sugared glass on the hearth; I looked at Finbarr slumped on a chair, his head in his hands and I turned back to catch sight of the tears forming in Céline's eyes. Nobody spoke as she turned towards the door and shuffled off to her bedroom.

Early next morning, we were still in bed when we heard the front door close and the sound of Céline's car leaving the driveway.

Later Finbarr got a phone call from Paul to say one of the paintings had been vandalised. Though it was Sunday morning, Finbarr got into his car and went to meet Paul at the gallery. It was only when Paul was locking up on Saturday evening that he noticed the vandals had struck. They had directed their ire at a single painting, 'La Danse Macabre,' the one which Céline had declared meant most to her.

Finbarr remembered that when he'd removed the offensive pig painting and hidden it in the storeroom, he'd used 'La Danse Macabre' to fill the gap.

A sharp knife had been used and part of the canvas hung in a limp flap over the bottom of the frame. The torn photo of a little girl which had formed part of the collage was missing.

When Paul suggested they call the police, Finbarr said no, he needed time to think.

"I wonder how she'll take it," said Paul.

"Céline? I hate to think."

However, her reaction when Finbarr broke the news to her at teatime that evening, wasn't the angry display I'd expected. Instead she listened in silence as he described the damage before subsiding into silent sobbing. It came home to me then just how much that painting had meant to her. I'd always suspected it might be related to the horrific events of her childhood and the trauma she carried within her.

In the days that followed, a sort of conflicted silence prevailed. There were complex tensions rippling beneath the surface. We both felt immense sympathy for her when she brought home the damaged painting to see if it could be restored. Still Finbarr refused to return the obscene painting which we found so offensive and this remained a source of conflict.

As happened so often before, I was the first to soften. When I'd time to think about it, it was clear she wasn't in control of her actions. I wondered if she was taking her medication or if she'd decided she could function without it. That was always the danger and yet it wasn't my place to act the nurse, chasing her around, insisting she follow the medical advice.

Finbarr wasn't as forgiving as I. He began to talk about how we could get rid of her. "Things can only get worse." I was shocked to hear him talk like that.

"How can you even think of it?" I said. "At a time when she's at her most vulnerable. Would you throw both her and Aline out on the road? Aline's your own child. Your child, Finbarr. Think about what you're saying."

He dropped that idea but his alternative was to stay away from her bed. He'd show his displeasure by refusing to sleep with her. I had misgivings even about that. It was a cruel punishment. While it was nice to know I was number one in his affections and I welcomed the closeness of his body at night, I wondered what it might do to Céline to be rejected like that. Such a drastic course of action might even make things worse. While they often fought, in some perverse way she loved him. Yet I didn't feel enough sympathy to send him back to her. Sooner or later, he'd mellow and things would be as before.

Saturday night had become established as Céline's night to be with Finbarr, while other nights were more ad hoc. All that week he stayed away from her. She must have noticed but probably put it down to the standoff between them about her wanting her picture back.

On Saturday she arrived home from wherever she'd been for the day. She looked into the sitting room where Finbarr and I were relaxing before the fire. She said a cheery hi folks before going to the kitchen and setting the kettle to boil. There was a distinct thaw in her attitude. I gave a knowing glance at Finbarr and saw that he too had noticed. She came back with a mug of instant soup in her hand.

"Either of you two want anything?"

"No thanks," I said, while Finbarr ignored her. He seemed absorbed in his book.

"What you reading there, Finbarr?" she said in a tone which suggested she was ribbing him.

"Middlemarch," he said, making no attempt to disguise his impatience.

"George Eliot," I added in case she didn't know.

"Old God's time," she said. "You'll find nothing in there to turn you on, sweetie." She seemed to be enjoying herself. I wondered had she been drinking.

Finbarr looked up for a moment but refused to be drawn in.

"I'm planning an early night," she said, still addressing him. "I don't suppose I could tempt you?"

Finbarr placed his book face down beside him and looked directly at her.

"You'd better get used to being on your own for a while. Don't think you've only to click your fingers for me to come trotting."

"Talk to him, Susan. Tell him not to be such a meanie." There was a pleading in her voice.

I was torn between them. That was my dilemma, that I could see it from both sides. I have to admit I had a definite sympathy for her needs. As a woman, I knew exactly how she must feel at his rejection. It must have been cutting her to the quick.

"I'm sorry, Céline, it's between you two. I can't force him if he doesn't want to."

"You too, Susan? You want your fingerprints on the dagger? Where's my friend when I need her most?"

I don't think I'd ever known her like this. This wasn't the fighting Céline we were familiar with. This was a different Céline, abject, defeated, and it frightened me to see her like that. There was nothing I could think of saying that wouldn't make matters worse. The awkward silence seemed interminable until Céline gave an audible sigh, stood up and without a goodnight to either of us went to her bedroom.

Forty-four

All night Finbarr tossed and turned and my own sleep was disturbed. I noticed the grey dawning of daylight and turned the alarm clock to silent, leaving it to nature to wake us. When next I looked at the clock, it was just after nine and the light seeping through the curtains was the sort of washed-out light that indicated rain or sleet outside. Finbarr was sleeping soundly. There was no sound from Céline's room and a flash of red through the front window told me her car was there in its usual spot. I peeped into Aline's room where the little girl was still asleep. The Christmas break had arrived, so no school for three weeks.

I found a half-empty coffee mug on the kitchen table, the brown mug Céline always used. I emptied the cold dregs in the sink. A sudden shower caused rivulets to form on the outside of the window and an icy draft told me the kitchen door was open. I wondered what could have taken Céline out into the garden on a morning like this. I threw a rain jacket over my head and shoulders and stepped outside. I called her name but there was no answer. I walked around the front and when there was no sign of her there, I turned and made my way into the back garden. The Sugarloaf was almost totally obscured by a damp misty veil. I picked my way along the muddy track between the winter skeletons of the fruit trees, down towards the rough part of the garden where bulges in the bedrock broke through the surface. I slipped in the mud and tore my hand as I came down in a clump of furze. For a few moments I sat there in that bush asking myself what madness had taken me down here in such messy weather. Common sense told me to get back inside and get dressed.

A last glance in the direction of the mountain and I noticed some stray pieces of clothing caught in the branches of the old hawthorn tree at the narrow apex of the garden. A gust of wind dashed cold rain in my face to blind me. I brushed the water from my eyes and for a moment the clothing seemed to resolve itself into human form. I recognised Céline's navy tracksuit bottom floating limp above the ground. I pulled myself free of the thorns and ran, slipping, sliding, to where she hung from the horizontal branch of the old tree, her white trainers with the blue stripe tracing random little circles about the tips of the brown heather, a length of nylon rope about her neck.

I cried out, but the scream broke in my throat. I threw my arms about her rain-sodden body and buried my face in her cold, damp bosom. "Celine, oh Céline." I sobbed her name over and over, begging her not to go, to stay with us, it didn't have to be like this. I knew I was making no sense, as if my choked pleading might entice her back from where she could never return.

"Why, Céline, why?" Words choked with tears. "You

didn't have to do it. Oh, my poor, poor child, you didn't have to, you didn't, you didn't..."

I wished it hadn't fallen to me to find her. I wished Finbarr had been there, that he might find a way to save her. But then he would be there to witness my despair and I his. After a long time, I dragged myself away and left her, still swaying in the gusting air from the valley, her skimpy white blouse soaked and clinging, and dragged myself back to the house to break it to him.

He cut her down with a Stanley knife, standing on a set of steps from the kitchen. He worked in silence, but his tears provided their own commentary. Between us we dragged her limp sodden body back to the house and got her onto her bed. Then we called the doctor, not that there was anything he could do for her, but formalities would have to be adhered to.

"Why did she do it?" Finbarr said over and over as we waited.

"We'll never know that," I said. "We'll never know what torment drove her to it."

"There was nothing so bad we couldn't have fixed it."

"I hope you're not blaming yourself, love. Nobody could have done more for her."

When the doctor arrived, we took him and showed him where it had happened. He picked up the severed end of the rope, looked at it as if it might yield some clue and tossed it back in the muck before retracing his steps to where her body lay inside. He felt Céline's icy forehead and frozen pulse, and checked his watch before beginning to fill in a death certificate on which he scrawled 'Death due to asphyxiation, self-inflicted.'

As I watched the doctor's almost ritualised movements, his professional detachment from the human tragedy, I too found that astonishing strength that comes to people faced with an emergency. I've seen it more than once, our ability to suppress the panic till the critical demands of the moment have been attended to. Only later comes the collapse when all defences crumble and powerful primal emotions come into play. So it was with Finbarr and me.

As the doctor drove away, we gave full vent to our tears, cried with each other, clung to each other, united in despair by a sense of irreparable loss.

Our Céline had been an integral, essential, part of the family. More than anything, we were torn by the terrible unexpectedness of it, horrified by the needless violence she'd been driven to visit upon her lovely fragile body.

We buried her in the local churchyard. Some friends of hers were there, a few artists and some who looked as if they might be from the hippy community. But it was a pathetic little band that didn't at all reflect the esteem in which her work was held. Her little girl, Aline, threw a flower onto the coffin, a mauve chrysanthemum, before they began to shovel the Wicklow clay on top of her mother's body.

"Your mamma's gone to heaven," I said as I took her up in my arms. I said it with conviction, for I couldn't bring myself to believe that someone as vibrant and gifted as Céline could simply have ceased to exist. "She's looking down on you from up there."

Afterwards, Finbarr said it was the grace of God Céline hadn't decided to take Aline with her and to tell the truth I'd always been conscious of that possibility. If anything had happened to the child, I could never have forgiven myself. As for Finbarr, life without his little daughter would have been unbearable. We'd had too much pain in our lives already. We couldn't have taken any more.

Maybe she did take another innocent life with her. This only emerged a couple of weeks after her death when Finbarr told me almost casually that he remembered Céline saying something about being pregnant.

"We were fighting at the time. I thought she was being histrionic. I dismissed it from my mind and forgot all about it until now."

"That must have been before you refused to have anything to do with her. You shunned her, remember?"

"Oh, no!" A look of anguish crossed his face. "There was no connection. I hope she didn't think there was."

Though we never spoke about this again, I've never been able to rid myself of the terrible thought that an unborn child of Finbarr's might have taken that grim journey with Céline into the world of shadows.

I turned the key in the lock of Céline's bedroom and hid it away until I got a chance to go through her things myself. There was no one else to do this for her and she had, after all, declared Finbarr her next-of-kin. In effect, we were the only family she had.

She hadn't slept in her bed on the night of her death. How long she sat alone in the kitchen with a mug of cold coffee, contemplating the last desperate act of her life, we'll never know. On the floor beside her bed, I found a scrap of a photograph. It was the missing piece torn from her painting by the unknown vandal. There was only one possible explanation. The deranged attacker who had viciously slashed 'La Danse Macabre,' Céline's favourite painting, could only have been Céline herself.

Later, in her scrapbook, I came across an intact copy of the same photograph. A little girl on her first Communion day, in a long white dress, a lace veil on her head and shoulders, a prayer book clutched in her hands. She'd managed a timid smile, no doubt at the prompting of the photographer, whose identity will forever remain a mystery.

Epilogue

Giltspur

Feb. 22, 2003

My dear Charles,

I'm thrilled you've accepted my invitation to stay here with me while we work through the sale of the magazine. It makes sense, doesn't it? I mean, you'd have to be mad to hole yourself up in some bleak hotel when this house is crying out for a semblance of human life. If nothing else, your just being here will bring a little more life to the place. Okay, let me say it straight out, it's a lonely spot now without him.

It's two months, would you believe, since Finbarr passed away. It hasn't quite sunk in yet, but there's this intense silence about the place that jolts me back into a realisation of what's happened. It's like a gaping hole. No one around to talk to and I end up talking to myself. But who am I telling? You've been through the same thing yourself, so you must know what I'm talking about. When you lost darling Emily, you still had

Rachel and David to distract you and keep you occupied. Even now you can call them up and ask them to come over for a meal or whatever. It must be a great consolation, that.

That's something I don't have. Aline's gone out of my life, gone with a huge chip on her shoulder. She's still convinced her mother was given a raw deal. The first time she ran away we tracked her down in Galway. She was only fourteen, imagine! Finbarr went and brought her back in the car. It seems she was looking for her mother's people, but got nowhere. Just as well she didn't find them. She'd most likely have got the cold shoulder, same as her mother.

She grew into a right little wild child, Aline. Always running away until no school would have her. I suppose we shouldn't be that surprised really. She's got a lot of her bohemian mother in her. And so different from her dad.

Finbarr was deep. You never really knew what was going on in that head of his. I knew he used to visit Céline's grave, but what I didn't know, and it was the florist told me this, that he always took a bouquet of flowers to the grave every December on her anniversary. That he should have picked that date and that spot to have his fatal attack, well that's something else.

I mean it's extraordinary, isn't it, how his stiff body, flecked with flakes of snow, was found stretched across her grave, almost as if he was begging to join her? Well, if that's what he wanted, he got his wish. The two of them lie together in death as they did so often in life. Do you know something, Charles? I think he loved her. Not just the physical thing. I mean deep inside. Okay, he loved us both, but I'd never really grasped the depth of his feelings for her. And do you know something else? I respect him all the more for it. I know his love for her in no way diminished the different love he had for me.

Do you think my book will make any difference to Aline? Do you think it will change her attitude? That's my dream, anyway. If she reads it, she'll know I harbour no bitterness against anyone, living or dead. Of course it's entirely up to her what she wants to do with it. In spite of your promptings, it was never my intention to publish it. What others decide to do with it after they put me in the clay won't concern me too much. I wrote it for Aline to help her understand.

See how I've changed? In the convent, it was all about the pursuit of spiritual perfection. When I lost my baby, it came home to me that life has to be about something more than a narrow self-absorption. I think Céline's arrival was the key. It allowed me to find my true meaning. I'll try to explain this better when I see you.

When you arrive, dear Charles, I'll have a blazing fire in the hearth and we can sit, two lonely middle-aged people, and reminisce about those who have passed on and the memories they have left us. Josie, poor Josie, had her work cut out trying to make me see sense and she probably had a better take on things than I gave her credit for. It wasn't my sister's fault that Blaithín has been turned against me. If Josie had lived, I'm convinced things would have been different.

Then there are Céline's diaries. I want to ask your advice about what to do with them. The parts I've read have given me some inkling of what lay at the root of her troubled existence.

Bring your walking boots, Charles, for I plan to take you across the moor to the spot where Kevin lies buried. And I want to introduce you to the mountain. My Sugarloaf Mountain, the one without whom I might not have survived. I feel certain you'll understand.

Susan

Meet

PJ Connolly

PJ Connolly lives in South County Dublin, Ireland, with his wife, Joan. Formerly a school counsellor he now devotes his time to travel and writing.